THE
LAST

VOLARI-

Other great stories from Warhammer Age of Sigmar

THE HOLLOW KING
A Cado Ezechiar novel by John French

HAMMERS OF SIGMAR: FIRST FORGED
A novel by Richard Strachan

GODEATER'S SON
A novel by Noah Van Nguyen

THE ARKANAUT'S OATH
A Drekki Flynt novel by Guy Haley

• GOTREK GURNISSON •
GHOULSLAYER
GITSLAYER
SOULSLAYER
Darius Hinks

BLIGHTSLAYER
Richard Strachan

DOMINION
A novel by Darius Hinks

KRAGNOS: AVATAR OF DESTRUCTION
A novel by David Guymer

GODSBANE
A novel by Dale Lucas

THE VULTURE LORD
A novel by Richard Strachan

CONQUEST UNBOUND
Various authors
An anthology of short stories

HALLOWED GROUND
A novel by Richard Strachan

GROMBRINDAL: CHRONICLES OF THE WANDERER
An anthology by David Guymer

A DYNASTY OF MONSTERS
A novel by David Annandale

THE LAST VOLARI

A SOULBLIGHT GRAVELORDS NOVEL

GARY KLOSTER

BLACK LIBRARY

A BLACK LIBRARY PUBLICATION

First published in 2023.
This edition published in Great Britain in 2023 by
Black Library, Games Workshop Ltd., Willow Road,
Nottingham, NG7 2WS, UK.

Represented by: Games Workshop Limited – Irish branch,
Unit 3, Lower Liffey Street, Dublin 1,
D01 K199, Ireland.

10 9 8 7 6 5 4 3 2 1

Produced by Games Workshop in Nottingham.
Cover illustration by Jodie Muir.

A CIP record for this book is available from the British Library.

ISBN 13: 978-1-80407-344-5

See Black Library on the internet at

blacklibrary.com

Find out more about Games Workshop
and the worlds of Warhammer at

games-workshop.com

Printed and bound in the UK.

---

*To Mimzy – for all the commas. the semicolons,
and everything else, thank you.*

The Mortal Realms have been despoiled. Ravaged by the followers of the Chaos Gods, they stand on the brink of utter destruction.

The fortress-cities of Sigmar are islands of light in a sea of darkness. Constantly besieged, their walls are assailed by maniacal hordes and monstrous beasts. The bones of good men are littered thick outside the gates. These bulwarks of Order are embattled within as well as without, for the lure of Chaos beguiles the citizens with promises of power.

Still the champions of Order fight on. At the break of dawn, the Crusader's Bell rings and a new expedition departs. Storm-forged knights march shoulder to shoulder with resolute militia, stoic duardin and slender aelves. Bedecked in the splendour of war, the Dawnbringer Crusades venture out to found civilisations anew. These grim pioneers take with them the fires of hope. Yet they go forth into a hellish wasteland.

Out in the wilds, hardy colonists restore order to a crumbling world. Haunted eyes scan the horizon for tyrannical reavers as they build upon the bones of ancient empires, eking out a meagre existence from cursed soil and ice-cold seas. By their valour, the fate of the Mortal Realms will be decided.

The ravening terrors that prey upon these settlers take a thousand forms. Cannibal barbarians and deranged murderers crawl from hidden lairs. Martial hosts clad in black steel march from skull-strewn castles. The savage hordes of Destruction batter the frontier towns until no stone stands atop another. In the dead of night come howling throngs of the undead, hungry to feast upon the living.

Against such foes, courage is the truest defence and the most effective weapon. It is something that Sigmar's chosen do not lack. But they are not always strong enough to prevail, and even in victory, each new battle saps their souls a little more.

This is the time of turmoil. This is the era of war.

This is the Age of Sigmar.

CHAPTER ONE

A hot wind blew across the Broken Plains, rustling grass gone dry and brittle as old bone, and I raced with it, staying just ahead of the mortals who hunted me.

I stopped at the top of the next hill, beside the basalt outcrop that jutted out of the crest like a shattered tooth. The wind moaned around the stone and I took it in, letting air fill the empty chambers of my lungs. Breathing was such a strange, invasive sensation, but I ignored the tickling touch of the dusty air moving in me as I searched for my hunters' scent. It was almost buried beneath the smell of dead grass and sun-hot stone, but my father's blood had gifted me with senses keen as my teeth. My pursuers reeked of their own mortality. Sweat, flavoured with fear and excitement, and beneath that the salt-iron-sweet smell of blood. My lips pulled back from my teeth as I breathed in again, baring my fangs in something like a smile.

There are many, Nyssa. The voice echoed through my head, her cool intrusion so familiar. *Enough to be dangerous.*

7

'Enough to be interesting,' I said. A full patrol. It had been years since Captain Takora had sent a patrol out this far, and I wasn't going to let them slip away. My heart gave one slow beat, stirring the blessed blood that filled my veins, and I stepped out into the open, exposed on the crest of the hill. I couldn't see the Sun Seekers, the remnants of the army that had been sent halfway across the realm of Aqshy years ago to destroy the Rose Throne, but I knew they were tangled somewhere in the scrub that lined the valley below. They would see me – a woman wrapped in dusty armour, carrying a pair of swords. They knew who I was, for I'd been fighting some of these mortals all their lives. But I was alone beneath the bright, hot sun, and I looked more like a girl playing soldier than the monster whose name they whispered in the dark.

Every enemy I'd ever faced had underestimated me. I hated that, but that didn't mean I wouldn't use it.

'See me,' I said. 'Underestimate me. Follow me.'

Just don't overestimate yourself.

I ignored that, staring down at a flash of gold that gleamed up through the brown leaves of the brush. The polished brass gilt of armour. I spun around, as if panicked by this glimpse of my pursuers, and started down the backside of the hill, heading towards the ravine that carved through the valley below. Careful to keep my speed in check, I timed my descent. The Sun Seekers had to believe that they were catching me, that this hunt was almost over. Which it was.

Just not in the way that they expected.

The ravine was a ragged wound in the bottom of the valley, a gash torn by the floods of storm season. Those rains were a distant memory, and the dirt crumbled into dust beneath my boots as I moved downwards. Stones rattled, and I had to stop myself from reaching out with my magic and wrapping silence around me.

8

That gift, the ability to kill every sound in the air encompassing me, had been very useful when I'd gone out to find these mortals. But now I wanted them to hear me, and I let every footfall echo.

The ravine was empty, the sandy ground unmarked except for the tracks of lizards. Everything was ready, and when I reached the sand the harsh daylight began to dim. Looking up, I found the distant summit of Temero rearing over the ravine's crumbling walls. The constant plume of smoke that rose from the massive volcano had grown, swelling enough to dull the day, and the shadows pooling at the bottom of the ravine increased. Better and better, even if the acrid stench of that distant smoke buried the scent of the mortals following me.

I moved to the far wall of the ravine and cocked my head. Stray wisps of my hair slipped from my braids and drifted across my face as I listened. Faint in the distance came the sound of boots, the clink of armour, the sound of harsh breathing and muttered curses. The Sun Seekers weren't fast, but they were coming, ready to fight.

'Good,' I breathed, and my heart beat again.

Reaching down I unsheathed my blades. They were ancient weapons, taken from the Crimson Keep itself – two slim, double-edged swords, finely made but lacking any ornamentation. In shape and size they were identical, but the metal of the one I carried in my right hand was as bright as a mirror, while the one in my left was as dark as shadow. Both were as sharp as terror. I spun them around me, listening to the thin whine they made as they cut through the air, waiting. But not for long. The beat of boots ended and there they were, standing on the edge of the ravine. A line of men and women, their orange uniforms mismatched, the brass gilding on their breastplates and helmets dull with dust and age.

Not a full patrol, Nyssa. Two. I count twenty.

'Nagash answers prayers,' I muttered.

How would you know? You've never prayed in your life.

'It is her.' A man in the middle spoke, and I could see the insignia of a sergeant worked into his dented armour. 'Nyssa Volari. Bloody Princess Bloodeyes herself.'

Bloodeyes? Is that supposed to be insulting? Those red streaks against the dark brown of your eyes are your best feature.

I didn't give a damn what the mortals thought about my eyes. Calling me princess, though. The mortal would pay for that.

The sergeant waved to his soldiers, and five of them moved up, pulling crossbows from their backs. 'You die today, Bloodeyes,' he said as they ratcheted back their strings.

'Do I?' I said, spinning my swords in smooth circles again. 'Try me.'

The Sun Seekers raised their crossbows, and my heart beat again – faster now, stirring the blood through my veins. The sergeant raised one hand and my heart started to squeeze again. Then his hand slashed down, and the soldiers pulled their triggers.

My blood was moving in me, and I could see the barbed bolts leap into the air like strange birds. I stepped back and turned, letting them pass through where I'd been. All except one. Its murderous metal tip would have sliced my cheek, but I spun the dark sword in my left hand and slapped it out of the air.

My heart finished its beat, and I looked up at the mortals with my blood-marked eyes and smiled. 'Try again.'

'Flank her,' the sergeant snapped. The Sun Seekers might have been ragged, but they knew their business. The ones without crossbows split into two groups, dropping over the edge of the ravine. They landed on either side of me, swords and shields ready, except for the last soldier. When her boots hit the sand it erupted under her and she staggered back, falling on her backside as a sand adder coiled and hissed, long fangs shining.

I couldn't help it. I should have used the moment to rush in

and attack, but the sight of the woman's startled face jerked the laughter out of me.

Don't bray like a beast, Nyssa. You are Kastelai. Hold yourself like one, and show these mortals what a warrior of the Crimson Keep can do.

'Yes, Mother.' I went silent and straightened, schooling my face into an appropriate expression of cold contempt. My blood was rushing through me now, pushed by the now steady rhythm of my heart. 'I'll do you proud.'

I raised my swords, dark and bright, as the adder slid away and the Sun Seeker regained her feet, face twisted with embarrassed rage. 'Are we ready?' I asked. 'Am I still dying today, or do you need more time?'

The sergeant answered by raising his hand again, and the fighters flanking me tensed while the crossbows drew aim. Then his hand fell, and everyone moved.

The shots were meant to throw me off balance into one set of swords or the other. But the mortals didn't understand how slow they were. I moved, faster than a snake strike, and was beside the sergeant. He didn't even have time to register my movement before I kicked him hard in the back, sending him flying to where I'd been standing just as the crossbow bolts ripped through that same space.

Most of the bolts flew past him, striking nothing but sand, but the last hit the side of his helmet straight on. It punched through the steel and the flesh and bone beneath, and the sergeant made a thin bleating noise like a startled goat and fell, thrashing his life out on the sand.

For a moment, the whole patrol went still around me, staring at their dead leader. Then someone shouted, an incoherent roar of fear and anger, and they were charging forwards again, swords raised.

I moved, my boots skimming across the sand so fast my tracks were barely more than the lizards'. I ran from one group and into the other, my blades whirling like shadow and light as I slashed the throat of one soldier, pushed back the blade of another, then danced away as they tried to pin me down.

It's time, isn't it?

It was almost tempting to ignore her, but Mother was right, and as I shifted, keeping the soldiers between me and the crossbows that were being reloaded above, I shouted, 'Erant! Rill! Time to come out and play!'

Do you have to say things like that?

'Father thinks they're funny,' I said, slapping a crossbow bolt out of the air.

Your father is amused by many ridiculous things.

Which explained me, she left unsaid. Spinning my swords, I charged the mortals that were running towards me, ducking another bolt aimed at my head.

I reached the soldiers just as the first of them were raising their shields, forming a wall to block me, but I threw myself to one side and dropped. My momentum sent me sliding boots first across the sand, under their shields. I came to a stop just behind the soldiers, and sprang to my feet, whirling my bright sword in a snapping circle that cut the tendons out of the back of the knee of the soldier closest to me, felling him.

I stopped then, watching the mortals stare at me with startled eyes. I spun one blade slowly, then ran the other past my lips, tasting the blood on its edge. Waiting for the Sun Seekers to realise I wasn't alone.

The first found out when an arrow took her in the throat. She fell, gurgling, and the ones closest to her backed away, cursing, searching for the archer who had shot her. Before they could find them, a broad-shouldered fighter armoured in red and black

with a massive two-handed sword crashed into their line. The Sun Seeker he struck barely had time to scream before that huge blade sheared through armour and flesh. The force of the blow sent the mortal flying across the ravine, to slam into the wall and fall, spilling blood and entrails.

Erant and Rill had hidden themselves against the walls of the ravine, crouching beneath overhangs cut into the dirt and veiled in shadows that had been deepened by Rill's magic. With my shout they'd charged out into the fray, and now the mortals weren't hunting me. They were trapped, caught between my paired swords, Erant's blade and Rill's bow.

The soldiers with the crossbows tried to pick off my companions. Two shot at Erant, hitting him in the chest. One bolt bounced off the red rose enamelled onto his black breastplate, but the other smashed through the steel faulds hanging below his belly and struck his upper thigh. Erant frowned when he was hit, then shattered a shield with his sword. He snapped the end off the bolt sticking out of his leg with one hand, getting it out of the way, then took off after the man with the broken shield. Rill dodged the three bolts aimed at her, disappearing into the shadows as she ran along the ravine's wall. When she reappeared, she was snapping arrows out of her short, heavily recurved bow of wood and bone at the Sun Seekers who were trying to reload their crossbows. Two went down fast, arrows punching into them, and then another fell, screaming, an arrow piercing his hand and pinning it to the stock of his crossbow. The last two turned, dropping their heavy weapons to run, and Rill vaulted out of the ravine to chase them.

My heart was beating, my blood singing through me as I moved, dancing away from every murderous swing aimed at me, ducking swords and slipping past shields. I was smoke, a shadow swirling through the mortals, my swords darting like striking snakes. Around me the smell of blood rose, thick and intoxicating, and

my rhythm began to falter as the bloodlust flared up inside me, ravening.

Control your emotions, Nyssa. Don't let them control you.

Even with all my speed, I didn't have time to answer, but my mother's voice helped me keep my control, helped me keep my skill and discipline married to the raw ferocity that came from the beating of my heart. I fought like my father had taught me, and in the end the mortals were sprawled across the sand beneath the red, smoke-tinged light. All except one.

I looked at her, staring at me with fear and hate and resignation, her sword still raised, and I rolled my shoulders. My armour was cut, and through the rents I could see the wounds that marked my arms. A few blows had got through, but they were already closing, red gashes turning into pink scars that faded away to smooth, unmarked brown.

The last Sun Seeker was the one that had landed on the snake, the one that had made me laugh, and I spun my swords one more time. Then I wiped them clean on the orange shirt of one of the dead before sheathing them.

'What's your name?' I asked her.

'Neria,' she said, and then she looked uncertain, as if she shouldn't have spoken. She was a new recruit, some poor Broken Plains native the Sun Seekers had pressed into service to fill their failing ranks. So young. She looked like me, that way, which made me sympathetic and annoyed.

'Your sergeant told me that I was going to die today, Neria.' Rill had returned and was standing on the edge of the ravine, pulling arrows from the bodies and licking the blood from them. The wounded soldier up there was groaning, trying to crawl away from her. Beside me, Erant was pinning a man to the ground with his knee, one hand holding the man's wrist, keeping him from stabbing at Erant with a dagger.

'But I'm not,' I told her, then I moved, smashing the sword out of her hand and catching her from behind. 'I'm not going to die, Neria. Not ever.' I looked at Erant and Rill and nodded, and they both dropped onto their captives, their teeth finding their necks. I could feel Neria jerk in my grip, but she didn't scream, didn't cry. 'Don't worry,' I told her. 'You're not going to die either. Not today. But I am going to feed.'

When Neria's head lolled back, I took my mouth from her neck and eased her to the ground. My hunger was still there, a ravenous beast demanding life, but I ignored it and wiped the blood from my chin, then licked that last remnant from the back of my hand.

No manners.

I ignored her and stretched, then looked for my companions.

'You could have called us earlier, Nyssa.' Erant was picking through the bodies, examining the dead with a critical eye. 'We're your guard, you know. You could let us guard you sometimes, perhaps?'

'Where's the fun in that?' I asked.

He grunted and nudged a severed head next to the body it had once been attached to. 'I can work with some of this. King Corsovo would appreciate it if we bring back more troops.'

Erant wasn't particularly gifted in necromancy, but he was the best of the three of us. The magic in Rill's blood ran more towards darkness, and me... My abilities to raise the dead were quite good, just so long as the dead in question were animals.

I looked down the ravine, reaching out with my magic and calling the steeds we'd hidden in the shadows beneath another overhang. The three Nightmares came trotting towards us, their hooves silent on the sand, their empty eye sockets streaming with glowing white mist.

I stroked the muzzle of the first, a mare whose pale hide was

almost perfectly intact. I'd made Thorn decades ago, and she was the best Nightmare I'd ever raised. I'd made Rill's and Erant's mounts too, taking fallen warhorses and giving them a deadly new life. But whenever I tried to animate anything intelligent the results were… singularly unimpressive.

'We'll be stuck shepherding them back with us,' I said.

'Magdalena will be pleased,' Rill said.

'Magdalena is never pleased.'

That would be your experience with her. Have you ever wondered why?

'No,' I growled, and Rill and Erant both frowned at me, but I ignored them. Rill shook her head and nodded at the woman at my feet.

'Are you going to finish her?'

I shook my head. 'No. I want her to tell Takora what happened. To remind her who rules the Broken Plains.'

'Do you really think–' Rill started, but I held up my hand, cutting her off. Something had just flapped down into the ravine, a tiny shape that dived through the air towards me. A bat, and I could see the red ribbon tied to its leg. A messenger.

'What in the amethyst hells is Arvan doing?' This little adventure of mine was supposed to be a secret. Sending me messenger bats wasn't very good for that. I held up my hand and the bat landed, little claws digging into my skin as it squeaked its pleasure at a task completed. I stripped the message from it, read it, and then read it again.

'Nyssa?' Erant asked, staring at my face. 'What's wrong?'

It's impossible.

My mother's voice was cold and certain in my head. 'Impossible,' I echoed, then moved to Thorn, grabbing her saddle and pulling myself up. 'Forget the dead. We go to the Grey Palace. Now.'

'Nyssa,' Rill said. 'What is it?'

I wadded up the tiny scrap of paper and threw it away. 'Corsovo. The king. My father. Arvan says he's dying.'

CHAPTER TWO

The sky was clear for once, the plume from distant Temero just a thin line, and the morning light gleamed off the white armour and silver spears of the soldiers drawn up in rows before the gangplank that led to the ship docked at Gowyn's greatest pier. Most of the port city's people were gathered around the pier, gawking at the polished might of the Church of Sigmar. The Spears of Heaven were dedicants of the Storm God, soldiers who'd sworn their lives to defending the Church and its followers, and the sight of them in their pretty white armour made the people murmur and my head ache.

That ache doubled when Galeris, my lieutenant, called out the greeting.

'To the Spears of Heaven, servants of the Storm Eternal, we, the Thirty-Ninth Regiment of the Sun Seekers, offer you welcome to Gowyn of the Broken Plains!'

Galeris' words echoed over the harbour, but the Church soldiers didn't move. They hadn't since they'd come off the ship and taken

their places on the pier. Their precision annoyed me. My 39th had been like that once, when I'd arrived with them at this cursed backwater thirty years ago. A girl of twenty, a naïve lieutenant on her first mission with the sun-bright host of Freeguild fighters from distant Hammerhal Aqsha, ready to scour the taint of undeath from these lands. Now... Now we were few, the polish stripped from our armour by ash and death, and I was too old to stand around in the sun like these fools.

We're all impressed, I thought, fighting to keep my face carefully blank. But can we get on with this? You're already decades late.

On the ship there was finally movement. Two more Spears of Heaven took their place at the end of the gangplank. One raised a banner, brilliant blue slashed with white lightning. The other spoke, his voice even deeper than Galeris'.

'He is here! Master of the Spears of Heaven, bearer of the sacred relic Heaven's Edge, the Abbot-General Celasian! He is here, bringing the blessings of heaven!'

A tall man appeared between banner bearer and herald. Armoured in white so pure it hurt my eyes, he carried a mirror-bright silver spear. Sparks danced along the weapon's edge, tiny bolts of snapping lightning.

'Celasian.' I didn't know I'd spoken aloud until I saw Galeris' eyes flick towards me. I pressed my lips together, but my thoughts were boiling. Even out here, I'd heard that name. Celasian was rising high and fast in the Church, an unforgiving prosecutor of anything he deemed unclean. The bitterness in me at this long-tardy arrival of reinforcements was suddenly replaced with something that was far too close to fear. Long before I'd received word that relief was finally being sent, I had set in motion plans to end this damnable war. But now–

'I am here.' Celasian's voice was not as deep as his herald's, but it was colder, harder. The crowd went silent and stared as he

spoke. 'Armed with spear and faith, to burn away the evil that taints this land.'

The abbot-general's words felt more like a threat than a promise, and the crowd remained silent as he strode down the gangplank. The waiting Spears of Heaven finally moved when he passed, forming into crisp lines, a guard that followed behind Celasian. He strode to me and stopped. 'Captain Takora of the Sun Seekers. I've come.'

I bowed my head, acknowledging him. The differences in rank between the Freeguilds and the soldiers of the Church were murky, but he was bringing a force that dwarfed the remnants of the 39th and it was best to be polite. The way he barely inclined his head to me made it clear that he believed he was the superior. It galled me knowing he was probably right.

Up close, I could see he was likely older than me, with thin lines on his skin and steel-grey hair, but his lean face was handsome in a stern sort of way, except for his eyes. They were a pale, washed-out blue, and flat, emotionless as glass. I met them and had to fight not to look away. Hard eyes I understood. After thirty years of fighting this damned war, my eyes were hard beneath the grey-black fringe of my hair. Celasian's eyes weren't hard.

They were repulsive.

'You have, abbot-general. Finally.' I couldn't help but let that last word slip in, but Celasian showed no reaction. 'We're glad to see you. But where are the rest of your troops?'

'They follow,' Celasian said. 'Ships are in demand. Sigmar's foes are legion, and his armies move in all directions to meet them. But I came first with my personal guard, to see what waits for us here.'

'I've sent reports,' I said carefully. 'Many reports, over the decades. I've copies of them all back in our keep.' The hot, dusty warehouse we called our keep.

'I've read them,' he said, not quite dismissively. 'I wish to see the situation myself.'

'Well, I can organise something in the next few days–' I started, but he shook his head.

'No. I've spent weeks on that ship, doing nothing. I want to ride out now, as soon as mounts can be prepared.'

'Now?' I said.

'Now.' He looked back at me with those flat eyes, but there was something there now, a tiny trace of consideration as he carefully sharpened his words before driving them in like knives. 'I don't intend to spend my whole life here, Captain Takora. Do you?'

Celasian took us straight towards Temero.

The volcano towered over the Broken Plains, dominating the horizon. The plume of smoke that rose from it grew thicker as the hours passed, and the sky darkened as the cloud of smoke and ash spread across the sky.

'It'll be dark soon,' Galeris said, 'with that cloud Temero is breathing out.' My lieutenant looked towards Celasian, who rode at the head of his guard. They made a pretty little parade across the rolling plains, with their white armour and banners, even mounted on the backs of a pack of lixx. The few mounted troops left in the 39th were all out patrolling, which meant that the lean, lethargic reptiles were the only mounts available in Gowyn. Celasian hadn't been happy about that, and he guided his poor beast with vicious jerks on its reins, making me wish that the ugly thing would shake him off. It seemed that even a lixx wasn't stupid enough to challenge the abbot-general, though.

'What do you want me to do about that?' I asked. 'Scrub the ash from the sky? The abbot-general wants to see the situation, so here we are.' I gestured towards the rolling hills surrounding us, empty of everything but the ruins of a village, its stone buildings burned out years ago. 'Seeing it.'

I kept my voice low, but Celasian looked over his shoulder towards me and waved his hand. I frowned at Galeris, then tapped the reins of my horse, Sugar, making her move forwards. Celasian had looked for a long time at Sugar, but I hadn't offered her to him. He wanted to see the Broken Plains immediately, he could see them from the back of a lixx.

'Captain Takora.' The way Celasian said my title set my teeth on edge. It was perfectly proper, but there was a whisper of dismissiveness to it that dug into me. 'That's the third abandoned village I've seen.'

'It is, my lord.' I was tempted to leave it there, but like the lixx I wasn't ready to challenge Celasian. 'The land between the cities of Gowyn and Maar was once well settled, but in the thirty years since the Battle of Ire Crossing most of the settlements have been destroyed. The people either died or fled to Gowyn or Maar. I outlined that in my reports.'

Celasian ignored that, staring past the ruins to distant Temero. Maar nestled near the volcano's foot, close to the ancient palace that the vampires claimed. 'Some joined the Soulblight vampires?'

'Some did.' Many, actually

'A mistake for them. One they'll regret.'

His words had an unsettling certainty to them, and I wanted to change the subject. 'Abbot-general,' I said, carefully, 'the day dims. How long did you wish to ride?'

'Until–' he started, but cut off. Across the plains, someone was moving, a figure dressed in orange. I stared at them, and my heart lurched. 'You have a patrol out here?' Celasian asked, his voice deadly calm.

'There was a patrol out, but they weren't supposed to be this far from the city.' I'd ordered Sergeant Jaral to stay closer to Gowyn.

'Perhaps they found something to hunt.' Celasian pulled on his reins, turning his lixx towards the figure. He kicked his reptilian mount hard in its ribs, and the lixx grunted in pain and started forwards at a shuffling run.

The man was one of Sergeant Jaral's, a recruit from Gowyn whose name I couldn't remember. We'd been drawing from Gowyn for years.

'What happened?' I said, riding to him. He was limping, but otherwise unhurt. His face was pale, though, eyes wide with fear, and I had a sick feeling in my gut. 'Where's your sergeant?'

'He told me to stay behind,' the man stammered. 'I rolled my ankle, and I couldn't chase that princess no more, so he told me to wait for them. But they never came back.'

Princess. 'Damn it,' I swore, and gestured for Galeris to pull the man up onto his horse.

'Who's this princess?' Celasian demanded.

'A Soulblight vampire,' I answered. I snapped the reins and got Sugar moving, heading back along the man's path. Celasian followed with his guard, pale eyes suddenly sharp.

We rode until we found the ravine, its sandy bottom covered with blood and bodies. Celasian drove his lixx down to the sand, his spear ready, and I was right behind with my sword in my hand.

But the enemy was gone.

There were only the broken remains of my soldiers, spread across the sand, and I cursed savagely. Jaral should've known better. Princess Bloodeyes and I had been picking at each other's forces for years. He should've known not to be drawn in, but if he thought he had her... I cursed again, and on the ground one of the bodies shifted, trying to sit up.

I vaulted off Sugar, avoiding a decapitated corpse, and fell to my knees beside the soldier that had moved. Neria. Another new recruit, but I knew her name because I'd practised with her a few

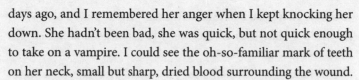

days ago, and I remembered her anger when I kept knocking her down. She hadn't been bad, she was quick, but not quick enough to take on a vampire. I could see the oh-so-familiar mark of teeth on her neck, small but sharp, dried blood surrounding the wound.

'They fed on her.' There was a kind of visceral abhorrence in Celasian's voice.

'Neria,' I said, ignoring him. Her eyes were closed, her face pale as snow, and I could feel how cold her skin was against my hand through her short-cropped hair as I cradled her head. Bloodeyes had taken a lot of blood, but not all of it. 'Neria!'

Her eyes opened, fuzzy, unfocused. 'Captain...' She closed her eyes again, a long blink, then fought them back open. 'Bloodeyes.'

'I know,' I said softly.

Celasian dropped off his lixx beside me. 'Who is this Bloodeyes?' His Spears of Heaven had arranged themselves across the bottom of the ravine, getting in the way of Galeris as he hunted for tracks. We'd grown used to scenes like this during the long war, and my lieutenant knew to look for the signs of where the vampires had gone, or warnings of traps they might have left behind.

'It's what we call one of the Kastelai,' I said, not taking my eyes from Neria. 'Nyssa Volari, daughter of Corsovo Volari, the one they name king.'

'Daughter?' Celasian snorted. 'Those abominations make no children.'

I didn't have time to explain the peculiarities of our enemies. I'd already put them in my damn reports. 'Galeris. Are they gone?'

'Yes,' he answered. 'Three riders left, fast, not long ago. No sign of any of their tricks.'

Tricks. Zombies left among the corpses of the victims, silent and hungry. Pits full of dismembered hands and heads, waiting to catch and bite. Vampires wrapped in shadows and silence, ready

to strike. There had been so many merry tricks played on us over the years we had learned caution. The abbot-general lacked that hard-won education.

'Not long ago,' Celasian said. He shifted Heaven's Edge in his hand, and sparks crackled up the weapon. 'We can catch them.'

'We cannot, abbot-general,' I said, leashing my impatience. 'We have to tend to Neria or she'll die.'

Celasian looked at me, his flat eyes flashing as they reflected the sparks that danced on his spear. Then he moved, touching its point to Neria's chest.

Just a touch, but when the silver blade met her armour a thick spark arced from it. I barely snatched my hand away as the electricity shot through my soldier's body, making her stiffen, mouth going wide in a silent scream. And then she went limp, lying on the sand before me, unmoving, a faint wisp of smoke rising from the spot where the spear had touched her.

I stared at Neria's still body for a moment and then I was on my feet, my sword point a hair's breadth away from the abbot-general's chest, and everything was silent except for the crackling pop of static arcs that ran up and down Celasian's spear. He stared at me with his almost colourless eyes, not moving Heaven's Edge, but behind him his Spears of Heaven had all aimed their weapons at me.

'She *fed* on the girl, Captain Takora.' Celasian's voice was cold and hard. 'That Soulblight vampire bit her, drank her blood, and she was about to die of it. A death most unclean. Sigmar's relic blessed her with better.' He placed the deadly spear against my sword, and the buzz of its power made the hairs on my arm stand up. 'Now. Let us catch this Bloodeyes, and avenge your fallen.'

I glared at him, every muscle poised for violence, but I kept my control and slammed my sword back in its sheath. 'They ride Nightmares. They're already gone, abbot-general. Gone as Neria.'

He studied me, and I wondered if he would argue, if he was so convinced of his own righteousness that he thought he could make a lixx move as fast as one of the tireless, death-wrought steeds the vampires rode. But finally he waved a hand, as if acknowledging the truth even as he dismissed it. 'They're gone. For now.'

He turned, staring again towards Temero. The column of ash and smoke had become a great plume whose dark threat mixed with the shadows of the coming night. 'But we know where they go. And soon, we will go there, and for Sigmar we shall burn them all!'

'For the glory of Sigmar!' his guard shouted, raising their spears, and in the distance lightning crackled up the storm of ash boiling out of the volcano, lighting up the sky. In the flash I saw something on the ground, a pale twist of paper. I picked it up and read the urgent message scrawled across it, then hid it in my hand.

So. That piece of my plan was finally falling into place. Right when everything else was falling apart.

White armour gleaming in the dark, Celasian raised Heaven's Edge, staring at the lightning that wreathed distant Temero. 'For his glory!' he shouted, and his voice echoed out of the ravine and over the night-drenched plains.

CHAPTER THREE

Built of black basalt, Maar was a dark city in the day. At night, under a cloud of ash, it was shadow turned stone.

I rode Thorn through the narrow streets, the mortals bowing as we passed. There weren't many of them. Maar had once been the greatest city in the Broken Plains, the mortals in it prospering after they had bowed to my father's rule, but now... The city was slowly emptying, despite the villagers who'd come in from the surrounding plains looking for shelter. The constant war, not enough food, not enough trade... The decline had been happening ever since the Sun Seekers had attacked thirty years ago, and nothing seemed to stop the bleeding.

Bleeding. How long will it be before there are no mortals left for that?

I ignored that cheerful question and guided Thorn towards the inn that rose ahead of us. The Black Stork's facade was ornately worked, but years of falling ash had half-buried the carvings. Much of Maar was neglected like that, all except the great temple

that sat at the end of the street. Once it had been dedicated to all the gods of Order, but the multihued stained-glass windows that decorated it had been replaced with panes of amethyst-coloured glass, glowing purple against the temple's clean, black stones. The temple belonged to Nagash now, as did this city and all the Broken Plains.

Whatever the Sun Seekers thought.

'Lady Volari.' The Black Stork's innkeeper looked familiar, but I couldn't remember if he was the man I knew, or the son that had grown up to replace him. Mortals were inconvenient in their constant change. I just nodded and swept past, heading for my rooms. When we reached the suite, carefully kept free of dust despite my infrequent visits, Rill frowned at me.

'We ran all the way back, and you stop here?'

'I do.' A great mirror stood in the room, flanked with panels of polished obsidian. I stopped in front of it and looked myself over. Ash dusted my hair, and blood stained my armour. 'If I went to the Grey Palace looking like this, I'd never hear the end of it from Mother.'

Erant sighed. 'How come you only listen to her now that she's dead, Nyssa?'

What an excellent question.

'Shush,' I said to them both, then there was a knock at the door. Erant opened it for a small troupe of serving women bearing pitchers of steaming water.

'For the princess,' I heard one of them whisper, and my lips curled back from my fangs. They quickly filled the tub that sat on one side of the room and were gone. I stripped and settled into hot water that smelled faintly of sulphur. The Irewater was a long, narrow lake that stretched from Maar to where the Grey Palace stood at the foot of Temero. Near the volcano the lake boiled and steamed, heated by the volcano's fiery heart. Here, near Maar, it was still hot, but not scalding. Convenient for baths, even if it did smell, and I cleaned the dried blood and ash away.

My scrubbed skin was deep brown, though it took a greyish cast when I needed to feed. My eyes changed when I fed – the chestnut irises coloured by strands of red that grew thicker when I was sated, or when I was angry. My hair was difficult, long and black and thick, just wavy enough to want to tangle in everything if left unbraided, but cutting it back was right out according to Mother.

I ducked my head beneath the water to wet it, and when my eyes closed I saw the words again, written in Arvan's cramped hand. *Come back. King Corsovo is ill, mayhap dying.* Mayhap dying? What in Nagash's lowest hell did that mean? My father was a vampire lord of the Kastelai. Vampires do not get sick, and they do not die.

Do we not?

Beneath the water, I shook my head. You were killed, I thought. By treachery and flame and my failure. You didn't just die, like a mortal.

Nyssa.

She said my name like a warning, but I didn't listen. I pushed myself out of the tub, splashing water across the floor. 'Clean up,' I said to Erant and Rill, and Erant went to the door, calling the servants for fresh water. Neither of them had teased me about the serving girl calling me princess, which meant they both knew my mood.

You call yourself the king's daughter. To these people, that has a title.

'A stupid one,' I muttered. 'If they want to give me a title, I can be royal executioner.'

An executioner is a commoner. You are a Kastelai, Nyssa. You are nobility. You must know that, the way these mortals know it.

Of course they knew it. One hundred years ago, Maar had been about to fall. A dozen bands of nomads had ridden in from the wastes that edged the Broken Plains, united in their greed. They'd laid siege to the city and were on the edge of victory the night the ruins that lay on the other side of the Irewater had blurred and stretched, and the abandoned castle had transformed into the Crimson Keep.

The nomads never understood what happened. One moment they were ready to claim Maar, and then had come catastrophe. An army of death, of vampires mounted on Nightmares and still more terrible things, had slammed into their flanks. Killing, feeding, smashing the nomads until each band had run, defeated.

We'd followed one of those ragged remnants. My mother and father and I, and the other vampires in our cohort. We'd helped shatter their army, now we drove them away. Not because we had cared what happened to Maar, we didn't even know the name of the city then, didn't even know which of the Mortal Realms we were in. That was the nature of the Crimson Keep. The home of the Kastelai was cursed to move, always, unpredictably. It would rest on the bones of some ancient fortress for a day, a week, a month, and then suddenly, as one day faded, the shadows would grow around the Keep and swallow it, taking it into darkness and then spitting it out somewhere else.

There was no telling where. It could be a different continent, a different realm. The only certainties were that the Crimson Keep always came to rest on ruins and that there would be a battle happening somewhere close. I could clearly remember the times the Keep had moved when I'd lived there. The thrill of feeling the darkness take us, knowing that when we came out into some new night, there would be a war waiting for us. We wouldn't know what the sides were, what the stakes were. We were just there to fight, and to feed, and we did both well that night.

Too well.

Temero had been spewing ash over the battle. The ash fall had been thick enough to hide the day when it came, and my cohort had followed the survivors of one of the shattered nomad bands far out into the Broken Plains before we stopped, finally sated on fighting and blood. By the time we'd returned, the cloud had thinned a little, enough for the last bits of daylight to slip through it and turn the churned earth around Maar red as blood. Night was coming, and we knew we should go to the Keep, but we were lazy with victory and the knowledge that it almost always lingered in its new spot. We joked about it as we rode, until the darkness gathered around those distant red walls and we saw the Keep vanish. Gone, leaving us behind.

That had been a long, terrible night.

Most of the vampires with us died. Some, tied close to the Crimson Keep and its curse, had crumbled to dust the moment it vanished. Others died a slow, agonising death over the next few days, wasting away to desiccated corpses no matter how much blood we gave them. We might have broken then, but for my father Corsovo and my mother Vasara. They kept us going. They were the ones who went to Maar, and discovered that the people there called us their saviours. They bent the mortals' loose legends about the return of the rulers of the Grey Palace to our ends. My parents saved us, ensuring we would not be refugees but conquerors. They made a broken cohort of Blood Knights into rulers, and became king and queen of the Broken Plains.

But just because I was their daughter didn't make me a princess.

I sighed, went to my wardrobe and began to pull out my things.

My court garb wasn't a gown. Mother wouldn't have minded that, though she'd seldom worn them. But armour was always appropriate for a Kastelai, especially at court. This armour wasn't worn or spattered with blood. Its leather was a lustrous black, perfectly fitted to me. Rose vines twisted up the legs and arms and

across the shoulders, intricately tooled so that the long thorns looked sharp as fangs. They flared into blooms around my collar and across my shoulders, roses of deep, deep red, the colour of blood in shadow. Across the back was a white skull with a rose blooming in each eye, one for Corsovo and one for Vasara.

I'd had this armour made for her funeral.

I frowned at myself in the mirror, dressed in that dark leather, my swords on my hips, a circlet of dull gold marked with one heavy ruby holding back my hair. I wasn't beautiful. My features were too hard and thin, my body too lean, long as a whipcord. But in this outfit, my eyes flashing red-brown over the rose-stitched collar, I was striking, and that was more important.

Adequate.

Despite the brevity of the word, I could sense her approval. I looked at Rill and Erant in the mirror. They'd dressed in their best, too, armour similar to mine if not as ornate. It was time to go, but despite all the speed I'd made getting here, I hesitated. What if Arvan was right? What if my father *was* dying?

Then you need to see him before he is gone.

There was no arguing with that, and I spun away from the mirror and walked out, my companions falling in behind.

We rode through Maar's gates, the hooves of our Nightmares tapping across the black bridge that crossed the river running below.

The hot, sulphurous Irewater poured itself into a rocky channel in Maar, and became the River Ire, looping through the hills and flatlands of the Broken Plains until it finally spilled into the sea at Gowyn, where the Sun Seekers plotted their raids. I stared at the boats scattered below, fishermen venturing out into the hot lake to catch the fish that surfaced each night. Every boat was draped with ribbons and pennants begging Nagash for full nets and a successful return.

Returns. Returns were hard.

The Grey Palace lay on the other side of the Irewater. I could pick out its lights in the dark, bright dots gleaming across the steaming water. We'd claimed the ruin where the Crimson Keep had briefly stood, dug a portion of the ancient castle out of the drifts of fallen ash and made it our home. My home. The other Kastelai had spread out over the years, starting their own holds in other parts of the Broken Plains, creating their own families of vampires from those they deemed worthy. But I'd stayed in the Grey Palace with Corsovo, because he'd made me, and with Vasara, who'd tried to remake me.

Stop being dramatic. I was just trying to educate you.

'There's a difference?' I said. My voice was soft, but the night was silent and I knew Rill and Erant had heard.

'Did you say something?' Rill's voice, of course. She was the braver one when it came to me. Her question wasn't a question, it was a reminder that my arguments with the ghost inside my head were audible to those around me.

She's right.

'Then–' I started, then caught myself and lowered my voice. 'Then why are you always starting arguments with me?'

Because you need my advice, Nyssa. And that advice right now is to school your tongue. The others have enough doubts about you.

I curled my lips into a silent snarl, but I didn't answer. It was unfair, the way she could speak whenever she wanted and I had to watch my tongue. It was unfair that she was right, too.

'No, Rill,' I answered, then followed that grudgingly with, 'Thank you.' Not for the question, but for the reminder to keep my arguments to myself.

They knew, of course. My father had made Rill and Erant, giving them his blood when they'd proven their skill and loyalty. But they'd been my companions, my supposed guards, since before they were born into their second life. They'd watched over me after Vasara's death, when I'd raged and mourned, and they knew how grief and guilt had become a ghost in my mind. The only ones who knew. I'd never told Corsovo about it, and never would.

And sure as all the amethyst hells, I didn't want any of the other Kastelai to know.

We rode through the dark, the lights of Maar fading behind us, the lights of the Grey Palace growing brighter. Beside us the Irewater lost its dark stillness, its surface marred with bubbles coming up from the boiling springs that fed into the lake far below. The steam rising off the water grew, twisting and turning into strange shapes, phantoms that stretched up from the water and then faded into the dark.

Black monoliths lined the side of the road. The massive stones were carved with names, a tally of the city's dead. It'd been their custom since Maar was founded, to wrap their dead in cloth weighed with stones and throw them into the Irewater. The corpses settled far below, their flesh dissolving in the boiling water, leaving their bones to pile in the darkness. Silent and gone, except for the thin wraiths that rose from the slowly roiling water and the names carved into the stones.

My father had changed the practice, told the mortals that they could still carve the names of their dead into the stones, could still cast a bundle containing the little fingers and toes of the bodies into the water, but that was it. We were the servants of Nagash, the god of the dead. We respected funeral rites, but we had other uses for those bodies.

When we passed the last of the monoliths, I was close enough to pick out the ash-coloured walls of the Grey Palace, rising high over the Irewater. Points of light had resolved into lanterns along the battlements, and I could see the narrow stained-glass windows glowing in the towers behind those walls. The ones that had been

repaired – my father had left half the castle in ruins. A place for the Crimson Keep to reappear, if it ever would.

Four pennants hung from the rebuilt walls, long shadows stretching against the grey stone. I could pick out the sigils woven into them: a raven in purple and black; a dire wolf's snarling head; a goblet of blood; a broken skull. Magdalena. Salvera. Jirrini. Durrano. The last of the Kastelai, the Blood Knights of the Crimson Keep who had survived our abandonment here. The blood-blessed nobility of the Broken Plains. My extended family.

The very last people I wanted to deal with.

My boots were dropping to the flagstones when I heard Magdalena's voice.

'Another adventure, Lady Nyssa?'

I took the time to hand Thorn's reins to the mortal groom, whose eyes had gone wide seeing my bared fangs. I closed my mouth and smoothed my face, then turned and faced the Kastelai. As always, Magdalena was perfectly if not prettily dressed in her usual court garb, a tunic and trousers coloured deepest purple. The tunic had a raven stitched over her heart and the symbols of Nagash embroidered up the sleeves. She'd always been pious and fussy, overcautious and demanding. Magdalena was shorter than me but broader, strong and tough as an old oak. Her dark, curly hair was cut into short ringlets that framed her round face, incongruously attractive around green eyes that were hard as stones.

Behind her, standing between the great doors that opened off the courtyard, Jirrini and Durrano were watching. Jirrini wore a gown and heavy jewellery of gold and rubies, the colour of the stones a perfect match for her dress. It all sat well against her dark skin, eyes and hair. Jirrini was beautiful and poised, a contrast to the deadly bearing she took when fighting, and Durrano

looked plain beside her. He was my height, though with broader shoulders, but his white hair, fair skin and bone-coloured clothes made him a palette of paleness. Even his eyes were white, the ivory pupils barely visible. His personality was as dull as his clothing, but he was my father's staunchest supporter.

'Lady Magdalena,' I said, without nodding my head. She was older than me, wise in battle and diplomacy, but we both knew I'd cut her to ribbons in a duel, so we acted as equals and kept our annoyance with each other buried beneath a veneer of politeness. Mostly. 'I *have* had another adventure. And now our Captain Takora is short a patrol.'

'Yet you return empty-handed,' she said.

'I return with the death of a score of our enemies,' I said. 'When's the last time you killed so many?'

Magdalena ignored the barb. 'All that death, and no bodies?'

'Do you think I'm lying?' I snapped.

Careful. She's baiting you, my mother said, but I ignored her. Magdalena had been sitting in Ruinview for years, doing nothing while I whittled away at the Sun Seekers, and I had no interest in hearing her critiques. Especially not now, when I was supposed to be on my way to see my father.

'I did what I said, and cost Takora. I fought her army and I bled her. I'm reducing her strength to a handful, which is how war works. Or have you sat in your hold so long that you've forgotten that?' I drew myself up, staring down at her, and for once I was glad my mother had forced me to dress for this. In my black armour, swords polished on my hips, I felt like I was driving through Magdalena's guard, ready to set the edge of my blade against her throat. And then she stabbed me back.

'Takora's handful has just been joined by an order of soldiers from the Church of Sigmar. They are called the Spears of Heaven, and they mean to end this long war by killing us all.' She glared

at me, her fangs flashing as she spoke. 'I learned that, sitting in my keep, studying how war works, Lady Nyssa. We're going to be doing more than these little skirmishes of yours soon enough, and we need those dead.'

Ah. That's what she was setting you up for. Note the others' faces. Jirrini isn't surprised, Magdalena already told her. But Durrano is. She's undermining you in front of him.

Her analysis of Magdalena's political manipulation wasn't helping me. Not at all. My hands gripped my swords, but I kept them still. I wasn't that way any more: angry, vicious, frightened, my only response to any attack a flurry of blades and fangs. I wasn't. Even if I wanted to be, sometimes.

Many times.

I opened my hands, collected myself and tried to organise a response, but there was a stirring near the door – Arvan, nodding respectfully to Jirrini and Durrano as he carefully slid his bulk past them. He was a tall, powerful man, his shoulders and arms heavy with muscle. He still wore his hair like a nomad's, bare on the sides with a wide strip of locks going from forehead to neck, all done up in a tangle of braids. The blood hadn't changed the light brown of his skin or the darker brown of his hair, but it had changed his eyes, made them blank and black as a night without stars.

Those dark eyes were on me as he approached. Arvan acted as though he were oblivious to the tension that filled the courtyard, but I knew that was a lie. He looked like a brute, but the mind behind those black eyes was sharp as obsidian.

'Lady Volari,' he said. 'The king will be happy to see you.' He straightened, and breathed, almost silently, pitched for my keen ears alone, 'They don't know.'

'I thought King Corsovo was unavailable,' Magdalena said, an edge of anger in her voice.

'He's never unavailable to family,' I said, then turned my back on them all and stalked away.

Corsovo's apartment was dark.

My boots clicked loudly against the tile, echoing in the silent chamber. No light, no other sound except the sighing of the breeze outside the wide windows. I looked over the room, keen eyes searching, and finally found him – one pale hand resting on the padded arm of a heavy chair that stood with its back to me. A hand that was as thin and still as a corpse's.

'King Corsovo,' I said. 'Father!' I came around the chair, facing him, and stopped.

Blessed Nagash. What's happened to him?

That was the question echoing in my head. When I'd left a few weeks ago, Father had looked the same as always, tall and broad, handsome with his long black hair and pale skin ruddy with fresh blood, dangerous with his purple-black eyes and the long, elegantly sharpened claws that tipped each finger. Now... Corsovo, king of the Broken Plains, sat crumpled in the chair. He'd gone thin, hollow and desiccated, his skin pulled tight over his bones, and his mane of dark hair was mostly gone, the few strands still clinging to his scalp now white. His skin had gone waxy and his claws were ragged, half of them broken, their lustre dulled and ugly.

'Father!' I said again, crouching before him, my hand on his shoulder. I wanted to shake him, desperate to make sure he was still alive, but I was afraid that if I did he'd crumble into dust, so I touched him gently. His head lolled on his neck as he stirred, his hands curling like dying spiders, his wrinkled eyelids twitching. They opened, and his eyes, eyes that had once seemed like thunderstorms, were the colour of bruises and rot. But they focused on me, and his lips moved.

'Nyssa,' he said, his once powerful voice a whispered croak. 'My child, you've come. Good.' He blinked, lids slipping over the ulcers that were eating away his eyes, and I wondered how much he could see. 'I need you. But where…?' He trailed off, confused. Like a mortal querulous with infirmity. Like a mortal, old and dying. 'Where's your mother? Have you been arguing again? Where is Vasara?'

CHAPTER FOUR

'What happened to him?' The question was all that had been running through my mind since seeing my father sitting broken in that chair. I hadn't asked then, not while I listened to him ramble through his delusions. Whatever had happened, it'd broken Corsovo's mind as much as his body. Sometimes he thought we were still in the Crimson Keep, sometimes he acted as if we were freshly arrived on the Broken Plains, and sometimes he seemed to be remembering something from his first life as a mortal. He wandered through those thoughts, telling stories that had no beginnings and no ends, a disconnected clutter of centuries of memories. Always, though, he returned to Vasara, the woman he'd met in the Crimson Keep, the woman who'd come to share her second life with his. His plaintive demands for her stabbed me like daggers made of ice. It was worse though, when he confused me for her.

'I don't know,' Arvan said sadly, and I wanted to strike him.

Arvan came to us shortly before my mother died. A warrior

from one of the nomad bands, a powerful, brutish-looking man with intelligence and ambition. Sick of the endless ride, the constant skirmishes with the other nomads, he'd sworn his spear arm to us. Corsovo had accepted, and just before the Sun Seekers had come he'd given Arvan the gift of his blood. Since then Arvan had become more than a warrior. He was my father's secretary and assistant, using his control over vermin to discover all kinds of useful information.

I'd never decided if I liked him or not.

'You don't know?' I rounded on him, both hands resting on my sword hilts. During that awful time I'd spent trying to speak with my father, Temero had stopped filling the sky with smoke. Now day had come, and the light struggled through the thinning cloud to fall harsh and red across my apartment. Arvan had taken one chair, while Rill sat cross-legged on my writing desk and Erant sprawled across a low leather couch. Rill was fletching arrows, and Erant was carving a cat out of a twisted piece of wood, but I knew they were watching me.

'I left four weeks ago.' I was pacing, feet moving along the path I'd worn across my parlour. 'The king was fine then. Now' – I stopped walking and slashed a hand towards the royal chambers – 'this! What happened, Arvan?'

'I've been working to find that out since it began, shortly after you left.' Arvan shook his shaggy head. 'It started with hunger. King Corsovo would feed, but the blood didn't satisfy him any more. That went on for two weeks, and then he stopped wanting it. His majesty will take blood now only if I force it on him. When his hunger ended, that's when the physical changes began.'

'Two weeks?' I said, unbelieving. 'He's changed that much in *two weeks?*' Arvan nodded and I spun away. I had to move, and I stalked the length of my parlour and back, trying to think. 'Did the mortals somehow poison him?'

'Your father's necromancer has examined him extensively. Shadas hasn't found any sign of poison. Or hostile magic.'

I growled. That scrawny necromancer had never impressed me, but Father trusted in him. If it wasn't an attack, though, what could be happening to him? The only thing I'd ever seen like this was the curse that had taken some of the Kastelai in the days after we lost the Crimson Keep. But that had happened a century ago, right after our abandonment. The same thing couldn't be happening to Father now. Could it?

'What else?' I asked. Arvan looked at me, unsure, and I barely checked my lunge at him, settling my hands on the arms of his chair instead of his throat. 'What else has been happening to him, besides this wasting?'

'Oh,' he said. He hadn't flinched. Arvan was a fighter, whatever else. 'You saw his confusion. Half the time he calls me by the names of vampires long dead or gone. He also sees things that aren't there, and misses things that are.' Arvan shook his head. 'At first it was just hearing voices. Vasara's, mostly.'

Vasara's. I jerked away from him, straightening up. Beyond Arvan, neither Rill nor Erant looked at me.

You're not going mad.

'*You're* not helping,' I hissed silently. 'Why didn't you send for me sooner?' I said out loud. Anger flickered through my words, and I welcomed it. Anger was better than the hungry dread I felt gathering in the dark corners of my mind, waiting for a chance to rush in.

'Your father forbade me,' Arvan said. 'He didn't want to distract you from your hunt.'

'He knew about that.' It wasn't a question. I'd always figured he knew about my raids, the way I baited the Sun Seekers. He approved, but didn't acknowledge them because they didn't fit Magdalena's more cautious battle plans.

Arvan nodded. 'Yes. So he told me no, and I respected his wishes. Until he finally got so bad, and the others came. Magdalena three nights ago, the others right after.'

'How did they know?' I asked.

'Magdalena is the *official* spymaster of the king, in addition to being his chief general.' Arvan's stress on the word 'official' conveyed his opinion of that title. He had respect for the Kastelai as a fighter, but he claimed his bats and rats were better than her network of informants with questionable loyalties. 'She's focused on Gowyn, but she has ears in the Grey Palace.' He drummed his heavy fingers on the arm of his chair, each tap popping like a bone cracking, then looked up at me. 'I think it's time for you to consider taking power, Lady Volari.'

'No,' I said, shaking my head.

'My lady,' Arvan said carefully, 'you'd not be usurping the king's power. Just the opposite. You'd be preserving it.'

'No,' I said again.

Arvan stayed deferential, but he didn't stop. 'Magdalena knows something's wrong. She's gathered the others as witnesses and demands an interview with the king. I've put her off for as long as I can, but I must cede to her soon. I may be the king's right hand, but she's his general, and she's Kastelai. She'll dismiss me soon, and what can I do? I've no power here. But you do. You're Kastelai, and you're his daughter.'

'My father rules,' I said.

Your father's gone.

I bit back my response, barely, and focused on Arvan. 'I know he's sick, but he's still king. I'll talk to Magdalena. She can wait until he's better, or until all light fades and Nagash takes us all, whichever comes first.'

'And if Magdalena calls challenge? Or Jirrini? Or Salvera?' Arvan asked. He saw my face and nodded. 'Yes, the Mad Dog is here too. How do you think your father will fare now against Salvera's scythe? How do you think any of us will fare if the Mad Dog becomes king?'

'That won't happen,' I snarled. 'If Salvera, Magdalena or one of the gods themselves challenges my father, I'll cut them to ribbons.'

'I think you would,' Arvan said. 'But when you did, you'd become queen.'

If you take his challenge, you take his power.

'No,' I said again, as if denial were a blade that could block. But my mother's voice would not be silenced.

You've killed for Corsovo, risked your life for him, but will you bind yourself to responsibility for the first time in your life for him?

Her words dug into my blood. *Will you bind yourself...* I shoved them out of my head. 'Corsovo is king. We will cure him.'

'How?' Arvan said, his voice soft.

I glared at him, and Rill and Erant shifted uneasily, clearly wondering what to do if I attacked. I wanted to. I wanted an enemy, someone I could cut and kill to solve this. I could feel my blood stir, on the edge of beating, and the temptation to draw my blades was strong.

Nyssa. Do you have control? Are you Kastelai?

Her words cut through me, and my heart stilled. I stared at Arvan, who waited calm in the face of my rage, certain in his correctness.

'Damn you,' I cursed uselessly. 'Damn this. Damn everything.' I turned and stalked out of my rooms, going out, going anywhere, going away.

Deep beneath the Grey Palace, tunnels had been carved into the roots of Temero, long halls that sweltered with the heat of the volcano's distant heart. We didn't know their purpose – the ancient rulers of the Broken Plains were legend when we took

their ash-buried home, and they'd left almost nothing behind. So we'd given the tunnels our own purpose, and in a chamber at the heart of their twisting labyrinth my father had built my mother's tomb.

You can't run from this.

I sat on the polished floor, my back against the great white marble cube. The tomb's walls were smooth, blank except for the single door. A heavy slab, recessed slightly into the rest of the marble cube. In its centre a likeness of Vasara's face had been carved, perfect, still, beautiful. I could never look at it for long. The memory of finding her skull, scorched black by flames, always intruded.

'It's what I do, isn't it?' I said the words quietly, but they filled the hall and sent echoes whispering around me. They were the only sound here, except for the subliminal sigh of air through the tunnels, a vague current of warmth that barely stirred the flame of my candle. 'That's what you told me right before you died. That I spent my time running from battle to battle like a child, thinking only about blades and blood, and that I was going to get someone killed. Then I did, and you died and I swear to Nagash I sometimes think you did it just to prove your point.'

Everything isn't about you. Even the things that hurt you the most.

She always did this. I'd bring up her death, my guilt, and Vasara would take the blade I'd given her to stab me and slap me with it instead and tell me to work harder. Gods, it was annoying.

I'd never got along with her. Not after Father had made me, when she ignored me with icy determination. Not after she'd finally accepted me, and began training me to be a true Kastelai.

We'd fought. Not with blades, but with arguments and etiquette, complicated battles I didn't understand and hated. A long war of education, so much more painful than the thousand cuts I'd taken learning the art of blades from my father. But she never let me go, never let me retreat. Of course she kept it up after death.

Forty years ago, ten before we'd met the Sun Seekers for the first time at the disastrous Battle of Ire Crossing, we'd been expanding across the Broken Plains, taking all the holdings between Temero and the sea. Folding in the bands of nomads who ranged across the rolling hills that spread out from the volcano, moving towards the wide, flat lands that surrounded Gowyn. There'd been a nomad named Celas, who united five of the bands together to oppose us. He was a thorn in my father's side, his forces always moving, hitting from unexpected directions, forever setting ambushes and traps. Magdalena had said he fought without honour, and she was right; Celas was not Kastelai, and I learned a lot from him that I later used against the Sun Seekers. But we didn't know how dishonourable he really was.

Celas set up a meeting, a plea for peace, to swear himself to my father, but it was a lie. Celas didn't want to serve us, he wanted to be us, to claim our power, our blood. When Vasara went to treat with him he set a trap, lured me away with a false attack and then went for my mother, trying to steal the blood gift for himself. She fought him and all the warriors he'd arrayed against her, but by the time I realised the trick and went back, the tent where they'd been was an inferno. She'd killed dozens before the flames got her.

She'd died because I wasn't there, but Father had never blamed me and did that make it better or worse?

Stop pitying yourself, Nyssa, and focus on Corsovo. He needs your help.

'I am helping!' I snapped, and the echoes mocked me from the darkness. Helping. Sitting beside a tomb, arguing with a ghost while my father fell apart in his rooms, surrounded by our dangerous little family. I was helping him as much as I'd helped Mother.

The past is the past. The present is happening right now, no matter how much you ignore it. What are you going to do about it?

'Do about it? I'm down here because I have no idea what to do about it!' I twisted around to face the carving of her face. It was gorgeous, but not lifelike. She'd never looked that serene, at least not near me. 'What do I do to save him?' I waited, but she stayed as silent as her tomb.

'*Now* you go quiet,' I muttered, and leaned my head back against the door. I'd used to hate setting foot in here. My father had to almost drag me when he came down on the anniversary of her death, to open her tomb and spill the blood of some mortal killer onto her blackened bones. Praying to Nagash that she would take the blood in and heal, be born again. Some vampires had come back from burning. The blessed blood was strong. But her bones never twitched, her flesh never regrew, she stayed silent and dead – except for the voice that had started to speak to me, quiet at first, a whisper in my head, then slowly louder, until Vasara was reborn not in the flesh but in my thoughts.

It was a problematic resurrection.

I was comfortable with coming down here now, though, to argue with her or to just sit in the silence and the dark. The dark that was fading. I stood, looking across the room at the faint light that was growing in one of the doorways, a soft purple glow. Rill or Erant, looking for me? Or Arvan come to sadly ask me to depose my father again? Instead I saw a thin young man at the door, wrapped in wrinkled black robes dusted with grey ash. A little cluster of purple flames drifted through the air around his head, lighting his way.

'Shadas,' I said, and my father's necromancer dipped his head, a gesture that looked like a scarecrow shifting in the wind.

'My Lady Volari.' His voice was better than it had any right to be, rising from his timorous frame, rich and deep. 'I am sorry to disturb you. I didn't know you were back.' He trailed off, uncertain. Shadas had been saved from his frightened family when he was

a boy. They'd been farmers, terrified by a child who could make the dead move. Corsovo had appointed him necromancer to the court, and provided what training he could. Not that any of us understood how mortal magic worked. I'd mostly ignored him, often forgetting he existed, but seeing him now I rose to my feet.

'I don't care about being disturbed. I care about what's happening to my father.' I took another step, closing on him. 'Arvan said you examined him, Shadas. What's wrong?'

He looked at the polished floor, not meeting my eyes. 'I don't know.'

I was on him then, one hand gripping his thin arm tight, shaking him until he looked at me, eyes wide. 'What do you mean you don't know? You study death magic. What's happening to him? Vampires – we don't get *sick*. What is this? Did the Sun Seekers do this somehow? Is this an attack?' The words came out in a rush, a demand for answers, a demand for an enemy, something I could attack. But the necromancer just kept shaking his head.

'I don't think so. I don't think it's an attack. I don't think–'

I let him go so suddenly he stumbled. 'You don't think,' I snapped. Useless. I remembered why I never bothered talking to Shadas. 'Is there anything you *do* do?'

He was fighting not to cower, and I could hear his heart hammering in his chest, could smell the fear stink on him. It made it hard to look at him. It made me hungry.

'Not a lot,' he said. 'I'm told I have talent with death magic. But my training...' Some other emotion besides nervous fear finally entered his voice. Frustration, marked with a lick of anger. 'You say I study. That's the task King Corsovo set before me, but how am I to do it? I've no teacher, I've no real books, just a few badly copied things that mostly don't make sense. Most of what I know are things I just *know*, and I don't understand how I do them any more than I understand how I make my heart beat.'

I was tempted to ignore him, but I'd heard my father make the same complaint. He thought that Shadas could be powerful if trained – but what training was there? When the Sun Seekers had sailed into Gowyn thirty years ago and then smashed themselves into the army we'd assembled to take the port city at Ire Crossing, they'd cut us off from the rest of Aqshy and the realms beyond. There was no way to train Shadas, no way to get teachers or books. But logic was a useless salve for my anger.

What will you do? Kill him for knowing only a little more than you? Tell me, how will that help?

'Fine. You know little,' I said, stepping back, trying to be less threatening. I looked away, knowing my eyes were probably more red than brown now, and tried to make my voice calm. 'Tell me what you feel, Shadas. Is there anything you *just know* about what happened to him?'

'Lady Volari.' He took several breaths, searching for words. Finally he spoke, slow, as if his tongue had to painfully pull out each word. 'There is… a flaw. In his blood.'

'A flaw?'

'Something related to the curse of the Kastelai. The one that bound you to the Crimson Keep.' He started speaking faster, as if he'd decided it would be better to get everything out all at once. 'The thing that killed the other Kastelai when you were left here a century ago.'

'They all fell within days. My father has been well for a hundred years!'

'Yes, I know. Why did it take them so fast, and him so slow?' He shrugged. 'I don't know. I know he told me that it took some faster, some slower. Maybe the curse is weaker in him and took longer, or maybe his majesty was stronger and he held it off. But I think it's finally caught him.'

Finally caught him. As if it were a monster in his blood. The same blood that flowed in me.

I looked at Shadas, an uneasy dread stirring in me, but he was staring at the white marble tomb. 'You call her Mother. And the king, Father. He made you, didn't he?'

'They both did, in their ways,' I answered. 'But it's Corsovo's blood that flows in me.'

'Ah,' he said, as if he understood, but I doubt he did. Our little family confused mortals and vampires alike. 'And he made Rill, and Erant.'

When you should have.

'He did,' I said.

The necromancer hesitated, and in that space I heard another set of footsteps. I raised my hand, stopping him from speaking, and we waited while another light grew as someone else approached. Someone big, alone, and I knew it was Arvan before he was close enough for me to see his features in the light of the lantern he carried, or to smell his scent.

'Good, you're both here.' Arvan set his lantern down, its light gleaming off his eyes and the eyes of the heavy corpse rat that curled across his shoulders. 'White Paw said she saw someone heading this way.' His hand dipped into a pouch tied to his belt, pulled out a piece of mummified meat, and gave it to the rat. She snapped it up, then ground her teeth contentedly as she settled onto his wide shoulders.

'What do you want?' I asked. I wasn't mad at Arvan, not any more. With time to think in the dark and the silence, I'd realised I hadn't even been mad at him then. Not exactly. My anger wanted an outlet, though, and he was so convenient.

If you don't control it, then it controls you.

I rolled my eyes, hoping the gesture was lost in the shadows, and waited for Arvan to answer.

'I wanted you to talk to Shadas. To understand what we know,' Arvan said. 'I wanted us both to have a chance to speak to you privately about what's happening. About what must be done.'

'I know what you want done, Arvan.' *And what* you *want done,* I said silently to my mother, to keep her quiet. 'But you can't push me.'

'I can't,' he said. 'But they can.' He waved up, in the direction of the other Kastelai gathered far overhead. 'Did Shadas tell you about his suspicion? That this might be a flaw in the king's blood, a weakness caused by the curse of the Crimson Keep?'

I bristled at the word 'weakness', but kept my anger leashed. 'He did.'

Arvan nodded. 'I've made sure that the only ones that know of this are Shadas and me. But when the others finally see the king, I believe they'll suspect something similar, and if they believe that this sickness is tied to his blood...'

The uneasy dread suddenly formed into a realisation. 'They'll think that the same will happen to me.'

He nodded. 'To you, to me, to Rill and Erant, to the Rose Knights who defend the Grey Palace, to everyone who has the king's blood. They may fear that all of us will fall to this, eventually.' Arvan's face was grim. 'That's why I'm telling you that you need to take power. Because if you don't, you may not be able to. Give them time to see him, time to think, they may decide that it's too much of a risk to let you rule in his stead, and if it's not you, then it has to be one of them.'

'Magdalena and Salvera will be at each other's throats,' I said. 'Salvera to gain power, Magdalena to ensure that Salvera doesn't get it.'

'Civil war within our ranks, and Takora and the Sun Seekers ready to take advantage.'

'Magdalena says new troops are coming,' I said.

He reached up and stroked the long, narrow head of his rat. 'I've heard. I think she's overly concerned. You've weakened Takora considerably, and from what little we hear, Sigmar has his hands full in every realm. I doubt Hammerhal cares what happens on the Broken Plains now. But if we're weak, that changes. If we fracture, Takora will take advantage and try to finally end us.' He stopped petting White Paw and looked at me. 'I'm sorry. I know what he means to you. But if you don't take control of this now, it's going to be ripped away from you. And then it probably won't matter if we're cursed or not, because we'll all be dead.'

I turned from him, and looked back at the tomb. It glowed in the lantern light, a white block in the darkness, my mother's carved face serene and still.

You don't belong here. Do what you have to. Not all battles are with blades.

'Damn me,' I said softly, then turned back to Arvan. Shadas was a shadow behind him, silent, looking away. 'Tell the Kaste-lai we meet. Tomorrow.'

CHAPTER FIVE

The Grey Palace's great hall was a massive, round room. Its ceiling was low around the edges, rising to a high peak in the centre where an oculus framed a circle of night. The room was a stylised volcano, Temero in miniature, covered in tiles of obsidian. They made the room a glossy black, except for a circle in the centre of the floor where the tiles were made of rare red obsidian. It was probably meant to represent the fire that burned in Temero's heart, but it gleamed like a pool of blood.

I stood on those red tiles and stared up at the dark sky, watching the stars fade as Evigaine, one of Aqshy's three moons, began to slip into the oculus, its red disc trailing glimmers of flame. We'd set the start of the meeting for midnight, when Evigaine would be in the oculus' centre, spilling its ruddy light down the black tiles. It was tradition, so of course Mother had insisted.

The appearance of power is power.

'So you've said.' I ran a hand over my armour, freshly polished like my boots and swords. Rill had worked my hair into

an elaborate braid that was ornate but practical. Bloodshed was always an option among the Kastelai.

'Lady Volari.' Arvan was also dressed in his best, brown leather armour with bands of rats and bats tooled in gold down its sleeves. He had none of his actual pets with him now, but they'd been flitting around all day, telling him what the others were up to. 'We're ready.'

Five massive chairs arranged in a circle on the red tile, facing each other. Durrano's was upholstered in white, Jirrini's was red, Salvera's grey and Magdalena's purple. The final chair had a back twice the height of the others and was upholstered in black, its wood carved with roses, petals red as blood.

Before it sat another chair, smaller and unadorned. This was the one change I'd insisted on, over Arvan's careful objections, and my mother's. But whatever else they might push me into, I wasn't taking Corsovo's throne.

I'd spent most of my day in Father's apartments. He sat in the darkest corner, staring into the black with ulcerated eyes, whispering to people long dead. I'd barely got him to talk to me, and when he did he thought I was Vasara. He was getting worse, his body falling in on itself like a tree rotting from the inside. The sight of him, the smell of him... I couldn't stay. I've never fled a battle, but when I left him it was all I could do to keep from running.

I'd come here and watched the mortal servants shift the chairs while a pair of clicking skeletons polished the floor tiles with mindless patience. I'd enjoyed the almost silence until Arvan, Rill and Erant had come, followed by the Rose Knights, the warriors my father had made to defend the Grey Palace. Each Kastelai house on the Broken Plains had their own order of vampire knights, but the Rose Knights were the most dangerous, of course, because my father had made them, and he and I had trained them, each and every one. At their head was Orix, the knight-

commander. He nodded to me as they took their places behind the throne, dressed in armour black and red, but I could see frustration in his eyes.

'How much does Orix know?' I asked.

'Little,' Arvan said. 'And he's unhappy about that. Here.' He held out a clay vessel, an amphora painted with runes. It smelled of blood, and when I took it I could feel its warmth.

'Shadas made these,' Arvan said. 'They keep blood fresh and warm for days.'

So Shadas knew one thing at least. The blood scent made me hunger, but when I raised the clay vessel to my lips I scented something else in that rich smell, something faintly acrid.

'It works, but the magic leaves a bitter taste,' Arvan said, seeing my expression. Then he suddenly looked towards the hall's entrance, where a tiny bat had flown in. 'They come.'

'Go.' I handed the amphora back, and he tucked it away as he took his place on one side of my father's throne. Erant and Rill took the other side and I stood beside the smaller chair, my hands touching the hilts of my swords.

Remember, Nyssa. You don't have to be your father. Just be what you have always tried to be. His defender.

I nodded, staying silent as I watched the door.

And wipe your lip. You've blood on it.

I growled a curse as I swiped a hand across my mouth. I dropped my hand as Magdalena swept into the room. She was first of course, appearing just as the fiery moon above centred itself in the oculus. Her clothes were similar to the ones from the day before, just more ornate. She stopped when she saw the added chair, but stayed expressionless, her face smooth as she started forwards again. Her house followed behind, Ruin Knights armoured in black and purple, lining up in neat formation behind her as she took her place beside her chair.

Jirrini came next, wearing a gown of gold studded with rubies and fire opals. Always careful with their resources, Jirrini's house was the largest, and her Knights of Plenty in their gold and crimson filled the space behind her. Jirrini looked at me as she stopped beside her chair, and a tiny frown touched her lips.

Then it was Durrano, wrapped in bone-white armour. His band of Skull Knights was much smaller than Jirrini's, their number greatly reduced by battle. He looked at the chair thoughtfully, then nodded to me, a tiny incline of his head.

And then... nothing.

We all stood waiting while Salvera's grey chair sat empty. Minutes stretched, and overhead Evigaine began to slip out of the centre of the oculus, moving on.

He's already testing us.

Of course he was. Salvera was always pushing against my father's power, but he'd never been this blatant before. I wanted to go and find him and drag him to his chair, but I didn't need my mother to tell me that I was stuck here, now. Which was why Salvera was daring this.

It was Magdalena who finally broke the tension. 'Should we throw his chair outside? Make him wait on the threshold like a dog?'

Don't say anything. Keep them at each other's throats, and away from yours.

I didn't, mostly because I didn't know what to say, but then I heard it. The rustle of cloth and the clink of armour, the sound of boots and the click of claws. I made my features blank of everything but thin disdain just as Salvera walked into the hall.

He was a lean man with short grey hair and an inhuman face. His eyes were yellow, and his nose and mouth had twisted together into a muzzle, something between human and wolf, filled with teeth. He wore chain mail and a grey cloak stained with mud and

blood, and his scythe was slung across his back, its blade arcing over his head like a gore-crusted halo.

Salvera's Wolf Knights were dressed the same, in tattered grey cloaks and patchy chain armour, carrying swords with curved blades and spiked pommels. Mixed with them were a dozen dire wolves, their grey fur matted with dirt and old blood, bony spines and dull ivory skulls visible through rents in their hides. Their eyes were black hollows with pinpricks of red in their centres, and they looked at us as if we were a banquet that was being kept from them.

At least he hadn't brought one of his monstrous vargheists with him.

'You're late, Lord Salvera.' Magdalena looked at the other Kastelai with contempt.

'Late?' Salvera's voice was a rough growl. When the Crimson Keep had left us, Salvera had almost fallen to his beast, but he'd chained it – until the Battle of Ire Crossing. His beast had saved him then, turned him into a whirlwind of blade and teeth, but he'd barely pulled himself out of that killing frenzy afterwards. Since then his savagery had lurked just beneath the surface, held back only by a thin skin of cunning. Father and I had speculated on how long it would be before that skin was finally ripped aside. Looking at him now, I thought we might have been fearing the wrong finish, for it seemed like Salvera had married his cunning to his anger and become something even more unpredictable, more dangerous.

'How can I be late when the throne remains empty?' His wolf eyes slid to me, and I could see red points glowing in his pupils. 'Where's our king, Lady Nyssa? Did he run off to find some other mortal child to pass his blood to? A new little jester, to make us all laugh?'

Don't.

My heart thumped in my chest, my blood moved, but that sharp command stilled me. If I attacked Salvera without offering challenge, his whole house would fall on me, and the Wolf Knights might take me before my house could help. I kept my hands still, staring at him with eyes that must have been as red as the tile below our feet, and he bared his teeth at me, his beast trying to call out mine.

'King Corsovo will not be attending,' I said. 'I sit in his stead.' And with that I dropped into the plain chair that sat before the throne. A moment passed with them all looking at me, plotting, until Durrano sat and I felt a touch of relief. His support was expected, but if it hadn't happened everything would have fallen apart right then. I turned my attention to the others, staring at each in turn. Jirrini was frowning, Magdalena was blank, and Salvera…

Salvera fell back in his chair as if he were crashing onto a couch in his own quarters. His bestial face was hard to read, but his eyes were glittering. Impatient.

He wants to start something, but he's unsure of the situation. He wants to see his quarry before he attacks.

Now it was just Magdalena and Jirrini. The two women exchanged looks, unreadable to me, but something passed between them. Jirrini gathered her skirts and gracefully took her seat, as if she'd been waiting for just that moment, leaving Magdalena standing alone. She gave me a long stare, then sat too. Across from her, Salvera opened his muzzle to speak, but Magdalena cut him off, her voice curt, commanding.

'You sit in our king's stead because something has happened to him,' Magdalena said. 'What?'

'The king, my father–' At this, Salvera snorted, a sound of contempt that became a growl, and Magdalena frowned. I lifted my head a little more, still looking at Magdalena, ignoring Salvera, and repeated myself. 'The king, my father, has been afflicted. We don't know the cause, but Shadas is working to discover it.'

'Afflicted?' Jirrini asked, her voice coloured with concern. 'How can a vampire be afflicted? We are not mortals, to grow ill from cold or miasma.'

'I doubt it's an illness,' Salvera said. 'Perhaps it's weakness of another kind.'

I wanted to snarl at him, but Durrano was already speaking.

'What affliction could affect us?' His pale eyes were troubled. 'We are proof against mortal weakness. The only thing I've seen that was like an illness to us was that curse–'

Durrano was an ally, but a poor one in both the strength of his house's numbers, and the strength of his thinking. The others might think of the curse soon enough, but he didn't need to bring it up, and that made me want to kick his fangs in. I reined in that impulse, and interrupted him instead.

'A curse seems unlikely,' I said. 'Shadas has found no signs of hostile magic.'

'Shadas.' Magdalena said his name dismissively. 'I don't care about the necromancer. I care about King Corsovo. There's something afflicting him, so bad that you won't let us see him. Despite how many times I've asked.' She tilted her head, studying me carefully. 'I came here days ago, brought by rumours of strange happenings in the Grey Palace, and I've not been allowed to see my Kastelai brother. I don't even know if he still lives.'

Fury flicked through me, but my mother was speaking, fast and certain, and her words cut through the anger.

Now it's her turn to bait you. But she doesn't want to fight.

'She accuses me of killing my father, the man whose blood made me, and you say she doesn't want to fight?' I had to keep my teeth locked together to keep the words inside, and I knew my mask of cold aloofness had slipped, that the red in my eyes was betraying my fury. But I held myself still, waiting for an answer.

No. She wants to see if you can control yourself. If you can't,

you prove that you're either guilty of something or that you're too dangerous to be your father's proxy.

Her words made sense, but that didn't matter to my stirring heart. We'd barely begun this meeting, and I already wanted to give up, to just challenge them all and smash them down with my blades.

But then I'd be showing Magdalena she was right.

'Of course King Corsovo lives,' I said. 'He will live forever, because of his blessed blood.' The words were a little hard, but with every one I pressed my anger back, and I could feel my mother's approval. A feeling that almost made me want to rebel and give in to my rage, but I fought that impulse too. 'You may meet with him if you wish, after we're done.'

'After we're done doing what, exactly?' Salvera asked. 'Making you queen?'

After Magdalena, that barely touched me. 'No. Corsovo is our ruler, since we came here, forever.'

'But he cannot rule us now,' Salvera said, leaning forwards in his chair, his eyes glittering. 'So someone else must.'

'I am his daughter,' I said, meeting his eyes.

'You're his,' he said, beckoning with his fingers. One of the dire wolves, almost twice the size of the others, came to him and Salvera ran a claw along the exposed bone of its skull, down the blood-matted fur of its ear. 'You're his the way this beast is mine.'

'Are you saying I'm his attack dog?' I said, my fingers touching the pommels of my swords.

'No,' he said. 'I'm saying you're his pet.'

Mother didn't have time to say anything. I was already up, starting to draw, and I would have been on Salvera if Arvan hadn't caught my shoulder. He was strong, stronger than me, but my hands were up, twisting his wrist before he could react and I was free, shoving him away. The moment it took me, though, was

long enough for my mother's voice to crack through my head, sharp as my swords.

Will you let him win?

'I will not let a dog shit on the floor of my father's house,' I said, answering her, Arvan and Salvera all at once.

Then answer him right. Call challenge.

I stepped into the centre of the circle of red. Overhead, Evigaine was already touching the other side of the oculus, the little moon continuing its rapid run across the sky, but its red light still spilled down over me. 'Lord Salvera. You have done insult to me, a fellow Kastelai.' He sat in his chair, watching me with glittering yellow eyes and shining yellow teeth. Salvera's lips were curled back, his pointed ears pressed tight to his skull. Eager? Afraid? Both, probably, but I would soon make him know that only his fear was valid. 'And for that, I will call–'

I stopped. Arvan had caught my arm again, and when I ripped it away I almost brought my fist around into his face. But he was shaking his head, pointing at a bat that was flying over the ring of chairs. 'Shadas is coming,' he said, his voice strange.

'Shadas?' I said, confused. My blood was moving through me, my heart beating, my body eager to fight. This was the best I'd felt since coming back to the Grey Palace, and I wanted to move, to take Salvera's blood and leave him crying for mercy on the tiles. 'What is he doing? He's supposed to be with–'

There was a clatter of boots at the door, and Shadas was there, his pale face sweaty, his breath ragged. 'Lady Volari…' he managed, then he looked around at the silent crowd of vampires. We were all standing now, still as statues as we waited for the one mortal among us to get his breath back and speak.

'Honoured Kastelai,' he finally said, drawing himself up straight. 'The king…' His eyes came to me, and then fell, staring at the crimson floor. 'King Corsovo is dead.'

CHAPTER SIX

Sugar crested another hill and I could see them in the valley below, the round hide-and-wood shelters the nomads called daciums built along a curve of the Irewater. A tall pole sat in the middle of the nomad camp, a pennant flying from it, yellow with a serpent stitched in red.

'The band of the Biting Flames.' Celasian reined in beside me, staring down at the camp. 'These are the ones you've spent so much time on, Captain Takora?' His face was its usual hard mask, but I guessed he was unimpressed.

'They're one of the largest bands on the Broken Plains, abbot-general,' I said. 'Our numbers being what they are' – because we'd been abandoned here, unsupported, for thirty years – 'we needed allies. Your arrival changes that, but they still won't hurt. And much better they come to us than join with the Soulblight vampires of Temero.'

'Yes,' he said, his voice hard. 'Better anything than that.'

I kept my face impassive as he dug his heels into the ribs of

the poor horse we'd finally found him and started down towards the camp. The people there were gathering, watching us. I didn't want Celasian here. To be honest, I didn't want to be anywhere with him after Neria, but here especially – today was the culmination of years of diplomacy, dealing with the nomads' suspicion and pride. Having him here felt like bringing an ogor into a glassworks. I watched Celasian move down the hill, trailed by his guard in their gleaming white, and decided I would probably be lucky if the band below was still speaking to me at all by the time we were done.

In the centre of the camp the Biting Flames had erected a circle of carved wooden supports that held up a roof of hides dyed crimson and yellow. The shelter was bigger than any of the daciums, its sides open so that the people of the band could stand outside and listen to us talk. There were two of us from each side seated in the shelter's shade on woven carpets, the nomads on one side, Celasian and me on the other. To my surprise Celasian drank the vesfire, the rough liquor that the nomads made from the thorny vesin trees that grew in the hills of the Broken Plains, easily. He made no complaint about the communal cup the nomads passed to us, and I wondered if I might be able to salvage something from this meeting after all.

'You offer us much, Captain Takora.' Rhysha, leader of the Biting Flames, sat easily despite her white hair and the deep wrinkles that marked her skin. Her voice was strong but harsh, made that way by the smoke she breathed out of her dragon-carved pipe. Her son, Shyn, sat beside her, watching us with open suspicion. 'Good blades and luxuries from far Hammerhal Aqsha. But we wonder, will you make us trade our freedom for things?'

In the gathered crowd behind her there were mutters of agreement. The nomads always did their negotiating in the open, letting

their people listen, and listening to their people. A cumbersome custom, but at least it meant that I had Galeris and a group of my best from the 39th at my back, along with the abbot-general's guard. I could see how the nomads watched them, especially the Spears of Heaven. Maybe the sight of Celasian's pretty troops would help bend the fractious nomads towards alliance.

'I've told you, Rhysha,' I said, 'the plains are yours. We ask nothing from you but your help in driving out your true enemy, the corpse king that lays claim to the Grey Palace.'

'So you say,' she said, as her people whispered and Shyn favoured me with a suspicious frown. 'So you say.'

'I do say–'

That was when Celasian spoke.

'Do you still remember Celas?'

Rhysha took a long pull from her pipe. When she finally spoke, smoke spilled from her mouth and drifted back into the nomads, who were watching us now with surprised silence. 'Celas and his Fist. That was years ago, but we still tell his story.' She looked at Celasian, her eyes sharp despite the haze of cataracts. 'What do you know of him?'

'The Fist,' he said. 'Five bands, united in one. The nomads of the Broken Plains haven't formed an army like that since the Siege of Maar.'

'He was powerful,' Shyn said, his first words since we'd shared drink. 'His Fist tried to drive us from our territories.'

'But he fell, and the Fist crumpled with him,' Celasian said.

'And we took back what was ours.' Rhysha took another pull from her pipe. 'You know some of our stories, servant of the Storm God. How?'

How. That was my question. I was staring at Celasian, confused. What did he care about some dead nomad warlord? How did he even know his name? I'd seen little evidence that he had

read my reports about the Broken Plains, so how did he know about… whatever this was?

'Because I lived them,' Celasian said. 'Celas was my father.'

The silence vanished as the crowd around us spoke all at once, questioning, demanding, trying to understand what was going on. I barely heard them as understanding swept through me. His father. That meant… Damn me. That meant nothing but trouble.

Rhysha raised the hand holding her pipe until her people slowly fell into silence. 'Tell your story.'

'I'll tell you all you need to know.' Celasian pitched his voice so that it carried to the people gathered behind Rhysha. 'I was a child when the Soulblight vampires came to us. They sent their queen, a monster with a beautiful face who promised my father gifts if he would slave the Fist to them. When he refused, she put her teeth to his throat.'

Celasian stopped, his pale eyes distant. 'I saw her, biting him, and I burned her for it. I've come back to see them all burn for that.'

'You've come back for revenge,' Rhysha said.

'Revenge,' Celasian said, 'and the glory of Sigmar. They are one and the same in me.'

Damn me, I thought again, and wished they were still passing around the liquor.

'So that is why you ask for our help?' Shyn asked. 'For your revenge?' He was staring at Celasian, his armour, his silver spear, and in Shyn's face I could see a mix of envy and jealousy. 'Why don't you and Sigmar do it yourself?'

'We will,' Celasian said with absolute certainty. 'You want a gift? Here it is. Join us, now, without begging for swords or carpets. Join us, because we are right and we *will* cleanse this land and take it for Sigmar.'

Whispers ripped through the crowd, but they were drowned out when the Spears of Heaven lined up behind Celasian spoke at once, their voices echoing through the camp, 'For the glory of Sigmar!'

The shout quieted the nomads, but I could see the mix of fear and anger on their faces, expressions that promised trouble, and I cursed silently to myself. Revenge. Celasian and his Spears weren't here to save the 39th, or the Broken Plains. They were here to destroy the Soulblight vampires of Temero, no matter the cost to anyone else.

Across from me, Rhysha was holding on to her pipe with white-knuckled fingers, and I could see the edge of fear in her old eyes. She understood how close this meeting was to riot. She started to stand, to speak, but her idiot son spoke first.

'This is how you come to us? Like conquerors?' He pushed himself up, standing over Celasian. 'We didn't ask for you, or your god. The Broken Plains are ours. They are not for you to take, whoever your father was.'

Many outside the tent stayed silent, confused or frightened, but there were enough of them who agreed with Shyn to make a roar that followed his words, a cry of defiance that echoed over the plains.

Celasian ignored the sound and stared at Shyn, his eyes as flat as a snake's. 'If you are not with us,' he asked, his cold voice a warning, 'then whom are you with?'

'We are with our own,' Rhysha snapped, still trying to stop the ruin that was coming. 'We are the Biting Flames. We have no allegiance to the vampires.'

'And why not?' Shyn turned towards his mother. 'At least when they come to us, they offer us their blood, their power, their immortality!'

'They offer you their curse,' Celasian said. 'They offer you their evil.' There was nothing in his voice now but certainty. No pity, no anger, just that, and I started to speak.

'Abbot-general. I think–'

He heard not a word. 'They offer you that,' he continued, his words rolling over mine, over the angry voices of the crowd. 'And you consider it. And so you are damned.'

Celasian was on his feet, his armour not slowing him at all, aiming Heaven's Edge at Shyn's chest. Sparks danced along the weapon's length, and from its tip a bolt of lightning cracked out. The white-hot arc smashed into Shyn and his skin burned black and split, the blood beneath flashing into steam, and before he could even scream, his body tore itself apart. Scalding shrapnel of burning flesh and melting bone flew back and struck the people gathered outside the shelter, searing into them.

Then the screaming began.

The day was fading, the light dissolving behind the haze of smoke that rose from the ruins below, and I stood on the hillside, trying to ignore the last screams.

Sugar snorted, tossing her head. The smell of smoke and blood made her uneasy – she wanted to go back to her stable in Gowyn, and I felt for her. I wanted nothing more than to turn my back on this day, this place, to ride back to that wretched port, get on a ship and leave the Broken Plains forever. But Sugar was stuck waiting for me just as I was stuck waiting for Celasian, and damn me, I didn't know which of us was more trapped. Sugar snorted again and I swore under my breath. Down the hill, Galeris was leaving the shattered remnants of the Biting Flames and walking towards me.

I threw him a waterskin when he got close enough, and he took a long draught. His face was streaked with sweat and ash, and he stank of smoke tinged with something else, something uglier – the smell of burnt meat.

'Is he done?' I asked, when Galeris had finished drinking.

'Almost.' My lieutenant's voice was thick with smoke and emotion, and he didn't look at me. He stared out at nothing, his thick fingers tightening and loosening on the neck of the waterskin. 'He's killed every adult and thrown their bodies on a pyre.'

'At least he didn't kill the children.' That... Gods, I hadn't even been aware of how afraid I was of that.

'No,' Galeris said. 'He wants them to help grind the bones to powder after the fire has cooled enough so there's nothing left for the vampires to raise up. He said it was his first lesson for them – that sometimes the greatest mercy is death.' He finally looked at me. 'We didn't stop him.'

We didn't. *I* didn't. There was no accusation in Galeris' voice. There didn't have to be. The accusation rode the smoke that filled the air, along with the thin sound of a child crying somewhere below.

Shyn's smoking body had still been falling when the warriors of the Biting Flames drew their weapons. I'd jumped up, shouting at them, shouting at Celasian, my hands out, trying to stop it all, and across from me I had seen Rhysha trying to do the same thing, her pipe still clutched in one hand as she stood screaming at her people to stand back. They had already been charging, though – until another bolt of lightning from Celasian's holy weapon had turned them into burning, screaming meat.

It had been blood and chaos then, the crowd exploding, some attacking, most running. The Spears of Heaven had rushed forwards, slamming into the mob that was coming for Celasian, their spear tips thrusting out, driving them back. I had seen Rhysha fall to the ground bleeding, her fallen pipe smouldering on a carpet, and then Celasian's boot heel had smashed down, crushing it into nothing as he sent another lightning bolt sizzling into the nomads.

I'd pulled my troops together as the Spears of Heaven drove forwards, spears flashing. I remember Galeris shouting at me, asking what we should do before he had to kick away a nomad

who'd rushed us with a sword. I'd looked past him, at Celasian standing in the centre of the shelter, Heaven's Edge blazing in his hand like a storm. The abbot-general's eyes had been as dead and empty as a skull's. I'd seen that and taken myself and the rest of my soldiers and left.

We'd walked out of the camp, careful to avoid the nomads fleeing the slaughter, taking our horses and moving away up the hill. We waited there, silent.

'I didn't stop him,' I said. 'He is an abbot-general of the Church of Sigmar.'

'He's…' Galeris said, and then shook his head. 'What are we supposed to do, Captain Takora?'

'Do?' I said. 'We go back to Gowyn. We wait for the rest of the Spears of Heaven to arrive. Then we go and kill the monsters that've trapped us here for so long. And when that's finally done, we leave these cursed lands and forget this damn place ever existed.'

'You think you'll forget this?'

I didn't look at him. I couldn't. 'No,' I said, finally, almost silently.

He didn't answer, except to move away to the little knot of soldiers from the 39th. Sugar pressed against me, and I turned to rub her ears. As I did, something caught my eye. A tiny message, stuck to my saddle. Similar to the one I'd found at the ambush site, but this one was meant for me. I snapped my head around, but there was nothing, no one. I was alone.

I picked up the scrap of paper and unfolded it. The message was short, four words in a neat hand.

'The king is dead.'

I crumpled the message into a ball, grabbed a handful of dried grass, and fed it all to Sugar. Dead. Now. Of course.

'Damn me,' I whispered, to Sugar and the smoke and the darkening sky. 'Damn us all.'

CHAPTER SEVEN

I had the coffin made of glass.

Not because I wanted to see my father like this. No. Stands of candles lined the dark walls of the chamber that housed my mother's tomb, and the glow of their flames danced off the polished floors and pushed the shadows back. That candlelight poured through the glass panes leaded together around my father, revealing every awful detail of dead-white skin and open sores, sunken eyes and skull-like face. That withered body wore my father's armour, clutched his sword in clawlike hands, but it looked nothing like him.

It was him, though. Corsovo Volari, Knight of the Crimson Keep, King of the Rose Throne. An immortal, granted life everlasting by the God of Death himself, dead. It couldn't be. It shouldn't be. So I'd made them make a coffin of glass so that I could see for myself, and know that I wasn't burying him alive.

It doesn't really help though, does it?

'Quiet.' The word echoed, whispering over and over until the

shadows swallowed them. I didn't care. The only ones to hear were Rill and Erant. Neither of them had left me since the night of my father's death, and they'd heard me snarling far worse at my mother over the last few days. She might be dead, but I didn't want her advice. Or her comfort.

Then what about another's?

I frowned, wondering what she meant, and then Erant was settling down beside me, his huge sword rattling as he laid it atop his crossed legs.

'How did it happen?'

Neither Rill nor Erant talked a lot, one of the reasons I'd chosen them to be my guards when Father had insisted, and I frowned at him. 'How did what happen?'

Erant had spent the last few days listening to me snarling at Arvan and Shadas, demanding to know *why* we were planning a funeral for an immortal. I knew Erant wasn't asking about Cors-ovo's death.

'How'd he become your father?' Erant asked. 'You've known us since before we took the king's blood, but we don't know any-thing about how *you* came to be born into your second life.' He shrugged. 'Except that you don't like to talk about it.'

'But you ask anyway,' I said. 'Now.' Now, sitting beside the glass box that held my father's body.

'Now,' he agreed.

'Another's,' I said, and Erant knew I wasn't talking to him. He was used to this. 'Why would I want his comfort and advice either?'

Because if you don't listen to him, I'll make you listen to me.

A threat, but I could also read the promise in her words. Put up with this, and she'd leave me alone.

'He made me the same way he made you – he took blood, he gave blood.' In my head, I could feel my mother's displeasure like

ice water, and I relented and went on. 'He killed me. After I stuck a kitchen knife in his eye.' Erant blinked at me, and Rill leaned in, listening. 'That was the only weapon he'd let me use at first, when I started training at the Crimson Keep. I got to throw it away when his eye finally grew back.'

I'd told Father I'd thrown the knife away. But I'd kept it in my quarters in the Crimson Keep, the only souvenir of my first life. I think I missed it more than the Keep.

'I don't remember anything from my first life. Not even my name.' I shrugged. 'It doesn't matter. I was a girl living in some forgotten part of Ulgu. Or Chamon. Or Shyish. Nobody could remember. It doesn't matter,' I said again. 'It was just another battle that the Crimson Keep found, a band of Chaos Warriors looting some city. The Kastelai hit them when they were drunk on terror and triumph and slaughtered them. Corsovo said he was drunk on blood, after. Riding through the ruins alone when a screaming wretch flung herself through a window and attacked him. That was me. He caught me, drank the blood from my veins, but then one of his bloody tears fell on my lips. And that's my first memory. Opening my eyes, aching, cold, and so hungry, looking up through the darkness to see him looking down at me, one eye a ruin weeping blood down on me, the other...' I looked at Erant. 'Do you know how he'd look at me, when I'd done something wrong, but that he found amusing? So serious but somehow still laughing?'

'I've seen it.'

We've all seen it.

'That's what I saw.' I looked at the coffin. That wasted face had no expression any more, locked in its rictus of death. 'I always remembered that, through all that followed. That twisted, secret pride in me for having caught him by surprise. He wanted me to do that to everyone else. The other Kastelai, the enemies we

fought, he wanted me to surprise them all, which is why he trained me so hard. The other vampires thought he'd made me as some kind of blood-drunk joke, and in a way I was. But I was a joke on them, and gods, how he laughed whenever I cut down the ones that challenged me.'

'That sounds like him,' Erant said. 'I'd heard so many stories of the vampires of Temero, but he was the first I met and he… confused me. I'd heard you were all cold and arrogant… but King Corsovo had a sense of humour. Dark and strange, but there.'

I remembered his sly smile, his fangs just exposed. 'Father was different.'

'He was.' Erant stayed quiet a moment, maybe considering how far he should push. 'Why did you call him Father? I've heard other vampires refer to the ones they've made as progeny. But none of them call their makers Father. Or Mother.'

'That was Vasara's fault. She hated it, but she started it.' That memory. The way it felt.

I'd been with the Crimson Keep for a year, spending day after day training with Corsovo. Fighting with that stupid knife, fighting with my hands and feet and fangs. Learning to read an opponent, to know how they were going to move *before* they moved so I could avoid the painful crack of a practice blade. Those wooden blades were my father's only concession to my training. He didn't slow down, didn't pull his blows, and he broke me time after time, to heal and be broken again. My healing was the only power useful to me then; my speed was wasted on clumsy lunges, mistimed blocks. I remember how other Kastelai would come to watch him train me, and how I hated their laughter as Corsovo smashed me down, or worse, their looks of sneering contempt. And I remember Vasara. Always there, always watching, her disapproval clear in her eyes even if her face was blank, indifferent.

A freak show, she told Corsovo, when the other vampires were gone. A stupid obsession that demeaned him. I lay on the ground, broken, and hated her for those words.

Then one day, not long after my father's eye had grown back, I was running through my forms with the wooden practice sword he'd finally allowed me to use and another Kastelai started to watch. Sevik, a vampire with a face twisted into something that looked more like a rat than a man. Sevik was a braggart, one of the fighters who always struck a defeated opponent one more time when sparring, just to make them hurt. He'd done it to a friend of my father's, and Corsovo had challenged him and savaged him. Sevik had wanted revenge ever since. I knew that day that Sevik meant to hurt me, the way he couldn't hurt my father. I knew, and didn't care.

I wanted to fight. I was aching from practice, the fingers of my left hand broken, my right ankle buckling every time I stepped on it, and one of my fangs had been ripped out after catching in my father's wooden blade. Still early in my second life, I didn't heal as fast as I do now. But when Sevik challenged me I went after that vermin-faced coward with everything I had, and almost won, would have won, except for his cheating.

I'd smashed Sevik's practice blade out of his hand, using the same move that my father had done to shatter my fingers, but instead of yielding Sevik had drawn his real sword. He cut my practice blade to splinters, and then it was just my hands and feet against his blade. It still galls me that I didn't beat him even so, but my strikes didn't hurt him. He took a punch to the throat, then drove his sword through my shoulder and pinned me to one of the walls.

Sevik was going to kill me. The beast was glaring out of his eyes, and when my blood ran down his blade, he'd howled and lunged at me. Grabbed my head, muzzle spreading wide, ready to bite… And then Vasara had caught Sevik by his hair and smashed his

face into the wall. She shattered his narrow muzzle against the stone, and broken teeth had rattled to the floor.

Sevik had tried to fight back, but Vasara had thrown him across the room into a rack of wooden swords. I remembered watching him rise, the beast blazing in his eyes. Remembered watching Vasara look back at him, her face a perfect mask of cold disdain, her only motion one finger tapping its red, three-inch talon against the sleeve of her gown. Remembered seeing the rage fade from the rat-faced vampire's eyes, swallowed by fear. And confusion.

'You defend it, Vasara?' His words had sputtered through his broken jaws. 'Your lover's pet?'

And I remembered what Vasara had said. 'He's more father to her than owner.'

Her voice had been scornful. That was the thing. It was a joke, but the truth of it was found in that scorn. The way Corsovo treated me was different to how most of the vampires treated their progeny. It was familial. That's why it bothered Vasara so much.

Her words had cut deeper than the sword that still pinned me to the wall. More father to her... I had no memory then, no past, nothing but Corsovo, and the word father gave me a connection, roots. A purpose to survive beyond anger.

I remembered the way I'd felt, and a new pang of grief stabbed through me. Something cold ran down my cheek, and I reached up and wiped away a tear. 'If these questions are supposed to make me feel better, Erant, you're failing.'

I'd called Corsovo 'Father' for the first time not long after Sevik's attack, and he'd just given me his smile and started our next bout of sparring, even though my shoulder hadn't healed from being stabbed through.

'They are and they aren't,' Erant said. 'When I was mortal, and one of our band would fall in battle, we'd get drunk and tell stories

about their life. We'd laugh and we'd cry and then we'd throw up and pass out and… It's what we did. We always felt better, eventually.'

'I can't throw up,' I said, 'and I can't pass out, and I don't know if I can feel better.'

I walked away, stopping in front of Vasara's tomb. In a few hours this door would be unsealed, and I would carry another coffin in to be set next to the one that held my mother's charred bones. Two dead immortals. My only family. My only past.

I stared at Vasara's carving, and I heard her voice in the aching vault of my skull.

Your past is behind you. Let yourself mourn, because you must, but do it fast so you can focus on your present. Or you'll join us in this tomb.

Night was fading into day, and the black circle of sky framed by the oculus at the top of the great hall was fading to grey. Then it went dark, blinded by the canvas pulled across it by skeletons that had been tied to the Grey Palace's rooftop for that purpose.

I stood in the hall below, in the dim glow of the few candles that were lit. The silence felt like a balm after the funeral. Magdalena had done the service, a harsh drone of words calling upon Nagash for his blessing… I hadn't listened. I was only there because Mother and Arvan forced me.

No.

They nagged me, but the truth of it was that I was there because I wanted to be the one to take my father into that tomb and set him beside my mother. I'd glared at the other Kastelai until they had fallen back and let me lift the glass coffin by myself. It weighed so little. My father's body was a husk, bereft of weight and soul.

'You're here.' Arvan strode into the room, boots cracking against the tile. 'I couldn't find you anywhere.'

'I wanted quiet,' I said, feeling too drawn-out to snarl. 'This palace is too full. Everywhere I go there's another bloody vampire.'

'The others… They're making ready.' Arvan looked around the room, at the empty chairs. 'If you want quiet, you chose the worst place, but it's the place you need to be. Magdalena has called council.'

'Only the king can do that,' I said.

'The king is dead.' His eyes stopped on the heavy chair that had been my father's. 'But someone must rule.'

Magdalena makes her move.

'Should I care?' Arvan looked at me, thinking I was responding to him. I shook my head. Did I care? Part of me, the part that wasn't wrapped in grief, did. Part of me was angry, looking to lash out, and Magdalena was setting herself up as a target. But my grief smothered my anger, and my heart stayed still in my chest.

'She'll be here soon, with Jirrini right after.' Arvan stared upwards, thinking. 'Durrano will hesitate, but he'll come. He won't know what else to do. And then Salvera. He'll hate giving Magdalena any pretence of support, but he knows he can't let her meet with the others alone. That leaves us. Your father's house. You.'

'That leaves me,' I said. Just me, two bodies in a tomb and a ghost in my head.

Nyssa. Do you know why I opposed your making?

'You've given me a litany of reasons over the centuries,' I said silently, bitterly. 'Am I supposed to pick just one?'

I mean the real reason. The one you just so clearly illustrated.

'What are you talking about?' I was barely moving my lips, but Arvan was staring at me, clearly wondering why I'd gone so still. I turned away from him, focusing on my mother's ghost. 'If you've some truth you want to spit out, just say it, instead of playing with words like always.'

Corsovo never should have given you his blood because you are a child. She kept speaking, before I could snap back my protest. *Your body may have finished growing, but your mind was still not fully formed. We have no idea how old you were when you tried to kill him, but you were at most eighteen. Likely less, still raw with youth. And on top of that, he found you in the middle of a battle with the servants of Chaos. Gods know what horrors you'd witnessed. Whatever they were, they were enough to make you throw yourself at a Blood Knight with nothing but a kitchen knife.*

She let her words sink in, then started again. *Corsovo should never have made you. Those traits, those emotions, you'll never grew out of them. That's why I was so angry with him, with you, for so long.*

'You always thought I was a freak.' I didn't care if Arvan heard.

Yes, she said. *And yet you grew on me. You have other qualities that make up for your faults. You're intelligent, loyal, driven. And vicious.*

That last word cut through my grief just enough to make me shake my head. 'You decided to make me a Kastelai because I'm vicious?' I kept the words silent this time. 'That fits.'

It does. But that's not it. I started to teach you because I realised you were no passing fancy of Corsovo. He was dedicated to making you a true Kastelai, one whose name would be whispered with fear through the halls of the Crimson Keep. You were his mad dream, Nyssa. A protege, a child, an obsession. I never truly understood his connection to you, but I grew to know its depth. He was tied to you, and because I was tied to him... so was I. Which meant that your successes, your failures, were tied to me too, whether or not I wanted that. So I started to teach you about honour and etiquette and politics, things that you hated but so desperately needed.

Now I'm teaching you this. You're flawed. You're over a century old, but you're immature and always will be. You hate hearing this, but you need to, because your immaturity is making you

weak, leaving you open for attack. Fight it. Get back your bearings, and use your strengths. You're smart enough to see what must be done. You're loyal to your father's memory, driven by his dreams, and you're vicious enough to tear out all their Kastelai throats if you have to.

'Gods damn you,' I said, out loud. 'Gods damn me.' My emotions were a tangle of anger and grief, shame and pride, and was this what she meant by immaturity? This knot of feeling that filled me, impossible to unravel? If so, she was right, because damn me, it was always there in the still chambers of my heart, wasn't it? Growing and shrinking but never gone.

But I could shove it down for my father. And my mother. For my vicious loyalty to them both, and the knowledge that if I failed here I would shame both their names.

'Arvan,' I said. 'Assemble the Rose Knights. Get them here, now!'

'Yes, Lady Volari,' he said, startled, and rushed from the room.

When he was gone, I went to the simple wooden chair I'd set before my father's throne, picked it up, and threw it across the room to shatter against the wall.

Arvan could move fast when necessary.

He had my house assembled before any of the others had made their appearance. They were probably all changing out of their funeral garb. I thought it appropriate that my Rose Knights were still dressed in theirs, weapons buckled over their dark finery.

When everyone was in place, the Rose Knights lined up behind Orix, Rill and Erant standing beside the Rose Throne, Arvan came to me.

'They're on their way,' he said. 'Sooner than I thought, but I expect Magdalena has had word that your house has moved.'

'Good. Let's get this over with.' I smoothed my hands over my hair, making certain that the braids were out of the way. I wore

my usual ceremonial armour, but the circlet in my hair was gold and obsidian, the closest I had to a crown.

'Lady Volari.' Arvan held up a painted amphora, similar to the one he'd offered me before. 'You need to feed. You're going grey.'

I didn't need to check my skin to know he was right. I hadn't fed since the fight in the ravine, and the hunger was in me, tangled with my emotions. I didn't need Mother to tell me that that wasn't going to help me in this meeting, and if fighting were necessary...

Pulling the plug from the vessel, I lifted it up and drained it. The blood was hot, and even though I caught a hint of that bitter tinge from Shadas' magic, I savoured it. It tasted like violence.

'A murderer?' I asked, handing the vessel back.

'Yes,' Arvan said. 'Sent here from Maar weeks ago. He'd beaten someone to death.'

It was part of the Kastelai code that we did not feed from humans or other intelligent creatures indiscriminately. Blood was taken from someone we'd defeated in battle, a willing servant who traded some of their life for our protection or regard, or a criminal sent to us for judgement. Those last we fought, and if they drew a drop of blood from us they were freed. Which never happened. We took them, and tasted their crimes as we gave them justice.

'Weeks?' I asked Arvan. 'Why did you not give him to my father?'

'I tried,' he said. 'But the king insisted he was for you. It was the last rational thing I heard from him.' Arvan watched me carefully, and the emotions that filled my blood-touched eyes must have been under control enough for him to go on. 'I was going to let you take him yourself, of course, but things spun out of control. I knew you were going to need blood for this, so I had him judged and drained for you.'

He was nervous, wondering if I would think his actions had somehow tainted this last gift of my father's. But I understood

the need. The new blood, the strength of life and death in it, was already flowing through me, helping me.

'Thank you.'

'Thank Rill,' he said. 'She took the man with a dagger stroke, kept him alive while she drained him, and she didn't miss a drop.'

I nodded to Rill and she nodded back. On the other side of the chair, Erant looked away, irritated. The last time he'd tried to kill and drain someone for me, he'd ended up severing both carotids and trying to scrape the blood off the floor into a bucket.

'They're here,' Arvan warned, as one of his bats flitted into the room and swung around his head. I swiped my tongue across my teeth, pulled myself up straight, and made my face a mask, haughty and impervious.

Better than adequate.

As good as I would get, and I held that pose as Magdalena swept into the room.

She'd come as the general, her formal wear replaced with armour. A cuirass was wrapped around her body, complete with shoulder plates, gauntlets and greaves – not quite full plate but close. It was black, with a raven embossed on the breast and the holy symbol of Nagash picked out in tiny inlaid amethysts on her shoulders and forearms. Her sword hung from her hip, and across her back hung a black shield, also emblazoned with a raven. Her head was bare except for a dark ring with one great amethyst directly over her brow. A crown and not a crown, just like mine.

Her Ruin Knights were also armoured and wearing their weapons, but they were polished and pretty, decked in feathered capes and pennants. A fine parade drew up behind her, all silent and waiting as she stared at me standing before the Rose Throne. I stared back, doing my best to keep my anger cold, controlled, even though I felt my heart quivering in my chest. We matched gazes

for a long moment, and then she strode to her chair, standing beside it as her house formed ranks behind her.

All was silence then. Even my keen ears heard nothing as we stood staring at each other, perfectly still. No breath, no beating hearts, just the poised perfection of vampires, waiting. Waiting. Until we heard the crack of marching feet coming down the hall.

I'm not sure what would have happened if one had arrived before the other, if it had been Jirrini first, or Durrano. I doubt we would have fought, we both had our prickly Kastelai honour, Magdalena from her centuries in the Crimson Keep, me from the constant presence of my dead mother. But there was a ruthlessness in all our kind that made us dangerous, and it was good, I think, that Durrano and Jirrini paused outside the door, then walked in together, their houses trailing behind.

They were once again in their court finery, Durrano's unchanged from the last meeting, while Jirrini wore a different gown that mixed crimsons and blues together like a twisting flame. Her skirts were divided, though; she wanted to be able to move if needed, and I could see the tiny bulges hidden in the flowing lines of her dress. She had knives, the small throwing ones she was so good with. Looking carefully at the Knights of Plenty following her, I could see the same hints of weapons hidden among their finery. Jirrini was trying to play this both ways, keeping the appearance of peace while ready for war. Which was better than Durrano. There were no telltale bulges of hidden weapons in any of his clothes, or on his Skull Knights, and I had to fight not to snarl at my one ally. My solace was the irritated look I caught flashing between Magdalena and Jirrini. Magdalena had no interest in being covert, and I knew she would have preferred Jirrini to come dressed in her armour. Which meant that while they might be allies, Magdalena didn't control Jirrini.

The other Kastelai took their places beside their chairs, their houses spread behind them. The numbers weren't encouraging. My house and Magdalena's were matched, but Jirrini had more than either of us, and Durrano's house was the smallest. There shouldn't be a fight. There wouldn't be a fight. But I couldn't stop myself from checking the disparity, and it was frustrating. Even without the wild card of Salvera factored in.

He came right on their heels. Last again, but not playing around with making us wait. Like Durrano, Salvera had dressed the same again in his blood-smeared chain mail and muddy boots and cloak. The one difference was that he carried his great scythe in his hands now, not across his back. None of the others of his house had their weapons drawn but it was still a clear message, and we all watched him cross to his chair with our lips parted, our fangs partly exposed.

Salvera made a point to look at each of us, me first, Magdalena last, as he took his spot. His Wolf Knights fell in behind him, the same feral bunch, though there were even more dire wolves mixed in with them now. The huge one from last time settled in beside Salvera, the glow in its empty eye sockets a baleful, hungry red. Salvera rubbed his pale fingers across the exposed bone of its brow and showed us his fangs. They were as stained with blood as the head of the beast that crouched beside him.

'I see we're done with posturing.' He turned his eyes, pricked with red like the dire wolves', to the Rose Throne. 'The king is dead. Now there will be a queen?' He looked at me, laughing silently like a wolf, then turned to stare at Magdalena. 'So which little lapdog will it be?'

He's certainly done with any posturing. He baits you from the start, but his focus... It's on Magdalena now.

She was right. The banal crudeness of his contempt was actually less annoying to me than what he'd said last meeting. But it was the kind of thing that Magdalena, with her stiff adherence to her

honour, could not stand. She kept her face cold, but I could see the tiny shifts in her stance, the way she was unconsciously readying herself to strike. I watched, and I wanted to encourage it. Let them fight. It was a strategy... but it was also an emotional, visceral response. I wanted them to hurt each other.

But you can't afford it.

And that was the painful truth. I needed them, all of them, otherwise all the work both my parents had done carving out this little empire after we'd been abandoned would be for nothing. I had to stop them, but at least I could make my own statement doing it.

I reached into myself and found my magic, the magic that flowed through my blood, sustaining me. It was cold and sharp as always, painful to the touch, but I grasped it with my will. Salvera had made a mistake when he'd come here with all his weapons out to intimidate. He'd forgotten my gifts.

'Lord Salvera. You dare!' Magdalena hissed. She was on the edge of drawing her blade, but I was focused on my magic, driving it out of me and into the monstrous dire wolf that crouched at Salvera's side. My talent for raising and controlling the dead, weaving my own death magic through the complicated collapsed architectures of a corpse that had once been home to a human soul, that was limited. Pathetic, my mother would say. That was what the other Kastelai remembered. But they had forgotten how good I was with animals.

Salvera was smiling his wolf smile at Magdalena as she demanded his apology, ignoring me as I stood still, silent. Ignoring me as I hooked my magic into the creature crouched beside him, stripped Salvera's will from it and made it mine.

'I think we're beyond apologies, my Lady Magdalena,' Salvera said. 'We've been together for centuries. We know who we are. Now we just need to decide–' He stopped when the dire wolf rose. His hand clutched at it, and it twisted its head, snapping at his fingers, just missing them as he snatched them away. Salvera spun his scythe down, prepared for an attack, but stopped when the huge dire wolf turned its back on him and walked away. It settled next to me, smelling of old blood and wet fur, but I let it lean the heavy bone of its massive head against my hip.

'Yes,' I said, stroking the bloodstained skull. 'Now is the time for many decisions.' I smiled at Salvera, showing my fangs. He looked back at me, the pinpricks of red in his yellow eyes glowing brighter.

Keep underestimating me, I thought, then deliberately turned away. I didn't underestimate him. I'd set Rill and Erant on that side of me and I knew they were watching. 'Isn't that why we're here?' I asked, looking at Magdalena.

'Very much so,' she said. 'I…' She paused, then went on. 'We must speak.'

Good. She changed her tone from command to cooperation. You've put yourself on better footing with her. Now let's hope Salvera can keep his beast on a leash.

'Then let us do so.' And with that, I sat upon the Rose Throne.

Though that may have pushed it, my mother said dryly.

I ignored her. I meant to have this finished.

'Are you trying to make us fight?' Jirrini asked. Her beautiful face was cool and still, her voice detached, but her eyes were a touch too wide. She was trying to act as if this were all beneath her, but she was frightened. She'd been struck from her mount at Ire Crossing, been forced to hold off dozens of mortals in the bloody mud of the riverbank before Magdalena had rescued her. Father thought she'd lost her nerve that day, and I agreed. She'd been cautious to the edge of cowardice ever since.

'Of course she is,' Salvera said. 'She's desperate to prove her dominance.'

I turned and met his ugly eyes. 'I need prove nothing. But if you wish to remind me of our unfinished business?' I left the question

hanging, and we stared unblinking into each other's eyes for a long, long moment. Until Magdalena surprised us both.

'We don't have time for this.' She sat down in her chair, steel thudding onto the wood. 'Or blood, to be honest.' She looked at the others. 'Sit, stand, I don't give a damn. We don't have time. The king is dead, we're bled almost dry, and the Spears of Heaven are coming. We need a plan, or we're all going to be sent back to Nagash with our fangs pulled.'

Jirrini's careful mask slipped a little more, and she frowned, but sat. Durrano sat as if the matter had been settled and was done. Salvera kept his feet. He leaned against his chair, his scythe in his hands, but he kept his muzzle shut.

'Their leader is already here,' Magdalena said, 'with his guard. No more than fifty fighters, but they wiped out the Biting Flames, one of the larger bands on the Broken Plains.' She looked at each of us, stopping with her eyes on me. 'These Spears of Heaven are mortals, but they're not like the Sun Seekers. They're fanatics, and Celasian, their leader, carries a relic that throws lightning. When their full strength is gathered we will face a force far stronger than the one that almost defeated us at Ire Crossing.'

'So you abdicate, Lady Magdalena?' Salvera asked, his words contemptuous. 'Because you fear these slaves of the Storm God?'

'I abdicate nothing,' she said. 'I'm just not going to waste resources in a pointless civil war.' Magdalena looked around the room. 'Look at us. We've barely half the number of vampires that we had when we fought at Ire Crossing. And our army of the dead? A handful of that force.'

'Whose fault is that?' Salvera snapped. 'All of you were turned into cowards by that fight. You kept us from rebuilding our numbers!'

'We kept you from slaying every mortal you could get your fangs into!' Magdalena retorted. 'We would have been reduced to

roaming the plains like beasts if we'd listened to you. How many mortals do you have left at your hold, Lord Salvera? None, except for those you've stolen from us.'

'I've had one of my outer villages go missing in a night,' Durrano said, frowning at Salvera. 'Which I've been trying to *discuss* with you ever since you showed up. But you've dodged me at every turn, like a cur fearing the whip.'

Salvera waved a dirty clawed hand at him. 'Keep your mouth shut, lapdog, or I'll take your hold next.'

Durrano rose to his feet. 'You admit it, you bloodless thief!' he shouted.

Salvera snarled, and the pack of dire wolves growled in support, their gore-crusted fur bristling. Magdalena was furious, ready to snap orders, and Jirrini had leaned back in her chair, obviously wishing she were anywhere but near the two shouting vampires.

Now, Mother said, even as I was starting to rise.

'Kastelai,' I said, 'silence!'

The insults, the threats, the arguing had made my heart beat, and my words rang through the chamber, loud enough to make the candle flames tremble. The Kastelai went silent, and the dire wolves sank to the floor, quiet, except the giant I'd stolen from Salvera. It bristled and growled, that low throbbing threat the only sound.

I had to fight not to smile at the looks on their faces. Then a chill swept through me, like a piece of ice had stabbed through my heart, but as suddenly as it had come, the cold was gone. My heart thudded again and I blinked, my anger almost fading into confusion.

'You have something to say, Lady Nyssa?'

Magdalena's voice hit me, and I realised I was sitting motionless, one hand on my chest. I brought it down to the carved arms of the Rose Throne and pulled myself together. 'What was that?' I thought, but for once my mother had no answer.

'I do,' I said out loud. The sudden silence in my head should have been welcome, but it wasn't. I brushed off the uneasy feeling and leaned back, the Rose Throne's high back pressing into my spine. 'Magdalena's right – and she's wrong. We're not going to fight each other, like starving rats in a cage. We are Kastelai, the deadliest warriors in all the realms, and in our blood is power. Immortality.'

They were all watching me closely now. Magdalena frowned, Salvera sneered, but they were silent, and Jirrini and Durrano were intent. I'd worked the shape of this speech out with Mother while getting ready for this meeting, and I was determined to see it work. I'd seen my father twist the others with words before, and while pretty speeches were something I'd had little use for previously, I needed all the weapons I could gather.

'That's what saved us, when we were left behind. Our pride, our strength, our heritage.' At least the speaking grew easier as I did it. 'Do you remember what Corsovo said when the Crimson Keep vanished? When we stood alone, with nothing around us but the mud and the ashes of our dead? He said we were not given the blood just to waste away. He said that we would live on, and be what we always were. Kastelai. Conquerors. That we would make this new land ours. We'd build our strength here, and prosper, and when the Crimson Keep returned we wouldn't be lost memories, ashes on the wind. We would be rulers, we would be kings and queens, we would be mighty, for we are Kastelai!'

I let that last word go, almost a shout again, and behind me Arvan led my house into a roar of approval. It was a risky thing, but now, as my house howled behind me and Durrano and his house joined in, my belief in it grew.

But the others stayed silent.

Some of the vampires among Jirrini and Magdalena's houses stirred, as if they would join the shouting, but they stayed quiet

when they saw the silence of their leaders. The members of Salvera's house just wrinkled their lips, as if annoyed by the noise.

'We are Kastelai,' I said when the cheers settled, 'and we were born into our second lives to conquer.' I looked at the others, trying to remember how it had been a century ago when we were all united behind my father and mother to claim the Grey Palace and the Broken Plains. It had been done, so it could be done again. 'I don't sit on this throne because I want it. My father should be here, and I believe that someday he will be again. He is not ash, and we know that vampires are, above all, the masters of death. Corsovo will be reborn, and when he is I mean to see that his throne is waiting for him. We will not lose what was his, not give up what is ours.'

The red in Salvera's eyes was dimmer, the gold brighter, as if his beast had stepped back, and the man was listening. Magdalena leaned forwards, looking at me. I'd seen her look the same way at battle maps, as she calculated the numbers of the forces. She was considering, and my heart was beating, stirring my blood.

This was almost as good as fighting.

Then she spoke. 'What do you propose?'

'That we be what we are,' I said. 'Kastelai. Warriors. You're right, we face a new threat. But Lord Salvera is right, too. We've waited to fight back too long. We must act. Now.'

'Now?' she said. Something in her voice made me cautious. I hesitated – waiting, I realised, for my mother to speak, but she was still strangely silent.

'Now,' I repeated. 'We gather our forces and we strike for Gowyn. We hit them hard, by surprise. We are reduced, but so are they. I've spent years seeing to that.' I looked directly at Magdalena, not challenging. Well, not quite. She looked back at me, with that same judging, calculating eye.

'What about the Spears of Heaven?' The question came from Jirrini, but I didn't shift my eyes from Magdalena as I answered.

'They're dangerous. So we attack now,' I said. Arvan had seized on the political elements when we'd talked this out. He saw this plan as a way of taking the throne and keeping it, but I believed in it. This was the only way that I could think of to get out of this long, grinding war. 'Before we hit Gowyn's walls, we'll hit the Spears. A small group of us will slip into the city at night and destroy this Celasian and his fanatics while they sleep. Then we'll open the gates and take the rest of the city. Hard and fast, keeping the destruction to a minimum.'

'Why?' asked Durrano.

'So it looks good when the rest of the Spears of Heaven sail in,' I said. 'Then we'll break their ships with the harbour's siege machinery, and send them to Sigmar before they even set foot on the Broken Plains.'

'That's your plan?' Magdalena's voice was neutral, her face a mask.

'Damn you, Mother, where are you?' I thought. I had no idea what my father's tactician was thinking. Her approach to battle had always been solid, but cautious. But Vasara was still silent, so I just nodded.

'A damn good one, I think,' Durrano said. 'Assassinate them, drown them, drive them out and they'll never dare oppose us again.'

'You would think that,' Magdalena said, shaking her head. 'Its boldness is outmatched only by its rashness, and it has about as much chance of success as you do in a battle of wits with a lixx, Lord Durrano.'

He sputtered, but I cut him off. 'You don't think it'll work.'

'I *know* it won't work,' she said. 'Something that complex, where so many things hinge on everything going right? No. Our army will be spotted coming in. The Spears of Heaven won't fall and will rouse the Sun Seekers. Our numbers will be too small to hold the

city. Or maybe everything will go perfectly right – which it won't – and then some bitter spouse of a slain guard will row out and warn the ships that they're sailing into a trap. No, it won't work, and the fact that you think it might means you're not fit to lead.'

She looked me in the eye and there wasn't challenge in her gaze, there was disappointment. It made the words I was about to shout back at her catch in my mouth, and Salvera took advantage of my hesitation.

'What would you do, Lady Magdalena? Run?'

'Yes,' she said. 'We don't have the forces to fight now. So we pull back to my hold. Ruinview is the most defensible of all our positions. When the mortals come, they'll find us gone, holed up somewhere impregnable. They'll try us for a while, but I have some idea of what's happening in the outside world. Sigmar is pushing on a thousand fronts, and being counter-attacked on a thousand others. He's bitten off more than he can chew in every realm. The Spears of Heaven were meant to destroy us, fast. When they find us gone, they won't wait around, they'll be pulled back.'

'And then what?' Salvera spat. 'Even if you're right, they'll leave a force of mortals to trap us, to starve us.'

'We're not mortals,' Magdalena said. 'We'll wait for them to weaken, then we'll strike.'

'So more of the same, then,' I said. 'Another thirty years of this war? Except instead of keeping our lands we give them up for one small keep overlooking a wasteland?'

'Better than death,' she said. 'Sometimes the only path to victory is patience.'

'Patience is just another word for cowardice.' Salvera was facing Magdalena, but he pointed a claw at me. 'This one's barely better than a child, but at least her fangs are sharp. Yours were pulled years ago.'

Magdalena showed Salvera her fangs. Anger filled me, and I

was ready to rise and challenge them both. But I thought of my mother's voice, and forced myself to speak. 'What would you do, Lord Salvera?'

'Your plan has some merit. It just doesn't go far enough.' Salvera shifted his scythe, arcing it slowly through the air as if pantomiming a peasant at harvest. 'Lady Magdalena says our strength is too low. She's right. But we have all the supplies we need just across the lake. I would lead us first to Maar. There are many living there, and from them we can have a feast. We'll claim our fill and then we'll raise an army from their dead that will let us smash the Spears of Heaven back into the sea.'

'You want us to kill them,' I said, unbelieving. 'Our own mortals. You want to reward their allegiance with slaughter?'

'So they are to be spared for being fools?' Salvera asked. 'They had legends of their rulers returning, and Corsovo was good at lying. That's no reason to spare them.'

'What about our honour?' I snapped. 'We promised to protect them. We did, we Kastelai. Is our word worth nothing?'

Salvera grimaced. 'Patience. Honour. Words for weakness. We are Kastelai, but you forget what that means. We are the teeth of Nagash. We are death. We cannot be beaten, and we do not shrink from doing whatever it takes to triumph. We have the strength to be savage, and because of that we will triumph.'

'That is the beast talking,' I said.

'So what?' He growled a laugh. 'The beast hungers, and hunger is strength.'

I felt a chill run through me, an echo of the cold that had touched me earlier, and with it came a pang of hunger, despite the blood I'd had. It didn't make me feel strong. It made the beating of my heart falter. But I forced the feeling away, focusing on Salvera and my anger, and the chill passed again.

'I won't let that happen,' I said. 'I won't let you make us into monsters, like the Avengorii, or the Vyrkos.' I'd never met vampires from those dynasties, but my mother had told me of them. They embraced their beast, and were warped by it, the way Salvera was warped.

'You won't?' Salvera asked, his voice mocking. He stepped away from his chair, his scythe ready. 'Do you think you can call me to your feet, too?' He bared his teeth, and the red had come back into his eyes, filling the dark pupils, so there was nothing but the dirty yellow rings of his irises and the crimson glow. 'Try,' he hissed.

I was on my feet before the Rose Throne, both hands on the hilts of my swords. Arvan had hoped we could get through this meeting without a challenge, but I'd told him that was foolish. I was trying to avoid a battle between houses, but I knew, *knew*, that blood was going to be shed, and I'd suspected it would be Salvera's.

But as I parted my lips to utter the challenge, Magdalena spoke.

'Your plan replaces foolish hope with sadism, Salvera, but it's just as ridiculous as hers.' She stood too, her face hard but resigned. 'You're both wrong, and if either of you get your way you'll drag us all down.' Her curls wreathed her face like a halo, startlingly dark against her pale skin, but her eyes were chips of emerald, hard and focused. On me.

'You remind us of what our king told us on that first day of our exile, Lady Nyssa,' she said. 'That our blood was meant to claim this land, not be destroyed by it. Destruction is what comes for us now, and we won't escape it if we're ruled by bestial anger, or naïve pride.' Magdalena drew her sword, and the steel made a low hiss that filled the silent great hall. She levelled her weapon at me, and spoke.

'Nyssa Volari, of the Kastelai. You wish to claim the place of Corsovo, our king, but I will not have it. I call challenge.'

Finally. My heart beat faster and my blood moved swiftly. I'd thought Magdalena would be cautious, would wait until I had

fought with Salvera first if she challenged me at all, hoping that I'd be weakened. But it didn't matter. Let her come first. I would settle Salvera after, and then we could be done with all this pointless posturing.

I drew my blades and crossed them before me, then bowed. 'Magdalena of the Kastelai. I hear your challenge, and I welcome it. Let our blades settle our differences, and let it happen now.'

Now. Right now. My heart was beating, my blood moving, and I could feel my body wanting to blur into motion. I ached holding myself still, waiting as the chairs were moved and the bounds set. I burned to fight.

Across from me, Magdalena knelt on the red tiles, her sword held before her. Motionless as a statue as she prayed to Nagash. I watched her and spun my swords in a circle, bright and dark slicing through the air. Now, I thought.

I waited for my mother to answer that, to caution me. We'd discussed what should happen if the challenges came. A death could lead to the civil war I was trying to avoid, and I expected her to remind me of that, to tell me that if I preserved Magdalena's honour, she could become a valuable ally. But my head was silent except for my own thoughts. It was a strange feeling, after decades of her ghost critiquing me. I should've been happy, but instead the silence ate at me.

'Are the challengers ready?' Salvera stood in the middle of the cleared space, head swinging back and forth between us like a hungry wolf sizing up its prey. Not my choice for a judge, but not Magdalena's either, and that had to do.

'I'm ready,' I said. More than ready, but Magdalena still knelt, still and silent, as if she hadn't heard either Salvera or me. I itched to give her a kick. Instead I spun my swords again, cutting the air, until finally Magdalena moved, opening her eyes and standing.

She made the sign of Nagash, her hand spreading out before her then closing and gathering in, as the Lord of Death gathered our souls to him, and then settled her shield on her arm.

'I'm ready,' she said, her voice grim. Magdalena was a deadly fighter. She'd been born to her second life over four centuries ago, and she'd survived countless battles with the Crimson Keep and on the Broken Plains. But she was also a cold realist, and she knew me. She was stronger, tougher, more experienced, but she couldn't match my speed or my healing. Her realism made her overcautious, but I wondered what she thought she was going to accomplish here. She had to know she would lose.

But she was also a traditionalist. Magdalena would go through every step before admitting defeat.

We stepped into the centre of the red circle that had been set as our boundary. The other vampires all waited outside it, silent, their eyes glittering in the candlelight, brown and blue and green, yellow and red and black. Waiting.

'Challenge has been issued,' Salvera said. 'In the name of Nagash, let it be answered. The circle is drawn, and no one shall interfere. The challenge will not end until one of you yields or dies. Do you understand?' I jerked my head, fighting to keep my whole body from vibrating, while Magdalena nodded, a tiny movement of her head, the rest of her perfectly still. 'Then begin!' Salvera shouted, and he pulled back, stepping out of the ring, freeing us to finally fight.

Don't shame her. My mother was still silent, but I knew what she would say. Fine. I could understand that necessity, even if I didn't want to. But damn me, I'd show her. I darted back from Magdalena, then lunged in, spinning. She waited until I was there and moved her shield, catching the flurry of strikes that I threw at her. My swords rang off her guard, blow after blow. She had no counter-attack, she was moving as fast as she could just to stop me

from touching her. Then I was away, on the other side of the circle, looking at her. Perfectly still except for the beating of my heart.

Magdalena faced me, her face grim. She'd barely withstood that, and she knew I wasn't moving my fastest. Not yet. But she took a step towards me, her sword raised, and I bowed my head to her. Whatever else I might feel about her, I respected Magdalena. She would fight for what she believed, until the end. Then I moved to meet her.

I let her strike at me and ducked the blow, using it to slip behind her. She turned, too slow, and I slapped my swords into her. One cracked off her armoured side, shifting her, while I smashed the butt of my hilt against her elbow as she tried to swing her shield around to block. The blows stopped her from turning, hurt her, but she moved forwards, pulling away from me to turn the other way. She was good.

But she was slow.

She got her distance, spun, and I was there. Inside her arms, our faces close enough to kiss – or bite. But my dark sword was between us, its point pressing into the underside of her jaw. She glared at me, then pulled her head back as she tried to slam her knee into my gut. But I was already gone, dancing across the circle to stop again.

'First blood,' Salvera said, his voice edging towards mockery. 'Will you yield?'

Magdalena didn't even acknowledge him, or the red trickle that ran down her throat from the tiny wound the tip of my sword had made in her skin. It was only a trace of blood, especially for how hard I'd pushed my blade up. If she'd been a mortal, my sword would have punched through the bottom of her mouth, through its roof, into her brain. But Magdalena was not mortal. My blade had barely marked her – but that was exactly my intent.

'Do you?' I asked, and I carefully kept my voice respectful.

'No,' she said, and she came at me again.

We moved like that twice more. I whipped around her, blades flashing, and she caught them on shield and sword, solid, determined. Slow. I left a mark again on the left side of her neck. Then the right. Two small cuts, just enough to bleed. They could have been death blows and she knew it, but Magdalena did not yield. I stood across from her, looking at the stripes of blood on her neck, hungry, but not letting that touch me. I couldn't. This was going to be the hard part. I was going to have to hurt her, but not kill her.

I raised both blades, waiting until she started towards me yet again. Then I moved, a blur around her, until I had an opening and I was driving forwards, my fist aimed at her exposed neck, ready to smash into it – and then the cold hit me again.

It swept through me, making my heart come to a juddering halt. I went still, hanging in the air, my arm outstretched. Until Magdalena smashed her shield into me.

I hit the red tiles and rolled across them, and as I did the cold faded back, went away, and my heart limped into movement again, my blood stirring sluggishly. But that was enough, and I was on my feet, swords up, sliding back and away from a vicious swipe of Magdalena's sword. She'd aimed the flat of it at me, not a killing blow, but if it had connected with my head I would have been laid out on the floor, dazed.

Moving away, I tried to will my heart to beat faster. I was surely angry enough, enraged at how she'd caught me. I felt a trickle of something running down my chin and swiped at it. Blood, running from my nose. She'd made me bleed, and how long had it been since that had happened to me in a duel?

'First blood for you,' Salvera said, and he sounded surprised, and eager. He wanted me to lose, I was more of a threat to him. 'Do you yield?'

I shook my head and charged.

Moving more carefully now, relying on skill and speed, I struck her, catching her shield and sword. But she had time to swing back at me, to change my rhythms, to make me have to block and dodge and move. I wasn't completely controlling the fight any more, and I could feel Magdalena gaining confidence as she swung back harder. I blocked a blow with my bright sword but it shoved me back, almost opened me up for a counter, and that was enough. I had to end this. I slid her blade off and drove forwards, the tip of my bright sword punching in.

It should have caught her under her sword arm, where the metal plates of her armour didn't protect her. Should have driven in and sliced tendon and muscle, separated the joint, and left her with a shattered, useless arm. Instead another wave of cold went through me, worse than all the others. It made my muscles seize, turned my smooth thrust into a lurch, and the tip of my sword wavered and hit Magdalena's armour, bouncing off uselessly as I staggered forwards. Off balance, exposed, and all the older Kastelai had to do was bring up her mailed fist and smash it into my chin.

I slammed into the red tiles. The blow had cracked my teeth together and sent a bolt of pain through my head that stunned me, but I could've shaken that off. What I couldn't shake was the cold that held on, chilling my heart. I lay on the floor, my body locked into a kind of spasm, and both swords rattled away from me, dropped from shaking hands. I fought to reach for them, but my body was stiff as a corpse.

Then Magdalena's sword was at my throat.

'Do you yield?' She stared down at me, and there wasn't triumph in her eyes. More a tired kind of acceptance, mixed with disappointment. Magdalena stood over me, the point of her sword digging into my skin, and she almost looked defeated.

Never. That's what I wanted to say. Never, as I rolled away from her weapon and took up my blades again. But I could barely move my lips. I couldn't speak, and she frowned at me.

'Say it,' Magdalena said. Then, in an almost silent whisper, pitched for my keen ears in this tomb-quiet hall, 'Do it. I don't want your blood. I don't want to kill Corsovo's daughter.'

I wanted to snarl, wanted to bare my teeth, but I couldn't move, couldn't speak, and I thought she'd have to kill me because I was too helpless to even cry mercy. I could feel the point of Magdalena's sword pressing in as her muscles tensed, and I saw her close her eyes as she prepared to thrust the blade home. Then the cold relented, just enough.

'I...' The scrap of a whisper made her open her eyes. I tried to shift, to pull away from her, but I was still so cold, so useless, frozen to the crimson tile. There was nothing else to do but yield or die, and I spent a long moment wondering which I should choose, wondering what words my mother would have told me. But it was just me in my head, alone and helpless, and I said the last word just loud enough for her to hear. 'Yield.' My heart twitched as I said it, shame and anger enough to make my arm unlock and push her blade aside, but that was all. I'd fought, and for the first time in such a long time I'd lost, and I let the cold take me, and fell into the darkness that came after.

CHAPTER EIGHT

'Captain Takora!'

The child shouting for me had a voice sharp enough to break glass, but I didn't bother turning. I was watching the waves crash into the rocky breakwater that protected Gowyn's harbour. Their mindless motion deadened my thoughts, a lulling reminder that the water, the realms and the gods themselves didn't care about what happened in this lost corner of Aqshy. I'd hated that indifference for most of my life. The knowledge that this long, ugly war was just a footnote in someone else's reports back in Hammerhal had made me furious, that all this blood and death was nothing to the lords of that great city.

Now though, after so many years of begging, the Broken Plains were finally being paid attention to. Here were Celasian and his Spears of Heaven to end this war once and for all, the answer to my prayers. Prayers. Finally, a god himself had spared me and this place some attention, and I wondered if I would ever be able to pray again.

'Captain Takora!' The child ran up and danced in front of me, his skin striped grey with volcanic dust even though distant Temero had settled days ago. 'I've a message!' The boy finally came to a stop and spoke in what was a pitiful attempt at a serious adult tone. 'Lieutenant Galeris sends word that you're to meet with the abbot-general at the Temple of Sigmar!'

'Did he say why?' I asked the child, who shook his dirty head.

'Nah. But he started swearing something fierce about those Church soldiers right after he told me to find you!'

I flipped the boy one of the small yellow pearls the locals used for trade and told him to tell Galeris that I was coming. Then I looked out over the harbour. It was quiet, only a few fishing ships drifting across the water. The rest of the abbot-general's forces were expected in ten days, if the winds stayed steady. The whole might of the Spears of Heaven, warriors who would march up the Irewater and tear down the Grey Palace brick by brick.

The thought should have pleased me, but after what had happened with the Biting Flames, it only made me shudder.

It had been bad enough a day ago when a single ship had sailed into the harbour, a heavy-beamed barque flying the blue-and-white lightning sigil. That ship's main cargo had been Erikil, Celasian's mount. Erikil was a griffon, a fierce beast with hooked beak, huge talons and shimmering azure wings. Seeing her climb out of the hold had sent a storm of emotions through me. I'd seen a battle lord riding a griffon as a child at some great victory parade in Hammerhal Aqsha. I'd wished then with all my young heart to be the lord who rode it, a warrior in gleaming armour mounted on a fierce, beautiful beast. Yesterday... I'd watched the griffon pace down the dock, the boards creaking beneath her, and dip her crested head to Celasian, and my heart had been filled with jealousy and a terrible sense of wrongness. I'd barely noticed the line of Demigryphs that had been led out of the hold after, fierce

beasts with their sharp-eyed eagle faces and lean, fast bodies. All I could think of was that lord mounted on his majestic war beast, marching through the cheering crowds... overlaid with my image of Celasian moving through the Biting Flames' camp, his holy spear dripping blood and his eyes dead.

'What are you going to do now, abbot-general?' I said to the waves and the wind. Better to ask them, for they wouldn't answer. When I got to the temple, I doubt I'd like what I heard when I asked that question.

I sighed and started walking back to the centre of the city. But I stopped after two steps, and sat on a heavy stone near the harbour edge. I pulled off my boot, shook out an imaginary stone, then as I pulled it back on I swept my fingers through a hollow just below one edge of the stone outcrop. There was a scrap of paper hidden there, and I tucked it into my palm and walked away.

I took the long way to the temple, walking through neighbourhoods populated more by vermin than people. Gowyn's population still hadn't recovered from Ire Crossing. Maybe it would, after Celasian was done.

And gone.

I stepped through a broken door into an abandoned bakery. A few rats stirred and ran, unhappy with my arrival, but I ignored them, waiting for my eyes to adjust to the dim light. When I could see well enough, I brought out the paper I'd recovered.

Trouble in the Grey Palace. The Kastelai have broken. All is falling, as I have promised. What of your promises?

I crumpled the tiny message. My promises.

With a whispered curse I punched the brick wall, stirring ash and dust from the rafters above. My promises. Damn me, they'd seemed so necessary not so long ago. This plan, this bit of treachery, had seemed the only way to end this damn war. Now... Now it was a complication that could see me in chains.

I snorted. As if Celasian would chain me. He'd kill me without a thought.

I needed time to think, to figure out what to do. Why had I let myself get pulled into this stupid plot? Bargaining with death. How could anything good come from that?

I pulled out a slip of parchment, a vial of ink and a pen. I scratched the words in tiny letters, slow and careful.

Our visitors make things difficult.

More than difficult. Impossible. How could I honour my promise with Celasian breathing down my neck? There was no way I could explain this, and it was driving me insane. The plan was working, the vampires' ruler was dead and their hold on the Broken Plains was fracturing. Would Celasian thank me for making his war easier? No. He'd kill me for it. He'd killed the Biting Flames for less.

So what could I do? Run? I smiled at the shadows. That wasn't in me anyway, and even if it were, Erikil would catch me. I put away pen and ink. I needed time. I needed to think. I shredded the message I'd been left and the one I'd started, pricked my finger, and smeared the tiny pieces with blood.

I left them in the dust for the rats to eat and walked away, heading towards the temple, trying to pretend that there was not only some way to save myself, but to save the Broken Plains, too.

Sigmar's temple was the grandest building in Gowyn, but that wasn't saying much. Its walls were hewn of dark basalt, and it was a squat, rude thing compared to the soaring spires of the great temples of Hammerhal Aqsha. But it was grand for the Broken Plains, and the inside of the wooden ceiling had been painted to look like the night sky with storm clouds ringed around it. Sigmar stood in the middle, lightning curling around his fist. The painting was crude, and Sigmar looked more like an angry farmer than a god, but there

was an enthusiasm to it which I admired. I couldn't guess what Celasian was thinking, though, staring up at that painted face with his dead eyes, and to be honest I didn't want to.

'Abbot-general. You sent for me?'

'And you finally answered.' His voice was flat but cutting. 'What matters are more pressing than my will, Captain Takora?'

'None,' I said. I didn't try to meet his eyes. I couldn't face their pale, empty blue even if I hadn't been lying. I just stood at attention and stared at his chin and waited, silent and obedient. Waited for a long time, while he considered me. Waiting to see if I would break under his regard, and spill ugly secrets like a shattered chamber pot? That's what it felt like, but that's what his dead gaze always felt like.

'None,' he echoed, his voice cold and distant as the uncaring clouds. Then he did something that surprised me. He reached out a gauntleted hand and the white-armoured guard standing beside him handed over a sheaf of notes. I recognised the cramped, narrow hand. It was a sheaf of my reports. 'You say that the leaders of our enemies, these Kastelai, each have their own holdings.'

'Yes,' I said. I hadn't thought he'd read any of those reports, no matter how much I pointed out that they existed. I was firmly convinced that the decades my predecessors and I had spent creating them were time wasted, as well used as trying to teach a lixx to read. 'When the Kastelai were taking over the Broken Plains, they seized the ruins of the hill forts that had been built by the old kings of Temero. They used them for the same purpose, to protect against raids from the nomads.' Or they used to. Now they used them to protect against raids from us.

Celasian picked out one of the sheets and held it up. It was the crude map that I'd sketched out, showing the position of the Kastelai holdings between Gowyn and Maar. 'These two are closest. Which would you target first?'

I felt a subtle pressure ease in my chest. Celasian was preparing for his coming battles, as he should. He wasn't focused on me. 'Skulltop,' I said. 'Durrano's hold.'

'Not the one that belongs to Salvera?' There was an edge of accusation in the question, but that edge seemed to be in every one of the abbot-general's questions. 'Bite Harbour? Your notes say that it is in worse condition.'

'It is,' I answered. 'But Salvera keeps better watch, and his force is more mobile. He'd see us coming, and if he thought he couldn't win, he'd run.'

'Is he a coward, then?'

'No.' Salvera liked to raid in Gowyn's territory, and I'd seen what he left behind. Whatever was wrong with that bestial vampire, it wasn't cowardice, but it was profoundly evil. 'He's practical and vicious. He'd leave us nothing but dust and traps, and then his forces would attack us where we were weakest. He'd hit our flanks and bleed us slowly.' Painfully. The Kastelai were all good at that, especially their damn little Princess Bloodeyes. Salvera might not be as effective as her, but the way he did it was uglier. 'The dead don't need supplies, or rest. They don't stop. Fighting them is… difficult.' I left thirty years of pain and frustration in that word.

'For you.'

When Celasian said that, with that thread of cool contempt in his voice, I couldn't stop myself from finally looking at him. Decades of bravery, decades of pain, of loss and heroism and sacrifice. My people and I had bled for years, fighting this forgotten fight, and we'd forced a stalemate with the monsters that lived in Temero. I wouldn't be denigrated so easily, but Celasian just stared back at me, as uncaring about the rage on my face as he'd been about the pain on Neria's before he killed her.

'We're not like you, Captain Takora. The dead will not stop us.' He handed back the sheaf of notes to his guard. 'But I'll listen

to your advice. I've no wish to spend the start of my campaign chasing a band of cowards across the plain. We will strike Skull-top first. Begin your preparations, we leave at dawn the morning after tomorrow.'

'The morning after tomorrow?' I asked.

'I would rather tomorrow, but your lieutenant was insistent that you wouldn't be able to prepare all your forces that quickly.' Celasian spoke as if he couldn't fathom how the Sun Seekers could be so incompetent. As if putting together five hundred soldiers and the supplies they'd need for battle were something that could be done in moments. Doing it in a day would be insanity, and I was going to skin Galeris, even though I knew it wasn't his fault.

'Why?' I said, making my voice stay level. 'Your army arrives soon. Why start now?'

'Because our foes surely know that too,' Celasian answered. 'It is an unfortunate truth that before every battle, traitors ply their trade. If we wait, we give the Soulblight vampires time to prepare. Best we hit them early, to put them on the defensive. Best we show them that the Spears of Heaven can be... difficult.'

So true, I thought to myself, so true. He turned his back on me, clearly done, and I walked away, leaving the Temple of Sigmar behind.

The ruined bakery in the deserted section of Gowyn was even more silent in the dark of the night.

I walked through the shadows, moving carefully. I couldn't be seen here, now. It would be difficult enough to justify coming here during the day, but this late? At least that made it easy to make sure no one was following me.

Before every battle, traitors ply their trade.

Celasian's words had kept echoing in my head as I worked with Galeris to sort out our forces, organising boots and blades, fodder

and bandages, all the thousand details necessary for moving even as small a force as mine. It wasn't a threat, wasn't some clever way to make me squirm. The short time I'd spent with him had given me a solid understanding of Celasian's character. If he suspected something of me, he'd have wasted no time forcing it out. But the realisation that his fanaticism didn't make him stupid, that he was as aware as I that the dead had eyes on us here in Gowyn, made me want to scream.

I wasn't a traitor. Everything I'd done had been to help my soldiers and the people of the Broken Plains. Damn me, I cared about them all, even if I hated them all sometimes, but I knew just how much mercy that would buy me from the abbot-general. Just as much as it had bought for Neria, and for Rhysha and the Biting Flames.

In the dark, I made my way to one of the ovens in the back of the ruin. I stopped in front of it, and pulled out a thin slip of paper, tightly folded. Much bigger than the messages I usually sent, but it had to be.

You've kept your part of the bargain. I'll keep mine. But the situation grows dire. The Spears move against you…

That was how it started. Damning words.

Damn me.

I reached up into the chimney, found a rough gap between two bricks, and pressed the message into it. Then I slipped back into the night, like a thief, like a spy, like a traitor. But I was just a soldier, doing everything I could to keep the world from falling apart into blood and ruin while hiding from the eyes of the dead and the blessed.

CHAPTER NINE

Vampires didn't sleep. But sometimes death came for us in small ways, and we were gone from the world for moments, days, years, millennia. When I roused from that fraction of death, I was hungry, angry, shamed and alone.

Alone.

My awareness came back, and with it all my senses, sharp and strong except for sight, and I lacked that only because my eyes were closed. First came the scents of my private room in the Grey Palace, the smell of dust and old blood, the oil I used on my swords, the familiar scent of myself. There was also the harsh odour of ash that was ever-present at the foot of Temero, mixed with the hot-sulphur stench of the boiling Irewater. The only scent out of place was something that smelled like old death and fur, but it had been here for a while, days at least, and I ignored it as I catalogued the rest of my senses.

The soft cushions of my favourite couch were under me, and the slick, silky touch of my robe was wrapped around me. Outside this

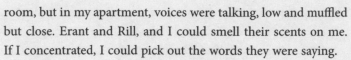

room, but in my apartment, voices were talking, low and muffled but close. Erant and Rill, and I could smell their scents on me. If I concentrated, I could pick out the words they were saying.

'Don't you have enough arrows by now?'

'Don't you have enough wooden animals?'

I stopped listening and opened my eyes. The room was dark, but I could see. A stand stood against one wall, holding my black ceremonial armour. The thin clothes I wore beneath my armour were laid out on a table beside my swords, a simple steel circlet for my hair, and my boots. Everything had been cleaned, though I could still smell a thin trace of Magdalena's blood on the swords.

Lying on the floor between me and the door was a heap of fur and bone and teeth, a monstrous pile of death that was the source of the familiar yet unfamiliar smell. The giant dire wolf that I'd taken from Salvera. The red points in the hollow black circles of its skull flared brighter as I turned my head to look at it, and its huge tail thumped against the floor.

Not totally alone then.

Never alone.

Vasara's voice was the same as always – quiet, calm, detached. Mine was not.

'Where were you?' I snapped as I jerked myself to my feet. The sudden motion made the hunger in me spike. It felt like I hadn't eaten in weeks, and I wondered how long I'd been out. But the fresh smell of Magdalena's blood argued only a little while. What was going on?

Where I always am. Here, haunting you.

'You were not!' I snapped. Across the room, the door opened and I could see Rill staring at me, Erant standing behind her. The dire wolf snarled at them, and Rill shot it an impatient look.

'Nyssa. Are you–' Rill started, and I waved a hand at her.

'A moment,' I said, and she nodded. She shut the door, leaving me alone with the wolf and the ghost in my head.

'You left me!' I said. 'Right in the middle of that council. Right before Magdalena called challenge on me!'

She called challenge?

'She did,' I said, and raised my hand to my throat. The place where her sword had pressed to my skin was smooth, unmarked, but I could still feel her steel. 'I lost.' The words came out of me soft, but the shame that followed burned.

To Magdalena? The usual smooth certainty was gone from Vasara's voice. She sounded confused. Confused! *How?*

'Amethyst hells, I don't know.' The memory of the fight was so clear. How my blood had been so liquid, pounding through me with every beat of my heart, and then that cold had come and made me slow, helpless… I raised my hands, looked at them, but all I saw was smooth skin. I spun and went to the mirror that stood beside the stand holding my armour. My face was the same as always, the skin unmarked, though the deep brown of it was tinged grey with hunger. When I ran my hands through my hair the thick strands fought me as much as they ever did, and my eyes… I moved closer, staring at my eyes. The red striations in my irises were thin and few, another mark of hunger, but in the left eye there were two stripes that weren't red. They were grey, grey as the ash that sifted down from Temero's peak, and a shudder went through me.

The curse.

'Quiet,' I snarled. 'You don't know that. You don't know anything. You weren't there.'

I wasn't, she said. *Something separated us, sent me back to death and left you alone. Something…*

I stared at those two tiny grey marks in my eye, and then suddenly they were gone, vanished into nothing as my fist smashed

into the mirror, breaking it and scattering its pieces across my room.

When I walked out of my private chamber, I was dressed in my armour, my swords on my hips. The skin over my knuckles was smooth and whole, the cuts I'd got from smashing the mirror healing as I dressed. I'd watched my skin knit together and wondered if I was healing slower. I didn't know.

Rill and Erant waited in my parlour, looking patient, calm, but I could read the tension in Rill's hands as she sharpened an arrow-head, and in the way Erant was hacking thick shavings off another piece of wood with his carving knife. He relaxed a little when I stepped out, though, and set down the blade. But Rill frowned, and if anything the tension in her seemed to wind tighter.

Arvan was there too, sitting on a couch in the centre of the room, and behind him Shadas sat in a chair beside the wide window that framed a view of the boiling lake below. Shadas barely turned his head enough to look at me, his eyes haunted, but Arvan jerked himself up when I appeared, like a clumsy animal goaded to its feet. The dire wolf, pacing protectively beside me, growled at him and I stroked the coarse fur of its shoulder.

'How long?' I asked, and Rill answered.

'Three nights.'

Three nights. With everything going on, that was far too long to have been dead to the world. I looked out of the window. The shadows were stretching long over the lake, and along the shore in the distance the great dark gravestones were gleaming with red, as if the dying day had coated them in blood. Three gone, and another night coming. I touched my tongue to my lips, my mouth dry, my throat swollen with hunger and all the emotions I'd shoved away after I'd broken my looking glass. I needed to speak, but couldn't, and I wanted desperately to pick up one of the

leather-cushioned chairs and hurl it through that window, break the silence with violence and make everyone stop looking at me.

You don't have time for a tantrum.

'I don't have time for *you*,' I said, angry, weary. Rill and Erant looked at each other, but Arvan's dark eyes were on me.

'Are you talking to me?' he asked. 'Or her?'

I frowned, and he shrugged. 'I've known about your conversations with Lady Vasara for a while.' I kept frowning, and he shrugged again, looking uncomfortable. 'Finding things out is part of my work. For your father. Was. It's part of my work for you now.'

'Your work is shit,' I said.

'I've been told that,' he said. 'But it's also necessary.'

'Did you tell my father?' I leaned back against the door frame. I felt drained, and I didn't know if that was hunger or... Or whatever it was that had happened to me. If I needed to stab Arvan, I wanted to do it from a solid start.

'No,' he said. 'He already knew.'

Already knew. I turned my frown on Rill and Erant. Rill stared back at me, her face blank, but Erant was staring intently at absolutely nothing.

They had to tell him.

I didn't answer her. I didn't trust myself to keep silent, and I didn't want to give Arvan any more information. I felt spied on enough. 'What did he say about it?'

'He said he hoped you were listening to her.'

That was too much to think about. I already had too much to think about, and I didn't even know what was going on. 'Is Magdalena on the throne?'

'No,' Arvan said. 'After you yielded, Salvera tried to challenge her, but she claimed the right to recovery.'

Right to recovery. Any Kastelai could claim that after a challenge, and get five nights to heal before they fought again. But

I'd barely touched Magdalena. She didn't heal as fast as I did, but she could've recovered in a few hours.

'Salvera didn't like it,' Arvan continued. 'He argued that it was unfair that Magdalena got time to rule with a challenge waiting.'

Salvera tries to act the wolf, but he was always more the weasel.

'What did Magdalena say?' Gods, I hated saying her name. She'd beaten me. No one beat me. She'd only done it because... Because of whatever had happened. But she'd done it, and I'd ended up under her blade. Still, even in all my anger, I would rather she rule than Salvera.

'She said the throne didn't belong to her. Or anyone.' Arvan looked almost apologetic. 'Magdalena said that the kingdom's dead, and that the Rose Throne and the Grey Palace should be left to be buried by ash. She said she's going back to her keep, and that anyone who wanted shelter from the coming storm should join her. Or run. She looked at Salvera when she said that.'

That's what she said, but what did she do? Whatever had happened to my mother, whatever had taken her away for a while, hadn't changed her. She was still pushing me.

And damn it, I was still stuck listening to her.

'What did she do?' I said, and Arvan hesitated, hearing the irritation in my words, not knowing it wasn't focused on him. Though that was changing every moment he didn't answer. 'After she gave her little speech?'

'She left,' Rill said. She was more used to my moods. 'Her and her house. That very night. Jirrini left the next.'

'Salvera?' I asked.

'Last night,' Arvan said, taking the telling back. 'He was skulking about for a while, but Durrano refused to leave while he was here and the Rose Knights were watching. So he went, vanished into the dark.'

'May the hells take him,' I muttered.

'Durrano left after that,' Arvan said. 'He said he needed to protect his hold from the mortals. And Salvera.'

I leaned against the door frame, thinking. It wasn't as bad as I
thought, and also somehow worse. 'They haven't united against
me,' I said. 'Nor have they jumped at each other's throats.'

'No,' Arvan said. 'Which means–'

'Which means they've given up,' I snarled, cutting him off. I
wanted to hit him. I wanted to hit something, anything. Instead
I slid down and thumped onto the floor with a clatter of swords.

The dire wolf was the first one there, its half-skull face close
to mine, one ear cocked forwards, but Erant was next, crouching beside me.

'Bugger off,' he told the dire wolf when it growled at him. 'What's
wrong? Is it the curse?'

'What bloody curse?' I said. This close I could smell his blood.
Usually the blood smell of another vampire was off-putting, but
my hunger was strong, and fighting the urge to slash my fangs
across his throat was hard.

'She hasn't fed in days.' Arvan handed over a clay amphora,
similar to the one he'd given me before that damned meeting.

I could smell it, that thick copper smell. I pulled the amphora
away from Arvan and raised it to my lips, drained it down, and
the deep hunger in me drew back. Not sated, but softened into
an ache I could ignore. I set down the amphora and I could see
that the grey undercast to my skin was almost gone.

Wiping my mouth off with the back of my hand, I pushed
myself up. Erant reached out to steady me when I wobbled, but
dropped his hand when I growled at him, a sound echoed by
the dire wolf. I reached out to touch the beast's shoulder, calm-
ing it, and surreptitiously using it to steady myself. Damn me, I
was weak, and was that hunger or–

I didn't want to think about that.

'Why is this one still with me?' I asked instead, my hand remaining on the dire wolf.

'He wouldn't leave you, after you fell,' Erant said. 'Almost ripped my hand off when I picked you up to bring you here. So we let him stay. Was that good?'

I ran my fingers through the beast's fur. Rip? No. Rend. 'Yes. Leaving Rend with me was good.'

'Told you it was,' Erant said, looking at Rill. She frowned back at him.

I let them glare at each other, their arguing familiar, and beyond them I could see Shadas across the room, his eyes on me, bloodshot and haunted. He turned away the moment my eyes met his, to look again out the window at the growing night.

'Better?' Arvan asked me, and I nodded. I set down the amphora, turned from Shadas. I didn't want to talk about hunger, blood or curses. I didn't want to think about them.

'They've given up,' I said. 'Are they right?'

He looked through the fringe of his hair at me, his black eyes dull, not reflecting the light of the few lit candles. 'Your father valued me because I was curious. Because I liked to learn things and share them. I liked your father because I knew I could share what I learned without fear.'

'Arvan.' I gave up, unbuckled my swords, leaned them against a chair and settled into it. The blood had helped, but it wasn't enough. Rend settled on the floor beside me, his half-skull face slightly higher than mine now that I was sitting. 'I'm not going to attack you if you say something I don't like. I don't like most of what you say, and I'm not sure I like you, but I'm not stupid. You helped my father, and now you're offering to help me, and...' I was going to say I needed it, but I couldn't. 'So do it,' I said instead. 'Tell me what you know.'

He nodded and folded his hands behind his back, the warrior-lecturer again.

'You're right about them giving up,' he began. 'And wrong. They've given up on King Corsovo's dream of a vampire kingdom. None of them think we can hold the Broken Plains against another army. Even Durrano knows that chance is slim, even if we were all united. Split like this, it's impossible. But I don't think anyone has given up on survival.

'Magdalena may be the closest to that,' he said. 'Her plan is a kind of suicide. Ruinview is the most defensible hold, and Magdalena would bleed the Spears of Heaven badly before they reached her. If all our houses joined her, she'd bleed them very badly. But enough?' Arvan shook his head, and his hair slid across his heavy shoulders. 'I don't think so. I don't think tactically like Magdalena, I think personally. If we were fighting Takora, it might work – she cares about her people and might be content to leave Magdalena trapped. Celasian, though. I don't know him, but I've watched him through the eyes of my animals. I've seen what he's done. I don't think he'll stop if Magdalena hurts him, he'll push forwards harder just to hurt her back. I think that if he has his enemies bundled up in one place he won't stop until they're dead, no matter how many of his own he kills to do it. I don't think Magdalena knows that yet, but I think that she'll find out.'

I didn't know Celasian either. I didn't know if Arvan was right about him, but I knew that I didn't want to trap myself like a rat in a hole. Or cede almost everything my father had won before the fight even started. 'What about the others? How do they plan to survive?'

'Jirrini has returned to her hold in Splitrock,' Arvan said. 'I know Magdalena wanted her to bring her house to Ruinview, but it seems their alliance is over. Jirrini is staying put.' Arvan picked up the amphora and ran a finger around the neck, coating it with blood. He held it up, and a bat flicked down from the shadows of the ceiling and began to lick it off. 'There are deep caves running beneath Splitrock. Your father and I long suspected that Jirrini was hoarding supplies down there. I think she plans to disappear, to fall back into the underground and wait this out. It might even work. I've never been able to find her secret stores, even with help.' The bat had finished cleaning Arvan's finger and he carried it to the door of my apartment, opened it, and tossed the little animal into the dark hall beyond. 'She might hide for decades, but what will she come out to? A new city of Sigmar, rising above the Broken Plains?'

Another hole, another trap. Another surrender. 'What about Salvera? I don't see him going to ground.'

'No,' Arvan agreed, shutting the door. 'I see him running. He won't name it as such. He'll say he's raiding the enemy, and he will. He'll range out from Bite Harbour and hit whatever targets he can find, but he'll retreat from Celasian eventually. He'll give up Bite Harbour, the Broken Plains, and run for the wastes.'

'Where he'll live in the wild and prey on the weak, like a beast,' I said.

And forget forever any notion of honour, any idea of what it meant to be a Kastelai.

'He's almost there now,' Rill said.

'True,' Arvan agreed. 'Which leaves Durrano. Durrano... I don't know, which is hard to admit. He's the simplest of you. He was dedicated to the king, and would have followed whatever your father said. He would have followed you, if things had worked out differently.'

I felt my fingers digging into the chair arm, my nails pressing into the leather. If I'd had claws like my father, I would have torn holes in the material. 'So without a leader, what does he do?'

'Stay at Skulltop, probably. Or run here. Or to Magdalena. I don't know.'

I flexed my fingers, made them relax. 'And the last house. My house. What happens to us?'

'We fall,' Arvan said, without pause. 'The Rose Knights cannot hold Maar or even the Grey Palace alone, but they are the targets that our enemy will focus on. The Spears of Heaven will come here and kill us all.'

I shook my head. 'That's not going to happen.'

'Good,' Arvan said. 'Can you stop it?'

'You think I can't fight?' I said, and Rend's growl throbbed below my words, emphasising them. I must have connected deeply when I seized the dire wolf, because he mirrored my mood now. I didn't mind.

'You still want to know what I think?' Arvan asked, eyeing Rend.

'I do.' I leaned back in my chair, leashing my anger, and the dire wolf stopped his deep rumble of displeasure.

'I think you should have beat Magdalena.'

Nyssa.

She cautioned me fast, and I kept my seat, but I knew Arvan could see the anger in my face, and definitely knew he could hear Rend growling again. He kept going though.

'I watched you take her apart.' He touched his left hand to his cheek, right below his blank black eye, the silent salute the Kastelai gave another warrior when they saw them do something worthy of respect. 'You were winning, until you lost. I don't know what happened to you, but I know what everyone said afterwards. They said the curse that claimed your father had come for you.'

'No,' I said. Had it? I didn't feel cursed. I didn't feel anything but hunger. Hadn't Arvan said my father had been hungry at first? That he couldn't be sated? I shook my head. No. I was hungry because I'd fought, then gone days without feeding. I wasn't cursed.

Then what are you?

'I'm not cursed,' I said, to her, to Arvan, to everyone and everything. But then what was I? I'd felt that cold knife through me. I'd

felt my heart falter in its battle rhythm. What was that, if not a curse? Some kind of sickness? I had no memory of being sick. I probably had been, when I was a mortal. But that first, temporary life was gone, lost to me, and so I had no idea what sickness felt like. Mortals talked about being cold... 'No,' I said again. Denial was stupid, but damn me if I was going to give in to anything, even truth.

'No,' Arvan repeated. 'No curse.' He looked at his hands, massive things heavy with scars and calluses from his spear. 'I want that. For you, for me too, for everyone here. Salvera was saying he could smell it on you. That your blood's cursed, that Corsovo's blood was cursed, that all the blood in this house is cursed.'

'He lies,' I said. 'Salvera just wants to see us fall.' Had we already? 'Maybe he did something. Some magic that hurt me.'

Arvan shook his head. 'We thought of that. Him, or Magdalena, though she seems less likely to try to cheat. But Shadas felt nothing.' He waved a hand at the necromancer. 'I asked him the minute we saw you slow, saw you falter. Then I asked him to examine you after. He found nothing.'

Examined me. I stood, hands on my swords. I didn't draw them, but I wanted to. My heart beat, once. Twice.

What else were they supposed to do?

'Quiet,' I snarled. It was directed at her, but Arvan blinked his black eyes. I ignored him and began to move, pacing back and forth across the room. Rend tried to follow but I pointed to the floor and the dire wolf settled, still and unhappy, his eyes glowing bright with our shared anger.

'Examined me. I yielded, and I fell into that black and they could have done anything. They could have burned me, the way you were burned.' I kept that all in my head, silent, but I knew it was obvious on my face, the anger, the frustration. I walked faster. Faster. Moving as fast as a mortal sprinting, I crossed from one

side of the room to the other, shutting out Arvan and Rill and
Erant and Shadas with speed. I didn't want them looking at me.

*Again, now is not a good time for a tantrum, Nyssa. Not that
there ever is a good time.*

I thought about denying it, but gave up. She was in my head,
she could read me from the inside, and most importantly I didn't
care. 'Why not?' My words were slipping out now, but they were
as fast as my motion, a buzz of sound to everyone but Vasara, so
I didn't care. 'Damn you, I did everything you wanted. Dressed
myself up pretty and kept my manners while Father suffered. Had
meetings and arranged chairs while he rotted away. And then
when he was gone I dealt with those carrion crows as if they were
equals. I did everything you told me, Mother. I was smart and
loyal and vicious and mature, and where in all the amethyst hells
did it get me? Sprawled across the great hall's floor, with Magdalena's sword at my throat!'

You're angry.

'Am I?' I snapped.

You're frightened.

I stopped. I was in the centre of the room, still, motionless. It
was dark, all the candles except the ones most distant blown out
by the wind I'd made, moving back and forth, but the dark didn't
affect me. I could see Erant and Rill, guarded but unsurprised.
They'd seen me argue with Mother like this. Arvan had shoved his
whole couch back, out of the way of my pacing, and his shadow
eyes were on me. Shadas had stopped staring out of the window
to gape at me, his face even paler than usual.

'I'm not frightened,' I said, and the words filled the silent room.
They all stared at me, none of them wanting to answer the words
that weren't meant for them. Neither did Vasara. And so the quiet
stretched until a knock boomed from the door.

* * *

There wasn't a youth in Maar who didn't dream of being one of us.

Erant had told me that once. The vampires of the Grey Palace were blessed by the blood. It wasn't surprising that we never had to tell the parents of Maar to send their children to us at the age of twelve for training. The children demanded it, dreaming of immortality.

Most of them never came close. They were given basic training so that they could help defend the city, and sent back to Maar. Some were kept to become servants. There were only a few deemed worthy of the training that might result in them taking the blood. But while they trained, one of their duties was to give it.

Arvan lined them up before me, five young mortals, barely adults. They wore no weapons, but even standing still they had the balance of fighters. Of course. They'd been taught by vampires trained by my father, only a generation of the blood removed from the Kastelai. They were already deadly, for mortals.

They smelled so good.

'You need this,' Arvan said. 'That little bit of blood wasn't enough.'

It wasn't, and all the churning emotions stirred up by talking to my mother had been... not dampened, not at all, but pushed aside by my hunger. I went to the oldest mortal, a tall, rangy boy. I remembered fighting him, my father laughing as the boy had tried to use his reach to touch me with his practice sword and the way I'd moved around it, the mortal's strikes so slow. I pushed that memory away with everything else, took the boy's head and bent him low. I could see the old marks on his neck, all well healed but there. We preferred to feed on those we fought, whether they were our enemies, the ones we judged, or the ones we trained. The boy didn't flinch when I set my teeth into him.

None of them did. They were used to it, and when I was finished they tried to keep their heads high as they followed one of the Rose Knights back to their tiny rooms beside the training yards. They staggered a little though, especially the last girl. I'd been careful, but I'd drunk deep.

'Two of them weren't fully healed from the last time they'd provided,' I said.

'There aren't that many in training, and we are low on criminals,' Arvan said.

'We have enemies in plenty, though.' I licked my lips. The blood, fresh and full of life, was spreading through me. It would go still soon, but the warmth of its spread was soothing. Not soothing enough to settle me, but I could hold myself in check. For now.

'That we do.' He went to a table, where a map of the Broken Plains had been set out. Carved bone tokens sat on it, a raven for Magdalena, a cup for Jirrini, a wolf for Salvera, a skull for Durrano, and a rose... a rose for me now. Not my father. They were each set on their separate holdings. In Gowyn, on the edge of the map, was a little golden sun, Takora's symbol. Joining it now was another, a silver spear. The Spears of Heaven.

Arvan walked around the table and put his hands on the other side, examining it. 'You say you're not cursed, even though all the other houses seem to think so. If they're right, and what happened to your father happens to you, you only have a few weeks left before you start failing as he did. A few weeks.' He reached out and picked up the spear. 'If we don't find some way to unite all the houses again, a few weeks won't matter. The Spears of Heaven will be here before you fall, and the Broken Plains will belong to Sigmar.' He let go of the spear and it fell on the image of Temero. A little silver icon, dominating the map.

'I swore to your father that I would defend him and the Rose Throne. I failed in the first.' Arvan looked up at me, his black eyes hollows of darkness in his rough, brutish face. 'But I didn't fail

the throne, and I don't plan to. We all have only a few weeks, my lady, whatever happens. Shall we talk about how we use them to defend that throne?'

I looked at him, then at the map. My emotions were still a tangled, angry knot, but Arvan was right. I didn't have time to waste. Whatever was happening to me. 'I think we should.'

How mature of you.

I ignored her, but her voice made my heart stir. I went to the map and picked up the spear, and my heart beat, once.

'Do you know what the blood of one of these Spears of Heaven tastes like?' I said, looking at Arvan. He shook his head, and I smiled, baring my fangs to the roots. 'You will. We all will.'

CHAPTER TEN

The ridge ran out from the side of Temero, a narrow crest of stone that stood high over the Broken Plains. I stopped Thorn at the top, uncomfortable in the light, but I wanted the view. Dropping Thorn's reins, I shaded my face and stared down. Far below was the Grey Palace, mostly hidden by the volcano's rough sides, but I could see the Irewater clearly. The steam-shrouded lake stretched out from the foot of the mountain, the steam clearing in the distance until the water stretched like a shining sheet to Maar, its buildings a black cluster of sharp-edged stone on the far shore. Beyond the city, the River Ire twisted through long hills and broad valleys, straightening out when the land went flat and running to the distant sea. Gowyn was visible mostly as a haze of smoke, but if I stared long enough my eyes could pick out gleaming sparks, flashes of light off glass and metal.

Was some of that light flashing off the Spears of Heaven? Off their white armour, their silver weapons? Arvan had described the enemy to me, the vision he'd seen of them through the eyes of his verminous

spies when the mortals had slaughtered the Biting Flames. I'd made him repeat it, over and over, until I could see them when I closed my eyes. A shining host in white, spattered in blood. These were the ones who'd come to claim my father's kingdom.

My kingdom.

Are you finally acknowledging his death?

I didn't say anything, just shook my head. I acknowledged nothing. Not his death, not the cold that had touched me and made me yield, not the almost certain futility of this fight. Nothing.

That furious, stubborn resistance to any reality that wasn't you winning is one of the things that endeared you to your father. It was one of the things I couldn't stand about you.

'What about now?' I said, running my eyes over miles and miles of heat-browned grass. There were two rainy seasons in the Broken Plains, when the wind changed and blew the storms in from the sea to drop a deluge on us. The grass grew and grew and grew when it rained and for a few weeks after. But the baking heat of Aqshy soon dried it out, turned its lush green into a brittle brown that flared into flames at the smallest spark. Huge areas of the land below were dark, burned already this season, and I could see the slow march of flames creeping across one line of hills. But the smoke rising from that distant fire didn't block what I was looking for. A smudge of dark stone, located out where the plains went dryer and dryer until they fell into sand. Splitrock, where Jirrini had her hold.

Now? Now I think that mad refusal to accept any failure has as much chance of saving you as it does of killing you. But I still hate it.

'What do you see, Lady Volari?' Arvan pulled his rust-red Nightmare up beside me. I moved Thorn away from him, and I wondered if I should have brought Rend instead of commanding him to stay at the Grey Palace. The dire wolf's bulk and growls would have kept Arvan further away.

'Splitrock,' I said, pointing at the dark smudge. I swung my hand over, to the other side of the plains, where they ended in a cliff that marked the start of the sea. At one spot a rough semicircle marked the cliffs. 'Bite Harbour.' Salvera's hold was impossible to see, camouflaged among the broken rocks. I shifted where I was pointing again, roughly to the centre of the land spread below us, where the Irewater made a wide curve around a roughly circular hill that marked where the Broken Plains began to flatten out. The top of the hill was white, a chunk of marble shoving out from the earth like bone through skin. 'Skulltop.' Finally, back to the end of the Irewater. 'Gowyn.' I turned to him. He was squinting his black eyes in all the uncomfortable light, trying to see what I could. 'Your map, laid out for us. The Kingdom of the Broken Plains.'

'It's bigger than when it's on a table. And brighter.'

'And we have to ride across it.'

'As fast as we can,' he said.

Fast. We'd left the Grey Palace at dawn, starting up the narrow road that led here. Thorn and the other Nightmares were tireless, but even they couldn't take this road quickly. I shifted in my saddle, looking down the other side of the ridge. Temero's bulk blocked the views of the wasteland that spread out on this side of the volcano. It was a place of lava flows ancient and recent, a scarred land marked with rough stone, hot lakes coloured with metallic poisons, and great flats of mud that boiled endlessly. The rough road we were on ran across the volcano a little way then divided, one branch running down to those wastes. I'd followed the road that way once, but not far. The ancient stones of it fell apart quickly, disappearing beneath a great oozing lake of sulphurous sludge. The other branch of the road led into a narrow, twisting valley – a crevice, really, that ended at the base of a tall cliff. I could see the narrow windows carved into it. Ruinview, an abandoned fortress guarding a road to nowhere. A fitting place for Magdalena.

Her beating you has only made this rivalry worse.

'Rivalry?' I said, taking up Thorn's reins. The Nightmare moved down the road, the sound of her hooves covering my whispered question. 'She said she didn't want the throne.'

She's been your rival ever since your father took her as an advisor. You had trouble sharing him with anyone. Her. Me. Arvan.

'You have trouble keeping quiet,' I said, and sent Thorn towards where the road split as Arvan, Erant and Rill trailed behind. It was only the four of us making this long ride. A danger, but it was the only way we could travel fast enough, and all the Rose Knights were needed at the Grey Palace to prepare the rest of the plan.

I took the split and rode up the narrow valley, sheer cliffs rising on either side. The road twisted through them, and all I could see was dark stone and a narrow slice of the sky above, clear except for where Temero's smoke drew a dark slash across it. I could see places up there where rocks were held in check by chains, traps meant to crush anyone who tried to force their way up here. Whatever else I thought about Magdalena's plan, she was right in this: any army that came for her hold would bleed.

The cliffs finally pulled back from the road, spreading out and making a short valley. A stream trickled through it, irrigating the gardens planted before the great wall of rock that ended the valley. Steps were carved into the rough basalt of that wall, twisting up to the gate that marked the entrance to the Ruinview. A huge raven was carved above them, the symbol of Nagash centred over its head. Beneath its spread wings Magdalena stood, looking down at me.

'Say it.' The memory of her whispered words went through my head, and I could see her standing over me, sword pressed against me. Shame and anger swept through me, and I wanted to ride Thorn up those stairs, to challenge her again. I wouldn't give her time to consider yielding, wouldn't worry about hurting her

dignity. I wanted to fight her, to beat her, to prove that I wasn't cursed. To prove that I was better. To prove myself.

What we want is not always what we need.

I didn't bother telling her to be quiet.

Ruinview didn't have a great hall or audience chamber, or anything like that. It was an ugly, practical thing hewn out of the basalt long ago by mortals over what must have been many of their lifetimes. Magdalena met us in her office, a bare room with a long window slit down one side that gave a wide view of the wastes. It suited her.

'What do you want?' Magdalena said as she sat at the end of a table strewn with maps. She had no guard with her, and hadn't asked me to leave anyone behind. Whatever else, she still trusted me. Or she underestimated me.

'The Broken Plains,' I said.

'Then go talk to the Spears of Heaven.'

'I plan to. But I want to make sure I'm loud enough to be heard.' I stood at the other end of the table. She hadn't offered us chairs and I didn't want one. 'So I need you and the others.'

'We already fought about that,' she said. 'I won.' There was no mockery in her voice, no sense of satisfaction. She stated it as the plain truth, and I hated hearing it. Hated that I needed her and couldn't challenge her again. Hated that she might take that as acknowledgement that she was better than me.

'We fought about my old plan,' I said. 'For taking Gowyn and stopping the Spears before they could step upon our shores. We don't have time to try that now. Thanks to your *win*.' She cocked her head, her curls brushing her shoulder, but she didn't respond to the rage barely buried in that word. 'You won, and came back to this hole to die.'

'Maybe,' she said, still infuriatingly calm. 'But if I do, it will be

after the halls of this hold run red with the blood of Sigmar's servants. If I lose, I'll make sure I keep them from winning.'

'It's still a loss,' I said.

'It's a loss with honour.' Magdalena leaned back, her armour creaking softly around her. 'It's death on my terms, as opposed to being hunted down like Salvera, or being killed fighting a battle that I've no chance of winning because I was too angry to accept the truth of my situation.'

We stared at each other for a long time, her face still serene while I fought to keep from baring my fangs, and I knew my eyes must be as red as the roses on my armour. But I held myself in place, waiting until I could speak without snarling.

'The truth of the situation,' I said, finally, proud that my words were even, 'is that you're alone here. As alone as I am in the Grey Palace. As alone as Lady Jirrini, and Lord Salvera, and Lord Durrano.' Durrano was a lie, he'd be pulling out of Skulltop as soon as he'd gathered his house together and stripped his hold of supplies, but it sounded better this way. If worse was better. 'When Celasian comes with his Spears, he'll find us divided, weak, ripe for defeat. That's our situation.'

Magdalena looked at me for a long time, her green eyes unreadable in her round face. A doll's face, framed with that curly hair, and for a moment I wondered how often she'd been underestimated by her enemies, and by other Kastelai. 'You want a different truth,' she said quietly. 'A better one. Corsovo wanted that too. When we were left here in this ash-smeared corner of the realms, it was his different truth that saved us. His dream of a Kastelai kingdom held us together, gave us purpose. I think it saved us from rotting away inside, like the others who succumbed to the Crimson Keep's curse. We went from being abandoned to being conquerors. We took the Grey Palace, Maar, almost all the Broken Plains. We weren't just knights any more, we were rulers

and Corsovo was a king. Then came Ire Crossing, when those mortals from Hammerhal almost beat us. After that...'

Finally, the mask slipped. Just a little, just enough for me to see the weariness in her eyes.

'Nagash gave us the blood, and with the blood came life.' Magdalena touched the holy symbol set on her armour. 'Life unending, on and on. A blessing, a burden, a curse. We live unchanging and watch everything around us fall apart. Apart, and apart, and apart, over and over again.' She looked at me with those weary, pretty eyes. 'That's why I serve the Lord of Death. So that I can serve his purpose and help him finally still the world and freeze all that ceaseless, awful change. But we are not Nagash, and we cannot stop things even in this tiny portion of the realms. Ire Crossing was the start of it. Corsovo knew. That's why the curse came for him. He saw the truth and tried to fight it, but it came for him anyway. You want me to say it, Nyssa? Then here it is. We're going to die, alone and forgotten by the Crimson Keep, and there's nothing we can do about it.'

'I don't believe that,' I said.

Magdalena's mask slipped a little more, and her lips twisted into a small, bitter smile. 'I didn't believe I could beat you. But the curse comes for us all.'

In my chest, my heart hammered. 'I am not cursed!' The words were a shout, ringing off the stone walls around us. 'Do you want—'

To fight me again, and find out. That's what I would have said, if my mother hadn't shouted in my head.

Nyssa, no! Not now. Not now!

I stopped. I didn't want to, but I did. I stopped and made myself listen.

You have her. Vasara's voice was controlled again, calm. *As well as you can right now. It might not seem like it, but I know Magdalena, I know her dark moods. She was listening to you, even if she wasn't showing it. But if you lose control now, she'll stop, and I doubt she'll ever listen to you again.*

'Listening to me? She was mocking me!' I kept the words silent, for Mother only, and even as I said them I knew they weren't true. Magdalena didn't mock, or ridicule. Those she thought of as fools she simply ignored. Though that didn't mean her words didn't twist like a knife.

'I don't believe I'm cursed.' Anger still crackled through my words, but I kept my voice low. 'I don't believe we're destined to lose. And I don't know what happened to my father, but I know he didn't believe that either. He didn't just give up and die. Neither should you.'

I looked at her table, at the papers scattered across it. One was a map, identical to the one I had in my rooms. I tapped my finger on it. 'This is your hold. Mine. Jirrini's, Salvera's, Durrano's.' I pointed to each drawn symbol. 'If we stay in them all, the Spears of Heaven will come to us one by one and destroy us. That's your plan.' I ran a hand over the map between the holds, the paper mostly blank except for marks where villages and towns had once stood. 'Salvera's plan is to hide here, in the hills and the grass, until we're hunted down or driven away like snakes. I don't like either of them. Here's my plan. We band together, as we should, as Kastelai, and we fight. But we fight on our terms, not theirs.'

I pointed to Durrano's hold. 'They'll hit here first. Skulltop is closest to them, farthest from us, and it's weak. It's still a holding though, and they'll have to fight and bleed to climb that hill. But when they finally break Skulltop's white walls, we'll already be gone. The hold will be empty, and as they search it they'll be hit from behind. They'll bleed again as their flanks are savaged, then when they turn, we're gone again.' My anger didn't go away as I explained. But it changed, blended with my eagerness for the

fight, and my viciousness, as Mother would say. 'We know these holds. The mortals who built them always left a bolthole. We'll use that. Defend each hold as it's attacked, then withdraw. Hold and bleed them. Run and bleed them. But bleed them, over and over.'

'They'll be wise to the strategy after the first time,' Magdalena said, frowning at the map.

'They will. We'll adjust.' That part of the plan wasn't nearly as fleshed out, but it couldn't be, not until we saw how our enemy reacted. 'Celasian came here not to beat us, but to kill us. They'll keep coming and we'll hurt them every time. By the time they get to the Grey Palace, we'll be able to take them by the throat.'

'Their commander is not a fool,' Magdalena said.

'Not a fool,' I said. 'A fanatic. You know what he did to the nomads.'

'Yes,' she said. 'One of my informants survived the massacre. She said that Celasian killed them all because one of the Biting Flames leaders hinted they might deal with us.'

'A fanatic,' I said again. Arvan had told me the same, and everything else he'd learned about the abbot-general. Which wasn't much, but it was enough to paint a bloody picture. 'He's here to hunt us down, Lady Magdalena. Every one of us. Instead of fearing that, let's use it. Make him run back and forth across the Broken Plains until he falls.'

'And if he doesn't?' She put her finger on the Grey Palace. 'If they're still strong enough to take your home, your throne, what then?'

'Then we come here, to the last hold, the one whose only bolthole opens onto ruin.' I waved my hand at the long window slit, and what lay beyond. 'It'll be your plan then. Except they'll be weaker from the battles before. Weak enough that the battle here might result in something other than your death.'

She stared at the map for a long time. 'It might work,' she finally said. 'If we had a leader. A king, like Corsovo, or a queen, like Vasara. But they're both dead, which just leaves us.'

I rolled my shoulders, forcing myself not to pace, not to scream. 'You don't think I can do this.'

'No,' she said. 'Nyssa. Listen. When Corsovo first brought you to the Crimson Keep, I had no idea why. You were like a feral cat, a fighter but wild, undisciplined, emotional. Over the years, I came to see what he saw, the potential in you. You became a great fighter, one of the best I have ever seen. But I also saw the weaknesses in you, the things Vasara saw, and was trying to correct. She made progress too, more than I ever thought she would. More, I think, than she thought possible.'

She has that right.

Magdalena took a breath, breathing air in just to push it out in a sigh. 'If they'd lived, I wonder what they could have made of you. I call us changeless, but they were changing you. Honing you into a weapon, and something more. A leader. But they died before they could finish, and the rot of the world closed in on us before you had a chance to change yourself. Maybe the Crimson Keep didn't have time to pass its curse to you, maybe it wasn't in Corsovo's blood, maybe there was some other reason you faltered during our fight, but you are cursed by time. You've run out of it. We all have.'

Damn her. I'd laid out the plan, and she hadn't torn it down like my first. She'd accepted it, but still rejected me.

She didn't want to. She wanted you to succeed, to convince her.

'What good does that do to me, if I failed?' I kept my response silent, barely.

You didn't fail. You started. Ask her what she'll do when you convince the others.

'What will you do,' I said, annoyed that I was using my mother's words exactly, 'when I convince the others?'

Magdalena laughed. 'If you do that, I'll join you too.'

Hooked. She's yours, now.

'Good,' I said. 'I'll hold you to that promise, after I go and collect them.'

Her smile disappeared. 'You really think you will,' she said, and I wanted to punch her. 'You really think you can win.' She paused, then continued on, carefully, precisely. 'Even after I beat you.'

She's testing you again.

'Yes, I damn well get it,' I hissed, letting the words slip just a little, and Magdalena cocked her head, staring at me. I focused myself on her, ignoring my mother, my anger. 'We are Kastelai,' I said to Magdalena. 'We cannot be defeated. Except by ourselves.'

I turned, letting my hair swing, going for drama, but she called after me and I stopped.

'Maybe you're right,' she said. 'I pray to Nagash that you are. I pray you succeed, and make me eat my words and my misery.'

I nodded to her, uncertain, angry. Magdalena was almost as good as my mother at putting me off balance, making me waver between hating her and admiring her, and it made me want to bite. But I held my anger in check, if only to keep Mother from giving me advice I didn't need. 'Thank you,' I managed.

'Thank you,' Magdalena said. 'For giving me something to think about while I wait to be destroyed.' She looked down at the map before her, as if considering something, then looked back at me. 'A gift, before you go. For the chances you gave me to yield in our fight. Jirrini will refuse you, the way she refused me. If you want to understand why, stand between Temero and Splitrock when the day is fading, and watch for where her hold bleeds.'

'I thought that would go much worse.' Arvan swung himself up into his saddle, his hair flying around his head.

'It could have gone much better,' I said, looking back at Ruinview.

I could pick out Magdalena's office, a shadowy slit cut in the stone of the sheer cliff face. Something moved in the middle of the cut, a flash of purple and black. Magdalena watching us go. Watching me.

It went as well as it could have. You handled her well.

As always, Mother's praise annoyed me as much as it encouraged me. I lifted Thorn's reins, and my Nightmare tossed her head, the white hair of her mane floating slowly through the air. Magdalena wasn't in hand, not even close. But if I could get my fists around the other two…

'Let's go!' I said, and Thorn took off, legs stretching into a gallop that the reborn horse could keep up all day and all night. The others followed, the clatter of their Nightmares' hooves sounding loud in the narrow valley until I reached out with my magic and quieted it, making us silent shadows racing along the narrow road, speeding back towards the Broken Plains.

There wasn't time to stop for the view on the way back. We rode down Temero's steep flank as fast as we dared, until the road levelled out as we passed the Grey Palace, barely acknowledging the startled salute shouted down at us. Day faded into night as we raced along the shore of the Irewater, passing the great memorial stones.

Such a waste. I had gone over the tallies with Arvan as we had planned, had counted the pitiful handful of fighting dead left to us. Maar and the villages that surrounded it had no graveyards, their dead were consigned to the lake. The villages and towns which had once dotted the Broken Plains had been looted of their buried dead years ago, either raised by us to their second life of battle, or dug up and burned by the mortals who sought to deny us foot soldiers.

War is a game of numbers, Arvan had said, more than strategy or skill. Numbers we didn't have.

Numbers. I looked ahead to Maar as we galloped silently

through the night, saw the sparks of candles shining from the windows dotting the dark walls of its buildings. Maar's population had declined over the years, ever since Ire Crossing, but… Damn Salvera for putting that idea in my head. Slaughtering the city just to raise them again broke the oath of protection my father had taken, the oath of servitude that the people of Maar had taken. Blood and loyalty were the underpinnings of Kastelai honour, and those kinds of oaths could never be broken. As Mother so often reminded me.

I did tell you that. Her voice was low, but it filled my head. *I also told you that everything ends in time. Anger. Life. Promises. All things fall eventually, except death, because it is an ending itself.*

'What are you saying?' Maar was flashing past now, hiding behind its walls from the night, not even noticing us as we flew past. We rode over the River Ire, shadows flickering across the black bridge. 'Do you think Salvera was right?'

No. There are not numbers enough in Maar to change the odds, and the cost of killing our mortal allies is too high. But if things were different, if their lives were all that stood between you and victory…

I heard her voice, and I almost lost my grip on Thorn's reins. What in all the amethyst hells was this? For years Vasara had been training me in the rules of being a Kastelai, all the things that lay beyond the use of blade and claw and fang. From before we came to the Broken Plains, while I was still growing into myself in the Crimson Keep's training rooms.

'We are vampires. In our blood flows the essence of death, and the power of its god, Nagash.' Vasara's voice had echoed in the stone room as she sat on a hard bench, watching me run through the forms my father had taught me. I'd practised them constantly in those early days, never stopping, never tiring, pausing only to feed. 'But we are also Kastelai, and alone among all the vampire dynasties we embrace a code of honour. The others may call it a

weakness, but that is their mistake. Let the Legion of Night have secrecy, the Legion of Blood cunning. Let the Vyrkos have ferocity, let the Avengorii become fear. We will have honour, and it will make us stronger than any of them, because it gives us discipline. With that we leash the beast that lives in our blood to our will, and become Kastelai. Unfailing in word and deed, forever.'

Back in the present, in the comforting darkness of the hills that spread beyond Maar, I picked out my words. 'Father gave an oath. He told the people of Maar, and all the ones that surrendered to us after, that if they gave us their blood, we would shed ours defending them. We would defend their city, their lands, them, from all who'd seek to harm them. It was a blood oath, the kind you said we could never betray. Because we are Kastelai, and we do not fail.'

In word or deed, she answered.

'Then how can you–' I started, but she interrupted my argument. *What form did Corsovo teach you first, Nyssa?*

'The pattern of six,' I said. 'What does–'

So if I were to stab my sword at your belly, what would you do?

'The fifth.' The pattern of six was basic, a series of blocks done with one sword. 'Blade descending.'

And so that is what you do every time someone tries to stab you in the gut?

'Of course not,' I said. 'It depends on how much they extend, what kind of weapon they have, whether they have armour or a shield, how fast they are, what their reach is.'

So if it depends, if that block is just one of a thousand possible moves, why did Corsovo tell you that it was one of the fundamental moves? Why did he teach it to you first and make you practise it over and over, if it was just one of many possibilities?

'Because you have to start at the beginning,' I said. 'Trying to teach all the possibilities is too confusing, so you begin with the first principles. Then you build on those as you grow.'

Yes, as in all things. Nyssa, I've spent years teaching you the first principles of what it means to be a Kastelai, of what it means to have honour. It's taken you so long to learn this, I had to keep going even after my death. But I think those first principles are finally sinking in, so now comes the harder part, the building through knowledge, through experience.

'Damn it, Vasara, what are you saying?' I said. 'That all the vaunted Kastelai honour you hammered into me is something that we only bother with when it's useful? When it's convenient? Because if you'd told me that from the start, I might have understood it!'

If I'd told you that first, that's what it would have been for you. Nagash knows there are enough Kastelai who are like that, Salvera being one. No, Nyssa, what I'm trying to make you understand is that before you can change something so fundamental as a first principle, you must understand what that principle means, so that you know why you need to change it when you do, and the hazards of that change. What the costs are. Corsovo gave an oath, to defend Maar and the Broken Plains. So what breaks that oath? Is it killing the mortals who live there? Or is it letting an army of invaders cut those same mortals down for made-up sins against a judgemental god?

I frowned into the darkness. 'I don't know. But I know the mortals in Maar wouldn't want either. They'd consider their deaths a betrayal, however they happened.'

They would, she agreed. *There are no easy absolutes, Nyssa. Not in fighting, not in leading. We bind ourselves to honour not because it makes things easier but because it makes them harder. Honour is the fire that tempers us and makes us stronger.*

'Damn me,' I swore. 'Honour and oaths, first principles and exceptions. When does it end?' Was she going to be critiquing me in my head, forever?

Never, Vasara said in answer. *When you stop thinking, stop trying to understand, when you just blindly follow a set of rules, it's as if you were allowing yourself to only fight using the pattern of six. It weakens you, even more than giving in to the beast and not having any rules or honour at all. You must think, you must grow, you must question and judge every moment you exist, or you risk sliding into poisonous fanaticism, and becoming a monster.*

CHAPTER ELEVEN

Dawn, and light, were spreading across the Broken Plains like liquid heat, making me sweat beneath the leather and steel of my armour, even in the shade of the fire-scarred trees that grew on the muddy banks of the River Ire.

'Captain Takora?' Galeris was sweating even more than me, the drops running down his face making tracks of grime out of the dust on his skin. 'We're ready.'

My lieutenant waved a hand towards the troops lined up beside the river, two companies of infantry and one of cavalry, though calling any of them companies was a stretch. The 39th Sun Seekers had fallen far in thirty years. The uniforms were a patchwork, few still showing the bright orange that had marched out of Hammerhal. Most were dull local imitations. Weapons were the same: spears, swords and axes of various qualities were distributed through the ranks. It was a collection of whatever we had available, not the unified equipment they should have carried. The cavalry rode horses that ranged from good stock bred in the Great Parch

to rough local nags. A rough, dispirited-looking crew, but mine. All of them survivors of this long, bitter war. Beyond them were the ones that weren't mine.

The Spears of Heaven were drawn up in perfect lines beside the river, the reins of their Demigryphs gripped in their white-gauntleted hands. The beasts moved sometimes, dipping their hook-beaked heads or shuffling their clawed feet, but the men and women standing beside them stood still as statues, seemingly unaffected by the heat despite their heavy armour. They were first off the wide-beamed barges that had been pulled up the river by teams of groaning lixx, and had waited through dawn as the 39th climbed out and formed up. It hadn't taken us long, but damn if their silent stares didn't feel like judgement.

Celasian waited with them, already mounted on the back of his griffon, who paced back and forth through the dry grass beside the Spears of Heaven. Erikil wore her armour now, and it gleamed white against her blue feathers. Every so often the beast would emit a low, keening noise that made the lixx groan and pull against the ropes that still tied them to the boats, trying to get further away from the predator.

'I think they're ready, too,' Galeris said, following my gaze.

'You think?' The griffon stopped, and Celasian looked to me. I couldn't read his face from here, but readiness radiated from his stillness as much as it did from the lashing of his mount's tail. I took a moment to look from them towards the sky, gauging the time. It would be almost noon when we reached Skulltop, the time when the vampires were weakest, and there was no reason to delay. I took a breath, thinking of all the messages I'd written in secret, of all the plans that rested on so many uncertain things. 'Go on his signal,' I said, and pulled myself up onto Sugar. I rode to the front of my troops, going slow to let Galeris get into place, then I nodded to Celasian.

The abbot-general didn't nod back. He jerked Erikil's reins and pointed the fierce-eyed beast towards the distant volcano and the hills between. He raised one clenched fist, and behind him the Spears of Heaven mounted their Demigryphs. In their saddles, they raised their spears as they shouted out in voices like thunder.

'For the glory of Sigmar!'

'For Sigmar!' Celasian echoed, and raised Heaven's Edge. Lightning crackled around the silver spear, sending sparks arcing out around the abbot-general as he started Erikil towards Skulltop, hidden somewhere behind the trees and low hills. The Demigryphs keened as the Spears of Heaven followed, their blue-and-white pennants streaming.

I took a deep breath, watching them go, then called to the boatmen who were tending the grunting lixx to get blankets and beat out the half a dozen little fires that sprang up from the brittle brown grass where Celasian had brandished his holy spear. When they set to work I pointed forwards, and Galeris raised the call behind me.

'Sun Seekers! The undying Thirty-Ninth! Forwards!'

When we crested the first low hill beyond the Ire, we could see Skulltop. The ancient hold was built on top of a great hill that reared twice as high as the others around it. Its summit was crested with a dome of white marble that glinted in the sun like fresh bone. Wisps of smoke could be seen rising from the hilltop and from its base, where a village nestled in a wooded valley.

I'd destroyed that village once. A raid ten years after Ire Crossing, when I was lieutenant to the man who'd led the 39th then, Captain Kota. Poor bastard. We'd burned the village then rode away, but not fast enough. When dark came we were still miles from Gowyn, our horses exhausted. That's when Durrano and his Skull Knights fell on us. I remembered riding as hard

as I could, trying not to panic as they picked us off. Remembered how Kota had shouted at us to keep going, that we were almost there. He shouted until we were almost at the city's gates, then there was a scream, horrible and inhuman and close, and Sigmar help me, I hadn't stopped. I'd spurred my horse on and rode through the city gates with the handful of survivors of that terrible night.

The next day, I'd watched in silence from atop Gowyn's walls as Kota's corpse stumbled down the road towards the gates. He'd been stripped of his clothes, and his body was as pale and white as sea foam except for the dark punctures that marked his throat, and the ragged wound that ran around the top of his head. They'd taken his scalp and hair, left the top of his skull bare over his dead, staring eyes. There was a candle burning there, on the very top of his head, and we stared in horror at the shuffling corpse as the candle burned low enough for the flame to touch the oil that had been poured over Kota's body. He burned then, shuffling down the middle of the road, skin going black and peeling, fat boiling away, stinking and smoking until he finally fell over.

I'd been made captain not long after that, and had never gone that close to Skulltop again. Until today.

Five hundred troops, the Spears of Heaven, and Celasian with his spear and his griffon. Was that enough? From my informant I knew there were something like thirty vampires in the hold, along with their lord, and maybe fifty shambling dead. A handful more of mortal warriors, and whatever villagers had run there for shelter. If it had just been my troops, I would never have attempted it. Cliffs guarded most of the white crown of Skulltop, except for a steep hillside that was protected by a marble wall. The 39th couldn't crack it, not without losing far more of my fighters than it was worth. How much did Celasian and his guard tip that calculation? I wasn't sure, but the abbot-general

was. He'd listened to my description of the hold, of its defenders and Durrano. The only time a flicker of emotion had stirred in his pale blue eyes had been when I described what had happened to Kota, the description of the bites on his body. Disgust had flickered across Celasian's face, fading away only when I said that the body had been burned.

Celasian had no worries about success. None at all. I wish I could say the same.

By the time we reached the village it was empty. It looked much the same as the last time I'd been here – they'd rebuilt on the foundations of what we'd burned, wooden and stone houses neatly laid beside a small stream. There were tools lying in the garden plots, food set out on tables, a few cats watching warily from windows and around corners. The other animals had been taken, along with whatever else the villagers deemed valuable, and hauled up to the hold. I'd had scouts riding back and forth, letting me know that our approach had been seen, that the villagers and the vampires were preparing for us. There had been a steady stream of messenger bats let go from Skulltop, and the scouts hadn't been able to shoot them all. Not that I think Celasian cared. He wanted the vampires to know he was here.

The abbot-general rode through the village as if it didn't exist, not worried about the possibility of a skeletal archer left behind as a trap. There didn't seem to be any today, but there had been enough in the past that my soldiers were looking around carefully. The possibility had me so on edge that I ducked when Celasian jerked on Erikil's reins, stopping in the middle of the village. But when I followed his eyes all I saw was a small shrine to Nagash. The abbot-general raised Heaven's Edge and aimed the spear. Lightning flew from the relic and smashed into the shrine, blowing the little wooden building apart, scattering smoke and charred wood through the village.

'Burn it.' Celasian was looking up, through the trees to the crest of the hill above, but I knew he was talking to me. 'Burn it all.'

I took a breath but nodded, and sent a group of soldiers off to torch the village. Then I led the rest of them after the abbot-general, marching up the hill towards the vampires that waited above.

It was just past midday when we reached the top of the hill, horses blowing and sweating, men cursing the heat and the steep climb. I reined in Sugar at the edge of the trees, staying in the shade and blinking my eyes against the glare as Celasian rode into the clear, the light gleaming off his armour and Erikil's azure feathers. Behind him, the Spears of Heaven had arranged their Demigryphs in perfect lines, the riders and beasts all motionless except for the slow stirring of the pennants that hung below the silver blades of their spears. The 39th stopped behind me, their lines not so precise. They clung to the shade, drinking from waterskins and staring at the wall that protected Skulltop.

It ran across the clearing in front of us, made of heavy blocks of marble. Bright in the sun, the wall was only half the size of the basalt walls that ringed Gowyn, but it was high enough. Only a single gate marred the smooth white face, blocked with two heavy doors of age-darkened wood.

Nothing moved along the wall, no sounds of boots or curses or clanking armour echoed from its other side. Skulltop seemed desolate, deserted, but from hard experience I knew different. The dead were patient. The moment Celasian or any one of us crossed the invisible line that marked the range of Skulltop's bows, skeletal archers would rain down death upon anyone who approached. For now it was all silence and stillness except for the waving pennants and the heavy breathing of the horses. In the quiet, it was easy to hear Galeris ride up, each crunch of his horse's hooves a jagged break in the hush.

'What are they doing?' he asked when he drew up next to me, his voice barely above a whisper.

'Damn me if I know.' I kept myself quiet too, though I didn't know why. It wasn't like we were sneaking up on Skulltop. But the sepulchral silence of the hold made me whisper. Celasian had given me precise instructions on what I was to do when he cracked Skulltop's gates, but he hadn't gone into how he'd accomplish that. As he'd brought no siege machinery, not even a ram, he must be expecting some kind of miracle. Or he had a plan to create one.

We sat, sweating, watching the Spears of Heaven do nothing. Waiting until we finally noticed a sound. Low, but growing. The Spears of Heaven were chanting. I strained, listening as the words grew louder, but their meaning was blurred. They were chanting in High Azyrite, the formal language of priests and scholars, and I couldn't make anything out but the words 'bless' and 'strike'.

'Go back to the infantry and get them ready,' I told Galeris, and he nodded, moving away. I gestured to the cavalry, using hand signs to warn them to prepare. They fell into position behind me, their ranks more practical than pretty, each rider holding their reins and staring ahead at the silent hold, wondering what was going to happen.

The chant grew louder, echoing off the wall, its rhythm reminding me of distant thunder. The air around me began to crackle with static. Tiny sparks flickered between the metal plates sewn onto my leather gauntlets, arcing out to tickle my flesh. The sparks grew, one snapping from my hand to Sugar's sweat-foamed neck, making her toss her head. I calmed her, and around me other riders were doing the same, trying to keep their horses from starting as tiny flickers of lightning danced across weapons, armour and harness. The same sparks were flicking from the white-armoured Church soldiers to their mounts, but the Demigryphs stayed still, as if the snap of tiny sparks meant nothing to them.

The chant grew louder still, and the Spears of Heaven were shouting it, bellowing their words up to the empty sky. It really did sound like thunder now, a deep rolling crash that went on and on as the sparks flickered through the air, dancing from their raised spear points, flashing and bright until Celasian suddenly raised Heaven's Edge high. The Spears shouted and arcs of electricity leapt from every one of their upraised spear points, flashing through the air to Celasian. The lightning twisted around him, shining off his armour, the little bolts like sizzling threads of white fire weaving together until they were one. A bolt as thick as a man's arm wrapped around Celasian like a serpent, so bright it was painful to look at. Then it exploded, the bolt flaring out as it shaped itself into something else. For a moment it was as if a huge drake had settled over Celasian, a great beast drawn from dancing electric light, and then the abbot-general snapped his arm down and aimed his spear at the gate. With a roar of thunder that shook the hilltop, the lightning drake darted forwards and slammed into the dark wood of the iron-bound gate. There was another roar and the gate was gone, smashed to flaming bits of wood and molten metal that pattered down into the courtyard beyond.

'For Sigmar!' Celasian bellowed, and Erikil leapt forwards, taking to the air just enough to bound over the wall. Behind him, the Spears of Heaven launched forwards, their Demigryphs pounding across the clearing and leaping through the flaming wreckage.

'The Thirty-Ninth! The undying Thirty-Ninth!' I bellowed, jerking on Sugar's reins to get her under control. Half our damn horses had gone crazy with the lightning and thunder. 'Get your blades out and ride, you luckless bastards!' I pulled my sword, aimed Sugar and got her running in the right direction. From the curses and the pounding of hooves it sounded like most of the other cavalry had done the same. Behind them came the sound of boots, the infantry rushing up. The lightning had scared us witless, but

damn the hammer, it had got our blood up too, and we charged after the Spears of Heaven, howling.

I raced across the clearing, heading towards the burning gate. On the wall I could see the hideous silhouettes of skeletons, ugly bone puppets holding the vicious little recurve bows that the nomads used. An arrow sliced through the air over me, and I ducked low, urging Sugar to run faster.

There were few arrows after that first, though. Most of the skeletal archers were firing into the fight going on inside the wall. As I sped through the gate I could see that the Spears of Heaven had smashed into the forces gathered there, and the courtyard was littered with corpses. Most of them still twitched and moved, and I guided Sugar around the ones that tried to bite or tangle her legs as we pounded towards the great white building that lay ahead. The hold proper, that was where I needed to be.

'Follow, Sun Seekers! On me!' I slapped Sugar's reins and the brave mare charged right up the marble steps. There were people packed at the door, villagers or servants who'd been outside the hold when the gate fell and were now desperately trying to get in. Stupid. They should have scattered and let the doors slam shut. I charged them, swinging my sword and howling, and they were smart enough at least to run then. The people inside tried to shove the door shut but I urged Sugar forwards, twisting her at the last moment so that her shoulder smashed into the closing door. It burst open and I was in, ducking my head just in time to avoid cracking it on the door frame.

The hall inside was big enough for me to sit back up, but I stayed low, catching movement out of the corner of my eye. Something swung through the space where my head should have been and I came up, snapping it aside with my sword. It was a bloody shovel, swung at me by a young man barely old enough to shave.

'Surrender!' I shouted, but everything was noise and confusion

as more of the 39th pounded in, horses and humans screaming. The man swung again, the shovel's blade missing me but heading right for Sugar's head. I blocked it and twisted my blade, flinging the tool out of the man's hands. A pretty move, but he tried to hold on to the shovel and stumbled. My sword clashed against the rusty shovel blade then came free, flying up and slicing across the man's face, cutting open his cheek and smashing out teeth, ripping through his nose and cutting one wide brown eye in half. He fell to the floor screaming and I cursed. Part of me wanted to puke, but my mind had gone into its battle place where things like that were carefully saved for later nightmares, but ignored for now.

I charged Sugar down the hall to its end then slid off. There were a dozen riders right behind me and I shouted at one of them to keep the horses under control. I ran along a corridor to a set of steps that corkscrewed down, opening at the bottom into an ancient storeroom. A cluster of people were huddled there, trying to squeeze into a narrow opening that was supposed to be hidden by the flagstone that sat tipped up beside it.

An old woman in black-and-purple robes who'd been helping people down the hole leapt in front of me. She had both hands out, open, but she was grim-faced, determined to stop me.

'It's just villagers,' she said. 'Let them go.'

'Sorry, ma'am,' I said, and deftly flicked my sword out, slapping her in one scrawny ankle with the flat of the blade. Harmless but damn painful, as evidenced by the wince she gave as she stumbled to the side. 'We'll take care of them,' I said to her, then turned to the soldiers behind me.

'Check it out,' I told them, and they headed for the tunnel, pulling people out and then dropping in to pursue the ones who were already in the stone throat of the bolthole. 'Bring them all back,' I called after them, and detailed more soldiers to guard the old

woman and the others we'd found here. Then I ran back up the stairs to the entrance hall.

My infantry was streaming in, men and women flying past me in squads as they tore through the hold, searching and fighting. I ignored them, except to shout at a woman who was looting silver candlesticks. That was for later. I made sure Sugar was being taken care of, then rushed for the door.

Outside, the courtyard was still a chaos of fighting. On one side a group of my infantry, led by Galeris, was forcing a clacking crowd of skeletons up against the white wall. The living outnumbered the fighting dead, but it was a grinding fight, blows being traded back and forth. I watched as Galeris swept his sword down, shattering the arm of a skeleton wrapped in the ragged remains of what had once been a dress. The undead lost its sword and much of its arm, but that didn't slow the horrible thing. It came back at Galeris without pausing, lunging at my lieutenant's face with dirt-stained teeth. He was hammering it away with the pommel of his sword when the fight swirled and I lost sight of him.

In the centre of the yard, the rest of the Church soldiers were battling the vampires of Skulltop. The enemy looked almost human, men and women, pale or dark, wrapped in ivory-coloured armour, but some had nails like claws, ridged ears like bats, or eyes that gleamed yellow, red or black. Every one of them had fangs that flashed as they shouted their prayers to the God of Death, or curses at the living that fought them. All were mounted on Nightmares, corpse horses with empty eye sockets that were streaming pale mist or weeping dark ichor.

They were half the number of the Spears of Heaven, but the vampire knights fought like disciplined daemons, sticking together in a tight squad of butchery. The Church soldiers were circling them on their Demigryphs, thrusting with their spears, but the undead were adept at smashing the long weapons away before

their sharp points found cold flesh. As I watched, one of the Spears of Heaven pushed in too close, trying to drive his spear into the chest of a female vampire whose skin was the same bone-white colour as her armour. She grabbed the spear behind its point and jerked it towards her, hard and fast. The Spear of Heaven holding it was too stupid to let go, and he was ripped out of his saddle. Another vampire caught the man as he fell and bit into his neck, ripping free a chunk of flesh. The undead drank for a moment from the blood that sprayed out of the gaping wound, then threw the body aside.

It was an uncertain, vicious fight, the vampires outnumbered but fighting hard, slowly moving towards the remnants of the shattered gate and escape. But then with a flash of wings and a shriek that split the air like lightning, Erikil slammed down into the courtyard. On the griffon's back, Celasian aimed Heaven's Edge at the undead, shouting a prayer.

The vampires paused only a moment, then drove themselves at the abbot-general, their formation shifting into a wedge as they thrust towards this new threat. At the point of their formation was the ivory woman who'd caught the Church soldier's spear, her eyes flashing as she pulled back her sword, ready to cut Celasian from his saddle. Before she could swing, though, Erikil slashed at the vampire's mount. The Nightmare stumbled and the vampire had to shift with it, giving Celasian an opening. He thrust Heaven's Edge at her, and she twisted, dodging most of the blow, but the edge of the spear touched her. A small, shallow wound, but the touch of the holy weapon was enough. An arc of lightning snapped out from Heaven's Edge and into the vampire. She went rigid in the saddle as the electricity coursed through her, and her sword fell from her hands.

Celasian pulled back his spear, but the arc of lightning stayed connected to the vampire, lashing out from the spear point into her shaking, smoking body. Her pale skin blackened, lips pulling back from her teeth, her gums and tongue smoking as her eyes boiled in their sockets. She burned until Celasian snapped his spear contemptuously away from her, as if shaking blood from its blade. The arc of lightning broke and let the smoking corpse fall. The vampire's Nightmare reared and bucked, screaming, but Erikil swept the undead horse down with her talons, tearing it into pieces.

The fury and the lightning of Celasian's attack had stopped the vampires, shaken their discipline as it bolstered the Spears of Heaven. The undead's formation was faltering, breaking as the Church soldiers drove in, their spears flashing and Demigryphs shrieking. Then came a different scream.

'Damn me,' I cursed, staring at the rider that stood on the other side of the yard. Durrano. The Kastelai rode a white Nightmare, its colourless fur wrapped in tendrils of mist. The vampire lord was just as pale, his ornate armour like a suit of bone wrapped around him. In his hand he carried a flail, its handle shaped like a femur, the chain on its end attached to a great club that looked like a length of vertebrae, the bone's strange protrusions spiked and sharp-edged. Durrano stared through his helmet at Celasian, and swung that heavy flail. The sound it made as it cut through the air was the same horrible scream I remembered from that terrifying ride back to Gowyn, the ride where Durrano had killed Captain Kota.

Durrano swung the flail, then charged straight at Celasian.

One of the Spears of Heaven foolishly reined her Demigryph around and put herself in the way of Durrano's charge. The vampire didn't even change his course. He just reared up in the saddle and swept that awful flail past the Church soldier's spear. The spiked head of his flail smashed the woman from her feathered mount, and she hit the ground a dozen yards away, choking and

spitting blood. Her mount got one startled squawk out before Durrano's Nightmare barrelled over it and crushed the Demi-gryph under steel-shod hooves, barely slowing.

Durrano kept going, his flail spinning over his head as he charged, and Celasian pointed Heaven's Edge at him, calling out prayers that couldn't be heard over the sound of Durrano's scream-ing weapon. But the lightning that shot from the holy spear was impossible to ignore. The bright bolt caught Durrano in the chest, leaving tangled black marks all across his armour. Dark smoke mixed with the white mist that poured off the vampire's mount, but the Kastelai didn't stop. He kept charging, sparks snapping over him, aiming straight at Celasian, and the abbot-general barely got his spear up in time to stop the crushing strike aimed at his head.

The flail bounced off Heaven's Edge, and sparks danced across the bone weapon as Durrano dragged it down. Its head bounced into Celasian's shoulder, denting the pauldron of his armour. Then they were moving, spinning around each other, flail screaming, spear sparking. The griffon shrieked and struck, and the Night-mare reared and lashed out with its hooves like massive clubs. Celasian's spear darted like a snake, and every time it touched Durrano lightning snapped around the vampire. But Durrano hit like rocks falling, his massive blows denting Celasian's armour. It was a nasty duel, and it needed to end.

There was a bow on the ground, still gripped in a skeletal hand. I picked it up and shook the bones off, then plucked an unbroken arrow from a pile of shattered ribs. Those around me who weren't battling for their lives were gawking at the duel, but I nocked the arrow and took aim. I waited for the fight to move the way I needed it, forcing myself to ignore the fear that came every time I heard that flail scream. Another nightmare for the future. I pulled back the bowstring, aimed the rusty steel-tipped arrow and let it fly.

The arrow flew true, but Durrano saw it. He ducked his head, letting the barbed tip slip by instead of slamming into the bridge of his nose. But that movement opened him up, and Celasian took advantage. The leader of the Spears of Heaven slammed his weapon forwards, driving Heaven's Edge into the seam between Durrano's breastplate and backplate. The holy relic buried itself deep in the vampire's chest and lightning poured into the Kastelai.

Durrano stiffened, his whole body going rigid as the electricity burned through him. Smoke poured out of his armour, thick and dark and stinking. It didn't rise, but pooled on the ground below, sluggish and dense as mud around the hooves of his Nightmare. The bone flail, hanging from the vampire lord's hand, rattled as he shook, then finally fell, vanishing into the black smoke. Even this far away, I could see the cold satisfaction on Celasian's face as he twisted his spear, grinding its edges against Durrano's broken ribs, then jerked it free.

A flow of blood followed, its red so dark it was almost the same colour as the smoke. Durrano slumped, no longer twitching, but he didn't fall. Smoking, his skin slowly turning black in thin, branching tracks as the lightning spread through him, the vampire twisted his head to look at Celasian. One eye was burning, going black, but the other was focused on the abbot-general and filled with hate. Celasian stared back with contempt.

'Return to your foul lord, you unnatural thing,' Celasian said, his voice cold and vicious with satisfaction. 'In Sigmar's name, die!'

'Idiot,' I said, scrabbling on the ground for another arrow. Vampires didn't die easy, and Soulblight vampire lords... I snatched my head back up at the roar that filled the courtyard. Durrano was burning from the inside out, but still he'd flung himself at Celasian, his mouth open wide to bare his fangs.

The abbot-general twisted in his saddle, trying to get his spear up, but he was too slow. Durrano was on him, and the straps

meant to keep Celasian on the back of his winged mount all ripped and popped. Both of them ended up on the ground in a crash of armour.

Durrano was on top, holding tight to Celasian as he tried to tear out the abbot-general's throat with his fangs, but Celasian had got one arm up to block the vampire's teeth. They scratched across white armour and bloody, smoking foam poured from Durrano's mouth and fell onto Celasian's face. The abbot-general tried to shove the vampire off him, his face twisted with rage and disgust.

Then Erikil's talons sliced through the air and caught Durrano in the back, sending the vampire rolling across the ground, trailing blood and smoke. When he stopped, Durrano tried to push himself up, but his whole body was shaking and both eyes were gone, black smoking holes over the bloody slash of his mouth.

Celasian pulled himself to his feet, staring at the dying vampire. His perfect armour was slathered with dark blood, and spots of the noxious fluid marked his face. The abbot-general reached up and touched one of the deep red spots, then looked at the stain the blood made on his gleaming gauntlet. With a guttural shout of revulsion he lunged forwards and slammed Heaven's Edge straight into Durrano's face. The vampire fell back, twitching, and Celasian stood over him, driving his spear down into the vampire's head over and over again, grunting, 'Bite me? Bite *me?*' – a chant of hate and disgust that went on and on as Sigmar's chosen smashed the vampire's head to pulp.

I was searching Durrano's office when Galeris found me.

'Anything?' he asked. I was sitting cross-legged, sorting papers on the floor because some idiot had shattered the desk and chair, knocked down the shelves and pissed on the cloth banner that bore dead Durrano's sigil. I'd got to the place in time to stop them from pissing on the papers, at least.

'Nothing useful,' I said, tossing away lists of goods, the detailed ancestry of various horses and a collection of surprisingly delicate poems that Durrano had been writing about Princess Bloodeyes. Were vampires romantic? If they were, could they do anything about it? Physically? It was a horrifying question that I didn't want answered. The next set of looters were welcome to piss on all of it. At least there was nothing incriminating in the papers, either.

'Has Celasian calmed down yet, or is he still desecrating corpses?'

'He's...' Galeris stopped, blowing out a deep breath. He was dirty and had a bandage wrapped around his forehead, covering a jagged cut from a skeleton's clawing grip. We'd done damn well from all I had seen. Only a few score dead, and three times that seriously wounded. The rest of the injuries were cuts and bruises, though I'd made sure that every member of the 39th washed those filthy wounds out with vesfire. That seemed to be the only thing that kept those injuries from going bad. From the scent of Galeris' breath, I knew he'd taken a healthy slug of the rough drink before he had poured it on his wound, as was traditional.

'He's had all the bodies thrown into the Temple of Nagash,' Galeris finally said. 'Theirs and ours.'

I winced, but it wasn't surprising. The dead belonged to the dead, and we'd have burned them anyway if we'd taken them back to Gowyn. Still, to mix them with the undead...

'That isn't the thing, though,' Galeris said. 'He's taken all the villagers we caught. He's got them lined up in front of the temple and I don't know what he plans to do with them. But I don't think it's anything good.'

'Hammer me to hell,' I said, and stood. I left the office and the hold, Galeris trailing behind, and headed towards the Death God's temple.

The building was the newest thing behind Skulltop's white wall, though it was a century old, a rough pyramid of dark stone. There

were no windows and only one door, a massive thing that had been left hanging open. Inside I could see little, just darkness broken by the faintest gleam of something white. Over the door hung a huge mask shaped like a skull, carved out of some dark wood. Two fist-sized amethysts were set in its eye sockets. The building, the skull mask, all of it, was crude and ugly, but effective, a glowering piece of darkness surrounded by all the shining white marble of the hold.

A good-sized chunk of the 39th had gathered in front of the building, men and women talking and laughing as they passed bottles and casks, liquor looted from somewhere. Trust a soldier to find any trace of alcohol after a battle. The crowd was loud, jubilant with victory and drink. They shouted at me as I passed, boasting of their kills. It was good to see them like this, laughing in their ragged uniforms, soldiers long denied even the hope of success finally tasting victory, but I couldn't focus on them. I was staring past their smiles at the white-armoured Church soldiers and the grey-haired man who led them.

Celasian was a sight, his face all hard angles as he frowned up at the skull mask. There was a bruise blossoming on one cheek, and the blue tabard over his white armour was spotted with blood so dark it looked black. But he stood straight, unaffected by the sun and the heat, Heaven's Edge clenched in one gauntleted fist, its shining blade pointing towards the heavens. I had no idea what he was doing, until I saw his lips move, silently tracing out words. Praying.

Celasian's guard, mounted on their Demigryphs, were set around him in precise lines. They barely looked as though they'd fought, and when I counted them I came up only ten short. None seemed to be injured badly. In a battle with undead and vampires, they'd lost fewer than a dozen, those killed outright, while all the injured had been completely healed of whatever wounds they'd taken. No

wonder they looked at their abbot-general like the holy light of Sigmar shone out of his arse. It apparently did.

The rigid lines of Church soldiers formed a box, and kneeling on the paving stones in the middle of that box were the prisoners. They were men and women, young and old, almost a hundred of them. The survivors from the village. They were roped together, silent except for some sobbing. They were all filthy and bloody and bruised, though few seemed badly injured. I didn't see the man with the shovel, which meant his body was probably with the others inside the temple. As I got closer, I could see that the blur of white in the darkness beyond the door was a figure in armour, the same bone-white colour as Durrano's.

I stared at the prisoners, at the open door, and I didn't like it. Not at all. 'Keep the Thirty-Ninth under control,' I told Galeris, and stalked across the white stones towards Celasian, walking wide around the holy warriors. No one blocked me, and I came up behind him, stopping almost in his shadow.

'What's going on?'

Celasian didn't stop his praying, didn't show any sign he'd heard or seen me. He kept going on, and my hands twitched at my sides. Grabbing him seemed a damn stupid idea, so I waited. Finally he whispered one last word and turned towards me.

'Purification,' he said. His eyes were as dead as ever. 'The battle does not end until the evil has been burned away.' He looked past me to the kneeling prisoners. 'All of it.'

I swore silently to myself. 'They're just people.'

'Just people.' Celasian raised his free hand and gestured at one of the prisoners. The two guards flanking him went to the woman and picked her up, hauling her in front of us. She was old, and dressed in a black robe marked with purple. The one who'd tried to stop me from pulling people out of the bolthole. She was a priestess of Nagash.

'Damn me,' I said wearily as she looked up at us with eyes untouched by fear.

'You said you'd take care of them.' Her eyes were on me, ignoring Celasian.

'Did you make promises to the damned?' Celasian asked, his voice flat.

'I tried to reassure the helpless and the innocent,' I said. 'Was I wrong to do so?'

'The innocent.' Celasian reached into the old woman's robe, grabbed something and jerked it out, making the priestess stumble. It was a necklace, a simple tarnished silver chain, but strung in its middle was the tiny skull of an infant. An amethyst was set in the centre of the high forehead. He held it out for me to see, then threw it over his shoulder into the dark temple. 'Is she one?'

'Fine,' I snapped, angry, trapped, disgusted. 'Burn her for... whatever. But those?' I pointed to the villagers. 'What did they do?'

The most frightening part of what happened next was Celasian's expression. It never changed. The abbot-general grabbed my arm and dragged me over to the prisoners as easily as if I were a child. His face stayed that same cold, emotionless mask. I stumbled with him, then got my feet under me, clenching my mouth shut to keep from cursing, hoping the 39th hadn't noticed anything. Last thing we needed was some drunk throwing a rock at Celasian and being fed to his griffon.

Celasian stopped in front of the first villager, some middle-aged farmer. He reached out and grabbed the man by the hair, brutally twisting his head back. 'What is this?' he asked, his voice deadly quiet.

I looked at the scar on the man's neck. 'A bite mark.'

Celasian nodded and let the man go. He went to the next prisoner, a woman, and did the same. 'This?'

'A bite,' I said again, my stomach churning. Celasian let the woman go, and I could see strands of her dark hair caught in his

gauntlet as he reached out for another, a girl of about nineteen. 'That's enough,' I said, as he grabbed her hair and jerked her head back, exposing another scar.

'Is it?' he said. Celasian grabbed another man's head, pulling it back, showing the bite. 'Is it?' He let the man go and grabbed an old woman's head. She stumbled as the abbot-general jerked back her head, showing the overlapping scars that marked her wrinkled neck. The old woman fell when Celasian let her go, but he didn't seem to notice.

'Enough!' I said. 'They all have it. I know! Giving blood, it's something the Soulblight vampires demand. They didn't have a choice, they had to do it, all of them.'

'All of them.' Celasian stopped in the middle of the prisoners and looked at me. 'Every one. Bitten. Tainted. Contaminated. By those things. And you ask what they did?'

'They survived!' I said.

'Exactly,' he said softly. 'They survived, when their only hope for salvation was death.' He looked at the Spears of Heaven gathered around us in their perfect lines. 'Take them in.'

Some cried, some struggled, but not many. Most of them didn't even sob. They just went limp and let the Church soldiers drag them across the white stone into the darkness of the temple. I stood there, silent, until I was alone, standing between the Spears of Heaven and the 39th. I could hear them, laughing, shouting. Drunk. They didn't know what was going on. They didn't care. Except for a few, who were turning their backs and walking away.

Gods hear me, I wanted to walk away too.

But I made myself watch as they nailed the temple's door shut. Watched them walk around the building splashing its wooden walls with lamp oil. Watched as the Spears of Heaven stood back, and Celasian raised Heaven's Edge and pointed it at the mask of Nagash.

Lightning cracked from its tip, struck the mask and sent it falling to the ground, shattered and blazing. One of the amethyst eyes rolled towards me, stopping an arm's length away, and I stared at the polished purple crystal. I could see the flames reflected in it as the temple caught, becoming a blaze, a pyre, and from it rose a great plume of black smoke that twisted high into the perfect blue heavens, carried up by the sounds of screams.

Just before night fell the last wall of the temple crumpled, turning the building into a heap of stinking ash and flickering coals. When it fell, a rumble ran through the earth, a silent tremble of the solid stone beneath my boots that made Sugar toss her head.

'Shh,' I said, rubbing my hand over her neck, trying to soothe her. I looked towards the distant horizon where Temero crouched. In the dying day I couldn't see the plume of smoke that rose from the mountain, but I could see a dull red glow, the colour of the coals that still flickered among the blackened bones of the temple. The mountain was flaring up again, and I wished it would let go, blow its molten heart out and bury this entire damned place under ash and fire.

I doubted I would be so lucky.

'There'll be ash falling again tomorrow,' Galeris said. He was sitting behind me, watching me check Sugar, instead of walking the camp like he should've been, keeping the troops from drowning in looted drink. 'Are you sure?'

'I'm sure,' I said. I let go of Sugar's head and faced him. 'I'm taking the cavalry now, while we've a little light left, to run the search. If anyone did get out of that bolthole, I'll get them back to Gowyn and see them safe.'

'And I tell Celasian…?' he said, waiting.

'The truth. That I'm making sure no one escaped. Just don't tell him I don't intend to let him know if they did.' I sighed. 'I'm sorry.

I know I'm leaving you to deal with him, but I want to help these people if I can. And… And I don't think I can be stuck on a boat with that pale-eyed fanatic without trying to shove my sword into him. Or falling on it.'

'And you think I can?' Galeris said.

'I do.' And I did. One of the reasons I relied on Galeris was his calm. He wasn't emotionless like the abbot-general, he could love and he could hate, but Galeris did both with the same unflappable equanimity.

'All right. I'll get the infantry aboard the boats and get them home.' He didn't walk off, though. He stood looking at me for a long time in the gloom. 'Captain Takora,' he said, 'I just want you to know… Things, all these things, they aren't your fault. They aren't none of our faults, except maybe the gods', and to be honest I don't think they really have anything under control either. So try not to beat yourself up too bad about them.'

'That's…' Sigmar's beard, I didn't know what to say to that. 'Just get the Thirty-Ninth back safe, right?'

'Right,' he said, and finally started to go. But not before saying one last thing. 'Good luck, captain. With whatever you're doing.'

I stared after him, a shadow moving towards the bright fires of the camp. 'With whatever you're doing.' Did he know? What could he know?

There'd been another message waiting for me beneath Sugar's saddle tonight.

Remember your promises.

My promises. What were they worth? The villagers of Skulltop would argue not much. But these promises… So many might burn if I broke them, so I'd written a message back, marked it with my blood, and spiked it to a twig on a branch over Sugar.

It was time to make one more gamble. To try to end this stupid war once and for all. And to see who I could save along the way.

CHAPTER TWELVE

From darkness through the painful light of day, our Nightmares bore us over the Broken Plains, silent, constant, unyielding. There's no sleep in the second life, and for those blessed with the blood, dreams take us when we're unwary, pulling us into fantasies of ambition unrealised or fear anticipated. As I rode Thorn across rolling hills, wrapping us all in silence, those waking dreams spun through my head. In some I united the Kastelai houses in my grip and crushed the mortal threat of Takora and Celasian. In others the cursed cold that had cut through me while fighting Magdalena came again, reducing me to ruin like my father. The other Kastelai stared at me with mad contempt as they laid me in the tomb beside him and my mother, sealing me in darkness: helpless, but still aware of everything, a ghost locked in a shrivelled corpse forever.

When Arvan reined in at the bottom of a narrow valley between tall hills, I had to shake myself out of one of those dark dreams, and its despair left a bitter taste. 'What is it?' I said, pulling Thorn to a stop and circling to face the black-eyed vampire.

'One of my spies.' Arvan held out an arm and a bat flew from one of the fire-twisted trees which grew beside the stream that marked the bottom of the valley. The leather-winged creature landed on his hand, sniffing at Arvan's palm, then sank its sharp teeth into Arvan's wrist. The vampire didn't move, letting the little bat lap up the blood that welled from the tiny punctures in his skin, his dark eyes staring at the feeding animal.

'The mortals at Gowyn are gathering,' he said as Rill and Erant rode up, both of them keeping a wary eye on the brush around us. 'Takora's pulling in all her patrols, and Celasian's guard has received reinforcements of a kind. Their mounts, some kind of Azyrite beasts.' Arvan spent a long moment staring at the bat. 'They're readying themselves for something.'

'An attack?' I said. It was too soon. By the hells, we had so little time, but we were supposed to have more. 'I thought you said the ships bringing the rest of the Spears of Heaven weren't supposed to be here for at least ten days?'

'They're not. This is just Takora's army, and the few new ones that have come.' Arvan tapped the bat with his finger and the little creature squeaked, took one last drop of blood, and flew away. 'An attack would be foolish with reinforcements coming so soon. Why would this abbot-general risk himself when most of his strength is so close?'

'I don't know,' I said. 'I don't know anything about this mortal, except that you and Magdalena say he's as dangerous as a spark adder. So treat him as such, and make sure you know where he is. Always.'

Giving orders like a leader now. Good.

'I've always liked yelling at people,' I said silently. 'Doesn't mean I want it to be my job.'

Vasara might have said more, but I'd caught something drifting in the air. A scent – old death, dried blood, earth and fur.

Vasara kept silent as I raised one hand from my reins and circled a finger, a tiny gesture but Rill and Erant caught it instantly. They shifted in their saddles, not drawing their weapons but readying themselves. It took Arvan a moment longer, but he saw the shift in them and looked up, his dark eyes flashing around the valley.

Maybe that was enough, or maybe he thought it was just time, but that was when Salvera appeared out of the tall grass that crowned the steep earthen bank on the other side of the stream. Behind him crouched two massive vargheists.

Colours flickered over Salvera and the beasts behind him. Browns and blacks, the colours of shadows and grass, melted away. Salvera had camouflaged them, made them invisible until he let his magic go. But I'd smelled him, and the vargheists he'd brought with him.

The hunched creatures looked like vampires and bats twisted together, with long-fanged maws and tattered membranes hanging from their arms. Their eyes were bestial, hungry, but there was a strange cunning that flickered through them. Vargheists were vampires who had lost themselves in their beasts, traded their humanity for predatory power.

Most vampires avoided those creatures and the fate, the temptation, that they represented. Salvera seemed to enjoy having them close.

'Young Nyssa.' Salvera smiled down at me, a wolf's smile, all threat and no humour. 'I thought you were locked in the Grey Palace, with Durrano watching over your slow demise.'

'I'm not dying, Lord Salvera.' Out here in the open, flanked by his monstrous companions, Salvera looked more the beast than ever. His yellow eyes gleamed over his muzzle, his pointed ears twitched at every rustle of the grass, and his nose quivered, testing the air. His hands moved restlessly up and down the handle of his scythe as if they didn't know where to settle, but I knew

that for a lie. I'd seen Salvera handle that heavy weapon as precisely as a razor.

'But you are,' he said. 'You all are. Jirrini and Durrano and Magdalena. Dying, every one of you, and all the ones you've spawned.' He paused, and an ugly laugh spilled from between his teeth. 'Except you never did make spawn, did you? Too afraid to leave the shadow of your sire? Or did Vasara tell you no? She kept you on a short chain when she was still alive.' He tilted his head, ears slanting forwards. 'I heard rumours she still might.'

Damn me, who didn't know about that?

It doesn't matter, Mother said. *See if you can sort some meaning from his madness, and find some handle to use to point his sharp edge away.*

'And what about you?' I said. 'You don't seem to be holding together yourself, Lord Salvera. Your beast has you by the throat, and I think it's doing most of the talking.' I breathed deep as I spoke, testing the air. Was the rest of his house close, sneaking up on us? I didn't taste them on the breeze that rustled through the dry grass.

Salvera shook his head. 'My beast saved me. It's why I didn't fall apart into dust like those others, caught in the curse of the Crimson Keep. I stayed alive because of my beast, not because of will, or honour. Those things don't make you strong, they make you weak. What has your honour given you? Blood out of fancy cups, gifted to you by mortals who want to earn your favour? No wonder your father rotted away from the inside. No wonder the same is starting to happen to you. The beast is strong in me, fed on blood torn from living throats, and I survive because that's what beasts do. They hunt, they feed, and they survive. If you want that, if you want your second life to stretch until the Mortal Realms fall to final ruin, you'll listen to me. Give up your vows. Forget the Crimson Keep, forget Corsovo, forget Nagash, forget everything

except the hunger and the hunt, and the curse will fall away. What happened to the one you called Father won't happen to you.'

'Oh, is that all?' I asked. 'Just be like you? Mad as a rabid dog, preying on farmers and children? Is that all? That curse is worse than whatever happened to my father. I'll give myself to the final death itself before I become what you're becoming, Lord Salvera.'

'Would you?' he said, smiling that wolf smile again. 'Because I can give you that, too.' His scythe shifted in his hands. 'It's said that the blood of another vampire can be potent.'

Rill, Arvan and Erant all put hands on their weapons, but I stayed still. I wanted to fight him. I wanted to call challenge and draw my blades bright and black and slide them both across his throat. I wanted to humiliate him and his stupid beast, but I didn't want to risk the cold curse that had taken me when I fought Magdalena.

What are you going to do, Nyssa? Mother asked. *He's awful, but we may need to use him.*

'I know,' I told her silently, and then I reached out with my magic, into the vargheists.

Their spirits were strange things, not quite beast, not quite human, but something in between. They slipped through the grasp of my magic, sometimes slick, sometimes painfully sharp, and when I tried to close my grasp on them it *hurt*. I made myself ignore the pain and gripped them as tight as I could. One of them slipped away, but in the other I found the spirit of its beast and took hold of it.

'You say the beast will save you?' I pulled on my connection with the vargheist, and it dropped one of its taloned hands onto Salvera's shoulder. 'I say the beast may end you.'

The Kastelai snarled, realising what was happening, and I felt him trying to flex his magic, to bring the vargheist back under his will. I bared my teeth at him and kept my control over the

creature. Salvera gave up suddenly and moved, jerking away from the vargheist's grip. When it went for him again, the other vargheist, the one that had slipped away from me, stepped in front of it. The two monsters faced each other, claws flexing, eyes burning.

Salvera glared down at me, his body as taut as Rill's bowstring. He was preparing himself to jump down from the bank, preparing to fall on me with his great curved blade. I could read his intentions in his coiled stillness, as easily as I could tell that his beast was taking over by the pinpricks of red that glowed in the centre of each yellow eye. In my chest, my heart thudded and my blood moved, but I didn't reach for the hilts of my swords.

'You speak of the power of the beast, Lord Mad Dog.' I flexed my magic, getting ready to try something I'd never done before. 'You forget, though, that beasts can be tamed.' I dropped the hold I had on the vargheist, and turned all my strength on Salvera, biting into his soul.

I couldn't control vampires, or even a mortal. My mother had those gifts – she could force all but the most wilful mortal to serve her, at least for a little while. But souls, the spirits of intelligent creatures, were harder for me to control than animal spirits. I could never grasp them right, which is why I had such trouble raising skeletons or zombies – finding even the fraction of a soul necessary to animate a corpse often eluded me. My strength was with animal spirits, and unlike Arvan it was with the ones that had already died once, whose spirits were set looser in their bodies.

Salvera should have been beyond me, his soul too hard for me to grasp. But he'd let his beast take much of him and that had scarred his soul, given me something to grip. He had let the animal part of him take control, and I could touch animals. So I grasped him, pressing my magic in tight, trying to crack his soul like a wolf cracked a bone to feed on the marrow, and for just one second I felt him in my grip–

Then he was gone. Salvera leashed his beast, pulling it back and shutting me out. He stared at me across the stream, the red once again absent from his yellow eyes, his nostrils flaring. Then he was gone, his magic wrapping around him and the vargheists, making them almost invisible, just a flicker of colours as they turned and vanished into the night.

It was late afternoon and our shadows were long when we finally came to Splitrock. The hold was a mass of basalt standing alone at the edge of the Broken Plains. Beyond it the land grew flatter, dryer, grasslands fading into a desert of rocks and scrubby thorn bushes, the barren territory of scorpions and nomads.

The sides of Splitrock were marked with great vertical grooves which gave it its name, rough open chimneys that stretched from ground to sky. A steep switchback climbed to the top of the great stone where the hold was built. The road was wide enough for two horsemen to ride abreast, provided that the one on the outside of the path was either very brave or very stupid. The rise ended at a gate at the top, guarded by twin towers. Splitrock might be easier to take by force than Ruinview, but the difference was slight, and the cost of attacking either would be too damn high.

'Jirrini has pulled her mortals out of their villages,' I said. Two small farming villages sat below us, built along the stream that curved around the basalt outcrop, the last visible water before the Broken Plains became desert. There was no sign of life from either, no people or animals or thin trails of smoke rising from campfires. 'She's brought them into the hold with her.'

'What is she up to?' That was the most Arvan had said since Salvera. Something about the encounter had shaken him.

You, Mother said. *Almost bending Salvera to your will.*

'You'd think he'd be pleased with that,' I whispered. I was. Jirrini I'd always thought I could reason with. She was cautious, especially

for a Kastelai, but she wasn't a fool. Salvera – I'd had no idea how I was going to convince that mad dog to join us. Now, though, I had a possibility.

Arvan would be thrilled to see you thrash Salvera. But binding him to you like Rend? Mortals are terrified of being caught like that, and vampires even more so. She laughed in my head. *I know. Even your father was wary of me. You were positively petrified of me doing it to you, as I recall, and I'd sworn to you that I wouldn't.*

I remembered. Very well. It was strange to think of someone fearing me that way. I was used to people fearing my blades. Fearing my magic felt strangely unfair, as if I were cheating, but at least I didn't care about cheating with Salvera. He didn't deserve anything.

'I don't know,' I finally answered Arvan. Did Jirrini really think she could weather a siege, if all the rest of us were gone? Her mortals would starve, and then the vampires of her house would grow hungry enough to turn on each other.

Jirrini's not stupid, Nyssa. Cautious, but not stupid. She's planning something.

'I'm going to find out,' I said, and urged Thorn forwards, cantering towards the hold in the last light of day.

We wound our way to the top of Splitrock in a single-file line well away from the sheer edge. We stopped before the gates at the top, massive wooden doors set in a heavy stone arch between the towers. The road curved and rose here, a twisting ascent that would be hell on horses and wagons, but made it almost impossible to bring a ram to bear against the gate. With a good-sized force, Splitrock could hold out for years, but to what purpose? It was meant to be a rallying point to defend against invasions from nomad bands, not a place to ride out a siege.

I pulled Thorn to a stop before the gates, took a deep breath,

and caught the scent I was looking for. Vampires, ten or so, the smell of their blood strong against the aroma of heated rock and ancient wood. But their scent was the only sign of them. No one stood atop the towers, no one called down to us. The red banners with their cup symbol that usually hung from each tower were gone. Splitrock might have been deserted, except for those scents on the wind.

'Splitrock!' I shouted, and my words echoed off the gates. 'It is Nyssa Volari, of the Grey Palace, come with urgency for Lady Jirrini! Open your gates!'

The only answer was silence.

'What are they playing at?' Erant said. 'We know you're there!' he shouted, but his words just echoed back, unanswered.

In my chest, I felt the first stirrings of heat. The vague ache that came before my heart began to beat. They were here and ignoring us, and I wondered how fast I would have to move to run part way up the gates and make the leap for the top. Very fast up that steep ramp, but I might be able to make it.

If I didn't go cold part way up.

I shoved that thought away with a silent snarl, but it made me pause and I took another breath, focusing on the blood scent. Jirrini wasn't there. I'd know her scent. But there was something I thought I recognised.

'Trevin! Knight of Plenty!' I called out. 'Answer the Rose Throne!'

There was a long moment of nothing. Then, finally, a shape appeared at the top of one of the towers. A silhouette against the glowing sky on a failing day. 'What Rose Throne, Lady Volari?'

'The one you took an oath to.' I tipped my head back to stare up at him. 'You and all your house.'

'The Rose Throne is broken, and so are our oaths.' His voice was as bleak as the stone we stood on. 'The king is dead, and so

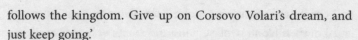

follows the kingdom. Give up on Corsovo Volari's dream, and just keep going.'

'Into the wastelands?' I said.

'Better than into the final death.' Trevin shook his head. 'Lady Jirrini won't speak to you. Go, Lady Volari. Find some new dream to replace this dead one. If Nagash grants you life enough to do so.'

He pulled back, disappearing into the tower, and my heart thudded in my chest. I wanted to try it. To see if I could vault my way up there. But...

'Damn her to the lowest hells,' I swore. And damn me too, for the doubt that kept me from trying to scale that wall.

It's likely you wouldn't have made it, and then you would have looked like a fool. Besides, you have other options. Remember what Magdalena told you.

'A riddle?' I muttered, but I turned Thorn carefully and faced the others. 'They've made their choice, then,' I said, loud enough to be heard in the towers. 'And you can't slip a stiletto between a coward and their hiding place.'

Maybe not the most diplomatic way to leave, Mother said as we started down the path.

'You would have just used your magic to force them to open the gate,' I said back.

Yes, but you can't do that. So, diplomacy.

'Diplomacy. Pretending to be nice when you can't take what you want by force.'

There. You're learning. Now get yourself between Temero and this rock like Magdalena said, so we can see if there is something useful in that riddle.

We found a place beneath a clump of vesin trees, protected from any eyes watching us from the top of Splitrock, and waited for the last bit of light to die.

'Where her hold bleeds.' Arvan had called a flock of ash ravens to him when we stopped, and the grey birds were muttering and croaking in the branches over our heads, staring down at us with black eyes. 'The birds say they've never found blood near Splitrock.'

'The birds are probably too literal,' I said, my eyes never leaving the hold. 'Magdalena likes to think she's clever. She–' I stopped. There was motion around the basalt pillar, a swirl through the air like smoke. Streams of darkness, pouring out of the crevices that gave Jirrini's hold its name, like rivers of ink spreading into the night.

'What's that?' Rill asked, her eyes not as sharp.

'Bats,' I said. They were the brown bats that fed on insects over the Broken Plains, and they looked nothing like blood. What had Magdalena… My thought stopped as I caught sight of a tiny bit of red mixed in with the stream of black.

One fleck of red, then there was another, another, then a whole line of crimson. A stream of blood-coloured bats pouring out of a crack on the lower part of the basalt pillar.

'There,' I said. It did look like Splitrock was bleeding, a thin line of crimson gore spilling out from its rocky flank.

Rill and Erant were cursing quietly, trying to see what I could see, but Arvan nodded. 'Gore wings. I've heard of them, but never seen one. They're rare. Can you see where they're coming from?'

'I can.' I searched around the crack as the stream of red began to flag, fewer and fewer of the red bats coming out. At the end of the dark seam in the stone the crack forked to either side, so that it looked something like a barbed arrowhead. 'And I can go right to it.'

We left Thorn and the other Nightmares under the trees and walked across the gravel waste to Splitrock. I wrapped silence around

us as we scrambled over the tumbled stones that surrounded the great basalt pillar, climbing up until we stood beneath the arrowhead-shaped crevice.

'What is it?' Erant asked. 'A way in?'

'Maybe.' I took a deep breath of the air spilling out of the crack. It was cool and damp, and I smelled stone, water, bats, guano and… something else. Something earthy, but alive, like a plant, but not. Almost buried under that scent, so very thin that it faded in and out, was the smell of mortal blood. 'There's blood in there. Human. Somewhere.'

I pulled myself up into the crevice, which shrank as it went deeper into the rock, becoming a narrow opening barely wide enough for me to slide into.

'Are we going in?' Arvan asked.

'No,' I said. '*We* aren't. Just me.'

'What?' Erant asked, at the same time that Rill said, 'No.'

'The space is too tight for Arvan and Erant' – I started taking off my boots, sword and armour, stripping down to the thin linen shirt and breeches beneath – 'and if it can't be all of us, it'll just be me.'

'If you can fit, I can fit,' Rill said, and maybe she was right. She was shorter than me, but her shoulders were wider, heavier with the muscle her body had grown to handle the bow when she was still mortal.

'No. I'm going in with just my teeth and a knife.' I pulled a dagger from my belt, ran a strip of leather through the ring on its sheath and hung it around my neck, as out of the way as I could get it. 'If I get in trouble, I'm fast enough to run away. You're not.'

'But what if…' Erant started and I frowned at him so hard he went quiet. I didn't want to hear any damn thing about a curse. Or think about it.

'I'm going to see what this is, then I'm coming out.'

'And if you don't come out?' Erant asked.

'Then go back to the Grey Palace and tell my house that they can join Magdalena, or run.' I reached into the stone, running my hand over the rock. It was smooth, at least, worn down by time and bat wings.

'Wait,' Arvan said. He reached into his pouch and pulled out another painted amphora. 'If you need your speed, you'll want this.'

I pulled off the cap, and the sweet smell of the blood hit me, mixed with that thin, ugly smell of Shadas' magic. I could feel the hunger surge up from where I'd been keeping it tamped down, and I nodded to Arvan. I didn't drink it right away, though.

'What about you? And the others?'

He pulled three more cylinders out. 'Enough for us all. I try to be prepared.' He smiled, his skin making furrows around the black pits of his eyes.

'Good for you,' I said, and waited for the others to open their vessels before raising my own. 'I pledge on this that I'll return, even if I have to pass through all of Nagash's hells to do so.'

They lifted their clay vessels silently, and we all drank the blood down, each of us wincing from the aftertaste of the charm. When I could feel the warmth of life spreading through me, I turned from them and began to work my way into the crack.

It was thin, and got even thinner. The stone pressed into my back, into my chest, against my head. I moved slowly, carefully finding where I could fit through.

Finally the walls began to pull back, widening until I could move almost normally. I increased my speed, and in the distance began to see something. My eyes had been useless so far, but now there was a glow up ahead – a faint ruddy light that made it possible to see the uneven gap I was moving down, and with the light came the thin sound of wind and water.

The crack became a tunnel, and stalactites hung from the ceiling like misshapen teeth, but the floor was smooth and soft. I realised from the smell that I was walking barefoot through a thick layer of waste, deposited over the centuries by the bats that nested here. Insects moved through the slime – pale, palm-sized cave cockroaches and the armoured centipedes that fed on them. I pushed through the muck, moving slowly to let the bugs scuttle out of my way. The light was growing, deep red and steady, not torchlight but something else, something strange. Finally the tunnel curved and I saw its source.

It was rooted in the muck, a ridge of something soft and fleshy that rose out of the filth like a pillow of fat. Some kind of fungus, feeding on the guano. Red light shone from it as if there were a candle hidden beneath its flesh. It was the source of the earthy scent I'd detected earlier – not a bad smell, but the fungus looked like a glowing, cancerous tumour.

'Disgusting,' I said silently, but Mother didn't answer.

There was more of the slick fungus beyond that, great beds of it feeding on excrement, dead bats and dead bugs. It grew in shapes like bloated corpses, and filled the widening tunnel with its dull crimson glow. The light gleamed off the water droplets that fell from the stalactites overhead, a steady patter which gathered into a little stream that carved its way through the slime. I walked alongside the water and pulled my knife out, the blade reassuring in my hand, but not nearly as much as one of my swords would have been.

Other passages opened up in the walls occasionally, and I wondered how vast this system was and where it finally connected to the hold far above. Then I smelled it. Blood. Human blood, maybe. It was close, but there was something strange about it.

'What is that?' I asked in my head, but again there was no answer, just silence. 'Mother?' I asked, but nothing, nothing.

'Vasara!' This time I hissed her name aloud, a whisper, but enough to make the roaches near me scuttle away. Again, nothing, and something went through me, a feeling that was too close to fear.

Was it happening again? I'd lost her last time and not even realised it until everything else started happening, the cold that had made me fall insensible for days. What if that happened here? Would I go face down in this muck, lie alone like a dead thing while the roaches and centipedes crept over me, devouring me? The thought of being so helplessly undone by such vermin was terrifying, and I almost turned and fled. Almost raced back to Arvan and Rill and Erant, to the people who could care for me if I fell.

No. That thought was almost as disgusting, almost as terrifying. I *wasn't* cursed. I *wasn't* helpless. I could do this without them or Mother or anyone. I was a vampire, blessed with a second life. I was Kastelai. I was Nyssa Volari. I was more than enough for anything, and I made myself walk forwards.

The stream grew, and ahead of me the tunnel opened up into a cavern. From that space came noise, the rustle of bare feet against stone and dirt, the sound of breathing, of teeth chewing, of hearts beating, slow and steady. Mortals – humans, the ones I'd scented. I crept forwards, picking my way around the fungus until I reached the cave's rocky wall. In its shadows I moved to the opening into the cavern and looked out.

The cavern was huge, carved out of the stone long ago by lava or water. Water shaped it now, forming the massive stalactites that grew down from the ceiling and cutting channels in the floor where other little streams flowed. They all ran together in the centre of the cavern, forming a small lake of clear water so deep the bottom was lost to darkness. The rest of the cavern floor was covered with guano and bones, most of them the tiny skeletons of bats, but there were larger ones mixed in, animals and human. Growing through the thick loam of faeces and rot were huge mounds of the fungus. It spread across the floor like thick roots made of rendered fat. The smell of it was thick in the cool air, almost choking, and I tried to block it out as I searched for the source of the blood odour. I could hear and smell them, they were here, but it took me a moment to find them.

It was their motion that let me see them. They were pale as the fungus that surrounded them, and their skin gleamed red with the crimson light. They were hairless, their bodies stick thin, their heads small, but their eyes were huge, unmoving saucers of red that bulged from their narrow faces. They wore nothing, and the only things they carried in their hands were bones, which they were using to tear through the outer skin that covered the fungi, bursting them open before ripping soft handfuls of fungal flesh out of the mounds to stuff in their drooling mouths.

'What are they?' I asked myself silently. Their blood smelled enough like a human's to fool me over a distance. Were they something related? Humans that had been changed by aeons of living beneath the ground? I didn't know, and there was no voice in my head to answer me, but I didn't have time to worry about that. From across the cavern, a shout echoed from one of the other cave openings.

'Here!'

I sank down further, pressing myself against the rock. A mortal stepped out into the cavern, followed by another, both of them dressed in Jirrini's red and gold, and behind them was Trevin. The mortals came out into the opening, waving long, thin staffs, and circled the white things, cursing as they did. But they seemed in a good enough mood, and though they used their sticks to prod the pale humanoid things back towards the cave mouth where Trevin was still waiting, there was no force behind their blows. They reminded me of shepherds shooing along herds of sheep.

I waited and watched as the humans drove their charges into

the tunnel. I could follow and see where they took them, but seeing Trevin had given me another idea, one that didn't rely on me slipping through unknown tunnels that could be full of other vampires whose intent was uncertain. I waited until the mortals had vanished, until Trevin was taking one last look around, before going after them, and stepped silently into the cavern.

He saw me instantly. His sword flashed out, so fast it seemed to just appear in his hand, and he stared over the blade at me.

'Is there something wrong?' I heard one of the mortals shout. I sheathed my knife and held out my hands, empty, stepping away from the cave I'd come down. Trevin frowned, but then he straightened up, out of his fighting stance.

'No,' he said. 'Just shadows. Take them.' Trevin sheathed his sword, and we both stood silent, waiting for the mortal voices to fade to nothing before we walked towards each other.

'How did you find your way in here?' Trevin stopped on the other side of the pool from me. It was only about five yards across, and both of us could leap it, or run around it in a flash, but it was somehow comfortable to have that barrier between us. I could feel my heart shiver as I waited to see if he would run or fight. Trevin was like me, fast, just not quite as fast, and I'd always beaten him when sparring before. But now he had armour and a sword, and I had just a linen shirt, breeches, a knife and the fear that the cold might come back and cut me down.

Still, I drew myself up, made myself as haughty and composed as I could. I might be dressed lightly, bare feet covered in bat dung and hair a tangled mass around my face, but I could still come the vampire lord. Vasara had taught me that, and taught me well.

'The same way you did. Following the scent of blood.' I folded my arms, making a point of looking around, as if taking my eyes off him was of no concern, no threat. 'How many of those things do you have?'

'The graz?' he said. 'A little over a thousand. But there are wild herds lower down from which we can harvest.'

'A thousand. And more below.' I looked back at Trevin. 'That's how Lady Jirrini plans to survive. Sealed in here, feeding off them. Is she even going to try to defend her hold?'

'No,' Trevin said. 'We'll leave the place empty. Let the mortals think we've fled.' There was a trace of bitterness in his words. Giving up, retreating, hiding. Maybe that didn't sit well with some in Jirrini's house.

'So you'll hide,' I said. 'Like mice beneath the floorboards, fearing the cat.'

He glared at me across the water. 'I faced the mortals at Ire Crossing, a few years after I'd been given the blood, promised immortality. I lost an arm and saw most of Jirrini's guard die.' He held up his sword hand. 'This came back. They didn't. Our immortality has its limits. You of all of us should know that.'

'I'm not dying!' I snapped. 'I'm–' I stopped. There was a smell in the air, something new. Faint and musky, animalistic. I looked around the cavern. There was nothing, but the smell was growing and–

They fell on us from the stalactites above. Things like bats, like apes, like Trevin's graz. The creatures were short, but broad as they were tall, squat bodies heavy with muscle. Their long arms ended in clawed hands, and their heads were eyeless, with great mouths full of sharp teeth and huge, wrinkled noses and ears. Short red fur covered them, and they had leathery membranes between their legs and arms, so their falling was controlled, aimed at us. I dodged the three that fell towards me and raised my knife, cursing its short blade. My heart was beating, pumping blood through me, and I spun away from the claws sweeping towards my throat. Coming up, I slammed my knife as deep as I could into the forward-facing ear of one of the things, driving in the blade until

I heard the crunch of steel against bone. I jerked it out and then stabbed again, punching the blade into the monster's other ear and pulling it back out before it even had a chance to start falling.

I could feel another moving up behind me and I kicked back, my bare foot connecting with the thing's chest. The fur covering it was slick and soft, like mucus-coated silk, and my foot almost slipped away. I kept driving into the thing, though, and sent it staggering back, its claws flailing. I twisted to face my last attacker, snapping out strikes. It raised its arms, too slow, and my blade carved a series of punctures into its domed belly, each one spurting blood that gleamed black in the red light. The creature made a sound, a high-pitched whine that I could barely hear, and fell backwards.

The one I'd kicked had fallen into a stream and was pulling itself up, crouching on all fours, fanged mouth gaping. I pulled back my knife, waiting, and that's when it hit me. The cold stabbing through me, dimming the red light, making my heart stutter. I staggered and the creature leapt out of the stream, claws sweeping for me.

I should've been able to evade it easily. Instead, caught in the cold, I barely got out of the way and its claws raked my side, carving four shallow grooves across my ribs. The blow knocked me back, and I almost fell into the clear water of the pool.

I hissed and caught myself, straightening up. The cold had gone away, as suddenly as it had come, and the wounds on my side closed as my heart beat a steady rhythm again. I could feel the blood that had come out of the wounds, though, sticky on my skin. I was used to blood on me, but not my own, and the touch of it made me fear that painful cold. The dread of it coming back rushed through me. Would it make me weak, make me helpless, enough so that I would die beneath the dirty claws of this filthy thing?

'No!' I snapped. Anger and denial were all I had, and I shoved

them up like a wall to keep the cold away and lunged at the thing that had dared strike me. It spread claws and jaws, trying to match my charge, but my speed was back and I reached it before it could strike. I slammed my knife into the top of its belly and pulled up. They were muscular things, but not big, and I lifted it up and tore its throat out with my teeth. Its blood was hot and full of life, and I spent a moment drinking it down, taking that heat and life before letting the thing fall backwards into one of the fungal mounds.

I spun away, looking for Trevin. Five of the beasts had come for him and I could see two had been slain, one in the muck at his feet, the other floating face down in the pool. But two more were moving around him, staying out of the reach of his sword as another rode his back, one powerful arm locked around his throat while its sharp teeth worried his shoulder.

There was a fraction of a moment where I hesitated, fearing the cold, and that lapse made my rage explode through me. I was a vampire. I was Kastelai. I was the blood daughter of one of the finest warriors the Crimson Keep had ever known, and damn me, I wasn't going to be slowed by anything. I ran at the pool, my feet digging into the muck, and jumped.

I flew over the water, heading straight for Trevin. He heard me and started to spin, his sword rising to meet me, but I snarled at him and he understood. He snapped his sword away, driving it towards one of the things on the ground that had surged forwards when he'd taken his eyes off it. I stopped paying attention to him, falling now, my arm swinging down with all the momentum I could give it. My blade hit the thing on Trevin's back on the top of its head, driving through fur and flesh and bone into whatever brain there was beneath, and the creature twitched and went limp, sliding off the Knight of Plenty.

Trevin had run his sword into the one lunging at him, through the top of the chest into its lung. The creature fell, spewing blood

through its pointed teeth. Trevin pulled his sword free and spun around, cutting the head off the last monster even as it was starting to flee.

'You're still slow when you pivot,' I said, jerking my knife free, and then the cold was back, slamming through me, freezing my blood, stopping my heart, and threatening to turn everything black. I fell forwards, uncontrolled, sprawling across the body of the bat-ape thing, fighting to shove the darkness back, to stay present, to stay alive. The shadows pushed in thick, but then they stopped, right on the edge of swallowing everything. I focused on the pale form of one of the cave cockroaches, scuttling close, attracted by the scent of death. I watched its antennae twitch, its tiny jaws working as they scooped blood from the filth on the cavern floor, feasting on it the way it would feast on me if the darkness took me. And then it pulled back, drawing away, leaving me to red light and furious terror.

'Nyssa!' I felt Trevin's hands on me, picking me up. He got me to my feet and kept a hand on my shoulder, holding me still as I swayed, unsteady. The darkness was almost gone from the edge of my vision, but my heart was still and I felt sluggish, aching. Empty.

'What is it?' Trevin was looking at me as he held me up, and I wondered how much grey marked my eyes now. 'The curse?'

'No curse.' The words sounded as useless and insane to me as they probably did to Trevin, but I had to say them. Had to believe them. What happened to my father wasn't going to happen to me. It wasn't. So I denied it, and jerked myself out of his grip, just barely keeping my feet.

'Nothing's wrong with me,' I said. 'I saved you, didn't I?'

'You helped me.' Trevin sounded reluctant to admit even that much. 'Now I'll help you. I'll take you back to the hold.'

I looked at him through a tangle of hair. It had come loose sometime during the fight and hung around me like a ragged

curtain. I could see strands of it gleaming in the red light. Were they grey? White? They hadn't been before. 'You will not. I'm going back.' I looked around, trying to figure out which cave I'd come out of. It had a stream, but most of them did, and right now I could barely tell which direction was up or down. The darkness was still on the edge of my vision, like a threatening storm, but I tried to ignore it.

'You can barely walk,' he said. 'And didn't you come here to speak to Lady Jirrini anyway?'

I had. But sluggish as I was, I knew going to her now, like this, would be the worst thing for me. 'Will she listen?' I asked. 'Or will she lock me away, to keep her secrets? Your secrets.' I picked a cave and started towards it. Behind me, Trevin stayed silent. Until I heard the grate of bone on steel. He walked up behind me, handing me my knife. I slid it into my sheath, and he pointed to the cave next to the one I was heading towards.

'You came out there. I can smell your track.'

I could too, once I started moving in that direction. Trevin came with me, silent, as we walked through the tunnel. He stayed silent as the mounds of fungus grew smaller and the red light dimmed around us. We kept going until we passed the last one and it was almost dark. That was good. It hid the dark borders that surrounded my world.

'You're right. She wouldn't let you out.' He stopped in that hazy twilight. 'Her plan is to disappear. That doesn't work if you tell anyone else where she is. She'd stop you leaving. I should stop you.'

'Then do it,' I said. I started walking forwards again, my feet so damnably slow. The walls were pulling in, and I knew soon I'd have to turn and slide sideways through the narrow stone gap. At least I wouldn't have to worry about falling.

'I won't,' he said. 'I understand Jirrini's plan. I understand that to survive, sometimes… we accept things we normally wouldn't.'

'You would trade your honour for your life?' I kept walking. Was the darkness rolling in around me in my eyes or in the cave?

'How can we have honour if none of us survive?'

'The graz smell like humans,' I said to him in answer. 'Were they people that lived on the surface once, before they fled to these caverns, seeking to *survive*? Trading your honour for survival costs, Trevin. Will you pay for yours by becoming like the graz? Or the things that prey on them?'

He stayed silent, long enough to make me wonder if he'd gone. Then, down the narrow crack the cave had become, I heard his voice.

'You never went easy on me in a fight, Nyssa. Don't go easy on yourself. Or those damned mortals.'

I didn't answer. I was in the dark, moving forwards. But I could feel the cold slipping into me again. Not like before, not a sudden wave that filled me, but a slow spread, making me numb, making me slow. I forced it back and pulled myself through the darkness, a little more, a little more, knowing that if I stopped I would be trapped forever in this place, a skeleton held up between walls of stone, powerless, forgotten, gone.

So I kept going, until there was nothing but darkness.

CHAPTER THIRTEEN

Another small death.

I opened my eyes to my rooms, dark with night, and that small death felt enormous. How long had I been out? Long enough for Arvan, Rill and Erant to find me in that hole and bring me back to the Grey Palace. Days probably. Such a small death when measured against eternity. An eternity when measured against my problems.

I pulled myself up. From the floor beside my couch, Rend lifted his head, but I wrapped silence around us both. I went to the curtains and pulled them back. I could see the stars and the little moon, Evigaine, glowing in the black sky, could see their light fracturing off the boiling waters below. Light enough to show me my room and myself. My skin had gone grey with the hunger that gnawed at me, and my hair… It tumbled around my shoulders, loose but untangled. Whoever had tended me had got the filth off my feet, the blood off my face, replaced my linen underclothes with a clean set and brushed out my hair. Probably Erant. He was better at that sort of thing than Rill.

There were strands of silver in my hair, glinting like the Irewater

in the moon and starlight. A lot of them. They probably matched the grey in my eyes, but I couldn't tell, since I'd shattered the mirror in here. I separated a strand out and pulled, ignoring the little pain of tearing it from my scalp. How long would it be before those strands came out on their own, falling free from my head in great clumps like my father's had done? How long before the grey pallor in my skin took over and I turned the colour of ash; before my eyes sank and my lips pulled back, my flesh melted away beneath my skin and I became a corpse like him? How long before my small death wasn't small any more?

How long?

I walked into my parlour. It was the same as before, yet so different. There was Arvan, frowning at a map, Rill fletching arrows, Erant making another pile of shavings as he carved a wolf. Shadas sat reading a book in the corner, his back to everyone else, the low beat of his mortal heart a nervous rhythm. They all stopped and looked at me when I came out, and that was what was so different. They looked at me with all their concern and instead of anger I just felt dead.

But you're not.

I stopped in the door of my room. I hadn't bothered putting on my armour or my swords, hadn't bothered to even pull back my hair. I hadn't bothered to reach out to see if she was there. I think I was afraid to. What if she wasn't? But now, hearing her voice, just as calm and clear as ever in my head, I did finally feel something. Relief, mixed with rage.

'No, I'm not dead. Otherwise you couldn't haunt me.' I stepped into the parlour, slamming the door shut behind me, almost catching the tip of Rend's tail. The dire wolf was bristling but uncertain, his joy at seeing me muddled with the storm of emotions spilling through our connection. I told him to sit and glared at the others, all of them staring at me, waiting.

'You're all haunting me too,' I said. My anger was growing, and I was grateful. It was so much better than feeling useless, impotent, weak. Dying. 'What are you doing, lurking in here? Isn't there a war coming?'

'Not if you're dead,' Arvan said, answering my anger with bluntness. 'If you fall, this house falls, and we all scatter to whatever hold will take us.'

My fingers tapped against my hip, not finding the hilts of my swords, and I regretted leaving them in the room behind me, even if I wasn't going to stab him. But the thought of doing so helped steady me, married my anger to some interest in something, anything, besides whatever was happening to me. 'Go to Magdalena. You'll die, but it'll be a better death than with Jirrini or Salvera.'

'What about Durrano?' Arvan asked.

'His house is our house. If the Rose Throne falls, so does Skulltop.' I looked at him, his dark eyes still staring down at the map. 'Why? Has something happened to Durrano?'

'I don't know.' Arvan looked up, his brutish face twisted in frustration. 'I told you Celasian was gathering Takora's forces back to Gowyn. They formed up and pulled out. I tried to track them, but...' Arvan's usual humble calm cracked, flared to an anger I'd seldom seen from him. 'Everything I send out after them, every raven, every bat, disappears, doesn't come back. They must be killing them before they can return.' His fingers clenched on the table, twisting the map, tearing part of it. He let it go and smoothed it out, smoothing the frustrated anger from his face at the same time. 'They're killing my spies, but I think the mortals are moving on us, even though much of their force isn't here yet. I think they're marching on Durrano.'

'Warn him,' I said. 'Tell him to pull back to us.'

'You think I haven't?' he snapped, his anger showing again, then he shook his head. 'My apologies, my lady. Yes, I've sent warnings.

But none of those messengers came back, and we've heard nothing from them. I sent riders last night. Still nothing. We're blind, and our enemies are moving against us.' He hauled himself up straight. 'I'm sorry, Lady Volari. I have failed you.'

'Damn you,' I swore at him. Durrano and his house were a third of the forces I thought I had for sure. If they were gone... I started to pace the room, my feet finding the shallow groove I'd worn into the stone. First I'd lost Mother. Then Father. Then everything, everyone, all the other Kastelai, except Durrano. He was the only one who'd held to me after the fight with Magdalena, and I hadn't even considered him while running off to try to grab the others back. And what had that done? I'd thought I had a chance with them, for a moment, but that all fell apart when the cold took me again at Splitrock. I'd lost my chance to gather any of them, and now I might have lost Durrano.

Durrano. Stupid, loyal Durrano who barely ever spoke to me, whose eyes had avoided me when he sat by my father in council. A good fighter but useless at strategy, at diplomacy, at anything and everything but loyalty.

'Damn you,' I said again, still pacing but moving slow. Not looking at Arvan or anyone else, just staring at the worn flagstones of the floor. 'Damn your failure, Arvan, and damn yours, Shadas, and most of all damn me and the curse that lays upon this house.'

Does it feel better, to finally admit it? Mother's voice was loud in my head, compared to the silence that had fallen across the room.

'Damn you too,' I snapped, turning away from the path of my pacing and walking out of my apartments, heading for silence, heading for darkness, as if my little death had given me a taste for oblivion.

I didn't bother with a candle this time. Or armour, or swords, or boots, or anything. I walked to my family tomb in darkness, a

196

dark so profound even I couldn't see, but I didn't need to. Memory guided my feet as much as my other senses, and I found myself standing before that door. I ran my fingers over it, and in the dark I could trace the carved features of my mother. And then, beside it, those of my father.

When had that been added? Who had ordered it? Arvan? Probably. I didn't know. I barely touched those features and had to pull my hand away. My mother's carving made me think of her charred skull. My father's, his face, wasted away beneath the glass of his coffin. Neither memory helped the darkness of my mood. My anger was still there, but it was a few weak sparks in the cold dark of all these endings, the ones that had happened and the ones that were happening.

Are you giving up, then?

'Giving up implies I have a choice.' My voice echoed, bouncing off the hard stone before it faded into nothing. 'You're dead. Father's dead. Durrano's probably dead. Salvera's mad, Jirrini's hiding, Magdalena is planning her suicide, and I'm cursed to die. What choices are left to me, Mother?'

I don't know, she said. *But neither do you.*

'That's what I just said!' The echoes shouted back at me, a gang of angry ghosts, before fading.

No, it's not. And you know it.

There was no sternness in her voice, and no sympathy. Just that smooth, cool poise that had driven me to a rage so often. Had. Still did, if not for much longer. Unless our spirits were bound, and she'd be lecturing me for eternity. I shook my head in the darkness.

'Are you telling me I'm not going to die? You just congratulated me for admitting I was cursed.'

Accepting that something bad is happening is not the same as deciding there is nothing you can do about it. What do you know about your enemy?

'Celasian?' The question didn't seem to fit, but I could feel her waiting for me to go on. 'He's a fanatic, one of the Storm God's mad pets, aimed at our throats.'

Yes. A dangerous man, and a mortal. Cursed like all of them to know that death is coming for them. Yet he makes his plans anyway.

'I don't remember being mortal,' I said. I stared into the darkness for a long time. 'I don't like this idea of dying.'

No one does. Even us, who dedicate ourselves to death. Because we don't want to be ended. We want to go on, the same, forever. That's what Nagash promised us.

'Does Nagash embrace the same fluid attitude towards honouring his promises that you were discussing?' I asked.

Don't let Magdalena hear you ask that, but yes. She laughed, low and quiet in my head. *The Lord of Death made a promise to us. Blood for life, life everlasting. But nothing lasts forever. Not vampires, not blood, not Nagash. But we try. We last as long as we can. Mortality and defeat are bitter, but if you don't swallow them you'll choke.*

'What are you trying to do, Mother? At the door of your crypt, below the ruins of a palace built by a dead empire, are you trying to give me hope?'

I'm trying to make you push away despair, so that you fight for one more day, one more chance to destroy the ones that want to tear you down.

That, at least, made me smile.

Then I smelled him.

The odour was faint, the air down here cold and still, and he was standing across the dark hall. But I caught the faint scrap of his scent, twisted in with the smell of stone and dust.

'Shadas.' I turned to stare in the direction the smell came from, and there was a noise, a tiny scrape of leather on stone. Then nothing but the faint beating of his heart. It had been too quiet

for me to hear before, when I was arguing with Mother, but now I heard it, focused on it, and knew exactly where he was.

'Lady Volari.' Light flared near him, dim at first, but it brightened into a faint glow no stronger than that cast by a candle, dark amethyst in colour. It came from a tiny flame that sat on Shadas' palm, dancing in an unfelt wind. 'I'm sorry to disturb you.'

'You didn't mean to.' I faced him, keeping my face smooth, poised, perfect, but in my chest my heart had started to beat. 'I didn't realise you could move silently enough to sneak up on me. Especially in the dark.'

'I had to use my magic,' he said. 'But you still found me.'

He was trying to stay calm, but there was a quaver of nervousness in his voice, and his heart was beating fast. His fear was reassuring, at least.

'What are you doing?' I asked him. No swords, but I could be next to him, my teeth in his neck, before he blinked. As long as the curse didn't touch me.

'I...' He paused, taking a breath. 'I want to give you something. I don't know if I should, but I want to.'

'Curses and armies, Shadas. We don't have time for riddles.'

Or despair?

I was too busy watching Shadas to answer that. He'd slipped his free hand into his robe and was pulling something out, something that glinted in the purple light. I tensed, ready to rush the young necromancer, but it wasn't a blade in his hand. It was a small bottle filled with something liquid and dark, its heavy stopper sealed with lead.

'You asked me for a cure for the curse.'

Shadas was used to vampires, was used to me, to what I could do. But still he stumbled back when I was there in front of him, the bottle in my hand, moving so fast that he probably hadn't seen me.

'Don't!' he said, his eyes wide. My fingers stopped, right on the edge of breaking the seals. 'Not yet!'

'Why not?' I kept my fingers still as I stared down at the bottle. The liquid in it had been dark, but now it was light, swirling beneath the thick crystal walls of the bottle. Then it darkened to grey, with swirls of dark and pale twisting over each other, forming patterns like chains of vertebrae, like overlapping sigils of bones. It felt cold in my hands, cold like the curse, and that, more than the fear in the necromancer's voice, stopped me.

'It's dangerous,' he said. 'And I don't know if it will work. But it can't work, now.'

I made myself look away from the bottle. Shadas had recovered his balance and was watching me. His brown eyes were wide, his heart hammering in his chest. 'I told you, none of us have time for riddles, Shadas. Me least of all.'

He nodded. 'I know, my lady. That has no chance of working now, when the curse isn't touching you. You have to take it when it's happening. When you feel the cold you were talking about, when you feel yourself slowing.'

'So I wait to be affected again, then drink it and I'm cured?' I didn't like the idea. The curse had fallen on me in the middle of a fight multiple times. Not the best occasion to stop and drink something.

And I didn't want to feel that cold again.

'Not cured. Not exactly,' Shadas said. Something in my face made him take another step back, to raise his free hand as if warding me away. 'It should stop the curse from affecting you. Make you better, for a while at least. It won't end it. It can't end it.'

Can't. Well, if it could drive it away, that was something. Something that would let me find one more day.

See?

'Be quiet,' I said to her, and Shadas winced. 'Not you,' I told him. 'Thank you, Shadas. It may not be a cure, but I need it.'

'I'm grateful to serve, my lady. The king, Corsovo...' He was staring at the tomb again. 'He saved me, you know. My family. I thought they loved me, but when I tried to help them, when I tried to stop them crying when my baby brother died of fever, when I brought him back...' Shadas closed his eyes. 'It was Arvan who heard what had happened, he came for me, he stopped my family from burning me. Arvan saved my life, so that I could use my gifts to serve the king. But the king, Lady Volari. He served me first. A boy, terrified and hurting. He came to me, so terrible, and he sat with me, talked to me, and eventually I stopped being scared, started listening, and he explained things to me. Explained that fear, ignorance and grief had turned my family against me, had convinced them I was daemon-taken, convinced them I had killed my brother so that I could bring him back. He made me understand that it wasn't my fault. That I didn't deserve it.'

That sounds like him. For once there was a smile in the tone of my mother's voice. *He could fight like a fiend and lie like a priest, but Corsovo loved nothing better than saving strays.*

'I could see why you called him Father,' Shadas said. 'And Vasara. The way he talked about her. I can see why you called her Mother.' He finally looked at me. 'I know you don't remember your first life, but I want you to know how lucky you are to have found a family like that in this one.'

'Found them and lost them,' I said, and he looked down at the floor, but I had seen his expression – sad and stricken – and I had to fight not to smash my fist into his sorrowful face.

What? You're the only one who can feel bad for you?

'No, you said I couldn't either.' I didn't bother seeing if that confused the necromancer. I was looking at the bottle. Not a cure,

but it was almost hope. Close enough, at least, to let me give up despair for anger.

'There's one more thing,' Shadas said. He'd shoved his unwelcome pity away too, and replaced it with his usual anxiety. 'Well, two more things. I don't know how fast that will take effect. Or how much it will hurt. But I know you'll need blood right after. Probably a lot of blood.'

'If the curse comes on me in battle again, that shouldn't be an issue.' I wanted to tuck the bottle away, but there was no place to do so in the thin linens I wore. Why in the hells had I come down here without my armour or swords?

Good quest–

'What's the *other* one more thing?' I asked Shadas, cutting her off.

'You shouldn't...' He trailed off, looking somehow even more anxious. 'I mean, it's probably not good to...'

'What?' I snapped, wondering if I would need to shake it out of him.

'Don't tell anyone about this,' he said, and seeing my face his words were suddenly tumbling out. 'I don't know how well this'll work. And, to be honest, there's a chance it won't work at all. That it'll actually make the curse worse, accelerate it. What happened to your father might happen to you in an instant.'

'In an instant?' The bottle felt even colder in my hand, a chill that almost burned. 'What, exactly, is the chance of that?'

'Small,' he said. 'Very small, I believe. But...'

'But if it did happen, and Arvan or Rill or Erant knew it was your fault and not just the curse, they'd tear out your throat.' I frowned at him. Our little talk had been making me feel better about Shadas, but this smacked of a particularly pathetic sort of cowardice. And made me suspicious. What if this cure were some kind of attack?

If it were, he'd have had you drink the stuff now. Or thrown his magic at you while you were arguing with me and didn't know he was here.

'Right.' I looked at the necromancer for a long moment. He stared at the floor, unable to meet my eye, and I could smell his anxious sweat, hear his hammering heart. And over that rhythmic thud, something else. The whisper of tiny wings.

The bat came through one of the arched doors that led into the chamber and chittered when it saw me. It started to swing in circles around me, bobbing and dipping in the air.

'Tell Arvan I'm coming,' I told it, then started walking. 'Come on,' I told Shadas, and started back to my rooms.

I dressed and pulled my hair back into tight braids in front of a mirror in my parlour, Rend pacing behind me, Rill sitting beside Shadas, both of them watching and waiting.

'What exactly did Arvan say?' I asked, staring in the mirror. My skin had lost its grey undertone, had gone back to red-brown with the blood I'd taken from the group of willing servants who had been lined up, waiting for me. Almost every mortal in the palace, and I still hungered, even though two of them had passed out from how much I'd taken. It was good though, I needed to feed. The blood hadn't made the grey leave my hair or my eyes, but it had put red in my eyes, a lot of red, from blood and rage.

'Just that Durrano was dead, and that he needed you,' Rill said.

'Then why isn't he here?' I growled, and Rend echoed me.

'He said he needed to get the house ready, and took Erant to help with that.' Rill stood, her hands touching bow and quiver, blade and knives, unconsciously making sure everything was there. 'He said he'd meet us by the gate when you were blooded and ready.'

'Bloody ready now,' I said. What was Arvan doing, rallying the house? Was Celasian heading here? It would take days for an army

to march that far, and the priest would be insane to come at us
without his full army, even reduced as we were. I had to know
what happened. I started to move, and didn't realise how fast I
was going until I noticed that Rend was loping after me, almost
running. Rill was still close, but we'd left Shadas behind.

He could catch up, I decided, moving even faster.

The courtyard behind the Grey Palace's main gate was crowded
with Nightmares and vampires, the Rose Knights assembling.
Arms and armour were being readied, the warriors moving with
efficiency. This was one of the things my father had learned well
from his time in the Crimson Keep, and he'd drilled it into all who
served him. The movements of that supernatural fortress were
unknown to anyone, and the warriors living behind its red walls
were practised in being ready to turn out at a moment's notice.

But why were they doing it now?

I spotted Arvan finally, a vortex of activity at one side of the
courtyard. Animals were swirling around him, bats and rats and
ravens and a few other things besides, including a marrow wing,
one of the great carrion birds of the plains whose wings spanned
more than twice my height.

'Arvan!' I shouted, striding towards him. Rill had caught up
with me, and Erant fell in beside her, leading our mounts. 'What's
going on?'

Arvan nodded to me, but his eyes were fixed on the marrow
wing. The great bird stood on the ground, its yellow eyes almost
level with Arvan's black ones. Marrow wings were bone eaters,
and Durrano had let a large colony of them nest on Skulltop. I
clenched my fists and let Arvan finish seeing whatever the great
bird was showing him, but the moment it turned from him and
lumbered away to find a place to take off, I was on him.

'What happened at Skulltop? Why have you called my house
to war?'

'Lady Volari.' He ducked his head, then reached up with one big hand to push his hair back. His long braids had come undone and tumbled around his shoulders like fraying ropes. 'I'm sorry, I sent my messengers to find you as soon as I had word. Skulltop is gone. Celasian attacked, took the hold, and killed them all.'

'All?' I asked. 'None escaped?'

'No,' he answered. 'They killed Lord Durrano and his Skull Knights, then slaughtered the mortals. Celasian burned them alive in the Temple of Nagash, with the bodies of all the others.'

'Burned them alive.' My blood went hot in me, my heart thumped. 'Burned alive the people my father swore to protect. The people I'm sworn to protect.'

He seeks to anger you.

'It's working,' I said. My heart beat again, moving all the new blood I'd taken through me, spreading heat and life and rage. This mortal had made my father a liar. He'd killed a Kastelai. My heart moved, and in my anger there was a twist of fear. What if the curse came again? What if the cold claimed me, halted my heart and stilled my blood and left me for the darkness? Just the thought of it brought the feeling back, and my anger dulled, my blood slowed. But I touched the bottle tucked behind my belt, and the feeling went away. Mostly.

'What's working?' Arvan was looking at me, his black eyes blank but his face confused.

'Celasian is trying to make me mad. To provoke me. That's what's working.'

'Maybe,' Arvan said. 'But from everything I've seen, the man is mad. The Storm God's fanaticism fills him. He burns anyone and anything that doesn't submit to Sigmar. I don't think this is a plot. I think he just wants to burn everyone on the Broken Plains, mortal and vampire, and claim the ashes for his god.'

'Celasian can want to burn the plains, the continent, the whole damn realm and the ones beyond,' I snarled. 'But he started at the wrong damned place. I'm going to trade his ashes for blood, and drown Celasian in it.' For Durrano, for my father, for myself and this fear that ran through me now, this sickening touch of mortality. Celasian might not be responsible for that, but he would pay for it anyway. Someone or something had to. I took a moment to rein in my anger, not to reduce it but to chain and channel it so that I could use it. And so Rend wouldn't tear some-one's throat out. The dire wolf was standing beside me, red eyes glowing malevolently as he glared at my dark-eyed counsellor. 'Now, Arvan. Tell me. Why in the hells are you arming my house?'

'Because I saw something else, besides Skulltop burning,' he said. 'A chance to strike back now, if you want it.'

'Speak,' I ordered him.

'Celasian brought his troops in on barges, pulling them up the Ire. From their movements, they plan to go back that way tomorrow, riding the barges with the current all the way to Gowyn. It won't take them long, and we've little hope of catching them even on our Nightmares. But he's not taking his whole army that way. Takora is taking her cavalry overland. I think they're running a sweep, searching for survivors.'

'Takora's cavalry.' The ragged wreck we'd left of it, at least. Their horses were no match for our Nightmares, their mortal riders no match for us. Takora had been very careful with them, mostly keeping them close to Gowyn, but there were a hundred of them left. About the number of my Rose Knights. Even numbers, but nowhere close to even odds. 'And Takora.'

'She's not their leader, not any more,' Arvan said. 'But she will know Celasian's plan.'

'And she owes us blood.' Takora had been a stubborn foe over the years, adapting well to the rough back-and-forth of our never-ending war. Better than her predecessors. We might have ended

this before Celasian had a chance to arrive if not for her. 'Where is she?'

'They were heading towards the ruins of Black Creek village before they stopped for the night. The place where Skulltop's bolthole came out,' he said. 'They must have made one of the prisoners tell them about it before Celasian burned them. I think Celasian is making sure he's got everyone.'

Or they're trying to bait us.

'Always the suspicious one,' I told her, keeping it in my head this time. But she usually had a point. 'Do we know that this isn't a trick?'

'I can't be certain,' Arvan qualified. As always. 'But I don't think so. Celasian's troops are all at the Ire, and they're too slow to come after us. The only other cavalry they have are the beasts his personal guards ride.'

'And if they come out, so much the better,' I said. 'What about the ruins? Have they hidden troops there?'

'No,' Arvan said. He waved a hand to his cloud of spies. 'I've sent scouts, there's no one out there but Takora and her horses. I think they don't believe we can reach them before they head back to Gowyn. And unless we ride soon, they're probably right. That's why I ordered the house to arms while I was still looking for you.' He bowed his head, his braids tumbling around him. 'Lady Volari, my service to you has been plagued with failures. I couldn't help your father escape the curse. I haven't been able to help you with it. I didn't stop Durrano's fall. Yet despite all that I am making presumptions for you. If you think I've overstepped, I will take a place with the newly blooded Rose Knights. Or offer you my neck.'

'Arvan, I think you've overthought as usual.' I went to Erant and took Thorn's reins from him. 'Do we have time for apologies or regrets?' I said, staring at my father's advisor. My advisor.

I still wanted to punch him, but this time he'd done right by me. I needed this. My hand touched the bottle hidden behind my belt again. This fight, this win, this blood. I needed to prove myself and the Rose Throne to my people, to the other houses, to Takora and Celasian, to all the Broken Plains.

To yourself.

'That too,' I muttered, swinging myself up into Thorn's saddle. I stared down at Arvan, who still hadn't answered. His black eyes were staring past me, past the walls, as if he could see the distant armies moving.

'No,' he said. 'There's no time for any of that.'

'No time at all.' I swung my Nightmare around and raised my voice. 'Knights of the Rose Throne! Mount up!'

There was a flurry of activity, the rattle of armour and weapons as they all obeyed, a hundred of the finest fighters outside of the Crimson Keep taking their places. It had been too long since we'd ridden in force like this. Far too long.

'Lady Volari!' Shadas had finally caught up, breathing hard, his face flushed. He came close, almost clutching my stirrup. He looked up at me and spoke, his voice so low that even with my hearing I barely made out his words over the thud of hooves, the clink of reins. 'Remember my warnings. Only when the curse takes you. Only then.'

'I remember,' I told him. 'As for you, remember this. However this battle goes, we still have a war to fight and I need troops. Find them for me, necromancer.'

'I will do what I can,' he said, stepping back.

'Do more than that,' I ordered him. 'Do more than you think you can. Whatever it takes, Shadas, or we're all going to find ourselves in Nagash's embrace.'

I spun Thorn from him and rose in my stirrups, standing high. 'Rose Knights! I am Nyssa Volari, Kastelai, blood daughter of

Corsovo, leader of this house and heir to the Rose Throne!' The
words echoed over the courtyard, brave and strong, but even as
I said them I felt doubt touch me. The vampires gathered here
had seen my mother fall, my father fall, had seen me fall to Magdalena. What strength did my words really have?

All the strength you can put into them, girl. Vasara's voice wasn't
calm. There was a crisp anger to it that was so familiar from when
she had first started teaching me. *You have your strength, Nyssa,
and our strength, and the strength of the blood. You have all the
strength you need. Use it!*

I had paused long enough that the echoes had died. All the
vampires were staring up at me, silent as death, waiting.

'We ride tonight,' I said, and I wasn't shouting. My voice was
just loud enough to be heard in the quiet. 'Not for the Crimson
Keep. Not for Nagash. But for Corsovo Volari, our king. We ride
tonight for him, and Durrano, and Vasara, and all the others
they took from us. We ride tonight for the kingdom they try to
take from us. For the honour, and the strength, and the place in
this world that they try to take from us.' Now I raised my voice
again. 'We ride tonight for vengeance. We ride tonight for blood.
We ride tonight to prove to these mortals that we are the lords
of the Broken Plains and that their priests and their god have no
power over us, for we are death, come for them on silent horse!'

The Rose Knights cheered, a shout that echoed from the walls of
the Grey Palace. Far above us, the glow at Temero's crown brightened as the volcano's fiery heart stirred. I unsheathed my bright
sword and raised it, letting its blade catch the crimson light so
that it glowed the colour of blood.

'We ride!' I shouted again, and sent Thorn forwards, Rill, Erant
and Arvan right behind me. As we went through the gate I leaned
forwards, urging Thorn on. She surged beneath me, falling into
a gallop, and I could hear the Rose Knights follow, the hooves of

their Nightmares flying. I listened to the thunder of their hooves, then I wrapped my magic around us so that we were all racing silent through the night as Temero spilled a new plume of ash across the sky. Silent as death, shrouded in darkness, we rode to battle and for that moment at least I could leave my doubt behind and ride, my blood pounding through my beating heart.

CHAPTER FOURTEEN

The sky over the Broken Plains was as black as the Death God's soul, but on the far horizon there were hints of a dull red glimmer, a spot of blood staining the sky. The only light in all that darkness, except for when the lightning lanced through the clouds and blotted out that malevolent glow.

It was metaphor blunt enough even for my tired brain, and I forced my eyes away, to stare out at the darkness that surrounded the camp spread below. A few low fires, some tethered horses, bundles of blankets on the ground. It looked good to me, but the vampires had keener senses. Still, they'd be coming in fast.

Maybe that would be enough.

Maybe, maybe, maybe. So many chances stacked on top of each other, all ready to tumble into ruin, but what else did I have? This was the only way out I could see for the people of the Broken Plains. This was the only chance to save them from the ones who would bleed them, and the ones who would burn them. And for me.

I sighed, trying to stop the thoughts from churning, when I heard the soft crunch of boots through the leaves behind me. I turned, ready to snap at whoever was making even that small noise, but the words died on my tongue.

'Captain Takora,' Galeris whispered, ducking his head in salute. 'We need to talk.'

We pulled back to the crest of the hill, far enough that I was willing to risk speaking.

'What are you doing here?' I hissed at my lieutenant. In the dim light I could see his face, battered and dirty. He looked like he'd been beaten, then dragged behind a horse through a newly ploughed field. 'What happened to you?' A fear seized my gut. 'Did the vampires attack?'

Was this all a set-up?

'No,' Galeris said. 'One of our scouts thought he saw some riders out in the hills, but they didn't come close. I came because of Celasian.'

'Who the hell did he set on fire now?'

'You,' Galeris said. 'Or at least he will when he gets his hands on you.'

'Sigmar save me,' I whispered, but that wasn't right, was it? Sigmar had sent his saviour, wrapped in white armour and carrying a silver spear, and my salvation seemed very much in doubt. 'What happened?'

'He knew you'd left. Someone in our ranks told him.' I could hear the annoyed disgust in Galeris' voice, but the small betrayal was predictable. Some in the 39th thought the abbot-general was practically a Stormcast Eternal. 'Celasian sent for me. He was in that office of Durrano's, looking through the papers. He said you'd been in there already, and the way he said it got me worried.'

'Got you worried?'

'Remember in training, when one of the sword masters would mention just offhand how some of the ale rations had gone missing and wasn't that mysterious, how strange... Then they'd run your squad until you were puking? Kinda like that. So I was already worried when he asked where you'd gone. I told him you were off looking for runaways, and he just looked at me with those eyes of his. Then he asked something.'

'What?'

Galeris was silent for a while, long enough that I almost asked it again, but then he finally spoke. 'He asked if I had ever had cause to doubt you, Captain Takora.'

'What did you say?' I said quietly.

'I was going to say no,' he said. 'It was right on my tongue. But he looked at me with those eyes, and something happened. I couldn't say it. I couldn't say anything. It felt like somebody had shoved a knife down my throat. I was choking, hurting, then I said it. How I'd seen you one night, on Gowyn's wall, throwing something out into the dark that spread its wings and flew away. A bat. I said all that, and then the pain was gone and I could breathe again.'

A bat. Galeris had seen that and kept it silent, even from me. Gods, I wasn't worth that much loyalty, was I? 'Priest magic,' I said. 'He called upon Sigmar, and made you speak the truth.'

'Yeah, well, it wasn't a truth I wanted Sigmar or Celasian to hear.'

I reached out in the dark and put a hand on Galeris' shoulder. Bless him, and damn Celasian. 'What'd he do?'

'Told me he'd talk to me more about it back in Gowyn. Then he had his Spears truss me up and throw me in the vampire's dungeon. Though really I think it was probably some empty storeroom, since the bloodsuckers just eat their troublemakers.'

'How'd you get here?'

'Celasian didn't want to waste his people watching me, so he put a couple of ours on guard duty. One of 'em owed me two weeks' pay from dice, and when the other went off to take a leak I told him that I'd forgive the debt if he'd let me punch him in the face and escape.' I could feel him shrug. 'We should maybe try to recruit more honest folk – he jumped at the deal. When I got out, I headed for the bolthole. Nobody was watching that, so I spent a few hours in the dark, running into walls, but it got me here so that I could warn you. Celasian is coming.'

I looked back down the hill at the dim light of the banked fires below. 'He was going to be doing that soon enough, whatever happened. But when we go back to Gowyn, I'll be ready for him.'

'Not in Gowyn,' Galeris said. 'Here. I heard him talking to his Spears as they hauled me out, telling them to be ready to ride as soon as dawn paled the sky. He means to take you out here, and bring you back to Gowyn tied over the back of your horse.'

Coming at dawn. I looked at the sky, black with clouds from Temero. Ash was beginning to drift down, tiny flakes so fine you could barely feel their touch. There wouldn't be a dawn this morning, but that wouldn't slow Celasian. Still. I'd made my plans. I wasn't going to abandon them now.

'Galeris, I've got something to tell you. I've tried to keep you out of it, but that didn't work worth a damn, so you might as well know what's going on.' I took a breath, and almost stopped. I'd kept this secret so long, but it was all going to come spilling out soon anyway. Once the throat's cut, there's no keeping the blood in. 'There's a traitor among the vampires of Temero. His name's Shadas, and he's been serving as their necromancer for years, but he wants out. Mostly doesn't want to die, I suspect, with our blades in his belly. He reached out to me two years ago, sent me messages with the vermin they use to communicate. Said that if I helped him get away, he'd help me end this war.'

'You believed him?'

'Sigmar's beard, no.' I shook my head. 'But I strung him along

and he fed me information and all of it was good. Stopped some ambushes, took some territory back, and as time went on, yes, I started to think this was something. A chance. So I took a risk, and we set up an endgame. He poisoned Corsovo.'

'The king?' Galeris said. 'So those rumours we heard?'

'Were true,' I said. 'He convinced them it was some sort of curse, and started in on Bloodeyes. She's still alive but weak. They're breaking up, Galeris, fighting amongst themselves, falling apart. The plan was to let them crumble, then we'd move in and finally end this damn war. Then Celasian showed up.' I spat into the dark. 'The Church of Sigmar's soldier. There was no way he'd understand. He's pure and blessed and true, but he hasn't been in the dust and the ash here for years, fighting an enemy that won't hold still. Fighting even though the local population spends all its time complaining about taxes instead of thanking us for saving them from being drained of their blood. Fighting on while those bureaucrats back in Hammerhal Aqsha quibble over sending us swords or the hands that can wield them. It's damn easy to be pure, to be righteous, when you've got soldiers and money and magic spears and a griffon to ride around on.'

My voice was starting to rise, and I cut myself off. The anger in me was bitter and deep, and I didn't have the time to let it take me. 'Celasian would burn me if he knew that I'd spoken to Shadas, much less cut a deal with him. He means to leave nothing behind but ashes when he finishes this war of vengeance that he's started.'

I had more to say, so much more, but I stopped. In the dark, I couldn't read Galeris' face. I might not have been able to read it in the light. But I needed to know what he thought. Did he think me a traitor, a fool, or as mad as Celasian? He stayed silent for an agonising moment, then finally spoke.

'So what's the plan?' His voice was flat and spare as ever, thank whatever gods would put up with me.

'Shadas wants out. Now. Celasian has him righteously scared. I want to end this too. Shatter the Kastelai and finish this, hopefully before the abbot-general gets anywhere near Maar. There are thousands in that city, and I think he'll burn them all. So I'm setting up the final battle right here. Shadas has been manipulating the information that Princess Bloodeyes has been getting this whole time. We're using that to bait her and her Rose Knights out. They're coming for me and the cavalry, now, tonight.'

'Nyssa and the Rose Knights? All of them?' Now Galeris' voice wasn't flat. 'They'll tear you to shreds, captain, and wring blood from every scrap!'

'They won't,' I said. 'We've set an ambush for them. They'll ride into that camp below and eat a storm of arrows.'

'That's not enough,' Galeris said, and I knew he was speaking from the same hard-won experience that filled me.

'I know. That's why there's another ambush. Shadas is going to poison the lot of them before they come in.' That was the part that worried me, of course. Relying on the necromancer this much, putting the lives of my troops in his hands. But I didn't have any other choice. 'It won't be enough to kill them, he says he doesn't have enough for that, but he claims they'll die easy. Easy as us mortals.'

'And if he's wrong?' Galeris asked. 'Or lying?'

'Then we die, and he dies.' That was the only surety I had on this bargain. 'He's following the knights. When they attack, he's going to get Bloodeyes away from the rest, so we can take her alive, and then I'll hand him over a map to a smuggler's boat hidden along the coast that will give him safe passage away from the Broken Plains. That and a bag of realmstone were my promises to him.'

'You think that'll work?'

Did I? By every god, I couldn't say. But I had to hope. 'I think so. I think by dawn the Rose Knights will be a story told to frighten

children, and Nyssa Volari will be in chains, ready to hand over to Celasian.' And damn me if I didn't feel a bit of pity for her. She'd been a knife in my side for years, fighting me back and forth over this useless land, killing my friends, almost killing me. She was a monster, a dead thing that fed on the living, but no one deserved to be handed over to that man.

'What about you?' The ash was falling thicker now, and I couldn't see Galeris' face. But I could hear his concern. Worried about me, even after all this. 'Even if you win, Celasian will know. He'll put the question to you, and draw out your answers with magic or something worse.'

'He won't have to,' I said. 'I'll tell him everything, though he'll still question me, I expect. But with a victory, my troops here… He'll have to haul me back to Hammerhal Aqsha for trial. And that'll go better for me if I've won. They might even let me live.'

'Gods, Takora!' For a moment, his voice started to rise, and I grabbed his shoulder again in the gloom, squeezing it hard, reminding him to calm, the way he'd reminded me so many times. 'Captain Takora,' he continued, quieter, 'why are you doing this? You can finish the battle and go. Run. Leave Bloodeyes to Celasian and ride away.'

'Where would I go?' I said, dropping my hand again. 'What would I do? This damned place, and this damned war, have been my whole life. When it's done, I'm done, Galeris.' I took a breath, tasting ash. 'This is the end, and I just want to make sure that as many people as possible make it out alive.'

'You don't even like people,' he said.

'I know. Especially the people that live here. But they don't deserve to burn.' I wiped a hand across my face, trying to brush the ashes away, but they just smeared across my skin. 'I don't want you to burn either. I want you to do something for me, lieutenant. I want you to take Sugar and ride to Maar. Tell them what'll happen here, tell them the vampires are dead and they're free. Tell them that when Celasian comes, they have to open their gates and greet him like a hero. That won't touch him, but by then the rest of his army should be with him and they can't all be fanatics, even if they're Church soldiers. They won't let him burn the people if they surrender without a fight. I hope.'

'You want me to go. To leave you to suffer, so that you can maybe save those people. Those enemies.'

'And maybe you.'

'And if I say no?'

'I'll order you to do it, lieutenant.'

We stood facing each other in the dark, ash settling silently around us, for what felt like forever before he finally spoke again.

'Of all the people I've ever met, you have spoken the most cynically, the most bitterly, about loyalty, mercy and honour. And you are the one who has the most of each of them. It's been a great honour to serve you, Captain Takora.'

Far away, around the peak of the volcano, lightning danced. In the scraps of light that made it through the dark and ash I saw him saluting me. I returned it, then put my hand on his chest and pushed him. 'Sugar is there. Take her and go. All hell is going to break loose here too damn soon, and I want you both gone.'

CHAPTER FIFTEEN

We rode through darkness made deep by the clouds that boiled across the sky. The Nightmares didn't tire, their hooves beating the ground with a steady, silent rhythm, racing on and on and on. We ran, and I could smell the ash, but we were too fast for it and it fell behind us like a grey shroud being pulled across the land.

With no stars or moons it was hard to gauge the time, but I could pick out landmarks in the dark which told me we were drawing near Skulltop. It was time to make a better plan than running fast.

In the next valley I began to rein in, bringing us to a stop. One hundred Rose Knights, silent shadows in the dark. I looked at them, and felt a fierce sense of pride and ambition. If I could smash Takora and her forces, if I could stop this curse, maybe I did belong on the throne.

More than maybe. Who else would you have? All the other Kastelai are too cautious or too mad. It's you, Nyssa.

'Stop,' I said, and my magic ate my words, but I knew she still heard. 'Every time you say something like that I want to argue, and this is the worst time for me to say that you're wrong.'

I swear I could feel her roll her eyes, though she had none, but Vasara stayed silent. I looked over my shoulder and gestured to Arvan, but he was already riding to me. When his stirrup was beside mine I raised one hand, fist clenched, the gesture for silence, and let my magic go. There was no sound, nothing but the distant call of a hunting owl and the whirring wings of bats as they circled around Arvan.

'Are they still there?' I asked him, my voice low. The mortals had learned to keep lookouts posted far from their camps if they dared linger on the plains at night.

'Yes,' Arvan said. He cradled a bat in his hand, letting it lick a drop of blood from his palm. 'They have their watch posted, but most of them still sleep.' In the darkness, Arvan's eyes were black holes over his teeth as he smiled. 'They didn't believe we could reach them. I barely believed it. Yet by Nagash here we are.'

'We're there when one of my blades is against Takora's throat,' I said. My heart had settled a little during the ride, but it was beating steady. 'Where are they?'

'The second valley over,' he said, pointing to the dark shapes of the land. 'The hills around them are thick with vesin trees. The terrain is bad on the right flank, but if we swing around there is a dry wash we can take straight into the middle of their camp.'

I turned Thorn to face the direction he'd pointed to. I didn't feel a trace of the cold that had come for me earlier; my anger was sharp and clear, and I almost forgot about the potion hidden behind my belt. Almost.

'Then that's how we'll hit them. Charging out of the dark, before they even know we're here.'

'There's a complication, though,' Arvan warned. 'My last scouts

said that Takora has shifted her position. Not far, but she won't be in the camp when we hit it.'

'How far is she?' Wiping out the mortal cavalry would be good, but it wasn't enough. Not with more of them coming soon. To make this strike worth it we had to take Takora.

And after years of fighting, I wanted to finally, truly beat her.

'Close. Just at the crest of the hill.'

Talking with her lookouts? Probably, but it meant that she'd see the attack as it hit and might be able to slip away.

'Can you take us to her?' I asked, and Arvan nodded. 'Then the four of us will separate from the main force and go for her while Orix leads the Rose Knights into the camp.'

'My lady,' Arvan said cautiously, 'we could send a squad. There's no need for you...' He stopped speaking when my eyes fell on him. 'As you wish. I'll guide us.'

He wasn't insulting you, Mother said. *A leader leads from the front of their army, not somewhere off to the side.*

'A leader makes sure that the biggest objective of the battle isn't lost in the first minute of the fight,' I told her silently.

Is that it, Nyssa? Or is it your need to humiliate her? I didn't answer, but she wouldn't leave it there, of course. *This is war. The stakes are too high to let the fight become personal.*

I felt my heart beating, pounding out the rhythm of my anger, the source of my battle strength. This was a division between us that I don't think we'd ever bridge, no matter how long Mother rattled around in my head. When she'd fought, she'd been cold, detached, unemotional. When I fought I brought my whole self, and everything was personal.

'Then it's time,' I said, and below me Rend rumbled a deep threat. 'Tonight we begin their end.'

It was a good line to ride to war to, so Arvan had to ruin it. 'Wait!' he said, and he turned in his saddle. There was a pack

strapped down behind him, and he pulled at its ties, opening it. 'Shadas has been working for months, preparing for something like this.' He reached into the pack and pulled out a handful of painted clay amphorae. 'Our mortals have been stretched thin, and none of us have fed to the fullest. This won't do that, but it will give us something.' He handed the vessels to me, Rill and Erant, and kept one for himself. Then he waved for Orix to come forwards and handed the rest of the pack to him. 'Enough for every Rose Knight,' he said.

'Theirs are a quarter the size of ours,' Rill noted dryly, watching as Orix started handing them out.

'Shadas can't work miracles, unfortunately.' Arvan cracked the seal of his amphora. 'As evidenced by the taste. But every bit will help.'

I held the warm clay in my hand, remembering that bitter taste. I had fed well before leaving the Grey Palace, or at least as well as I could. But my body still craved blood, still craved life. The cost of the curse. So I kept hold of the amphora and rode out into the middle of the Rose Knights. I could see they all held their portion now, drops of life given to us by the mortals back in Maar and the Grey Palace.

The night was silent, black except for the distant light of Temero, the red of the mountain's sullen anger, the flickering white of lightning dancing around it. The ash had finally caught us and was drifting down now, a silent storm of darkness. I raised my amphora, and when I spoke my voice was a whisper, but it spread through the silence to them all.

'This is the life of those who bow to us, given freely in exchange for our protection. A sip of life that will sustain us until we reach our enemy.' I cracked the seal with my thumb and brought the vessel to my lips, drinking deep, and all the others followed, swallowing the blood sealed inside. The taste of it made my lips

wrinkle, but I could feel the heat spreading through me. 'And now, let us be done with sips,' I said, dropping the amphora. 'Let us meet our enemy and drink torrents from their throats!'

I barely raised my voice, but as soon as I let that last word sound I drew both of my swords and raised them, bright and dark, over my head. Around me, there was the low hiss of steel as the Rose Knights followed suit, pulling their weapons and holding them high. Wrapping my magic around us, I spun Thorn about and started to ride, cutting through the darkness and the falling ash, leading an army as silent as death.

I felt the cold touch me as we peeled off from the Rose Knights, turned our Nightmares and sent them climbing up the hill beneath the tangled, thorny branches of the vesin trees. It was just a touch, a momentary chill, a brief pause in the steady thrum of my heart, but the dread it brought tore through me like a knife.

'Vasara,' I said, and my magic ate the sound of her name, left me in a silence that matched the silence in my skull. My mother was gone, and I was alone with the curse.

I started to reach for the bottle, but forced myself to stop. Shadas had said to take it when the cold had me, when I felt myself slowing. The cold had barely touched me, and the slowing hadn't begun. Did that matter? I should have asked more questions, but it was too late now, best to focus on what I could do. Which was to finish this before the curse sank its cold claws deeper.

I could hear the sound of hooves as the Rose Knights left my magic behind. In that moment Orix must have called the charge because the hoofbeats became a rolling thunder as the vampires of the Grey Palace charged. They would be upon the camp in moments, and when the screaming started I needed to have Takora in my hands.

The Nightmares were surging up the slope, unaffected by the darkness. Beside me Arvan was pointing, and I could see a clearing at the crest of the hill. I headed towards it, broke through, and there was Captain Takora at last, standing alone in the clearing.

Waiting for us.

I stopped Thorn, and Rend fell in beside her, jaws wide and eyes bright, eager to keep charging but staying with me. Takora was waiting, alone, and as I stared at her I could hear the sounds of battle erupting in the valley below. Not the screams of mortals, trampled and cut down in their camp, but the twang of bows and the high-pitched shriek of Nightmares falling, mixed with the curses and snarls of vampires.

I'd ridden us into a trap.

My swords were in my hands. Rill was pulling her bow free, while Erant grabbed the hilt of his sword, sliding the huge two-hander out. Beyond him, Arvan had his spear in his hands, but he wasn't raising it. He was staring across the clearing at Takora, his eyes blank as the sky overhead. Then he swept his gaze over to me, and Thorn went berserk.

The Nightmare twisted and bucked as if she were on fire, and when I tried to reach her with my magic that's all I found, pain burning through her dead nerves, and I couldn't touch her mind. Thorn reared up then toppled back, falling over, and I barely managed to leap away before she slammed into the ground. She rolled and I had to duck, my speed saving me as her hooves whistled past where my head had been. Then she was up, on her feet and galloping away, Erant's Nightmare right behind her. Rill's mount lay still on the ground, its bony head shattered against a stone outcrop.

I came up, swords in my hand. Beside me, Rend was shaking and I reached for his mind. In it was nothing but more pain, and the dire wolf howled and ran away into the dark. Something had caught the spirits woven into the bones and dried muscles of our

beasts' bodies and wrapped them in pain until they ran away as fast as they could. Something. Someone.

Arvan sat on his mount, his blank eyes on me. There was no anger on his face, no twisted pride, no satisfaction. Only a kind of impatient annoyance.

'You're supposed to be fast, Lady Volari. Can you not solve a riddle, when all the hints have been laid out for you?'

'You,' I said. 'You betrayed me!' Anger filled me, and my heart was a war drum. Then I moved, tearing through the space that separated us in an instant.

If he hadn't been mounted, I would have had him. Arvan's spear was coming up, but I was already there, the point of my dark sword driving towards his chest – and then his Nightmare twisted its head, putting it between my thrust and Arvan's traitorous heart.

The point slammed into the Nightmare's eye socket, passing through the pallid grave light gathered there before crunching deep into the bone. The beast shuddered and tossed its head, wrenching the sword out of my hand as it staggered and fell. I pushed off its chest, flipping backwards and landing on my feet. Arvan had thrown himself free and came up with his spear ready. His eyes were on me, which meant he didn't see Erant rushing up behind him, sword pulled back to swing at his head. But Arvan heard him and started to spin, turning to block Erant's attack while not giving me his back.

Too bad, I was going to take it anyway, and I started to rush forwards – then the cold hit me. It struck me like an avalanche, a wave of deadly chill that made my heart stutter, made my blood stop in my veins, and my sprint turned into a stumble, sending me to my knees. I could hear the clash of weapons, Erant's angry shout, but I was fighting not to collapse under the weight of the cold and darkness that was pounding down onto me, threatening to swallow up the world.

'No,' I gasped, trying to shove back the cold with the heat of my rage, trying... and then it let me go. Death pulled back its shroud and the dark night was suddenly bright to my eyes. I blinked, and ahead of me I could see Rill.

She was kneeling next to the still body of her Nightmare, her bow in one hand but her arrows laid out in front of her. She was reaching for them, hand moving across the ground, and her eyes were wide. I could hear her whispering to herself, 'Damn this cold, it's taken my eyes, *I can't see!*'

This cold. Rill had been given the blood by my father. Was all of it tainted with this curse? I struggled to my feet, the empty hand that once held my dark sword going to my belt, fumbling for the bottle hidden there, but just as my fingers found it something slammed into my back, sending me down once again. I tried to catch myself but my blood was sludge in my veins, and I hit the ground hard. I struggled up to my knees as Arvan stood over me. Behind him I could see Erant struggling to pull himself to his feet, his sword hanging from one hand as if he could barely lift the weight. Erant, who I'd seen pick up a boulder almost as big as I was.

Cursed? All of us? All except Arvan, whose spear was levelled at my throat. 'You did this.' I shifted my bright sword, but there was no way now I could strike at him before the razor point of his spear tip caught me. 'You cursed us all.'

'Cursed?' Arvan shook his head. 'You had it right the first time, Nyssa, back in the Grey Palace. I poisoned you. You, these two, all the Rose Knights, poisoned with the same thing I used to kill the king.'

My father. Not caring about his spear, I was on my feet, charging him, clumsy, slow, but that didn't stop me. The poison might stop my heart and freeze my blood, but it didn't take away the anger that burned through me. I struck out at him and he slapped my

sword away with his spear, then caught me by the throat with one hand. He slammed me down and dropped his knee onto my back. My sword was gone, but on my belly like this I could feel the bottle digging into me. I squirmed, trying to reach my hands down to get it, but Arvan caught them, hauled them back behind me and wrapped a cord around my wrists, binding them.

'You're slow,' he said. 'I thought I might be in trouble when your first guess as to what had happened to Corsovo was poison. But you swallowed the story about the curse so easily.' He wrapped his fingers into my hair and hauled my head back. 'Shadas made the poison. Do you know what from? Vasara's bones. I killed Corsovo with the bones of his lover, then I poisoned you and his whole court with them.'

Rage filled me, hot enough to push back the cold. My heart thudded, slow, but it clenched and my blood stirred. I jerked beneath Arvan's knee, threw myself to one side, hard and fast enough to slip away and roll to face him. The black-eyed vampire sighed and reached for me, careful of my snapping teeth, and didn't notice Erant until my guard's sword fell on his neck.

It would have killed him if Erant had not lost his strength. The blade bit through Arvan's skin, cut into the muscle beneath, but it stopped against the bone of his vertebrae. With an angry growl, the traitor slapped the sword away, picked his spear up from the ground and slammed its point into Erant's chest.

It took Erant in the heart, and he hissed as it passed through him, blood exploding from his mouth. Red mottled with something else, clots coloured grey and white and black, the colour of ash. But Erant didn't fall.

'Run,' he said, his eyes on me, and then he drove himself forwards, sliding down the spear's bloody shaft to grab Arvan's chest, trying to bring him down.

Trying, and failing.

Arvan jerked back his spear and kicked out with his foot, shoving Erant off. Then he thrust it back in. In and out, slamming the spear through the cold flesh until he had dug a pit in Erant's chest, destroying his heart.

Erant staggered backwards beneath the blows, and when he finally hit the ground his body came apart, became like the ash falling from the sky, shattered into dust, gone.

I hadn't run. I hadn't even moved. I just stared at where Erant had been. I'd known him so long. Quiet, strong, protective of me and Rill, who always ignored him. Arvan had killed Erant, had killed my father, and now he was trying to kill me. I moved then, lunging at Arvan again, not caring that my hands were still bound behind me. This time he turned and caught me with the butt of his spear, smashing it into my face, sending me falling onto my back into the ashes that covered the ground like snow.

'Nyssa? Erant? Arvan?' Rill was standing, an arrow nocked against her bow, but she wasn't even facing us. 'I can't see. I can't hear. What's going on?'

Arvan shook his head, walked over and stabbed her in the back. Rill stiffened, bow dropping from her hands. Arvan picked her up, holding her off her feet on the end of his spear, then threw her down the hill.

'There.' He looked at Takora. At some point she'd drawn her sword, but she hadn't moved, hadn't fled. 'That's the bargain honoured. The king dead, the Rose Throne fallen, the vampires divided, and the princess all wrapped up for you. Now where's my due?'

'You're not Shadas,' she said, watching him the way a mortal would watch a viper.

Shadas. He'd had Shadas make the poison for him. From the bones of my mother. My mouth was filled with the bitter taste of the blood that had flowed from the amphora Arvan had given

228

me. Was that what they'd used to disguise what they'd hidden in the blood? Or was that the taste of the burned bones of my own mother, which they had made me drink?

Shadas.

I could feel the bottle he'd given me. His not-cure for the curse he'd made for me himself. The thing that had given me hope: a poisoner's cure. I snarled to myself, my anger trying to burn through the cold. Trying to give me strength, enough to bend myself back. To pull my arms wide and down, to jerk them apart far enough that I heard the soft pops of dislocation in my elbows, my shoulders. I barely felt the pain, lost in another wave of cold washing over me. It was trying to take me again, to freeze me into stillness and death, but I moved, pulling my body through the loop of my dislocated arms so that my bound hands were now in front of me.

Takora had seen me. 'She's trying to get away.'

'My Lady Volari doesn't know when to give up,' Arvan said. 'It's one of her charms, one you should be familiar with. She'll stop when the poison takes her. She'll seem dead but she won't be, so you'll have a prisoner to hand over to your Celasian. Now settle your side, Takora, or face the consequences.'

She held out a pouch, heavy with something, and a folded piece of paper. 'A fortune in realmstone, and a map to the boat that waits. Though they're expecting a man, not a bloody Soulblight vampire.'

'Same as you.' Arvan took the pouch and paper, and Takora stepped back quickly. 'I'll make it work.'

I watched them as I tried to make my hands work. I was used to my body mending itself moments after being hurt, but like everything else my healing had slowed. I could feel my shoulders shifting, the ligaments in my elbows weaving back together, but not fast enough no matter how much I cursed at them. It hurt

too, like saw blades running through my joints, more painful than when I had wrenched them apart. I could fight the pain, but it brought the cold back, and I felt it spreading inexorably, ice water rising around me. When it closed over my head it would drag me to darkness, and when I woke I'd be in Celasian's hands.

It wouldn't matter if I was free of the poison then, that fanatic would chain me down and use my powers of healing to burn me slowly.

I stretched one hand, feeling the tendons pop into place, and my fingers touched my belt. The bottle was there. Shadas' cure for his own poison. What game was he playing when he gave me that? When he told me not to tell anyone, which kept me from telling Arvan? Where was the lie and where was the truth and where was my damned mother to help me sort this out?

'Lies,' Takora said. 'That's how you made it work for me.'

'They're a convenient currency.' He looked past her. 'Do you have a horse? My Nightmare has a sword through its head.'

'Afraid I just gave mine away.'

'Too bad.' He tucked the bag and map away in his armour, then nodded to Takora. 'Do you know what the nomads say after haggling? Good trade, good luck. Good trade, Takora. Now good luck with your fanatic.'

'Walk fast or we'll both need luck,' Takora said. 'Celasian's on his way here, now.'

'Then I'm best off.' Arvan turned, the wide black holes of his eyes staring at me through the falling ash. 'I never liked you, Nyssa, but I never hated you either. You Kastelai were too stupid to deserve my hate. But I'll wish you luck, princess. I think you'll need it more than either of us.'

Then he was gone.

Killed my father, killed Erant, killed Rill, killed me. Killed me. The cold was running through me, stopping the healing in my

arms, stilling my heart, my blood. The darkness was rising in my eyes, slowly eating the night, the ashes, Takora, the distant sounds of battle. There were just my hands, pulling up my chest, the cord binding them rasping against my armour. The bottle was there, between my fingers. I could barely make out the strange patterns swirling in the liquid, the marks like chains of vertebrae, beads of bones. Shadas' potion. I could drop it, bite through the cord that bound me, reach for my sword and–

And what? Death was coming for me, would claim me for a little while again, and then spit me out into a new kind of hell where Celasian would have me and I would spend every moment of that slow death knowing Arvan had got away.

'Damn me.' Takora's voice, Takora's words, as she stared into the dark where Arvan had disappeared. Then she was turning. She would see the bottle and smash it away from my hands, and all would go dark.

'No,' I hissed, and with my teeth I ripped out the stopper. The liquid came out, splashing across my chin, my hands too numb to place the opening against my lips, but it didn't matter. Whatever potion Shadas had made, it was eager for me. It ignored the tug of gravity and flowed up my neck, my chin, my cheeks, found my mouth and poured inside. It ran into me, and it felt like swallowing razors. A storm of blades shredded my tongue, my gums, the lining of my mouth, then poured down my throat. They shredded me from the inside, pouring into my belly, slicing it apart and then spreading. I shuddered, my whole body convulsing with pain. I was coughing, choking, blood spilling from my mouth. Takora was screaming something, but her voice was a distant whine, fading away to nothing as my hearing went, my taste, my touch, my sense of smell. There was nothing but pain and the sky above me, black with clouds and falling ash, and that was going too, the last darkness swallowing it all as I was torn apart.

I was cold, I was dying, and I was alone.

Except for the scrap of a whisper.

Nyssa. What have you done?

CHAPTER SIXTEEN

'Damn me.'

The words fell heavy in the quiet air. Below I could hear the fight, soldiers shouting, Nightmares screaming, but in this clearing there was nothing now but my breathing.

I always knew there would be some kind of betrayal. I'd expected it, half expected to die tonight on this hill. I didn't really care. Death didn't worry me as much as Celasian. My only desperate hope had been that I hadn't led my soldiers into a trap with me.

It was hard to accept that I wasn't the one betrayed. I stared through the dark at the spot where the vampire had disappeared. Had he always been the one I'd been dealing with? Probably. Did Shadas even know what had been done in his name? I didn't know. Didn't care, really. The entire point of this was to turn the vampires against each other, to break their leaders down.

That thought jarred me out of my reverie. I turned, sword in hand, and peered through the gloom at my captive. Princess Bloodeyes, the monster that'd been haunting me for decades, deadly and... doing something.

I lunged through the gloom, boots slipping on ash. Nyssa was lying on her back, her bound hands holding an empty bottle. Just before I reached her, one last drop of dark liquid fell between her sharp white teeth, then I smashed the bottle out of her grip. The vampire princess barely reacted. Her hands fell and her head tipped back, eyes staring blankly at the sky. In the dim light I could see that her eyes were marred not with red, but with grey, the same colour as the streaks that ran through her hair.

'What was that?' I shouted. Her only answer was a trembling that started in her hands and spread, becoming a convulsion as blood spurted from her mouth. Red blood marked with bits of black and grey and white, as if mixed with ashes. I skipped back, getting away from the foul stuff, and cursed. Was this more poison? Had Bloodeyes chosen to go to whatever hell took her, rather than face Celasian? It wasn't a bad choice, but it wasn't something I would have expected. The traitor had been right when he said that Nyssa didn't give up. But as I watched, her convulsions slowed and she went still. Blood stopped coming from her mouth, and her eyes stared blankly up at the sky. I approached her slowly, waiting for the trick, but she didn't move. I crouched down beside her, careful not to let her blood touch me, and looked at her face.

She looked so young, like a girl asleep. But her eyes were open, and as I watched a flake of ash drifted down and landed in the centre of her pupil. Bloodeyes didn't move, didn't blink.

'Damn me,' I said again. I rose and kicked her shoulder with my boot. Nothing. But the traitor had said she'd seem dead, hadn't he? Dead and still, not dead and moving. He'd better have been telling me the truth. If I didn't have a toy to distract Celasian, my chances of making it back to Hammerhal Aqsha for a trial were slim.

'At least you're not fighting me,' I said, and that was important. I'd spent too much time up here already. I'd cut the head off the snake, but its body was in the valley below, trying to kill my

soldiers. I needed to be down there, fighting, and that meant dragging Bloodeyes with me. I took hold of her beneath her shoulders and started down the hill.

I barely reached the trees before I was attacked. She came at me from the side, lunging out from behind the twisted trunk of one of the vesin trees – the vampire guard who had been stabbed and knocked down the hill. Not dead. Of course not, these damned things never died properly, but she was weak. Even hampered with Bloodeyes, it was easy to step out of the way and let her stumble past. Her bow was gone but she was holding a knife in her hand, big enough to be a short sword.

I dropped Nyssa's body and drew my sword, and at the steely rasp the vampire spun, facing me. Her head was turning, eyes searching through the shadows, but she couldn't see me. The poison she had been given had taken her senses, but it must be wearing off now. She could hear, but her vision was still gone, which made her only a little less dangerous.

'Lady Volari?' the vampire said, her voice low. 'I smell you.' She was circling, feet moving in a careful slide through the ash as she looked for me. 'I smell a mortal too. Takora. If you've harmed her–'

She left the threat hanging. She'd kill me? She'd kill me no matter what. I slid to the side, circling with her, keeping my feet silent. If I could get behind her I'd get one clean shot. A chance to take her head off, and that was usually enough.

Then a hand closed on my shoulder, and another on the wrist of my sword arm.

'She has not.'

A voice in my ear, cold as death, and I tried to jerk myself away, but I'd barely started moving before I felt teeth plunge deep into my neck.

* * *

235

I was lying on the ground, and the world was spinning around me.

'He killed Erant.' A monster's voice, low and deadly. 'I'll kill him.'

'No.' Another monster's voice, coming from right above. I blinked against the darkness, trying to decipher the shadows. 'Arvan is mine, Rill.'

'Where is he?' The one who'd attacked me. Rill. I shut my eyes, but the world kept spinning, and I could feel the pain in my neck, the warm liquid heat on my skin. Something had hurt me. I'd bled. I'd almost bled to death once, not long after I came to these damned Broken Plains, when a skeleton had planted an arrow in my arm and nicked an artery. It had felt like this: the pain, the cold, the swirling, dizzying world.

Blood. Pain. A vampire had taken me from behind, had fed on me. I shook, cold and horrified, and wondered why I wasn't dead.

'I don't know,' the one that wasn't Rill said. I opened my eyes and there was a face in front of me. Dark skin, flashing teeth, and eyes, great brown eyes marked with striations of red. Bloody eyes.

Nyssa's eyes.

'But she does.' Nyssa picked me up and handed me to Rill, who cradled me against her as if I were a child. 'Take her. Keep her alive. We'll need her to tell me where he's gone.' I turned my head, staring. Nyssa was not still any more, not dead. She was undead, and very much in motion. She stepped back from Rill and was gone, vanished. Had I blacked out? No. Rill growled, and her cold fingers pressed against the wound on my neck, not gently, stopping the slow seep of blood. Then Nyssa was back.

The darkness was fading a little. Somewhere behind the clouds Temero had spread across the sky, dawn was breaking, changing the darkness to a grey murk filled with drifting flakes of ash. The light was enough now that I could see the swords in Nyssa's hands, one bright, one dark.

'Can you see?' she asked, and I muttered something slurred and idiotic, but Rill ignored me and answered.

'A little.'

'Then stay close. When I tell you, stop and stay still. Keep Takora, and keep safe.'

'What are you doing?' Rill asked. 'Why aren't we questioning her? Why aren't we going after Arvan *now*? He's getting away!'

'I know,' Nyssa answered, and there was a tightness in her voice that sounded like pain. 'But I led the Rose Knights into this ambush, and the poison that makes them weak comes from my family. I have to help them first.' Her face suddenly twisted into a frown, and her eyes slid up and towards the left. 'I know!' she snapped suddenly, as if arguing with a voice I hadn't heard. 'I'm doing it, like I said I would! Now leave me alone!' Then her bloody eyes snapped back to us. 'Come on.'

We moved towards the sound of the fighting, and through the slow sludge that was my thoughts I realised what Nyssa was about to attack. She was going to kill my soldiers, while I hung here, weak and helpless. I took a breath and then shouted, as hard as I could. I screamed a warning so hard my wound started to bleed again, but there was nothing. No sound came from me, just silence, and I realised that one of the vampires must have wrapped us in their death magic, and I couldn't warn anyone of anything.

I struggled in Rill's arms, trying to get away, but I was so weak all it did was make me dizzy. I collapsed, breathing hard, help-less, useless, forced to watch what was happening.

In the grey gloom, shapes flickered through the trees. My soldiers, bows in their hands, firing into the valley below. I could see fallen Nightmares, their bodies full of arrows, and with them the still bodies of vampires in armour coloured black and crimson. There were not nearly as many as there should be, and the cries coming from my side weren't reassuring. Sergeants were

snapping orders, someone cursed a broken bowstring, a lieutenant called for archers to shift positions, but I had been in enough battles to hear the edge of panic in some of the voices. Something was happening they hadn't expected.

Mixed in with the shouting was the rising sound of steel on steel, the brutal crunch of blades shearing through flesh, and the awful tearing noises that happened when a Nightmare caught someone's face in their flat, awful teeth. I'd split the 39th's cavalry, sent half to each side of this valley for the ambush, and from the sound of it the vampires were ripping through my forces on that far side, fighting them hand to hand. That was a battle my troops couldn't win, poison or not.

Bloodeyes touched Rill's shoulder and her hand brushed past me. I tried to twitch away but Rill just clamped down tighter, holding me still as Nyssa gestured to her. Their hand signals were only a little different than the ones we used when keeping silent on the lines before an attack. Stop. Stay. Rill frowned, but she nodded. Nyssa stepped away, flipping her swords in her grip so that she was holding them points down, and then she was gone.

Gods, the speed of her was terrifying. One moment there, gone the next, running so fast I lost her. I only saw her again when she slowed down to kill. Bloodeyes slid her blade across the belly of one of my men, the sword cutting through his leather armour, biting through muscle and bowel, and blood burst out like water. But there were no sounds. It was Nyssa who had carried that magic, and her killings were wrapped in silence.

Despite this, I tried to shout, but her magic still reached me, and even though I howled until my throat ached my warnings were as noiseless as Nyssa's attacks.

The man pitched forwards, hands clutching at the wound that almost split him in half, but Nyssa was already gone. She vanished into a blur, only to reappear next to a woman who was suddenly

lurching backwards, the bow she'd been about to fire cut along with her throat. Blood pulsed from the wound and I saw Nyssa stop, holding the woman up as she pressed her mouth to the wound, drinking. Then she was gone again, moving, the black blade in her left hand slicing out at the man who'd been standing next to the archer. He didn't even notice the person next to him falling, dying, didn't notice his own death slashing at him, and his eyes widened in surprise as his head tumbled away.

I'd seen the sword masters in Hammerhal Aqsha. I'd even seen Stormcast Eternals, once, sparring in that great city. I'd seen Soulblight vampire knights fight and kill over the decades. None of them terrified me the way watching Nyssa Volari cut her way through my soldiers did. There was the silence of it, the way that wherever she moved, wherever she killed, there were no screams, no sickening squelch of flesh splitting beneath steel, no sound at all. Then there was the grace: the precise, perfect way she moved, gliding through the people, a beautiful dance that left a wake of carnage. Finally there was the speed. Nyssa was stronger than a woman her size should be, but she wasn't strong like the Stormcasts. She didn't knock her victims through the air, didn't split armour or flesh with massive strikes. But she moved faster than anything I'd ever seen, and combined with her grace that speed was deadly. She cut exposed flesh, sliced through the weak points in armour, and was behind opponents before they even knew they were fighting her. She flashed across the hillside like darkness fleeing light, and behind her my soldiers fell to the ground, bleeding, dying.

I stopped trying to shout. My throat was raw and the world was spinning around me. It was useless. I was useless. I'd led these soldiers here on a gamble, and it was costing them their lives and me my soul. I shut my eyes and wished the darkness would take me, pull me down into death, but it didn't. Damn me, of course it didn't.

I don't know how long I hung in the black behind my eyelids, trying to push away the images that crowded in of swords, of blood, of teeth, of faces stretched in silent screams. It ended when Rill started moving, walking down the hill, and the motion made me open my eyes. The ash was still falling, grey flakes that brushed my face and gathered in my hair. My soldiers were sprawled in it, their blood turning its grey black. Down at the bottom of the hill, in the narrow valley, the dead had been still long enough to gather drifts around them, powdery blankets pulled over bodies twisted in death. So many dead.

It was too much, my failure written across the ground in carnage. I raised my eyes, and concentrated instead on the ones still standing. The ones who'd won. The undead.

Nyssa stood in front of us. Blood marked her, but less than I would have expected. She moved so fast she'd barely been touched by the gore. She stood straight and tall in her black armour with its skull and roses, her swords sheathed on her hips. Some of her hair had escaped her braids and the circlet holding them back. The loose strands were black and glossy, none of them grey now, and the grey was gone from her eyes. There was just red there, almost glowing against the brown. Her skin had lost the grey pallor that had underlain it too, had become a smooth, ruddy brown, a perfect contrast to her gleaming white fangs. She looked young and ancient, handsome and horrifying. Whatever injury that poison had done to her, it was gone, wiped away by blood.

Bloodeyes was beautiful and terrifying and victorious, and I hated her as much as I hated myself.

'Put her down,' she said, and Rill set me on my feet. The world swung around me, but I made myself stand. I wasn't going to fall in front of them. Behind Nyssa was a group of mounted vampires, Rose Knights by the markings on their armour and the banners

they bore. I watched one of them snap the fletched end off the arrow embedded in his neck, then shove the rest of it through his dead flesh so that it slid out the other side.

'Lady Volari,' he croaked, his voice like gravel. 'Thank you. Something happened to us, just as we began to fight. I don't know how to explain it. We went weak, and so many fell to the mortals. Without your aid, and Magdalena's, we might all have fallen.'

Magdalena. I knew the name, and now I had a face. A face that looked nothing like I expected, sweet almost, especially surrounded by the loose curls of her hair. The Kastelai sat on a Nightmare with ten other vampires, their armour coloured black and purple, marked with ravens and the symbols of the cult of death. They must have been the ones that attacked my forces on the other side of the hill. Maybe the vampires weren't as divided as the treacherous Arvan had assured me. Except Magdalena's face was as hard as stone, and Nyssa looked like a cat watching a stranger approach. But as I watched Nyssa, her eyes shifted up again, and I saw her lips move as if she were whispering something to herself. Then she rolled her shoulders and nodded.

'Thank you, Orix. I know what happened to you, where the weakness came from. It wasn't your fault, and it won't happen again.' Nyssa looked from her warriors to the other group. 'Lady Magdalena. It's good to see you out of your fortress.'

'My spies told me that Sigmar's dog was on the march,' Magdalena said. Her mask slipped a little, still grim but not as hard. 'I went to warn Lord Durrano, but we were too late.' She made the sign of Nagash, and I shuddered. 'We didn't dare close on the forces around Skulltop, but we found the tracks of this group and decided to follow.' She looked at the Rose Knights, at me and Rill, at Nyssa. 'What happened?'

'Treason,' Nyssa said. 'Betrayal. Stupidity.' She snarled, seemingly to herself, then looked at me. 'Arvan made a deal with Captain

Takora. He had Shadas make some sort of necromantic poison, and they gave it to my father. That's what killed him. Not the curse of the Crimson Keep.'

Magdalena looked at me, her eyes incongruously terrifying in that round face. 'Captain Takora. I am unsurprised. You have always fought without honour.'

'You drink the blood of my soldiers, then raise their corpses up to kill us.' I managed to keep myself from swaying as I spoke, managed to keep my voice level, my words clear. 'I've seen thirty years of what you Kastelai call honour, and it sickens me.'

'Does it?' Nyssa was suddenly right there beside me, so fast I didn't see her move. I tried to draw the sword that still hung on my hip, but she reached out and slapped my hand away, as easily as a mother correcting a toddler. 'Was fighting your dead worse than finding out your enemies had killed your father with poison they'd made from the body of your mother? Worse than finding out they were slowly killing you with it? Is that your idea of honour?'

I made myself look her straight in her red eyes. 'No. There was no honour in that at all. I lost my honour a long time ago, fighting this ugly war in this ugly place with you, and I just wanted to end it.'

'You could have ended it whenever you wanted,' Nyssa said, her voice low. 'You could have gone home. The Broken Plains don't belong to Hammerhal.'

'Do they belong to the Crimson Keep?' I said.

'No,' she said. 'They belong to the Grey Palace. To the kings and queens of Temero. To me.'

She walked away, moving like a human, and I wanted to draw my dagger and stab her in the back but... I'd already tried that, hadn't I? Arvan and Shadas had been my dagger before, and look how well that had gone.

'This one bribed Arvan,' Nyssa said, anger flashing in every word, 'to poison me and divide us. To have him lead us into this trap, where he poisoned us all with tainted blood. That's why you were weak, Orix. That's why the Rose Throne almost fell today. But it didn't, and now it is time to end this treachery. To end this war.' She turned and looked at me again. 'We have Takora, and soon we'll have this Celasian. The head of this mortal snake is coming to find his wayward soldier. And when he does, we'll take him.'

CHAPTER SEVENTEEN

Magdalena stopped in the middle of the hillside, untroubled by the ash that drifted through the trees to land in her dark hair. Her face was calm as she bowed her head and clasped her hands in front of her. She whispered her prayer, but I could hear every word of it, a long string of praises to Nagash and a request for him to bless his children as they began their second life. Then she opened her hands and let her magic go, and throughout the woods the soldiers that I'd killed began to move.

Legs twitched and fingers curled, eyes blinked and mouths opened, groaning, as Magdalena's magic pulled back bits of their souls and planted them in the cooling flesh of their bodies. The newly made zombies began to drag themselves up, staggering to their feet, weapons clutched in their hands.

'She does good work,' Rill said. She was standing beside me, Takora by her side. 'Maybe I should ask Nagash for his blessing next time I try a raising.'

'It's not the prayer,' I said. 'The blessed blood may have come

from Nagash long ago, but the magic in it belonged to us. 'The dead look good because I didn't hack them to pieces.'

'I'm sure they count that as a blessing,' Takora said, her voice wooden, emotionless. She turned her head away, refusing to watch as her troops rose and shuffled down the slope to the valley below.

'Should I have tortured them?' I asked her. 'Maybe given them a poison that slowly, painfully killed them, instead of a quick, clean death? Is that the *blessing* you'd have had me give them, captain?'

Takora didn't look away from the tree trunk she'd locked her eyes to. 'I did what I did to save lives. I wanted to end this war with as little bloodshed as possible. Unlike you.'

Blood. Oh, I wanted blood all right. My lips parted, and I bared my fangs. Shadas had been right. I'd needed so much blood after his cure for his not-curse. And I'd fed very well, but not on the blood I wanted.

You have to do this first. You can deal with Arvan after.

After. After wasn't soon enough.

'That's right,' I said. 'You mortals don't dirty your hands with blood. You cover yourselves with the ashes of your enemies.' I moved to her, so fast she stepped back in surprise. 'Did they smell like this, after?' I ran my fingers through her short hair, too quick for her to avoid, and then held them out, coated with ashes. 'Or did they still stink of burning flesh?'

'That wasn't me!' she snapped. 'Do you want me to admit that Celasian is as much of a monster as you? Maybe worse? You don't have to push me into that. I know what he is. That's why I made this stupid gamble. I was hoping that if I gave you to him, if I destroyed the forces of the Grey Palace, he'd spare the people of Maar!'

'You could have spared them if you had slit his throat, got on a boat with your people and left. Then those nomads and Durrano's villagers would be alive too.'

I could hear Takora's heartbeat quicken as fury washed through her, and I knew what she was going to do before she even moved. My hand flashed out and pulled the longsword from the sheath on her hip, then threw it away. It landed point first in the ground, and one of the freshly risen zombies dropped the broken bow it was holding and picked it up, then kept walking.

In my chest, my own heart beat a steady rhythm. It stirred all the new blood flowing in me, warm with life and anger. When the darkness had broken for me, when I'd come back to myself after the vicious pain of Shadas' potion, my heart had begun to beat and it hadn't stopped since. The chill dread of the poison had been cleaned out of me, and all that was left was anger, speed and the need for revenge.

Takora was a distraction. I could have snapped her neck and run after Arvan, tracked him by his scent until I found him and tore his throat out with my fangs. I didn't want to make him beg or torture him, or draw it out in any vengeful way. I just wanted his blood on my teeth and to see him dead.

But Mother had stopped me. Damn her.

No. Her voice filled my head, clear and calm. *I just broke through your anger long enough for you to see what was going on. You were the one who made the right decision.*

The right decision. Saving Orix and the Rose Knights. But then that decision became the right decision of dealing with Magdalena, of staying here to set the trap for Celasian. A whole series of right decisions that let Arvan get further and further from me, and in my chest my heart beat a little faster and I wanted to scream.

Killing Arvan and losing everything else is a greater loss than letting him get away.

'Is it?' I said. 'I think if he lives, it will eat me alive as much as his damned poison.' Rill knew to ignore that, but Takora looked

at me, eyes narrow. I watched as Magdalena directed the zombies to their places and made them quiet, still. Preparing for Celasian. My fingers tapped on the hilt of my swords, an impatient dance. 'Takora, where is Sigmar's boy? You told Arvan he'd be here soon.'

'He'll get here when he gets here,' Takora said, her voice hollow. 'But he's coming. The only thing the abbot-general cares about is hate, and he's found a reason to hate me. He'll come for me. Then he'll come for you. He hates you more than he hates anything, I think.'

'He can hate us in Nagash's lowest hell.' As I spoke, a look twisted across Takora's face, a mix of bitter resignation, as if she doubted that was Celasian's fate, and was disappointed. 'Why does he hate us so much? Because we kill with our teeth, instead of a torch?'

'That's part of it,' she said. 'He finds you disgusting. But I think it's more than that. I think he fears it. Being bitten, having his blood taken. Being fed on, the way you fed on me. It's a violation for him worse than death. Because of what happened to his father, I would guess.'

'Did a vampire kill him?' I asked.

'Yes,' she said. 'Vasara.'

Now I did care. 'Vasara? How?'

'His father was a nomad leader. A man called Celas, who allied five of the bands together. Celasian said Vasara came to him, to offer him an alliance with the Rose Throne, and when he refused she killed him.'

That is an interesting interpretation of those events.

'It's a lie,' I said. Celasian, son of Celas. My heart thrummed in my chest, alive with anger. The fanatic wasn't just here for his god, then. He was coming home for his family, for revenge. I understood that, with every drop of blood flowing in me, but revenge was a blade with two edges, and I would press mine into the abbot-general's throat. 'Celas started that fight, and Vasara died in it.'

'That's not what Celasian believes.' Takora shook her head. 'He thinks the vampire you call Mother killed his father, and now he's back for vengeance with a god on his side, a spear made of lightning, and an army of soldiers from the Church of Sigmar. He's not going to stop until he wins, and he *will* win. You can deny him though. Keep him from getting what he really wants. You. Go. Get on those dead horses and ride, and leave Celasian holding nothing but a ruined palace and useless, half-burnt grasslands. Leave him with nothing but impotence and ashes.'

'And victory.'

'Such a hollow thing to give your life for,' she said. 'Especially if you're supposed to be immortal.'

'Hollow.' I looked at her, filthy with ash, her neck caked with blood, her eyes filled with despair, but still pushing, still fighting. 'If it's so hollow, why did you want it badly enough to make a deal with Arvan?'

'I keep telling you. Because I thought it might end this sooner. With fewer people dead.'

'You do. And I'm starting to believe you.' I caught her chin in my hands and tilted her head back. She winced as the motion stretched the wound in her neck, but kept her eyes on me. 'You were always dangerous, Takora. Smart. I always respected you, but you went too far. My mother once told me not to make war personal. I think it's far too late for that now. What you did to me, to my family, is as personal as it gets.'

She stared back at me, frustrated, opened her mouth to argue again, but in the valley ahead of me a vampire broke through the trees. One of Magdalena's scouts. She spoke to him, then raised her hand. They were coming. Finally.

* * *

Standing behind the wide, twisted trunk of an ancient vesin tree, I readied myself for our ambush. Rill was beside me, still rubbing her eyes, but when I looked at her she just held up her bow, signalling her readiness. Takora stood on my other side, shifting uneasily. My hand was wrapped around the back of her neck, my fingers close to the bite wound I'd given her. Waiting like me for the abbot-general to arrive, but there was none of my angry eagerness in her.

I wrapped silence around us, then spread it as far as I could. Rill was working her magic too, making the shadows deeper. Other vampires with similar blessings were doing the same, hiding us from hearing and vision. When Celasian and his guard crested the last hill and looked down into the valley they would see the remains of a camp, the signs of a fight, and nothing else. As if the battle had begun here, but moved on. It was a trick that probably wouldn't have fooled Takora – she was used to our magic after decades of ambushes. Celasian lacked that experience. Perhaps today he'd learn something, right before we killed him.

We were at the end of the valley. A steep hill rose up here, studded with chunks of basalt, like broken ribs from some gigantic corpse. There were few trees on that steep slope, and I could see Celasian's guard easily when they crested the hill, men and women armoured in white, carrying banners with a lightning sigil on it. The Demigryphs they rode were fierce-looking creatures, hook-beaked and sharp-clawed, and they picked their way easily down the rough slope. There was no Celasian though.

I growled to myself. If he wasn't here, if I'd wasted all this time on a patrol, I would hang Takora upside down and drain every drop from her. Then a shadow swept over me.

It was thin in the ash and shade of the clouds. Only a tiny bit darker than the rest of the day, but my eyes picked it out and I looked up. Over our heads a griffon circled, and on its back I could see a man in white armour. Celasian, high above, and even as I

watched I saw him picking out the position of a group of zombies we'd hidden deep in the woods.

'Sigmar sends a warning!' he bellowed, my magic not reaching high enough to silence him. He levelled his spear at the newly raised soldiers and a bolt of lightning shot from it, lighting up the clearing with a sudden glare that washed away the shadows hiding us as it incinerated the zombies. I cursed and let my silence go, shouting for the vampires around me to attack.

The fanaticism of the Church soldiers had some limits. Celasian's guard took in the sudden appearance of the Rose Knights and twisted their mounts around, urging them back up the hill, their talons tearing great rents into the ground. Magdalena and her soldiers had been hiding on their mounts among the trees, waiting to ride in and cut off the escape route, but now she was leading them out at a gallop, chasing after the Demigryphs. But the hard hooves of her Nightmares struggled for purchase on the ash-covered hill, and she wasn't going to catch them.

'You didn't tell me he had a griffon,' I snarled at Takora.

'You didn't ask,' she answered, and there was a tiny hint of satisfaction in her voice. One last trap in our long war, and I thought about ending her. But Celasian was still circling overhead, and I could see him staring down at us. At me, at the woman I held.

'Rill,' I said, almost silently, too quiet for Takora to hear with her mortal ears. 'I'm going to draw him in. Try and get a shot.' She nodded and disappeared into the trees, wrapping shadows around her as she pulled out her bow. I walked out into the open, dragging Takora with me.

'Celasian!' I shouted, and he levelled his silver spear at me. Would he throw lightning at me while I held Takora? Was I fast enough to dodge it if he did? There was only one way to know. 'Looking for someone?' I shook Takora, and she almost fell, still unsteady on her feet.

Celasian swung his winged mount away, and for a minute I thought he was going to ignore me, but he guided the griffon over to a thick pillar of basalt and brought the beast down on its top. He stared down at us, a grey-haired man with a face that could have been handsome if the eyes weren't cold as ice, unfeeling and expressionless.

'You found my traitor.'

'I'm no traitor, Celasian!' Takora shouted.

'Is that what you told your men when they were drained of their blood?' he asked. 'Or did you wait until your undead allies destroyed the peace of their death and made them into monsters?'

I could feel Takora wince. She was about to shout back when I tightened my grip on her neck, just enough to prod my bite and make her hiss in pain. 'Enough.' I looked up at Celasian. He was a long way up that pillar. Rill would have to get very close to try a shot.

'Errand boy of Sigmar, what are you doing here?' I moved closer to the spire, bringing Takora with me. Keeping those pale eyes away from Rill. 'The Broken Plains belong to us, not to your Church.'

'Sigmar is the lord of the sky. Everything beneath the heavens belongs to him.'

I stopped and looked up through the ash. 'I don't see any heavens up there. Looks like you've made a mistake.'

'The heavens are everywhere, you walking corpse.' He turned his head, just for a moment, likely to look for his guard. 'Sigmar cannot make mistakes, and this land belongs to him.'

'The way it belonged to your father?'

That pulled his attention back.

'Celas had greater claim to this land than you, dead thing. And you killed him for it.'

'We killed him because he betrayed us,' I called out. 'Vasara, my mother, met with him to discuss an alliance. One he wanted

dearly. Your father was getting old, and he feared that decline. Feared it enough that when my mother refused to pass our blessed blood to him as part of the bargain, he sought to take it.'

There was a moment, a second when Celasian stared down at me with eyes that finally showed some emotion: disgust, complete and absolute. So he hadn't known the truth of what happened. Then his eyes narrowed, and the only thing in them was anger, cold as the poison that had been burned out of me.

'Shut your unclean mouth, you evil, lying beast. My father wanted no part of your cursed blood.'

'He wanted it so much he lied and betrayed to steal it,' I said. 'He wanted it so much he killed my mother for it.'

'That woman was a monster like you and she deserved to die in that fire!' Celasian shouted the words down at me. The cold disdain he'd held around himself was gone. 'I was a child, they kept me from attending the negotiations. But when I heard the noise, the shouting, the clash of blades, I ran to the tent and I saw that thing you call a mother covered in blood, her teeth dripping with it, saw her holding my father down and biting his throat!'

Covered in blood because they'd already stabbed me a dozen times.

'I saw her killing him, taking his blood!' Revulsion and anger twisted Celasian's face. 'That's why I threw the oil lamps at them, that's why I set the tent on fire, to save him from that, from her!'

Now it was my turn to go still. For my heart to pause, for me to stand like a statue beneath the falling ash. The only motion my lips, shaping my words. 'You started the fire.'

'I burned them both.' Celasian forced his features back to cold disdain. 'I knew even then that fire was the only way to cleanse your kind from the world. I have dedicated my life to the purity of heaven's white fire.' He lifted his spear high, and in the gloom I could see the sparks winding their way towards its tip like thorny rose vines made of lightning.

In my chest, my heart started beating again. Hammering inside me, making my blood race. 'You killed my mother.'

'I killed a monster. The first of many.' Celasian snapped his spear down and an arc of lightning cracked through the air at me.

I shoved Takora away, pitching her across the clearing, and threw myself to the side. Electricity snapped across my skin, sparks buzzing off my swords and the steel buckles of my armour. The heat of the bolt washed over me, and my right arm sizzled, the pain of it sudden and enormous. But I'd dodged the bolt itself, and it smashed into the ash and left a white-hot scar of molten glass where I'd stood.

I glared up at Celasian. My swords were in my hands, drawn the moment I'd landed. I flicked the right one, the bright one, and the blackened layer of skin on my arm sloughed off, falling beside me. The muscles and vessels beneath were already knitting back together, smooth brown skin running over them like water as my arm healed. The regeneration made me hungry, but my thirst for blood was much, much deeper. I stared up the basalt column of Celasian's perch, and barely noticed the snap of Rill's bow.

She'd got close. Celasian, arguing with me, had never seen her creeping up. The arrow flew from her bow, straight at his face, the only unarmoured piece of him. But right before the barbed point sank into the fanatic's eye, a flicker of blue flashed over his face and the arrow cracked off as if it had hit a wall. Some kind of blessed shield, some protection the priest had begged Sigmar for in prayer.

Celasian flinched back from the arrow, jerking the reins of his mount, and the griffon reared up, talons slashing the sky. Then it crouched, wings rising, ready to take off, and my heart beat. One hammering strike in my chest and I slammed my swords back in their sheaths and was running forwards, my blood surging through me as I raced over the ground. I hit the bottom of the

column and ricocheted upwards, my hands grabbing for holds as my feet kicked off the stone, climbing so fast I was almost flying. I could hear the griffon's wings coming down, beating against the air as the huge beast launched itself up. Faster, and I was shredding the tips of my fingers as I hurtled straight up the spire. Then I was at the top, looking up at Celasian as he rose into the air. I pulled a sword free and jumped, slashing as I went, and watched the sharp tip flash inches below the hind leg of his mount.

'You are filth, and you lie, and I will cleanse you from this world with all the fires of heaven!' Celasian shouted down as he rose higher. 'You and all your kind. I'm going to burn you, the way I burned that thing you called a mother.'

I landed on the top of the spire, and I felt my heart beat again, a sickening lurch in my chest, and I had to stop myself from throwing my sword up in the sky after him like a child having a fit. Instead I watched him disappear behind a curtain of ash, listening to the voice of my mother echoing through my head.

That thing I said about not making war personal. I think maybe you're right. Maybe it's time to make this very personal.

CHAPTER EIGHTEEN

'I found her. And someone else.'

Rill walked out from under the trees, leading Thorn. The Nightmare looked just the same as she always did, untroubled by whatever Arvan had done to make her run. But behind her, Rend walked with his head down. He'd been tricked into betraying his pack, and felt it. I reached out a hand, and he pressed his massive head against me as I stroked his ear.

'It's okay,' I told him. 'He tricked us both.'

The woods were busy around us, Orix readying the surviving Rose Knights. Celasian was gone, his Spears were gone, and the fight was gone, over before it started. Now it was time for the knights to be gone too, back to the Grey Palace. Without me, Thorn and Rend.

We were going to find Arvan before he reached the sea, and send him to Nagash.

Beside me, Takora stopped drawing lines in the ash at our feet to look at Rend and shuddered. She started drawing again before

I could say anything, finishing her crude map with the stick she held in her left hand. She'd broken the wrist of her right when I'd thrown her out of the way of the lightning, and she cradled that arm next to her.

'That's where the ship will be waiting,' she said, tossing down the stick. Takora had been more than willing to draw the map for me, once I told her that I'd no interest in killing the mortals crewing the boat. I didn't even want to see the damn boat. I wanted to catch Arvan before he reached the coast.

'You're going after him.' Magdalena looked at the map with a tactician's eye, calculating. She'd returned with her Ruin Knights empty-handed and angry. The Demigryphs couldn't gallop forever like the Nightmares, but they were faster in a sprint, and had built too much of a lead for them to catch. Which meant this whole ambush had ended up a waste of time, and time was something we didn't have.

If a 'we' existed.

Everything had been a whirlwind since Arvan had revealed his betrayal. I'd barely had time to acknowledge Magdalena's presence, much less gauge what she thought of me now. She'd given me that tiny opening at her fortress, but since then everything had mostly gone to hell. Except I knew I wasn't cursed any more, and my anger had grown into a bonfire in my heart. Arvan had killed my father, Celasian my mother, and I was going to destroy them both.

'I am,' I told her. 'He's had enough time to get a mount and get halfway there. I'm the only one that has a chance to catch him.'

She nodded, looking through the trees, in the direction of the distant sea. 'You would have had him, if you had gone after him right after you recovered.'

Nyssa. My mother's voice was a warning, ringing through my head as my anger tried to break free and lash out. *She's testing you.*

Magdalena was always testing me, and damn me if I had time for it now. Only Vasara's warning kept me from grabbing her by the throat. 'I would have. But then I would have lost my Rose Knights.'

'I know,' Magdalena said. 'Which would have left me here alone when Celasian and his guard showed up. Sigmar's dog might have taken two Kastelai instead of one, had you not made that decision. One I wouldn't have believed you would have made until this day.' She finally looked at me. 'Nyssa Volari. Do you truly claim the Rose Throne, and the Broken Plains?'

I stared back, hesitating, but I knew my answer. 'I do.'

'Then I would pledge fealty to you,' she said. 'Not because you might have saved me from Celasian. Not because I know you are not cursed, and that if we met in challenge again you'd beat me. But because when you had every reason to give in to rage, to the need for revenge, you did not. You showed me that despite the unfortunate circumstances of your birth into your second life, you can mature.'

I desperately wanted to say something snide, but I buried the words and nodded. I drew my bright sword and held it out in front of me, blade facing her. She knelt, and reached out with her sword hand to grip my blade tight.

'I am Magdalena, Kastelai of the Crimson Keep, Mistress of Ruinview, servant of Nagash. I pledge myself now to serve you, Nyssa Volari, ruler of the Broken Plains, Queen of the Rose Throne, from now until the final death welcomes us.'

She opened her hand, and I could see the blood pooling there. 'Lady Magdalena, I accept your fealty to me, Nyssa Volari, Queen of the Rose Throne.' My tongue almost stumbled on the word 'Queen'. Princess had felt like an insult. Queen felt...

Like too much? You will grow into it, Nyssa.

'I hope so,' I thought, and raised the sword up, kissing the spot

where Magdalena had gripped it, licking the blood off the steel. Then I slid the sword back into its sheath, and gestured for Magdalena to rise. The Rose Knights and Ruin Knights crashed their fists into the armour over their hearts in a thunderous salute, but I raised a hand, silencing them.

'You did not pledge to me at an easy time.'

'I do not think any of us are going to have an easy time for quite a while,' Magdalena said. 'But Nagash bless me, this feels right. We were not meant to be divided, to be picked off one by one by the mortal servant of an interfering god. Let us at least fall fighting together.'

'Better yet, let's not fall at all,' I said. She nodded, but I knew that fatalism still infected her. I didn't care. I'd had my taste of mortality and hated it. Now I was going to force-feed it to my enemies. 'I have to go. Now. I'll be back as soon as I can, but Celasian will move against us as soon as the rest of his soldiers arrive. We have to be ready. Take the knights and the dead you raised back to the Grey Palace, then send emissaries to the others. They must join us.'

'I will,' she said. 'They probably won't listen.'

'I know. I'll deal with them.' Without that poison in me. 'And when you get to the Grey Palace, seize Shadas. Make sure he can't escape, but don't harm him. I'll handle him myself.'

'It will be done. Shall I attend to preparing the palace's defences?'

I almost grinned, but fought to keep my face as serious as hers. My father had always admired and hated the way Magdalena could tell him what must be done with her suggestions. 'Of course.'

She nodded, then looked at Captain Takora. The mortal was watching us with dull eyes. 'And her?'

Her. I frowned at Takora, thinking. My hate for Arvan and Celasian had shoved my feelings for her down. She'd always been an enemy, and she'd been the one bargaining with Arvan, even if she didn't realise it was him. But.

'Takora.' I walked over to her, deliberately keeping myself slow. I watched her straighten up, raising her dirty face high. Ready to die. She had her own kind of honour, one she'd fought for over the long, grinding years of this war. Part of me wanted to see her survive, but it couldn't entirely overcome the part that wanted to see her suffer for what she'd done. 'You claim you did what you did to save the lives of others. Including people not under your protection, my people. But you also plotted my father's death, and nearly killed me. There must be consequences. Give me your hand.'

Takora took a breath and held out her left hand, the uninjured one. What was she expecting? For me to bite her wrist, drain the rest of her blood? After my healing, I was hungry enough. But when I took her hand, I didn't raise it to my mouth. Instead I held it gently. 'But they'll be the consequences that you bought.' I twisted her hand suddenly, too fast for her to move with it, and the joint snapped with an ugly crunch. Takora made a noise, the start of a scream, but she locked her teeth and stopped it. She stood before me, swaying, somehow not falling despite the pain. She stared into my eyes, still defiant.

'If you won't use your own hands to strike your enemies, you don't need them,' I said. 'Think about that, as you go.'

'Go?' she asked, her voice tight with pain. 'Go where?'

I shrugged. 'Wherever you want, captain. Go to Gowyn, where Celasian waits. Go to Maar, beside my Grey Palace. Or go to the wastes beyond the Broken Plains and explain to the nomads what happened to the Biting Flames. Go wherever you want, captain, and face the consequences of your failures.'

Thorn's hooves cut through the ash as we left a trail across the plains, heading to the sea.

Rend ran beside me, surging through the brown grass and the drifts of grey. The dire wolf would stop occasionally to lower his nose, just to shake his head and snarl. There was only the bitter, greasy scent of the falling ash. Temero had covered Arvan's trail, and all we had was my memory of Takora's crude map.

It had to be enough.

I leaned forwards over Thorn's neck, urging her to go faster, but she was already at a gallop. We were tearing across the flat-lands that spread between the hills and the sea, but Arvan had a long head start. If he reached his boat before us, he'd be gone. If he was, I thought my heart might burst. We had to go faster.

I shut my eyes, concentrating on the beating of my heart, my connection to Thorn and to Rend. I could feel their spirits bound to mine, feel them more clearly than I ever had before. There had been a shift since Shadas' poison had been purged from me. I had always been fast, but I moved faster once I began to take the blood of Takora's soldiers. Faster than ever before. When I spread my silence, it went further, covered a wider area around me. Now this. I'd always been connected with animal spirits – similar to Arvan's ability to control them, but different. I could raise them and I could bond with them, and now that magic felt stronger too.

Some effect of the poison? Of its cure? Of touching true death and coming back? I didn't know.

They said you were poisoned with me. My body. Maybe you have taken some of my power into you.

I shuddered. 'That's awful. The thought of consuming you.'

In my head, Mother laughed. *I forget you don't remember being mortal. Children consume their parents. That's how mortal life works.*

'Mortality is awful,' I told her, then reached out with my magic, through the bonds that connected me with Thorn. I reached into her body and found her heart. Touching it with my magic, I made it give a slow, shuddering beat. Then another. Until it was moving

on its own and her cold, clotted blood turned liquid and flowed. Below me, Thorn shot forwards, her speed almost doubling.

I laughed. The wind of her running was tearing my hair from its braids, sending it streaming behind me, and it was like we were flying. I wanted speed, and now I had it, and I laughed until I caught the mournful distant howl behind us. Rend.

I reached out for him, through the bond that connected us. The distance made it harder, but I better understood what I was doing now, and I felt his dead heart twitch into motion. Soon he was catching up to us, flying through the ash like a storm wind, and he howled as he came. I could feel the hunger for lifeblood growing in me, the cost of this magic, but we were streaking across the Broken Plains now. A blur of motion through the murky day, heading towards the sea, towards vengeance.

We were still too late.

On the beach, the churning waters washed across the sand, taking away the ash. The cove where the boat was meant to be waiting was empty, and for a moment I wondered if Takora had lied to me, but no. I could see it in the grey water, a small, single-masted sloop, sailing away.

'No,' I said, to the waves and the gulls and the grey sky. 'No.'

There were no other boats. Nothing on this coast for miles, just driftwood and sand, stones and ash. Nothing. My need went through me, through the bonds I'd just deepened, and Thorn tossed her mane and whickered, the noise a hollow sound that startled the gulls. But Rend raised his head, smelled the air, then started down the beach.

'What?' I snapped, but my magic hadn't changed like that, I couldn't talk to him like Arvan could. So I followed, until I caught the scent too. Death, tangled in with the smell of salt and ash. I followed Rend up the beach until I saw it. A monster lay on its side on the beach, the waves lapping at its sleek, dead flanks.

Some kind of massive shark, its streamlined body as big around as Thorn, dead for days at least. The gulls had picked out its eyes and torn at the flesh of its sickle-shaped fins, while crabs crawled in and out between the rows of massive triangular teeth, patiently taking the beast apart.

I slid off Thorn and touched Rend's head. 'Good boy,' I whispered, then walked over to the corpse. I put my hands on it, and reached out with my magic. The traces of its spirit were weak but they were there, and I reached with my power and caught them. I teased them out like threads and wove them through the body, until it gave a twitch. Its body shuddered, and the gulls shrieked and ran across the sand. The great shark moved its massive tail, and the wet sand hissed around the corpse as it righted itself and twisted its great head towards me. In its empty eye sockets two wisps of light gleamed, like emerald candle flames. The shark opened its huge mouth wide, and the shadows behind the countless lines of sharp teeth seethed with crabs and worms.

'Welcome to your second life,' I said, considering the view of its dark, ravaged throat. 'I am Nyssa, and you are now Maw, and I need you to do something for me.'

Maw swam beneath the waves, her great tail moving through the water with steady, tireless strokes. I held tight to the fin on her back with one hand, the other pressed over my nose to keep the sea from filling my dry, empty lungs. The water was dark and shapes swam beneath us, dark shadows much larger than Maw. Whatever they were, they were not drawn to the zombie shark's scent. We were left alone as Maw closed on the sloop tacking slowly along the coast.

When we caught up it was close to night, and the warm water around us was growing dark, except for the gleaming red-and-yellow wake the boat was trailing behind. Sparktides, the sailors

called them, tiny creatures that flashed when disturbed. I kept Maw deep enough not to trouble them, and followed the trail of false fire to the shadow of the sloop.

We came up below it, Maw matching its speed, and I touched the wooden bottom. Almost. In my chest my heart beat faster. I needed to get out of the water and onto the deck above, but I lacked the claws of my father. I wouldn't be able to climb the boat's side. So instead I used my magic to stir the remnants of Maw's heart. The great muscle beat, and a dozen crabs scuttled out through the slits of her gills, disturbed by the motion. Then Maw dived.

I grasped her sharp-scaled hide, holding tight as Maw swam down into the dark, paused, then started up, tail beating hard against the water. We rose fast, faster, until Maw exploded out of the surface, sparktide flashing into life around us.

Using all the speed I'd given her, we arced high out of the water, flying through spray that gleamed like fire around us. The sloop's deck was below me, and it was easy to launch myself off Maw's back and land on the wooden boards. Maw fell back into the waves with a sound like thunder as I straightened up, dripping, beside the sloop's mast.

I stood in the centre of the deck, lit by the shifting glow of the lanterns swinging from the rigging. A few sailors stared at me, open-mouthed, but they backed away when I unsheathed my blades.

'Nyssa.' Arvan stood at the prow of the ship. He'd got rid of the complicated braids of a nomad, pulling his long hair back into one simple tail bound by a strip of cloth, and on his face he wore round discs of smoked glass, hiding his black eyes. 'I'm surprised, and I'm not. You've always refused to know when you're beaten.' He shifted his weight, and I could see that he had his spear in one hand, the butt of it resting on the deck, the gleaming point

aimed at the sky. This one wouldn't throw lightning at me, but I knew the strength of the man who wielded it.

It wasn't nearly enough to stop me.

'Arvan.' I spun my blades, doing it slow, not letting him see my recovered speed. 'It seems we're both bad at endings. You told me what you'd done to me, what you did to my father, and then you left without finishing me. Ending me was something you should've done when you had the chance.'

'Maybe.' He shifted his spear to both hands. 'But that wasn't the deal I made. Takora wanted a sacrifice she could serve to Celasian. Corsovo was already dead, and he was too dangerous anyway. So it had to be you.'

'Me,' I said. 'Not dangerous?' I stayed in my spot, letting my senses take everything in. The rocking of the boat. The swaying of the lights. The breathing of the crew. They were staying back, not interfering.

'Don't get me wrong, princess.' He wasn't moving either, just watching me from behind those blank circles of glass. 'You're a true killer. Or at least you were. Corsovo taught you that. But he couldn't teach you how to be clever like him. And even though you have her voice in your head, you don't have Vasara's intelligence. That's why you were never dangerous to me.'

'Never?' I spun my swords around in a slow circle. 'If I never seemed a threat to you, it was because I believed you had some shred of honour. That you served the Rose Throne like me. But now I know the truth of your betrayal, and you should know this. Because of you, the Rose Throne now belongs to me. Because of you, I am queen. And I am very, very dangerous to you.'

Yes, but you're not charging in yet. Because you know that is what he wants you to do.

'I do know,' I said, almost silent, but Arvan tilted his head and smiled at me.

'Is she telling you to be careful, queen?' Arvan spoke the title mockingly. 'Probably. She knows you're not that smart either.' Arvan took one step towards me, then stopped again. 'It's too bad the nomads killed her. Corsovo was charming, and he knew how to manipulate people, but she was the only smart one of you, the only one I respected.' He took another slow step, stopped, and I had to fight the urge to throw myself at him. Was he counting on getting his spear down, hoping that I would spit myself on its point for him? I could be on him before he got it between us, my swords tearing at him before he could stop me. But I held myself still, suspicious.

'When my mortal father died, my family tore itself apart, everyone fighting to see who was the strongest and the mean-est. Those were the only things they valued in a leader. They didn't care if they put a fool in charge, as long as they knew how to use a spear.' Arvan took a step to the side, starting to circle me, and I moved just enough to keep him in front of me. 'That's why I left. Why would I want to lead them? Idiots, fighting over who got more wasteland to feed their goats. I left that life behind and went to the Grey Palace because you Kastelai were supposed to be ancient and evil and wise.' He shook his head. 'But then it turned out you were just the same – a group of fools fighting over worth-less land, choosing your leaders by how well they could swing a sword. Gods. Why couldn't you have been part of the Legion of Night, or at least the Legion of Blood? Why did you have to be Kastelai, a bloodline cursed with stupidity and honour?'

'Is that what you want?' I said. 'To join with a different blood-line?' One that didn't care about honour, I thought, watching him. There was something about the way he was holding his spear. It was subtle, but he was gripping it differently, as if he had some-thing concealed in his right hand.

'I want to live, Queen Volari,' he said, still slowly circling.

Moving so that if I came straight at him, the way I usually did, my left side would be open. What was he hiding? A knife, for when I closed the distance? A small knife wouldn't stop me, even if he jammed it between my ribs.

'You're all going to die here. The fight was decided years ago, at Ire Crossing. It's all just been a slow downward spiral since.' He kept moving, ignoring the crew crammed into the stern of the boat, staring at us wide-eyed. 'That abbot-general is going to kill you all and burn your teeth on his shrine. I tried telling Corsovo that, but he didn't listen to me, the smart one who knew what was happening. He wouldn't listen to me because I wasn't Kastelai. I had never walked the halls of the Crimson Keep, so I would never be as good as any of you. No matter how smart I was, no matter how well I fought. I'd always be lesser to him, to you, to all of you.' Anger and hate twisted Arvan's face, and I knew that this was the truth of his betrayal, this jealousy of being denied the name and rank of Kastelai.

'I was smarter than you all, but did King Corsovo listen to me? No. He listened to you, his Kastelai pet, even though your stupidity is outmatched only by your arrogance. Even though you got Vasara killed.'

I moved then. I couldn't not move. My blood was roaring through me, my heart pounding like a mortal's. But I was also my mother's daughter, and I knew what she would say. So I started towards him, a blur of motion, and then stopped when I'd only covered two steps. Froze in place as fast as I'd started moving, but it was enough. Arvan shifted his right hand and I saw what he held. A stiletto, long and thin. He hid it again when he realised my feint, but it was too late. Not because I'd seen his hidden weapon, but because I had caught the faint scent of the dark substance that covered its thin blade. That same ugly smell I'd caught in the blood that he had given me in the amphorae. The smell he

claimed was a side effect of Shadas' preservation spell. The smell of the poison that had killed my father.

He wasn't trying to trick me into drinking it any more. This time he meant to stab it straight into my heart.

'Arvan,' I said softly. 'You can stop trying to make me mad. It's already worked.' Then I really did move.

I didn't charge straight at him. I spiralled in, circling to his left. Arvan tried to spin with me, but he was too slow. I caught the shaft of his spear with one sword, moving with him as he parried me away, turning his strength against him. Using the momentum of his block, I spun behind him, and with my other blade I stabbed three blows into his back that hit like lightning. The point of my bright sword punched through his leather armour, his skin, and into muscle, scraping off the bone beneath. The first two cuts did little, bouncing off vertebrae and his ribs, but as Arvan lifted his arm up to sweep the stiletto back I drove my sword in, letting the point slide until it lodged in the deepest part of his armpit. Then I drove it deeper. I could hear the crunch of bone, the snap of tendons, and Arvan's arm lost its strength, unmoored from the heavy muscles of his back. It was easy then to slide away and slam the hilt of my other sword into the back of his wrist.

The blow made him drop the stiletto, and I slapped the weapon with my bright sword, sent it spinning over the rail to fall into the dark water below. Then I danced back, getting out of the way as Arvan slashed his spear point at my face. I took my stance, staring at him. He'd lost his dark glasses trying to strike me, and I could see the lamplight gleaming in his black eyes.

'I have a fortune in realmstone,' he said, not to me. 'Help me take her down, and you'll all be rich.'

One of the men packed into the back of the boat spoke, his voice wavering. 'I think if we move, sir, she'll kill us all. Good luck with your fortune.'

I spun both my blades, baring my teeth at him. 'No more tricks, Arvan. It's just you and me and steel, and I call challenge.' I didn't give him a chance to answer. As soon as the word left my lips, I was on him, blades bright and dark slicing through the air so fast they barely made a sound.

I cut him. Arms and legs, belly and back, face and throat. Ten cuts, fifty, a hundred. A whirlwind of slashes, the edges of my swords slipping through his armour as if it were water and parting his flesh. I carved off the edges of his ears, the tip of his nose, his lips, took pieces of his hair away by slicing off parts of his scalp. I took his fingers and made him drop his spear, I opened ladders of cuts up every limb. I carved my anger into him, and it happened so fast he could do nothing but stumble back, his flesh flying from him like ash blowing off a stone. I was taking him apart, and I would have done it until he was a bloody skeleton, but he backed into the sloop's rail and threw himself over, diving away from me into the sea.

I came forwards, sheathed my swords and then dived off the top of the rail into the water even as I reached out with my magic. I saw him sinking, surrounded by a glittering wake of sparktide. That light was fading, though, and I might have lost him in the depths, but another shape swam through the dark, wreathed in tendrils of glowing red. Maw surged through the water towards Arvan, and snapped her great teeth shut on his legs.

He twisted in the shark's grip, pounding on the jaws that held him, but Maw didn't notice. She turned in the water, heading towards me, and that's when I felt Arvan trying to break my control. I was ready for that this time. I clamped down on the zombie shark's spirit, shutting Arvan out, and the beast brought him to me.

I met them in the darkness, lit only by the sparktide that swirled around us like red stars. Arvan tried to slap me away, but I ducked

his maimed hands and clutched at him, holding what was left of his hair in one hand and his shoulder with another.

It was too bad we were underwater. I couldn't ask him how clever he was feeling, couldn't ask him how it felt to have mortality come crashing down on him. But I'd heard enough of him talking. Forever. I clamped my mouth to the side of his neck, buried my teeth into vessels that lay there, and pulled every drop of blood out of him. I took back the blessing my father had given him, took back his immortality, and when I was finally finished I told Maw to let go. Weighed down by his armour, the withered husk that had been Arvan sank into the darkness, his dull grey eyes the last thing to vanish into the black.

CHAPTER NINETEEN

Temero still glowed on the horizon, a sullen red that mirrored the dawn spreading on the other side of the sky. The ash had stopped falling, though, and the air was clear except for grey veils pulled up from the thin drifts covering the ground by the hot wind blowing in from the wastes. I rode Thorn through those veils, heading for the stone tower of Splitrock.

When I'd left the sea, sending Maw off into the sparktide, I had to make a decision – to ride straight back to the Grey Palace, or to swing back to Jirrini's holding, where I'd failed so miserably before. Remembering that, how I'd fallen into the black wondering if vermin would strip my flesh from my bones to leave me truly dead, I'd turned Thorn towards the wastes.

The only solution for fear was anger.

I never taught you that. Neither did your father.

'Life taught me that,' I said as I reined Thorn in, Rend falling in beside me. 'My second life.'

On the edge of my sight, almost lost in the growing light and

the distance, there were people moving towards the base of the stone spire, making their way to the narrow road that wound up to the gate that stood on its top. The emissaries I'd told Magdalena to send. With a tap on the reins, I started Thorn moving towards them.

I was going to speak to Jirrini this time, and offer her a choice. She wasn't going to like either option, but my second life had also taught me that choices were often like that.

'You killed him fast.'

Rill was with the Ruin Knights Magdalena had sent, and she rode out to greet me. I was halfway up, and they were coming down, their faces hard. Her eyes were on me as she came close – intent, hungry.

'Yes,' I said. 'But I still made him suffer.'

'Good.' Rill looked away from me, looked away from everything, staring out past the edge of the narrow road to the wastes that spread beyond Splitrock, and whispered a short prayer, something twisted together from the traditions of the nomads and the Crimson Keep. I'd never heard her pray before. Erant had been the one to do that for us.

Damn you, Arvan. I couldn't make you suffer enough.

'Did they turn you away again?' I said, pushing the thought aside. Arvan had got off too easy, but he was done. Let Nagash sort him into one of his hells.

'Not even that. The gate is shut, and there's no answer.' Rill shook her head. 'It seems Lady Jirrini has gone to ground.'

'Underground,' I said.

'Exactly. I was going to go down to the crevice you tried and see if we could get in that way.'

'They'll have sealed it after my visit.' Trevin would have told Jirrini I was there, after giving me time to go. 'Besides, I'm done

with sneaking in the back. If I'm to be queen, she can open her door for me.'

Rill didn't ask me my plan. She just moved her Nightmare aside so I could pass. The Ruin Knights did the same, all of them nodding to me, their eyes evaluating. They'd seen their mistress beat me. Magdalena had told them the curse was a lie, and they'd seen me fight the mortals. Judging from the space they gave me, I think they believed the story of Arvan's treachery and my recovery.

I passed them and went towards the gate. It loomed above me, silent, desolate, and I returned its silence with my own as I measured its size. Then I led Thorn to the front of the gate and told her to wait. I backed away, moving down the road until I had enough space, then sprinted forwards.

The world blurred as I raced towards the gate, then leapt. I hit the saddle on Thorn's back with one foot and pushed off. I sailed up, slapping the top of the gate with my hand as I passed over it. I dropped to the other side and turned back to the gate, reaching for the bar that held it fast. Then I heard a scrambling sound from the other side, and something huge sailed overhead. My swords were halfway out before I realised it was Rend.

'Find their hidden entrance,' I told him as I pushed the gate open. Rend tilted his head, the red light in his eye sockets tightening to points, but he didn't move, and I wished that I'd taken Arvan's ability to control animals when I'd taken his blood. Instead I'd have to rely on my own powers.

I crouched close to the ground and breathed deep. I took in the scents of Rill and the other vampires, their Nightmares and Rend's musky scent of decay. Buried beneath all that was the thin scent of Trevin. I rose and followed it through the empty holding, past the guardhouse and storage buildings, until it finally led me to an ancient stable, half-collapsed and abandoned. Inside, the trail led to a blank stone wall.

Excellent, Mother said. *Now, how do you open it?*

That, unfortunately, took hours to figure out, and by the time it was done my heart was beating a steady rhythm of fury in my chest.

They were waiting for us beyond the door. A line of Knights of Plenty, grim-faced and silent, but they did not draw their swords. Trevin stood at the front, blocking the narrow hall that stretched behind him, a long, low passage designed for defence. Or collapse, as I noted that the arches supporting the ceiling all had rings set in their keystones and a chain linking them together. At least they hadn't pulled the roof down on us.

'I'm going to see her,' I said.

'She doesn't–' Trevin stopped speaking when he felt the touch of my dark sword's point against his right eyeball. When he blinked in surprise, his eyelid tapped the black metal and snapped back.

'I'm going to see your mistress,' I said again, letting my anger fill my voice. 'And if you want to continue seeing her through two eyes, you'll get out of my way.'

He stared at me, very still, until a voice echoed up the hall. 'Enough. Let her through.' Jirrini's voice, and I had my sword back in its scabbard before Trevin could blink again.

'You seem recovered,' he said, touching his eye. A tiny speck of red marked it.

'I'm much better,' I said, and pointed down the hall. He took the hint and the knights formed into something like an honour guard and escorted us to the stairs twisting downwards to Jirrini's hold.

'Is it a trap?' I said silently as I walked.

I don't know. Annoyance ran through my mother's words. *I normally wouldn't think so. Jirrini always had her secrets, but she was prickly about her honour. Or at least the appearance of her honour. She wouldn't attempt something as crass as an ambush*

unless she were desperate. Which she is. There was a long pause as Vasara thought it through. *Be ready. Jirrini fears true death, and if she thinks that's what you're offering her she's capable of anything. But you should know that there are a few things that she fears even more...*

The stairs corkscrewed down through the stone until they opened into a chamber that almost matched the great hall of the Grey Palace in size, but certainly overmatched it in opulence. The walls were panels of red sandstone, intricately sculpted and lit from behind. In its centre rested a great chair carved to look like a goblet, brimming with cushions of crimson silk. Jirrini sat upon them, but not comfortably. She leaned forwards, staring at me with a frown.

'This is the second time you have broken into my hold, Nyssa,' she said, her voice cold.

'This was the second time you tried to deny me entry.' I walked to stand in front of her, gesturing to the rest of my retinue to stay behind. Jirrini's guards were behind her, not her whole house, but the best fighters of her Knights of Plenty. They stayed back, leaving the centre of the room to their mistress, so I met her alone – except for Rend, who stalked behind me like a hungry shadow. 'And the second time I've let myself in. That doesn't seem to bode well for your cunning plan of hiding like a gut-cut dog.'

'At least I have a plan. What is yours?' She shook her head, her carefully arranged hair gleaming in the crimson light. 'To see us all dead in battle before your cursed blood rots you from the inside?'

My heart thumped in my chest and I bared my teeth in a smile. 'No.' Then I crossed the floor to her chair, settling into the cushions beside her. In the time it took me to do so, Trevin had started to move forward to stop me, but he was barely halfway to his mistress before I'd wrapped one hand in Jirrini's dark hair and tipped

her head back. I leaned forwards, my teeth close to her neck, and slowed myself, so that my words were clear in her ear. 'My plan is to kill those who seek to destroy the Rose Throne. *My* throne. And I've already started.'

I leaned back from her, letting her go. I could see the anger in her eyes, but she held herself still, not lunging for me with her teeth or the knives I knew she'd hidden in her gown. Instead she raised one hand, holding it out to Trevin, who stopped a sword length away.

'What has happened?' she said, her voice perfectly calm.

'I wasn't cursed. Neither was my father.' I leaned back in her chair, my armour brushing her gown, ignoring her predatory stillness. 'Arvan used some kind of necromantic poison on us both. He did it for Takora, promising that he'd destroy us and our kingdom in exchange for an escape from Celasian's attack. And because he couldn't stand not being Kastelai.' I picked up one of the cushions that covered Jirrini's throne and spun it in my hands. It was amazingly soft. 'Arvan betrayed my father, and me. He broke his promises to us and was a traitor to the Rose Throne. So I drained him of every drop of blessed blood he had and destroyed him. The way I'll destroy anyone else seeking to betray me or my throne.'

However cautious Jirrini could be, she was no coward. She faced me when she spoke. 'Your throne. You claim an inheritance that none of us recognise. If you want to call your maker Father, that was between you and him. But we're not mortals, and we don't pass power that way. You had a chance to prove your worth, and you failed when Magdalena beat you.'

My blood flowed faster, but I kept my anger in check. 'Lady Magdalena has pledged herself to me, and acknowledged me queen. You'll do the same. Now, or when you lie at my feet after I've cut you down.'

'Is that it then?' Jirrini drew herself up. 'Obey you, or face you in challenge?'

'Is that not the way of the Kastelai?' I said softly.

'No.' She shook her head. 'You've been with us for over a century, and you still don't understand our traditions. You've the mind of a child, and the understanding of one. We didn't battle to determine that Corsovo would be king. We chose him. Because we knew he'd be the best among us to do it, to hold us together. You might be a great fighter, but you're no leader. The only thing I would get in pledging my blood to you is the chance to be burned on one of Celasian's pyres.'

My hands were on my sword hilts, ready to show her what kind of death her refusal would earn her. But I heard my mother's voice in my head, and I didn't draw. Instead I spoke, my voice a whisper between us.

'Remember the ravine, Lady Jirrini. Remember when you fell there, fighting the orruks.'

'What do you know of that?' Her voice was almost as quiet as mine, but there was a thread of fear laced deep within it. 'That happened before Corsovo brought you to the Crimson Keep.'

'Mother told me. About how she thought you were dead until she heard your screams. About how they spent hours digging you out from under dead orruks.'

'She told you that story?'

'Not before she died,' I said. 'After, though…'

'You're mad,' she hissed. 'A mad child, pretending to be queen.'

'I'm not pretending anything,' I told her. 'But I am mad. I am furious, and I am your queen, and you and your house owe me your service and I will have it.' I made myself go quiet again, my words just for her. 'I need the blood you've hoarded here, Lady Jirrini, and I need your Knights of Plenty. The supplies I can take, but the knights are loyal to you. If I challenge you and kill you, they may not serve me. So, I'll do as my mother suggests and use diplomacy. You can fulfil the oaths you gave to the Rose Throne and keep your honour. Or you can refuse, and I will challenge you, and beat you. But I won't kill you. I'll bury you in one of these caves instead.'

Her eyes were wide, and a spark of red burned in their depths. Terrified and furious. 'You wouldn't–'

'I'll bury you,' I said again, 'and tell your people that when we win, they can go dig you out. They'll fight for me then, because they'll be fighting for you.'

'You'll die, and–'

'I won't,' I said. 'You'll be dug out in a few days. That's not so long, though it is longer than you were trapped in that ravine. Buried alive, crushed in darkness, alone and screaming.'

Her hand moved towards a fold of her gown, and my hand was on hers, holding it still. I could see the glint of the blade she'd grasped. 'Is this your challenge, Lady Jirrini? Are we going to fight?' I pulled the blade out of her hand, held it up between us, a sharp sliver of metal. 'I've told you how that ends. With you buried. Waiting.'

Jirrini glared at the blade, but the red spark in her eyes was fading, her mouth twisting into a frown of frustration. 'I am not challenging you.'

'Then you're pledging yourself to me.' I stood and flipped the knife towards Trevin, who plucked it out of the air. 'And you're not dying on a spear. We're going to take those mortals apart, show them that the Broken Plains belong to the Kastelai.'

'So you say.' Jirrini looked at me. 'What does Vasara say?'

I listened to my mother, and buried my smile. 'She says what do you care? You never liked her.'

'I never did. I feared her. All those monsters in the Crimson Keep, and I feared *her*.' Jirrini stood, looking into my eyes. Peering,

as if she could see through them, like windows. 'You're probably mad. But if she is in there... then maybe.'

She turned and looked at Trevin. 'Get the rest of the house. I have to pledge myself.'

'Maybe what?' I asked, as he bowed and strode away.

'Maybe Celasian will be the one to burn.'

CHAPTER TWENTY

I watched Jirrini lead her house out of Splitrock, a line of Nightmare-mounted vampires armoured in scarlet and gold, carrying banners showing roses and blood-filled cups.

'Impressive,' Rill said, moving up beside me, ignoring the low growl Rend gave her.

It was. The Knights of Plenty were greater in number than the Rose Knights. Especially now, after Arvan's betrayal. But…

Not enough.

'Not enough,' I echoed. 'So we get more.'

'Salvera.' Rill said the name as if it hurt her mouth. 'What are you going to do with him? Whisper in his ear, like you did with Jirrini, and convince him not to be a bloody monster?'

'No,' I said, then reached out with my magic to Rend, to Thorn and to Rill's Nightmare. I moved their hearts and gifted them the speed we'd need to cross the plains in a night and a day. 'Just the opposite.'

* * *

Bite Harbour had been a ruin since long before we arrived on the Broken Plains, an ancient keep half tumbled into the sea. Now its crumbling stones were marked with smears of blood, and the cold air spilling from the empty hollow of its entrance reeked of corruption: a stink strong enough to overwhelm the smell of the sea.

We reined in before the ruin, and below us the sea churned, a dark cauldron of waves in the semicircle of the ancient harbour. The docks had fallen apart long ago, and the waves crashed against their skeletal remains, making a sound like thunder.

Sound and stench and growing dark, but none of it mattered. I didn't need to hear Rend's warning growl to feel the presence of Salvera's feral house around us, the touch of their hungry eyes on our throats. They were gathered in the shadows and behind the broken stones, wrapped in their magic and malice, waiting.

Waiting for their master, I was certain.

Are you sure you know what you're doing? Mother asked, and at the same time Rill whispered, 'I hope you know what you're doing.'

'I know exactly what I'm doing,' I said as I dismounted Thorn and handed her reins to Rill. She took them, frowning, but led both Nightmares away from the crumbling cliff edge then nocked an arrow. I couldn't shed Vasara though.

You want to fight, she said as I drew my swords and stepped towards the empty black of the door. *So does he. You're going to have to spill his blood, but after...*

She stopped speaking as the shadows around us split and Salvera's house revealed themselves. Vampires stood on broken walls, clung to battered battlements, hung from arches with clawed, bat-like feet. All were marked with the signs of the beast, their faces twisted into muzzles or stretched out like rats, their bodies covered with fur or scales, their fangs enormous, their nails long claws. They were the children of Salvera's blood, and if there was a cursed line among the Kastelai of the Broken Plains, it was his.

They waited, silent, malevolent, ravenous. A house of monsters, and I wanted them, each and every one.

'After, they'll be mine,' I told her silently. 'All of them.' A piece of darkness moved in the gate, becoming a man with the face of a wolf, carrying a scythe coated in rust and gore. 'Salvera included.'

'Have you come to surrender, princess?' Salvera's voice was a purr, his words smooth despite their passage through the fangs that filled his jaws. 'To give yourself to me? You should. The strength in my blood might be enough to drive off your curse.'

'There is no curse,' I said. 'Only betrayal, and I've been settling that issue, traitor by traitor.' I stared into the vampire's rabid eyes. 'You're next, Lord Salvera. Give up your pride, your rage, your stupidity, and swear yourself to me, Queen of the Rose Throne, or face my challenge.'

'Queen of the Rose Throne.' Salvera didn't stop circling me like a wolf. 'Have you already given up on the pretence of holding the throne for your father?'

'If I can bring back Corsovo, I will,' I said, turning with him, always facing him. 'But until then, I rule the Broken Plains, and no mortal or vampire will challenge me.'

He spun on his heel, circling back the other way, yellow eyes on me, each one marked with a red spark. 'No?' he asked, his voice still smooth. 'I brought none of the beasts for you to control this time, princess, no dire wolves or vargheists to turn on me. When you fight me now, you'll be by yourself. You didn't do well the last time I saw you fight alone. And Magdalena is nowhere near the fight you'll find in me.'

I kept moving with him, my blades still held low, easy in my grip. 'Do you challenge me?'

He stopped his circling and faced me, his scythe gripped in both hands like a grim promise. 'To surrender, or death.'

'Fight me, then,' I said, taking my stance. 'And make your choice.'

He snarled, his eyes on me, the red in their depths brighter.

Have a care. Salvera is mad, but he is Kastelai, and you've touched his pride. He'll bring forth the beast, and kill himself to cut you down.

'I know.' Leaning forwards, I met Salvera's eyes and pulled back my lips, matching his fanged snarl with my own. 'I'm counting on it.'

When Salvera came, he came fast. He was a blur of motion, and his scythe cut through the air like a whirlwind, every blow powerful enough to shatter my swords and then cleave me in two. His ferocity matched his strength and I was driven back as Salvera charged forwards, unrelenting. Forced to move away, blocking and weaving as I searched desperately for an opening, I almost forgot that in all his madness Salvera was clever too.

The heel of my boot scraped over the edge of the cliff. The wind howled up from the waves in the harbour far below, whipped my hair around me as Salvera swung again, a great arcing cut that would have bitten through my armour, my flesh and my bones to send me over the edge in pieces. But while the Kastelai was fast, he wasn't nearly as fast as I was now.

I sprang up, and Salvera's scythe sliced through the air beneath my boot heels as I slammed a fist down on one of his shoulders. I shoved hard against him, using him to vault through the air as I pushed him towards the edge he'd tried to send me over.

My boots hit the ground and I spun. Salvera stood teetering on the edge, fighting to shift back, and I moved towards him. One kick, and he'd have fallen into the thrashing waters below.

Instead, I grabbed his hair and sent him sprawling as I spun away, my blades raised. 'What are you playing at, Lord Mad Dog?' I asked, my voice a purr. 'I thought this was supposed to be a challenge?'

What are you doing? You can't play with him like you did Arvan! He's dangerous!

'I know,' I said, as Salvera lunged to his feet. 'That's why I'm trying not to kill him.'

Mother never had a chance to answer that. Salvera charged, and we were fighting again, spinning across the damp stone as the other vampires watched. They were waiting for blood. So I gave it to them.

Salvera's scythe whipped past me and I ducked beneath it, the great blade taking a few strands of my hair as I moved in, not out, so the edge of my dark sword could slide along the outside of the Kastelai's thigh, below the ragged edge of his rust-and-blood-splotched chain mail. I opened up a cut on his leg and blood sprayed out, thick and cold. Then I was gone before Salvera could bring his scythe back around. But he let go of the weapon with one hand and slashed his claws across my face. They carved furrows across my forehead and nose, just missing my eye. I felt my blood splash out and then the cuts were closing, healing shut in seconds. We both stopped, looking at each other. First blood on both sides, but my wounds were gone already, the only trace of them the blood on Salvera's nails. He licked it off as he glared at me, and I raised my dark sword to my lips. Then I shook my head and snapped the blade away, sending the blood across the stone.

'You talk of blood curses?' I said. 'When the smell of yours would make an Avengorii retch?' I saw the red grow in his eyes, and he charged me again before I could even smile.

Ferocity versus speed, we moved in circles across the stone. I felt the touch of his talons, a clipping kick, the hard shock of the handle of his scythe, but never the touch of that great blade. I ducked and weaved and danced and he couldn't reach me, I was beginning to find his patterns. My blades touched his hands, his neck, his face. I cut him a dozen times. His blood was as dark as the seawater churning below, and the smell of it made me hunger

despite my taunting. My heart beat harder, making my blood move, making me fast, and I kept striking, moving, taking only small wounds that closed as fast as they opened.

What are you doing? You can't keep playing with him!

'I'm not,' I whispered. 'I'm negotiating his surrender.' I ducked another slash, then slid in and ran the edge of my bright sword along the side of his neck. A little more pressure and I could've buried the blade in his flesh, but I pulled it away and flashed my teeth at him. Let him know that I was toying with him. Hurting him, when he couldn't hurt me, and I could see that the yellow was disappearing from his eyes, iris and pupils swallowed up by red. Now.

'You call this a challenge?' I let my pride fill me, my disdain, stood as tall as I could and laughed. 'This isn't even a fight.'

The last thin edge of humanity vanished from Salvera's eyes as crimson overcame them. He threw back his head and howled, the full-throated cry of the beast. He flung his scythe at me, blade whistling as it cut through the air. I ducked, and the gory weapon flew over the cliff and into the sea. Salvera didn't care. On each finger his claws were lengthening, thickening, and when he threw himself at me he slashed those claws in a blur of savagery.

Now I could block and I did, smashing back his strikes with my blades even though I still had to move with them, to absorb the hideous strength behind them. Every parry opened up wounds on Salvera's monstrous hands, but the vampire didn't feel them. He was raging, and he caught my blades in his grip, clutching them tight, not caring about the blood that poured down his arms. He pulled my swords apart, his muzzle opening, fangs flashing as he prepared to drive them into my neck, and that's when I smashed my magic into him.

I'd felt it before, when I'd touched his mind. Felt how loose his soul was, how thin it had become. Like a beast's.

I touched him now and felt nothing but the beast in his head. The man that had been Salvera was gone, pushed aside by the animal rage, and that I could dig my magic into. I wrapped my mind around what was left of Salvera's soul, made my magic into a leash, and jerked it tight.

My bond took Salvera, and it broke him. He let go of my swords and staggered back, howling again, and that howl twisted and deepened as his body warped. The blessed blood, freed by the loss of his humanity, rebuilt Salvera into the shape of the beast. His body changed, his armour and clothes shredding off him as he swelled with muscle. In seconds he looked nothing like a human. He was wolf, he was bat, he was a thing of night and death. He was no longer a vampire but a vargoyle, a leader of the fallen vargheists, and he was mine.

'You always were a monster, Salvera.' I walked towards him, and he leaned down, red eyes filled with hate, jaws slavering. But when he tried to lunge for me I squeezed the bond I'd forged between us and he shook his head, bestial rage twisting into confused obedience. 'But now you're my monster.' I looked up from him, his head bowed, then at the silent vampires gathered around. 'You're all my monsters, Wolf Knights. And you will swear yourselves to me as your master has done.'

CHAPTER TWENTY-ONE

The cell was a square barely big enough to lie down in, lit only by a window slit cut high in one wall. The scrap of light slipping in was just enough for me to see the body slumped in the dirty straw covering the floor, but not enough to tell me whether they were man or woman, alive or dead. But as soon as the guards had slammed the door shut behind me, the shadow on the floor stirred.

'Captain Takora. I'd say it's good to see you again, but it's really not.'

'Lieutenant Galeris.' I breathed out his name, and I was happy and hideously sad all at once. I carefully slid down the wall to sit, making sure not to touch anything with my aching hands. 'You're supposed to be in Maar.'

'I was.' He pulled himself up, reaching out a hand. I kept mine away.

'They're broken. Both of them.'

He grunted, then reached for them again, gently, and I let him

291

take them, breathing hard through my teeth as he examined the breaks. The swelling had gone down, but my wrists were ugly, twisted, especially the left. 'Celasian?'

'Bloodeyes.'

'Your plan didn't work.'

'No,' I said, the word soft but so, so bitter.

'I didn't think so.' He set my hands down carefully. 'When I got to Maar they were calling her queen. Saying that Magdalena and the other Kastelai were all pledging themselves to her to fight against Celasian. They were uninterested in capitulation. So I left – well, I fled before they killed me for being a spy – and came back here.'

'That was stupid,' I said.

'Yes,' he agreed. 'I notice you're here too.'

'Because I am also stupid.' I'd managed to sneak into the city, got all the way to the docks and found the smugglers I'd hired to take Arvan away. They told me what happened before they handed me over. They probably would have done it even without the abbot-general's reward. They hadn't liked Arvan, and they really hadn't liked Nyssa's visit, or the undead shark that had followed them all the way back to Gowyn, tearing at their hull and almost sinking them.

'Now what?' he asked.

'We wait for Celasian to burn us,' I said. I could feel the fleas and lice that lived in the dirty straw working their way under my clothes, nipping into my skin, but I couldn't slap at them with my aching hands.

The pyre couldn't come fast enough.

It was only a few days before they pulled me out of my cell, dragged me through the baths and dressed me in rough clothes. I might've appreciated that – my body was covered with bites – but they cared nothing for my broken wrists, and by the time they were done my arms were howling. I clenched my teeth, fighting not to vomit, and didn't notice where we were going until they stopped dragging me there.

It was Gowyn's central market square, cleared of every stall and stuffed instead with soldiers, each one of them carrying a gleaming spear. Rank after rank, dressed in white armour burnished to eye-aching brilliance, carrying banners marked with lightning bolts. Celasian's Spears of Heaven, his full army finally assembled, thousands of men and women filling the square and spilling out into the streets that surrounded it. And there he was, standing on the steps of the Temple of Sigmar, his griffon crouching behind him. A tall man with empty eyes, gazing out at the army that would let him end this long war and seize the Broken Plains for Sigmar's glory. For Celasian's revenge.

Celasian raised his spear, and a bolt of lightning snapped upwards from its tip, slashing into the clear sky above. Thunder followed the blinding flash, and through its echoes I could hear the chime of falling glass from shattered windows, the howl of dogs, the wail of frightened children. But in the square there was silence. Every soldier was still, their eyes on their abbot-general.

'Holy Sigmar, father of us all, I raise my voice to you!' Celasian's prayer filled the square. 'I call on you to see us, your faithful servants, gathered to do your will! Darkness has fallen across this portion of your everlasting realm, and seeks to claim it for evil. Death is here – corrupt and predatory, restless and malign, the hideous undeath of the traitor god Nagash! His vile blood has touched this land, and from it monsters have grown, ones that feed upon the living. So we have come, holy Sigmar, to cleanse this land of these beasts and all who serve them. We have brought your holy fire to these Broken Plains, and we will not rest until we have burned every drop of Soulblight vampire blood from this land!'

Celasian thrust Heaven's Edge towards the sky once more, and electricity ran through the relic, snapping arcs that sizzled around the abbot-general. 'Holy Sigmar, we beg your blessing today, for we ride forth to destroy those who would taint your creation with darkness and blood! Bless us, and bless our weapons, the Spears of Heaven!'

With a shout, every soldier raised their weapons. They held them high, and there was another boom as lightning flashed again, this time falling from above. It struck Heaven's Edge and split into a hundred rivers of light, arcing away to touch all the upraised spears. It rippled between them, a web of brilliance snapping from point to point, and on the face of every soldier I saw the same expression – a rictus of pain as the lightning jolted through their spear, followed by the madness of ecstasy. They shouted again, a frenzied roar that made me shudder and close my eyes, but I could still see those twisted faces glowing in that burning light.

I kept my eyes closed until they dragged me to the steps and threw me at Celasian's feet. I knelt there, hissing in pain, hands cradled to my chest as the Spears of Heaven marched away behind me, off to finish the war I never could.

'Takora.' Celasian's voice was as cold as ever, but when I looked up at him there was something in his eyes, a faint satisfaction that made me want to shudder again. But I kept myself still, waiting. 'It is good that we were able to find you.' He crouched down, resting easy on his haunches, looking at me from almost eye level. 'You've been in this fight longer than anyone. Except me. You should see the end.'

'You're taking me with you?' I asked.

'Of course,' he said. He reached out and took my hands. 'You're hurt. Did this happen during your capture?'

'No,' I said, fighting to keep from jerking away from his touch. 'Bloodeyes did this.'

'Queen Nyssa,' he said, and the cold in his voice was sharp with hate. 'Was this her reward for your treachery? Probably not what you expected, but what would one expect from the servant of the traitor god? Soulblight vampires are liars.' His voice went lower, more dangerous. 'Her most of all.'

'She wasn't...' I gave up. I didn't care. The truth didn't matter to fanatics, especially if it inconvenienced them. But I'd already said too much.

'She wasn't lying?' Celasian said, his voice almost a whisper. 'Did you believe her? Did you believe the falsehoods she spoke about my father?'

I looked into his eyes, empty of every feeling but deepest hate, and stayed silent. There was nothing I could say.

'Both wrists are broken,' he finally said. 'The left is bad, but the right is starting to heal.' He pressed his fingers into my right hand, gently, and I remembered how he'd healed his soldiers at Skull-top. But his grip grew tighter and tighter, until pain was roaring through my head.

'The Soulblight vampire is a liar, and you're a traitor. And for that, you both deserve only one thing. Pain, and the flame.' Celasian suddenly twisted his hands and the partially healed bone broke again with a dull snap. Pain smashed through me. I hit the stone of the steps, retching and convulsing, and Celasian straightened up over me.

I could barely hear him as he gave his orders. 'Bring her. And the other one. They'll burn in Maar with the rest of the traitors.'

CHAPTER TWENTY-TWO

We crested the last hill and the Grey Palace lay before us, its towers rearing up in Temero's vast shadow. The citadel glowed with light, while bats swung through the great clouds of steam that rose from the Irewater. Magdalena had been busy, and I looked down the long road threading between the boiling lake and the hunched shadows of the memorial stones. Maar glowed with light too, the city readying its own defences, and beyond it there was nothing but darkness. No torches, no campfires, no approaching army.

Not yet. I'd beaten Celasian back to the house of my father, to my house, with the Wolf Knights at my back.

'Home,' Kill said, reining in beside me.

'For now,' I answered, and below us the ground trembled. High above, the dull red glow crowning Temero brightened, then dulled again as a great cloud of ash rose up, swallowing the light. But arcs of electricity, blue-white veins of brilliance, ran through the black. Then they vanished, swallowed by the dark. 'And forever.'

* * *

'You did it.' Magdalena bowed to me as I slid off Thorn, then touched her hand below her eye. I see your skill, the Kastelai salute.

She's showing you respect.

'I know,' I said silently, but I had stopped, confused. This was the kind of behaviour the older Kastelai reserved for each other, not for me. This was how they treated those they respected. Those they feared.

'Where's Lord Salvera? Did you kill him?' Jirrini was standing behind Magdalena. She'd bowed with the other Kastelai, but she kept her hands folded into the sleeves of her gown. Not disrespectful, but not friendly.

'No,' I said, and nodded to the knot of vargheists coming through the gate into the courtyard. The vargoyle that had been Salvera was in their lead, its jaws open, its nose twitching beneath red eyes as it searched the air for the smell of blood. When it saw me, it snarled but ducked its head, not a bow but a bestial act of submission. 'I brought the Mad Dog of Bite Harbour to heel.'

They stared at the vargoyle, puzzling out the lines of the bestial face. Magdalena's face went hard, her eyes faintly sick, but Jirrini's mouth quirked into a terrible little smile, and now she raised her hand to touch beneath her eye.

'It's good to see you found a use for him,' she said.

'It's good to see you brought him – however you brought him – and his Wolf Knights,' Magdalena said. 'We need every blade and fang we can get.' She looked at me, her eyes hard in her pretty face. 'My spies report that Celasian's forces have arrived, and they're wasting no time. The Spears of Heaven are on their way, and they outnumber us at least ten to one.'

'Good,' I said, handing Thorn's reins to Rill. 'There'll be blood for us all then.'

* * *

Magdalena had made the Great Hall her war room, and we gathered around the table now set there to stare at the maps spread across it.

'They're bringing the troops by boat,' Magdalena said. 'All the way to the rapids that lie just beyond Skulltop. There they'll have to get out and march. That'll slow them, but they'll still get here in days.'

I traced the path Magdalena had marked as the easiest route for Celasian's army. If I had time, I could have set a dozen ambushes, made them pay for every step taken towards the Grey Palace. As it was, we barely had time to prepare to meet them here. Still...

'We should–' I started, and was cut off.

No should. Be sure. Be a leader.

'And follow your orders?' I whispered, then pointed at the map. 'We'll send the dire wolves into the hills, to encourage the Spears to keep to the path we expect, and to take out any scouts they try to send ahead.'

'Done, my queen,' Magdalena said. She seemed content to take my orders.

She was never comfortable as a leader. Prove yourself half-competent, and she'll follow you happily. Just make sure you encourage her to push back when you're only being half-competent.

'I'm never half anything,' I muttered. Magdalena ignored it, but Jirrini raised an eyebrow. Still, she didn't look concerned. More curious. 'What do you think?' I asked Magdalena. 'How will we beat them?'

'With difficulty, and loss, if at all.' She sighed, looking at the map, then picked up a handful of carved bone tokens. 'The army we have is mostly our mounted knights. Fast, hard-hitting, deadly. Trying to hold the Grey Palace or Maar for some kind of siege would rob us of most of our strengths. It would be best to meet Celasian here, in the open. And he'll know that, but he'll let us,

because the Spears of Heaven are almost the perfect counter to our forces. Disciplined spearmen, they'll form tight units that will be murderously hard for us to take. They'll not be drawn out and killed, they'll stay together and wait for us to charge them, and when we do we'll die on their spear points.'

Magdalena laid out the tokens, silver spears and golden suns for the mortals, while ours were red and marked with roses, wolves, cups and ravens. There were far fewer tokens on our side. 'We're stronger. Faster. Deadlier. But the numbers are against us. We're too few. We can't break their units without losing too many of ours. We are unlikely to win this kind of fight.'

'Then why are we fighting it?' I asked. 'What if we...' I stared at the map, trying to think, but coming up with nothing.

'We're fighting it because it's all we have,' Magdalena said. 'If we don't meet them out there, they'll take Maar. The mortals are preparing to defend themselves, but if Celasian's army falls on them with its full force, they'll be destroyed. Then they'll come for the Grey Palace, and we can't hold a siege long. Cut off from blood, trapped, Celasian would destroy us slowly. If I wanted that kind of miserable death, I would have stayed at Ruinview.' She drummed her fingers on the table. 'Numbers. In the end that's what it boils down to. They have them, we don't. That's why Salvera wanted to kill everyone in Maar and raise them to fight.'

'We're not doing that,' I said. 'We made an oath to those mortals. We are Kastelai and we do not fail.' I thought about what Mother had said, about oaths and honour and thinking things through. 'Besides that, I want a kingdom, not just a victory. If Maar falls, so does the Rose Throne.'

'But we may still stand,' Jirrini said, almost silently. But I heard her.

'I'll find another way,' I snarled. Somehow.

Across the hall from us a group of mortal servants staggered

by, loaded down with baskets. In each I could see dozens of clay amphorae. 'What are those for?'

'We've set up a supply line between here and Splitrock,' Jirrini said. 'We're harvesting as much blood as we can from the graz and bringing it back here.'

I stared at the vessels, and remembered the bitter taste of the poison that Arvan had given me in them. The poison Shadas had made.

'Keep planning, Lady Magdalena,' I said, turning away from the table. 'And try to think of something better than suicide for once.' Then I strode off, heading into the bowels of the palace, to speak to the last of those who'd betrayed me. And the one who had saved me.

They had locked Shadas in a chamber deep beneath the palace, not far from the tomb where my mother and father lay. It was a vast space spanned by heavy arches, lit by the dim amethyst light of necromantic magic. Shadas sat in the middle, surrounded by amphorae, painting symbols onto the clay while muttering incantations. I stood in the doorway, watching him, and when he finished he awkwardly pulled himself to his feet and bowed.

'My queen. Apologies, my work kept me from sensing your presence. Have you come to kill me?'

'Probably,' I said. I walked into the room and shut the door. I felt a surge of caution from my mother, wordless but clear, but I closed it anyway. Despite all that had happened, Shadas didn't feel like a threat.

'You have every right to,' he said. 'It's probably your duty, actually.' Shadas sat back down on the stone floor and picked up another amphora. 'But I'm almost done with these, if you don't mind waiting. I told Lady Jirrini I'd make as many as I could.'

I walked towards him, hands light on my sword hilts. He seemed even paler, the skin around his eyes was dark, and he stank. He hadn't bathed or changed his dark robes in days.

'When I went to Arvan, he couldn't stop himself from boasting about why he'd done it. Part of it was to distract me, but I think he really wanted me to know how he betrayed me. You don't though. You don't want to boast.'

'No,' he said quietly, not looking up from his work.

I stopped in front of him. 'The last time I saw you, you told me how much you owed my father. How he'd saved you. Why did you betray him?' And why did you save me? was the question I kept back.

He sighed. 'I did owe Corsovo, and was desperate to repay him. More, to prove myself to him, to be valued by him. I wanted him to look at me like he looked at you. I told you I lost my family because of my magic. I thought my magic might gain me a new one. So I tried and tried, but… I already told you I had nothing to work with. No teacher, just a few old books that were mostly useless. Until I found a spell in one of them, tucked between the pages, something someone had copied from another work and hidden there. A formula for a potion that would increase the power of an undead creature.' Shadas set down his paints. 'It was exactly what I needed. Something that would make Corsovo stronger, something that would make him realise my potential, something that would make him see me. So I studied it, learned it, but there was a problem. The spell required a piece of another of the undead, of equal strength or greater than the one being enhanced. And where would I find something like that?'

'In my mother's tomb,' I said.

'Vasara's tomb,' Shadas agreed. 'I knew Corsovo would never allow it. He believed Vasara could come back, no matter how many years passed. I knew this, so I set the spell aside. But it wouldn't let me go. So finally I did it. I took the bones of her smallest toes.

What would they matter? I took them, and I did the spell, and I made the potion and… it didn't work.' Shadas shook his head. 'I knew it when it was done, the same way I know things about my magic. It was flawed somehow. I didn't understand why, but it wouldn't work. I had desecrated Vasara's body for nothing. So of course I had to try again.'

Of course.

'Another failure,' Shadas said. 'I went through her whole left leg up to the knee before I finally gave up. I couldn't make it work. All those attempts, and all I could make was…'

'Poison?'

'Poison,' he sighed. 'I didn't know it then, I just knew it was wrong, so I hid it away. I didn't get rid of it because I thought maybe I would understand, maybe I'd figure it out. I kept it, and thought about it, and was terrified that someday Corsovo would open Vasara's tomb. Then he started to get sick.' Shadas looked at me. 'I kept this to myself for so many reasons, but this might be the biggest one. I didn't want to admit how stupid I was. When Corsovo got sick, I didn't know why. I tried to help him. I was *desperate* to help him. But I didn't know what was happening until the day before you came back. On that day he spat up some of the blood Arvan was giving him. I saw the potion mixed in with it, and I knew. Arvan was feeding him my failure, and it was killing him.'

'And you didn't stop him.'

Shadas smiled without humour. 'Oh, I told him to stop, and he did. Why not? The king was already dying. Arvan stopped, but he told me that if I breathed a word of what he'd done I'd be just as dead as him. I'd made the poison, hadn't I, from Vasara's bones.' His dead smile became a frown. 'Arvan spied on me. He had watched me through the eyes of his animals and knew exactly what I'd done, and he used that to attack the person I most wanted

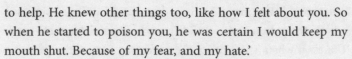

to help. He knew other things too, like how I felt about you. So when he started to poison you, he was certain I would keep my mouth shut. Because of my fear, and my hate.'

'You hate me?' I asked, and he nodded.

'Not because of anything you've done,' he said. 'You mostly ignore me. I hate you because Corsovo treated you the way he'd never treat me. Maybe hate is the wrong word. I'm jealous of you. Like a sibling rivalry, except I was never even part of the family.'

'If you hate me, if you thought you would be killed if this came out, why did you save me?'

He looked down at the amphorae crowded around him. 'Mostly because I wanted to see if I could. I came up with the idea right after the king died. If I could make that spell really work, then it might counter the failed versions and burn out the poison. And I had an idea of how I could make it work. So I stole one of Vasara's femurs, and I did my magic, but this time I didn't just do it as it was outlined on the page. This time I added your blood to it. It was easy to get, after your first poisoning. I wove your connection to Vasara into the spell. Bodies hold an echo of the soul that animated them, so I used that to make the potion... personal. When it was done, I knew it was right. I knew I'd finally done it, and I wanted to try it, even though I'd be saving you and that you would kill me for it.'

'You said mostly,' I said. 'What else was there?'

'I heard you in their tomb. Right before I gave you the potion. Talking to them.' He shrugged. 'I wanted what you had, that family, but I couldn't have it. I'd never have it. But damn me, I never meant to take it from you. Sibling rivalry...' He sighed, and looked at me with eyes bleak and exhausted. 'I wanted to be something like your brother. Instead I became your betrayer, and however jealous I was of you, I couldn't live with that. So I saved you. If curing you of the poison I had made counts as saving.'

'It counts as something,' I said. 'Which is one reason you're still alive. There's one more. You owe me for what you did. You owe me a lot more than these stupid jugs.' I kicked over the one he'd been painting, sent it rolling across the floor, knocking over others. 'The Rose Throne is mine now, Shadas, and so are all who are sworn to it, including you. That throne is under threat. Tell me, now, can you do anything with your magic to help me defend it, besides making these damn pots?'

He shut his eyes as if in pain and whispered, barely at the edge of my hearing. 'Nagash help me. Yes.'

CHAPTER TWENTY-THREE

You can do this.

I leaned my head against the smooth marble tomb of my parents, my fingers tracing the carving of Vasara's face.

'Can I?' I said. Can I? Could I? Should I? 'I know I killed you once. Do you think that means it would be easy to do it again?'

Killed me? Mother sounded irritated. No, she sounded angry. Angry in a way I hadn't heard in a long time. *You've wallowed in that guilt long enough, Nyssa. It's time you gave it up with your other childish things. I am responsible for my death. I am the one who walked into that trap, I am the one who underestimated that barbarian, I am the one who let myself get burned to blackened bones by a child. Me. You like to think yourself the centre of everything, but your role in that debacle was strictly limited because I wanted it to be. I didn't want you anywhere near those negotiations. I was convinced you'd take offence to the way Celas was breathing and skewer him, ruining the chances for any alliance. So I sent you off on guard duty to get you as far away as I could.*

I stepped back, blinking at the face carved in the marble. 'You sent me away?' I'd carried this guilt for so long... Damn me, I'd carried *her* in my head for so long. 'Why didn't you tell me this before?'

You should have figured it out on your own, she snapped. But she followed up in a calmer, more resigned voice. *Also, I did not want to face the idiotic circumstances of my death, how much of it was my own fault. I was known for my cunning, my ability to see through things. And what happens? I'm tricked by a goat herder with ambitions.*

I couldn't help it. I laughed, and after a moment I heard her chuckle in my head. But when we both went silent, I shook my head. 'I still don't want to do it. I don't want to give you up.'

Loss is hard. Why do you think Nagash wants to rule the realms? If everything is dead, then nothing dies.

'Would that really work?'

I don't know, I'm not a god. I just know that the brief taste of immortality I had only meant that I lost more. But I learned to gain new things, like you're doing.

'What?' I said. 'Am I to replace you and Father with Magdalena and Jirrini?'

And Rill, and Shadas.

'I'm probably going to kill Shadas,' I said.

Not if this succeeds. He'll have proven his worth.

I frowned at that, but before I could argue I saw a flash of light. I turned, and Magdalena was standing at the entrance to the room, a torch in her hand.

'My queen,' she said, sketching a bow. 'They're coming. They'll be here in two days. You're needed.'

Her face was flat, but I could hear the disapproval in her voice. She thought I was mourning. And I suppose I was, for a resurrection that would never happen.

'Thank you,' I said. 'I'll be there soon enough, with an answer to our numbers problem.' She frowned at me, and I waved a hand. 'Go.'

The bow she gave me as she left was even more perfunctory, but I was already forgetting her as I pushed the tomb door open. Inside, the withered corpse of my father lay in his glass coffin, beside the bloodstained marble rectangle of my mother's sarcophagus.

'I know she forgives me,' I told him. 'Or at least her voice in my head does, and whether that's her or just some kind of madness, that's what I have of her. But will you, if I ever succeed in reviving you?'

His only answer was silence, and eventually I nodded and went to Vasara's sarcophagus, pulled away its lid, and began to gather the charred bones that lay inside.

It took nearly the entire two days for Shadas to finish.

I sat in his chamber the whole time, assisting him when I could, and making sure that his helpfulness wasn't a mask over betrayal the way Arvan's had been. Shadas ground my mother's remaining femur to dust and mixed it with a dozen other things, muttering incantations, drawing symbols, working without food or drink or sleep. He only spoke to me once, when he told me to come close so that he could stab a silver knife into my palm and add my blood to his ingredients.

Even with the increase of my healing powers, that wound took a long time to close, and it burned the whole time.

Rill came and went, carrying messages from Magdalena, urgent warnings of Celasian's approach. I responded enough to keep Magdalena from coming down here herself. She had her work, and though she didn't understand it, I had mine. Finally, on the second night, a handful of hours before the Spears of Heaven were supposed to arrive, the necromancer was ready.

'Finished.' He handed me the flask. The potion inside looked just like the one he'd given me before, black and bright, swirling with half-seen skeletal shapes.

'Not poison?'

'No,' he said. 'Will it work as we wish, though?' He shook his head. 'I don't know. The original spell was meant to make every part of your blessed blood stronger, but I've focused this on one ability, and one only. I don't know if it will work.'

'If it doesn't, I'm going to throw you into the Irewater,' I said.

'I know,' he said. 'Shall we?'

I stood on the shore of the Irewater, staring out at the boiling black water. The potion I held was almost a mirror of the deadly lake, dark and light and always moving.

'Ready,' Shadas said, standing up beside me. We had walked to where one of the great memorial stones had fallen, its worn list of names facing towards the sky for the stars to read. The necromancer had drawn a series of arcing lines over the flat face of the stone and spread the bones of my mother in the centre, where all the arcs intersected.

Ready?

Her voice seemed to stir strange currents in the potion. Ready? No. Yes. I raised the flask towards the dark sky, and whispered back to her.

'Thank you, Mother.' Then I drank the flask down.

I had forgotten how much it hurt. The potion poured into me like a storm of blades, and I had to fight to swallow every drop. But this time the agony didn't spread through my whole body. Instead it rose into my head and a ball of razors spun behind my eyes, trying to take me apart. But unlike the poison, there was a purpose buried in this pain and I reached my magic into it.

The magic became a rope of razors, twisting through my brain,

but I controlled it. I tied one end to the bones of my mother, then drove the other end into the water before me, down into the boiling depths, searching. Finding.

The dead were there, so many of them. Bodies reduced to bones by time and the boiling water flowing from Temero's heart. I touched them and found the thin echoes of the souls that were once bound to them.

Such tenuous connections. I felt for them, and some shattered beneath my fumbling magic. This power should have been given to someone more skilled at raising something beyond animals, but Shadas said it had to be me, that the only way he could make the magic work was to use the connection between me and Vasara. So I reached for that. Reached for my memory of my chosen mother, my love for her, my hate, my fear, my respect, and through that bond I could do it. Could connect the bones of my mother above to the bones of the lost dead that lay below. The death magic flowing through me touched them both and I snarled, holding on to the power flowing through me. I kept it focused on the dead, kept it from tearing me apart, and slowly, slowly, the bones began to knit themselves together. Feet to legs to hips, vertebrae to vertebrae, fingers to wrists, jaws to skulls. The magic flowed through me, and the dark water of the Irewater shone with an amethyst glow.

At my feet, the rest of my mother's bones burned as the necromantic magic tore through me, hungry for more power. They flared to ash, one after another, then they were gone, just scorch marks left across the worn names of the dead. Lost, along with any chance of her resurrection. I stared down at those black marks, the pain from the magic slowly fading from my head as the roiling surface of the Irewater broke and the first skeletons began to pull themselves up and out of the lake.

* * *

They were waiting for me at the gates of the palace. Magdalena and Jirrini in front and all the knights behind, standing silent as I walked towards them with an army of skeletons at my back.

Their bones were dark, ragged, pitted by the acidic water, and then built up again, bone replaced by the metal and mineral contaminants from the volcano. They were skeletons of bone and rust, of stone and sulphur and obsidian. The contaminants had made them impossible for our magic to touch before. Now, raised again, the ghosts of their souls glowing in their eye sockets, they were stronger for it. They were dead but their twisted, encrusted bones moved with a deadly celerity.

When I reached them, Magdalena swept into a deep bow. Jirrini followed, uncharacteristically clumsy in her confusion. Behind them, all the rest bowed too.

'These last few days,' Magdalena said, 'I've spent praying to Nagash that I hadn't made a mistake when I pledged myself to you. Now, I see my prayers are answered, and I give thanks to the Undying King, and to you, Nyssa Volari, Queen of the Rose Throne!'

Behind her, the gathered vampires raised their weapons and shouted my name. Day broke over the Broken Plains then, and I stared at them, my people, great and terrible. I clenched my fist, feeling the pain of the two fangs I held as they bit into my skin. The cracked, blackened teeth of my mother, the only pieces of her left after my magic had burned through her bones.

You did well, Nyssa. You did well.

The words rang through my head, even as I shouted. 'Our enemies approach, and so does our feast! Let us remind the slaves of the Storm God what the word mortal means!' I raised my fist like a challenge towards the brightening sky, my fingers pressing the teeth into my palm, and down my arm ran a ribbon of blood, hot with the anger that made my heart beat like a drum in my chest.

CHAPTER TWENTY-FOUR

Morning stretched our shadows long, and the heat was already building even though the day was minutes old. But the march was almost over.

'How long, Takora?' Galeris asked. Well, partially asked. He started coughing in the middle of the second word, a harsh bark that went on and on. When it finally settled, I answered him.

'Not long now.' We'd spent the night camped a mile from Maar's black walls. I'd never been this far across the Broken Plains, but I'd studied the maps for years. 'We'll see the Grey Palace soon.'

'Good,' Galeris said, swiping at his mouth with manacled hands.

They hadn't bothered chaining mine. They hung before me, twisted and ugly on their broken wrists, aching with every step. But they had locked an iron collar around both our necks and bound us together with a length of chain, to hold and humiliate. 'Are you so eager to burn?' I asked. I'd lain awake most of the night, staring at Temero, wondering if it would hurt more to fall into the lake of liquid stone inside the crater, or to die tied to a

stake in a burning city. When sleep finally had come, the dreams had been unpleasant.

'Better to be ash than choke on it,' he said. His face was grey with the stuff, like almost everyone's. There hadn't been a drop of rain since the last ashfall and the long march towards the Grey Palace had taken place in a cloud of ash kicked up by the column of soldiers that marched before us. It was awful, choking stuff, but I wasn't sure I agreed.

I wasn't looking forward to becoming part of the ashes covering the ground. I'd had more than my fill of this land. Becoming part of it forever seemed a special sort of hell.

As I mused, the column of marching spearmen came to a halt. I could see nothing, stuck back here at the end of the line with the creaking wagons and grunting lixx. 'We're probably there now.'

'Good. Let's get this done.'

Galeris had never seen a battle like this. I remembered Ire Crossing, the hours spent drawing up the lines, both sides fussing with equipment and placement before they finally flung themselves at each other, screaming for blood. I wasn't surprised when we just stood there waiting in the hot sun for a long while. But I was surprised when a pair of Celasian's guards came for us and marched us to the front of the line.

From there the view was much different. The steep hills pulled back from Temero, as if they were intimidated by the looming volcano. I could see a wide, flat plain stretching out before us, and in the distance were the walls of the Grey Palace, set between the steaming Irewater and the volcano's dark bulk. In front of those grey walls I could see the army of the vampires spread in neat formations, perfectly still beneath the bright day, unmoving, waiting.

Huge.

There was a clap of wings, and then Celasian dropped down

beside me, the wind from Erikil's landing stirring up the ashes. Galeris started hacking again, but the sound didn't cover the abbot-general's voice.

'What is that?'

He stared down at me from his perch on the griffon's back, eyes ablaze with icy anger. I wanted to quip something back at him, but I checked my tongue. If he stabbed that silver spear of his through me, he'd probably kill Galeris too. So I just said the obvious.

'Bloodeyes has added to her troops.' I blinked against the ash. I could see blocks of riders, the cavalry I expected, and I could pick out each house, all except dead Durrano's. Four blocks of vampire knights, but between them were arranged two huge blocks of foot soldiers. From the strange shape of them they were probably skeletons, though at this distance it was hard to say. As I looked at them, I saw a ripple of movement go through their ranks, and across the distance I heard a deep, booming noise. They were beating their bony hands against their ribs in a simple menacing rhythm. *Thud thud. Thud thud. Thud thud.* Like the sound of an enormous heart beating. There had to be thousands of the undead warriors, and they kept the beat in unnerving, perfect unison.

Celasian glared at the army, then back at me. 'You said you'd destroyed most of their undead legions. That it was just the Soulblight vampires left.'

'We did. But that's the problem with fighting the dead,' I said. 'There's always more.' What was Celasian thinking? That he should pull back? That was probably the tactical move. Pull back and then what? Burn Maar and everyone inside, and this war would go on and on. I was done with it, done with all of it. I just wanted an end.

'You'll have to retreat.' I used the voice I employed with my rawest recruits when I was explaining to them which end of the sword to hold.

'Retreat?' he said, his voice cold and sharp.

'Of course,' I said. 'You came here thinking you'd have a ten to one advantage. Enough, if barely, against superior troops. But now you're only ahead two to one, if that. You'll get taken apart on these odds. Skeletons aren't that tough, but they'll bog you down while their knights cut you to ribbons.'

'Superior troops? Those *things*? Superior to Sigmar's chosen?' Celasian's pale eyes were almost glowing with rage.

I shrugged. 'You brought me up here to tell you what I saw, and I told you. Or do you prefer lies now?'

Celasian snapped his spear up, its razor edge swinging at my face. Maybe he meant to stop it at my chin, or maybe he wanted to cut my tongue out along with my cheeks and teeth. I'd never know, because Galeris caught the chain connecting us and yanked me back, away from Heaven's Edge. I stumbled, almost falling, but I could see the flicker of annoyance on Celasian's face. It only lasted a second, just as long as it took the abbot-general to shift the aim of his spear and drive it into my lieutenant's chest.

I saw the spear moving, saw the blood, and I was reaching for Heaven's Edge, to pull it out. But there was a snap of power and electricity coursed through Galeris, burning his pierced heart. The jolt ran down the chain connecting us and made me spasm and fall.

'I hate lies. I hate liars. Like you. Like *her*.' Celasian stared down at me with his terrible eyes as I convulsed on the ground. 'Understand this, Takora. These lands are tainted, and I am *meant* to cleanse them.' He swung his spear, flicking Galeris' blood off its tip. 'Watch and witness, traitor. Beneath the eyes of Sigmar, I will turn those unclean things to ash.'

I pulled myself up to my knees, the collar hot against my throat. Galeris lay on his back beside me, his eyes staring blankly at the sky above, a curl of smoke rising from the red wound in his chest. 'I hope she kills you,' I said. 'You're more monster than Blood-eyes could ever be.'

'So you believe,' he said. 'And so you will burn with her.' With a thunder of wings, he took to the sky, Erikil shrieking. Far above he levelled his spear at the army of the dead – lightning flashed around him and his command roared like thunder.

'For Sigmar! Forwards!'

The Spears of Heaven shouted back, raised their weapons high, and began to move, spreading out into their formations: a perfect, shining army marching forwards, leaving me and my dead lieutenant behind in a cloud of darkness and choking ash.

The Spears of Heaven were standing across the valley, a column of white, and at its head was the flicker of wings, feathers bright and blue as a morning sky.

Celasian.

My heart beat as I stared at the man who'd murdered the woman I'd called Mother. The man who was coming now to kill me and my house, to tear down our cities and slaughter every mortal who'd sworn themselves to us. I watched Celasian's army gathering, preparing to attack, and my magic reached out, touching the skeletal legions I'd gathered before me. They'd been dressed in every scrap of armour the servants of the Grey Palace could find, and ancient weapons hung from the bones of their hands. When my magic shivered through them, they raised those dead hands and struck their knuckles against their ribs all at once.

A booming rattle, the click of bone on bone. The drums of the dead, beating out the rhythm of my heart.

'Ready yourself, Kastelai.' I turned to face the vampires arrayed behind me. Magdalena and Jirrini were closest, Magdalena wrapped in her black-and-purple steel, Jirrini in crimson scale mail. Behind them waited the knight-commander of each remaining house, banners on their backs, wolf heads and bloody cups, ravens and roses. Lurking behind them like a pale shadow was

Shadas, leaning on a staff of twisted vesin wood, its end crowned with thorns.

'I stand ready, my queen,' Magdalena said, sounding righteous and eager. Jirrini stayed silent, but she made a quick bow, her armour chiming like bells.

I gathered my magic, the thick rope of invisible strands connecting me to the skeletons, divided it into two halves, then I pushed them out. Magdalena took one, Jirrini the other, and then the skeletal legions were bound to their will, a smooth transition of power that did not cause their steady beat to falter.

I was interrupted by a flash of lightning and a crack of thunder. Celasian was flying high above his troops, his silver spear sparking. His voice came across the valley, like an echo of the thunder he'd summoned.

'For Sigmar! Forwards!'

Across the valley the Spears of Heaven drew themselves up, and I felt my heart begin to beat faster, out of sync now with the steady drum of the skeletons.

I flicked out my magic, and Thorn and Rend came to me, the Nightmare tossing her head, the massive dire wolf snarling in eager hunger. Behind them came Rill, a black banner on her back marked with a skull with rose eyes. I vaulted into my saddle and Rill and Rend took their places to either side of me as I looked down at the other Kastelai and the knight-commanders.

'Thirty years ago, the mortals came for us at Ire Crossing. Thirty years ago, they tried to kill us and failed. They have failed every year since, and today we end the war that they began. This day—'

The ground bucked beneath my feet, hard enough to make Thorn stumble. There came a sound, a growling roar from Temero as the heart of the mountain beat a glowing gout of fire into the sky. It fell behind the mountain, into the wastes, and the smoke rising from the volcano became a thick and heavy cloud, veined

with lightning. I bared my teeth at that bright light, but the cloud was already dimming the morning sky, its shadow falling across my army to reach for the Spears of Heaven.

'This night,' I called out when the echoes of the eruption faded. 'This *night* thirty years of war end in blood!'

Forty years. That's when Celasian's father betrayed me. That's when Celasian burned me. That's when this war really began.

Mother's voice cut through the shouts of the vampires gathered before me, and I raised my hand to touch the leather pouch hanging around my neck, the one which held her fangs.

'What was that about not making war personal?'

Be quiet and kill him.

I smiled, baring my teeth, and drew my swords. 'For the Rose Throne!' I shouted, and the knight-commanders mounted up, riding back to their troops. Magdalena made a sign.

'For Nagash,' she said.

'For blood,' said Jirrini.

They mounted their Nightmares and took position to lead their skeletal hordes. Shadas followed Magdalena on foot, and as he passed he ducked his head, bowing to me.

'Don't die today, Shadas,' I told him. 'Or I'll raise you and kill you again.'

'I'll do my best, my queen.'

He went, and I stared at the troops that remained. With the growing darkness, the vargheists had left the shadow of the palace walls and crept forwards, their noses wrinkling as they caught the distant smell of blood. I looked at the greatest of them, the vargoyle that had been Salvera, and wrapped my magic and my will around it.

'Go where you were told. Then kill.'

The vargoyle snarled at me, looking past me at the distant army. Foam dripped from its muzzle and its claws twitched, eager to

rend. I felt its mind press against mine, felt something like Salvera's hate pushing against me. But then it fell apart, shattered by the hunger of the beast, and the vargoyle loped away, angling across the plains as if running from the battle, the other vargheists following. I watched them go, satisfied.

Then I turned back to the Spears of Heaven. And the man who flew above them.

I leaned forwards and started Thorn into a trot. Rill and Rend followed, and we rode towards Celasian and his army.

'Time to end this,' I said.

Finally.

CHAPTER TWENTY-FIVE

The day was gone, swallowed by smoke that boiled with lightning, and on the ground far below the living fought the dead.

The Spears of Heaven drove themselves forwards like a dagger, its point aimed at the Grey Palace. The fanatics of Sigmar had split into dense phalanxes that pushed ahead with deadly inexorability. The Church fighters moved with a trained precision that made it impossible to fight them one on one. Each formation of soldiers was its own monster, scaled in white armour, bristling with spears that slashed like terrible claws whenever an enemy pressed close.

Watching them work as I rode through the battle, I understood what Magdalena had meant when she spoke of the terror of numbers. Our knights were faster, deadlier, but alone against these steel-spiked beasts we would have fallen fast, impaled on those silver spears on every charge. But that wasn't happening now.

The dead I'd raised from the Irewater came forwards in two great blocks, the skeletal fighters moving with perfect precision, guided by the Kastelai. They marched towards the Spears of Heaven,

steaming eyes empty of fear, and where the mortals met the dead of the Irewater, their perfect formations faltered. Their advance ground to a halt against a tide of bone and rust that drowned the Spears of Heaven in fear and death.

Then the knights struck. They thundered across the field, Nightmare hooves pounding into the ash-covered ground. Swinging around the edges of the phalanxes, they struck and pulled back, hitting their flanks, disrupting the careful formations, reaping death over and over again.

'Lord of Death, take them all!' Rill said, snapping shots from her bow as we rode past one of the mortal formations which was slowly drawing tighter, shrinking in on itself as they fought. The Knights of Plenty swirled around the mortals, sending waves of arrows into the close-packed ranks as they passed. It was a brutal, effective tactic, the favourite of the nomad tribes Jirrini recruited from, and her red-armoured knights seemed to be wreaking greater havoc than the other houses. But on every side my army was pressing against the mortals' advance, grinding it to a halt even though they still outnumbered us.

Except for a wedge in the middle, where the lightning wasn't confined to the churning dark above. There it danced along the ground, and where it passed it carved holes through the ranks of my army, blasting apart lines of silent skeletons, sending Nightmares to the ground, their manes flaming, glowing eyes going dark. Vampire knights tumbled from their fallen mounts, convulsing and smoking, blackened husks in half-melted armour.

There.

As if I didn't know. I spun Thorn towards the unit forming the sharp point of the enemy's attack. There was Celasian atop his griffon, flanked by his guard on their Demigryphs. The beasts were as terrible as their riders, shattering skeletons with clawed talons and hooked beaks while the men and women on their

backs struck with spears that danced with sparks. Whenever they hit, there was a *snap* of light and their target would crumble to charred bones. The silver spear in Celasian's hand did the same, cutting down any skeleton that came close, but every few strikes he would raise the relic, thrust it forwards and unleash a bolt of lightning that crackled through the ranks of my dead, leaving a trail of broken skeletons. 'There,' I said, and Rill snarled a curse as she drew another arrow. I turned Thorn towards Celasian and sent her charging forwards.

I pressed my magic into Thorn, into Rill's mount, and into Rend. They surged ahead and we were at the edge of the skeletal formation in a heartbeat. The undead opened their ranks for me, moving out of our way as we raced through them, and we were passing before Celasian's guard before they realised we were coming.

Rill snapped out arrows, the first glancing off a guard's helmet, the next taking a Demigryph in its feathered throat, another smashing into a guard's face, the steel arrowhead breaking teeth before burying itself in the roof of the man's mouth.

Rend was racing beside us, snapping at the leg of a Demigryph, nearly tearing it off, then leaping to hurl a guard from her saddle, ripping her throat out as she fell.

My blades were flying, cutting as I went down the line. I took a hand from one guard, cut across the eyes of a Demigryph that snapped at me, and then I was at Celasian. Moving fast, streaking past him, I barely saw his pale eyes as they turned towards me. I slashed at his face, but the wing of his griffon snapped up, catching my blade. Blood gouted, and the scent of it made me growl as I flashed past, my bright blade catching another guard under the arm as he tried to stab at me. I heard him scream as he fell from his mount, then again as Thorn's hooves smashed over him. Then we were gone, racing through the ranks of the skeletons again, leaving Celasian shouting behind us.

'Abomination!' A bolt of lightning cracked by me, shattering a skeleton, but I was twisting Thorn already, turning her with my knees back towards the abbot-general. I could see him trying to aim his spear at me and I drove Thorn forwards in a twisting rush, avoiding that gleaming point, trying to reach Celasian again before he could release another bolt.

'Liar!' he shouted as I flew at him, and his griffon reared up, talons slashing, blue feathers stained red with blood. I bared my teeth, pulled back my sword and then ducked as he shot another bolt straight towards my face.

I could smell the stench of my own singed hair, could feel the prickly sensation of electricity dancing across my skin. But I was blind, my vision gone white, and deaf from the thunderous crack that came with the strike. I dropped to Thorn's neck as I made her turn, and I knew we must have made it past because I didn't feel the bite of a spear.

The world was coming back, my ears and eyes healing quickly as my blood raced through me, but not fast enough. A Nightmare was screaming, and then went silent, and Rill was cursing, but her voice was fading behind me, lost in the battle. When my eyes finally began to work I was almost at the end of the block of skeletal warriors. Jirrini was ahead of me, shouting, asking if I was all right, but I just waved at her and spun Thorn away, racing back towards the front.

Halfway there I found Rill, pinned beneath the smoking carcass of her Nightmare, skeletons moving in uncaring lines around her. I reached down for her, my eyes on Celasian as he stared across the ranks of dead between us. 'Grab hold!' I shouted.

'No! Both my legs are shattered,' she said, pulling herself free. 'Keep moving, before he can use that damned spear again!'

I cursed, but my being near her made Rill a target. I left her to crawl and sent Thorn forwards, barely getting away from my guard before another white bolt smashed a skeleton to pieces beside me.

'We have to get him clear of this mess.' That cursed spear made it hard enough to reach Celasian, but with his guards and the chaos of the battle raging around him I'd never do it.

He's not going to take your challenge, she answered. *He's trying to drive a wedge through the middle of your army so that he can catch your skeletons between his phalanxes and crush them. It's a gamble, but he might be able to do it with all the destruction he's dealing with that lightning.*

'Like I said, I have to get him clear.' To save my army, and to tear out his throat. I watched him, and when he cast his lightning again I was ready. I sent Thorn to the side as the bolt sizzled past us, then drove straight in, Rend right behind. I was trying to hit Celasian before he could throw another bolt, but a Demigryph rider drove himself into the path of my charge, his spear aimed at my face.

I blocked the weapon away, but I couldn't stop Thorn's momentum. She smashed into the Demigryph and everything was a sudden confusion of hooves and talons, feathers and hide. I hit the ground and rolled up, my dark blade stabbing between the Demigryph's ribs and into its heart, making it drop. Beside it, Thorn was thrashing, attempting to get up, and I could see the guard trying to stab his crackling spear into her. She caught the back of his neck with her teeth, lifted him off the ground as she stood and shook him like a dog with a rat. Then she threw him towards the Spears of Heaven.

I jerked my sword out of the twitching Demigryph, but before I could launch myself onto Thorn's back Celasian was there, his griffon rearing up, talons tearing into Thorn.

She screamed, a terrible shriek that cut through the battle's roar, and then the griffon's beak closed on her head. The glow vanished from her eye sockets as the griffon cracked her skull, and Thorn collapsed into a pile of dust and ruin.

I screamed in rage and pain and slammed my sword into the griffon's chest. The bright blade cleaved through the blue feathers stained red with blood, but the point hit the thick bone of the griffon's sternum and stopped. I started to drive my other blade forwards, but a gleam of silver made me raise my dark sword up to catch Celasian's spear. He was thrusting it down hard with both hands and all his weight, and I had to slip to the side. Still, I felt the tip of it cut across my forehead, slicing through my eyebrow and down to my cheek before bouncing off the shoulder of my leather armour.

I moved back, hissing. The wound on my face sizzled and I could smell my flesh burning. Electricity buzzed through the cut, making my eye twitch, the muscles of my jaw spasm.

'Now I have you,' Celasian said. 'Strike, Erikil!' As he gave the order, his griffon shrieked and dived at me with talons as long as my forearms.

I danced back, dodging blows I couldn't block.

Run.

The command echoed through my head, and I knew she was right. Celasian's guards were moving to surround me, pushing back the skeletons with a fevered surge of slashing spears, determined to cut me down, but damn me, he was right there.

I tried once more to drive into the fray, but a wing caught me and slammed me down. I was on the ground again, the griffon ripping at me with her beak, trying to pin me. Until a furry shape crashed into it, teeth snapping.

Rend's teeth tore at Erikil, raking across an eye. The beast shrieked and reared up, just as Celasian unleashed another bolt. The lightning flashed, striking nothing, and Celasian cursed as the griffon smashed Rend away with one great talon. Erikil shook her head, showering me with blood and the hot, viscous liquid spilling from her ruptured eye. Her remaining eye was filled with rage as

she struck at me again. I twisted away and slammed a sword at her ravaged eye, trying to send the blade into the beast's brain. But Celasian cut at me, the point of his spear slicing through the black leather covering my arm, and the spark that snapped into me made me convulse and fall back before I could finish my thrust.

The strike was enough though to make Erikil shriek in pain and jerk her head away. She spread her wings and beat them once, twice, rising above the battle as Celasian shouted and pulled at her reins. I scrambled up, my body still twitching from the spear's touch. The guards were already rushing into the gap where Celasian had been, charging in to kill me.

I danced through their attacks, a blur whirling away from their strikes, stabbing and slicing where I could, never stopping. But they were all around me, trying to fall on me and bury me in the inexorable mass of their numbers, until the screaming started.

I heard it above the clash of spears and the curses of the guards trying to kill me, the desperate shrieks of mortals being ripped apart. Below the din there was another sound, a thick, growling howl, and I knew what had come. I didn't need to see the bestial shapes tearing through the heart of Celasian's phalanx to recognise the stink of the vargheists and the sound of vargoyle Salvera, a thick growl spilling through its teeth as it tore through the Church soldiers.

They'd done as I'd told them, crept around the edges of the battle to hit the Spears of Heaven from behind, and now their violent bloodlust sent them careening through the ranks of mortals, tearing their formation apart.

Their attack gave me time to pull myself back. The guard before me were breaking ranks, some trying to spin to face the new threat, some trying to run. One still came at me, stabbing for my heart, but I caught her and ripped her spear away, then bit her throat out.

The blood filled me, made my heart thud faster, my wounds smooth away. I threw the guard down and sprinted away until I found a clear space, empty of everything except the dead, the battle raging around it. I spun, searching with every sense until I found him.

Celasian had regained control of Erikil and brought her down on a low rise not far from where I stood. A band of Ruin Knights rushed him, their lances lowered, but the abbot-general smashed a bolt of lightning into them and they fell.

Is that clear enough?

'Yes,' I said, and charged.

I flew over the ground, heading for Celasian. Erikil saw me first, and the beast turned to face me, hissing, her wounded eye still oozing blood over azure feathers. Celasian twisted in his saddle and saw me, and a light touched his faded eyes. He leaned forwards with spear at the ready. I raced at him, and when the sparks began to climb I threw myself to the side, rolling away from a strike that never came. When I looked up, Celasian had raised his weapon towards the sky and was beckoning me with his other hand.

'Come, liar. Monster. Abomination. *Biter.* I want to see you burn up close. The way I saw Vasara burn.'

I crouched, feeling my heart beating hard in my chest, and then I moved. There was satisfaction in seeing his eyes widen as I streaked towards him, as he saw my speed, but there was no time to savour that. I was there, swords swinging, trying to cut him down. The griffon saved him again. Erikil rose on her haunches, talons flicking at me, massive wings striking. I dodged her blows, but the bulk of the beast kept me from striking her rider. My swords swung and cut, making bloody lines across the scales of her forelegs, slicing through the feathers on her wings, driving back her head when she tried to tear at my face with her

beak. I was laying cut after cut into the beast that destroyed my Thorn, but she was too big, too fierce to fall. So I danced around her, searching for an opening. When it came, it came at a cost.

I twisted around a slashing talon and I was at the side of the griffon, Celasian suddenly exposed to me. I drove forwards, ducking his spear point, ignoring Erikil's talons reaching for me, and struck. My bright sword stabbed straight at the gap in the abbot-general's armour where his leg met his body, but then there was a flash of blue and the point of my blade bounced away as if it had hit stone. That damned defensive prayer, the one that had stopped Rill's arrow, deflecting my strike.

'Sigmar protects!' Celasian shouted, and then agony ripped through my back as the griffon punched her talons through my armour.

Caught in the beast's grip as I was, my speed meant little. I thrashed, trying to get away, and I could feel the scrape of talons against my shoulder blades and spine. I ignored the pain and twisted, trying to bring my swords around, but I couldn't move and Erikil dropped her other forefoot on me, digging those talons into my legs, preparing to tear me apart.

And then there was Rend.

The huge dire wolf's body was twisted, the splintered ends of broken ribs punched through his hide, but his red eyes were blazing and fresh blood dripped from his jaws. Rend stopped before Erikil, meeting her one eye, and snarled his challenge. The griffon shrieked and reared up, spreading her talons at the foe who had taken her eye. Freeing me.

The moment Erikil's weight was off me I moved. My body was screaming with pain, my right arm wasn't moving, my legs were shaking, but I drove the dark sword in my left hand up. I punched its sharp tip into the spot just below the griffon's sternum, driving up through the beast's diaphragm, into her lungs.

The griffon's shriek cut off into a coughing gurgle as blood gouted from her beak. Erikil trembled, wobbled, and then collapsed beside me.

'That's for Thorn,' I snarled. I was shaking, but I fought to stand despite the damage the griffon's talons had done to me. My rage helped hold me up as my body knitted back together, but I barely kept my feet as I stepped back, jerking my dark sword out of Erikil's still-twitching corpse. As I did, Rend stepped beside me, staring at the collapsed griffon with slowly dimming red eyes. Then he gave a low whine and fell over, not dissolving but on the edge of it.

I understood the feeling. But I wasn't done.

Celasian was struggling out of his saddle, cutting away the straps that had kept him tied in. His white armour was stained with blood but it was all from his mount. The grey-haired mortal was uninjured, and he swung his spear around to point at me, sparks flaring.

'I don't know why you refuse to believe your father would want to steal our blessed blood,' I said, trying to work my right arm back into place. I was healing, but that arm was still mostly useless, and it was a fight just to hold on to my bright sword. 'Look how you cower. Fear of death runs in your family.'

'You have a filthy, lying mouth.' Celasian stepped closer, his spear still crackling, but he didn't send the lightning. 'My father didn't want your curse. Why would he want the half-life of an abomination?'

'Because he was afraid,' I said. 'He feared death, so he begged for life, even as my mother's teeth tore it from him. The same way you'll beg when my teeth fasten in your throat.'

Celasian raised his spear, but he didn't throw the lightning at me. He came forwards instead, driving his holy relic at me, desperate to see me burn. It was exactly what I wanted and I swung my dark blade up, smashed away his spear and drove my sword at his neck. But sparks arced from his silver weapon, electricity running down my arm and ruining my strike. I hit the heavy steel pauldron that armoured his shoulder instead of the side of his head, and he swung his spear back around, slashing its sharp edge towards my eyes. I ducked the strike and kicked out, connecting hard with his armoured belly, sending him sliding back. I followed with a thrust that should have taken him right below the chin, should have sent my blade sliding through his throat and out the back, but the protective prayer he'd wound around himself like a second set of armour flashed again, and the moment the tip of my dark sword touched his throat it skittered away.

Celasian skipped back, boots landing against the fallen bulk of his griffon, and raised a hand to touch the tiny wound on his neck. He stared at the drop of blood, then his pale eyes went to me. They were filled with icy fury, but there was fear there too. I shrugged my shoulders, feeling my joints sliding back into place as they healed and now I could swing both my swords in whistling arcs.

'You can't hide behind Sigmar forever, Celasian.' I smiled, showing my fangs. 'There's another god waiting for you, and Nagash is impatient.'

Now afraid and angry, Celasian struck. He pointed his spear at me and lightning cracked, but I was ready. My heart was hammering in my chest, my blood flowing fast, and my wounds gone. I spun away, slipping the bolt, ready to rush in, but Celasian was shouting, screaming a prayer to his Storm God, spear pointing to the dark cloud of ash and smoke that boiled above us, and lightning began to fall.

Bolts flickered all around, slashing down to hit the earth like a hail of white fire. I moved, fast as I could, spinning through the bolts hammering into the ground around me, but they were getting closer and one was going to find me soon, find me and burn me the way my mother had burned.

No. You're faster than me, Nyssa, you're more skilled than your father and you're more vicious than us both! Make him *burn instead!*

Her words cut through the thunder, and I knew what to do. I twisted through the falling lightning, moving towards Celasian. The bolts fell like rain, trying to catch me, stop me, kill me, but I danced through them. Drawing closer, closer, until the priest of the Storm God was almost within reach. But the lightning was a white curtain between us, a crackling wall of burning death. I could feel its heat, its painful itching touch arcing through my body. I knew just how much this was going to hurt, but wrapped in my rage I didn't care. With a shout I lunged forwards into the lightning, my dark sword raised over my head.

A bolt found that dark metal instantly. The electricity drove its way down through the blade and into my cold flesh. It poured like a river of fire through me, tearing and twisting, and my muscles started to lock. Sigmar's lightning was trying to shatter me, trying to turn me into convulsing, burning meat, but my newly healed right arm was snapping out, moving as fast as I had ever moved. Just before the shock made me useless, the tip of my bright blade touched Celasian's armour.

It wasn't a strike, just a brush of metal against metal, but it was enough. The lightning pouring into me had another channel, and it flowed through me, from dark sword to bright, and then into Celasian.

The connection lasted only a moment. The instant the energy bit into Celasian his arms flew out, spasming in pain from the angry touch of his god's blessing, and the silver spear tumbled away. With his grip on the cursed artefact broken, the lightning storm flashed away, gone, and I was left standing beneath the grey sky, smoking, shuddering with pain, surrounded by a circle of molten glass.

Celasian lay sprawled before me, just beyond that glowing circle. A man in scorched white armour, without his monstrous mount, without his god-given spear. He was helpless, still twitching from the aftermath of being touched by the lightning that he had brought to burn me.

'Abomination.' The word fell blurry from the abbot-general's quivering lips. He was trying to crawl towards his silver spear, but his trembling limbs weren't working well. 'I'll kill you! Burn you from this world!'

'You tried,' I said. I stepped over the cooling glass, moving carefully as I fought the painful spasms that still ran through my body. When I reached him, I kicked him over, pinned him down with one boot pressing into the lightning sigil that was stitched into his bloodstained tabard. 'And you failed.'

I leaned over him, and I could see my teeth reflected in his pale eyes. 'I won,' I told him softly. 'Now it's time to feed.'

'No,' Celasian said, his voice cracked, the fury in his eyes melting away into fear. 'No! Not me! You can't feed on me!'

I smiled, spread my jaws, and bit.

CHAPTER TWENTY-SIX

After the lightning, after the battle, the ash finally began to fall. Big flakes landing soft and silent. I watched them fall on my broken hands, sticking to the spots of Galeris' blood that hadn't yet dried on my skin.

It was still falling when true night came. When darkness swept across everything, and I couldn't see his body, or anything really. There was the red glow from the top of Temero, and in the distance faint lights which might have been the Grey Palace, and fainter ones that might have been Maar. I could hear sounds from both directions, the distant sounds of victory.

I listened for a while, and decided I should probably live.

In the dark, I went down to the battlefield, dragging Galeris' body with me. It took longer than I would have thought to find what I needed. There'd been so many bodies before the night had come, but in the blackness I went in circles before I stumbled over one. I landed on my hands and bit down a scream.

Noise wasn't a good idea. I could hear the sounds of scavengers

335

all around me, carrion bats, rats and bigger things. The howls of dire wolves. The snarls of vargheists. Even with all this plenty they might come for me, so I stayed silent until the pain faded. Then I slowly reached around until I found the body. My hands flinched from the wounds that covered it, but I finally found the hilt of a heavy belt knife. Gritting my teeth against the excruciating pain of my fractured wrists, I pulled it slowly free and went to Galeris.

'I'm sorry,' I whispered to him. Sorry for him, and for me, sorry for all these dead, sorry I'd ever come to these damned Broken Plains. A good name, I thought, as I found the collar locked around Galeris' neck – this land broke me. Then I began to cut, hacking through his cold flesh.

It felt like it took forever, but it was still night when I finally finished. I coiled the chain around me, the bloody collar hanging over one shoulder. I stood, and looked for the faint lights of Maar. There. If I walked past there, I'd find the Ire, and Gowyn, and the sea, and lands beyond this hideous place.

I started forwards, silent, miserable, and was barely a hundred paces before I stumbled and fell again.

Only one hand touched the ground this time, only half the agony, and I breathed deep. But I could feel something through the pain. I struggled to close my fingers around the thing I'd almost tripped over, and felt a buzz of electricity.

The dark was nearly absolute, but I could still see the spear, gleaming silver in the black. Runes ran down its perfect blade, symbols of power centred around the hammer sigil of Sigmar.

Celasian's spear.

I stared at it and sighed, then stood. Leaning on Heaven's Edge like a walking stick, I staggered forwards, into the dark.

You did well.

I stood in the tomb of my parents, staring at the empty marble

box that had once held my mother's bones, at the glass coffin that held my father's corpse.

'So you say.' I spoke quietly, but my voice made soft echoes. 'But you're both still gone.'

Are we? There was humour in her voice. *I still seem to be here. And your father... Well. The blessed blood is strong, and death for us can be a transitory thing.*

'It's what he believed,' I said. I moved to his coffin and opened the lid. 'It's what he hoped it would be for you. Do you think he'll understand what I did? The sacrifice you made?'

We *made. And yes, I do.*

I wasn't as sure. I reached down and tucked the pouch that held Vasara's teeth beneath his armour, placing them over his heart. 'I'm sorry I couldn't stop this from happening,' I told him. 'But know that I've broken the ones behind it.'

It was as close to a prayer as I could get.

Finally, light spread into the room, spilling through the open door of the tomb. Amethyst light from pale purple motes that drifted like candle flames that had lost their candles. They came at the head of a short procession. Shadas led them in, then Magdalena and Jirrini, walking on either side of a mortal man, grey-haired and pale-eyed.

Stripped of his spear and his armour, dressed in tattered under-clothes stained by ash and blood, Celasian looked nothing like the man he'd been the day before. He moved in silence, his eyes staring at nothing. Periodically he would raise one hand to his neck, but always flinched away before his fingers touched the wound my teeth had made. I hadn't taken much blood, just enough to render him senseless and helpless, enough to let me heal Rend and go back to the battle to finish off the last of the Spears of Heaven.

I had wanted Celasian alive. I had wanted him for this.

They led him to my father's open coffin. When he saw the corpse

there his face twisted, and something came back into his eyes, a flash of fear and disgust.

'What is happening? What are you going to do?'

What was I going to do? Vampires were already walking through the ash-covered valley outside, raising the dead Church soldiers, adding their spears to the army I'd raised out of the Irewater. Magdalena wanted me to march on Gowyn immediately, to take the city and all of the Broken Plains, while Jirrini wanted us to ready ourselves for retribution from Sigmar's Church.

Weighty decisions, and a thousand others beside, but all that could wait.

'Every year, ever since you killed Vasara, my father Corsovo Volari, the king-that-was, tried to revive my mother with blood and magic.' I nodded towards Shadas, and he nodded back and began to softly chant, using an obsidian knife to scribe glowing runes in the air over the glass coffin. He carved them smoothly, and I thought to myself that whatever else I did, I needed to acquire books for him to study.

'He would send for the worst criminal found on the Broken Plains, the darkest, most twisted heart we knew of. He believed that such a sacrifice carried power. I'm not sure he was right, but I vow to continue his tradition, in honour and in hope.'

Shadas completed the final rune, then held the knife out to me, and I took it.

To new beginnings.

'I will build something new, Mother. I will forge a new family among the ashes of this broken land.' I said the words aloud, uncaring that they heard. 'But I will never forget those who made me.'

Then with a single slash I cut Celasian's throat.

He choked and tried to stagger back, but I grabbed his hair and pulled him forwards, slamming him down so the wound on

his throat was pressed against the fangs of my father. He jerked, convulsing, trying to pull away from the corpse's mouth even as he died, but I held him there until he stilled. Until the glowing runes faded from the air. Until it was certain that my father was not coming back.

Not this time, my mother said. *There will be others.*

'I know,' I said softly. Some part of me wanted to rage, to smash Celasian's throat against my father's teeth again and again, forever. Instead I tipped his head back and stared into his pale eyes, empty now of everything.

'Pray for him,' I told Shadas. 'Pray that Nagash takes his soul and locks it in the same hell as his father's.'

Then I turned and walked away, out of the tomb and into the amethyst dark, the smell of blood heavy around me, my dead mother's words running through my head.

You are learning to make your anger a tool, instead of being a tool for your anger. And that, Nyssa Volari, is what makes you a true Kastelai.

ABOUT THE AUTHOR

Gary Kloster is a writer, a stay-at-home father, a librarian and a martial artist – sometimes all in the same day, seldom all at the same time. He lives among the corn in the American Midwest and his short fiction can be found in *Analog*, *Apex*, *Clarkesworld* and others. For Black Library, he has written the Necromunda novella *Spark of Revolution*, and a number of short stories.

An extract from
The Hollow King
by John French

The girl ran through the wood under the grin of a skull moon.
Breath panted from her lungs. The roots tangled the ground
under her feet. A branch caught in her hair, and her head
snapped back. She pulled at the branch. The thorns tangled
deeper. She yanked, panting, tears running through the blood
smearing her face.

A howl came from the direction of the road.

'Please...' she cried, the words dissolving into a gasping ball
of panic. She wanted her mother, her father, her elder sister. She
wanted to be back in the rocking dark of the wagon as it jolted
along the road in the twilight. She wanted the world to be a
shape she understood, to hear a voice say that everything would
be all right. She wanted someone to reach down and pick her up.

The thorns sliced into her fingers. The branches of the trees
thrashed. She saw crimson eyes, pinpricks of ember red in the
dark, behind her, coming closer.

Branches whipped Cado as he ran. The moon poured silver down
on him. He could smell blood. Could taste it. Death was howling

through the forest. The quarry was out there, running, flooded by fear, bleeding. It was fast too. He reached a thicket of trees. His eyes had become red flames in their sockets. The skin of his face pulled back from his teeth. The world was silver and red. It had taken too long to catch the caravan. Too long running along the lich-marked paths, hunger growing inside, as the prey sent a fraying thread pulling him on. Now the wagons of the caravan lay behind him on the road, tipped over, spattered with blood, dying horses thrashing in the harnesses. Now there was just this chase and a world redrawn by hunger.

· His senses were singing. The reek of blood was a crimson haze. Magic spiralled through the bare branches. The gasp of breath. Bones rattling. Close. An abyss of hunger open and waiting to swallow him. He reached a rock, bounded onto its top and launched up into the branches of the trees. Birds took flight, cawing, their song splitting the air.

She had been asleep in the wagon, and then there had been shouting. She had come awake blinking, thinking for a second that the shouts were echoes of her dreams.

'Stay here,' her father had said, and she had clutched at the cold-iron hammer amulet and pulled the furs close. The rock and sway of the wagon had slowed, and then the vehicle had kicked, and she had heard voices shouting to ride fast. Her heart jolted. The grave-coins, bone amulets and dried roses hanging from the wagon's roof swung on their cords. She hoped they would keep them safe again. There were things in the forests. For as much as her parents and the other adults tried to hide it, she knew this land wanted them dead.

Two nights ago, she had heard muttering and the click of cocking crossbows as she lay awake. She had sneaked up and opened the hatch at the back of the wagon. Peeking out she had seen something drifting through the trees. At first it looked like nothing, just a smudge of pale light. It was no more than two hundred paces away. It glowed, fizzed. Dead leaves rattled on tree branches above. The more she looked, the more she thought it had a shape – like an old person bent under a cloak, long arms and thin fingers trailing. She had wanted to duck back into the wagon but stayed, watching as the shape crackled past. Once it turned, and for a held breath she was certain she could see a head, the curve of a hood hiding a face and eyes. It had looked at her while the breath she was holding burned in her lungs. Her fingers had gripped the little iron hammer. She whispered what she could remember of the names her mother had spoken while hanging the charms inside the wagon: Sigmar, Morrda, and others that were just sounds.

Please let all the cruel things of this realm pass... Please protect us... Please let us reach a safe place... Please.

The blurred figure had drifted away through the trees. The guards settled again as she went back inside the wagon and watched the amulets turn on their cords as the wheels rolled on.

Tonight, as she heard the guards shout, she had begun to plead to the names and amulets again. Not whispering. Calling. The wagon had started to shake, wheels bucking over earth and stone. They were going fast, trying to outrun something coming after them. Then the world had tipped over. The wagon rolled and skidded, and the amulets clanged against each other. Toppling bundles of clothes half buried her. She heard the horses cry, and her father shout, and then another sound. A sound that froze her in place. A howl that passed through the wagon's walls like they weren't there. More shouts and then a loud, wet crunching. She had lain still, hardly daring to breathe.

Then she had heard claws on the outside of the wagon. She had looked around at the hatch-door, now on its side and level with the ground. Its bolt had broken, and it lolled on its hinges. The scrape of claws came closer. Her eyes stayed fixed on the hatch, waiting for a shadow to blot out the sliver of moonlight falling between it and the frame. Then there was a shout from somewhere nearby and the scraping of claws paused. She had not waited. She was up and through the hatch and running before her heart beat again.

There had been an instant when she had seen the shadow, looming close, ragged under the moonlight, eyes red. She had run into the trees. She saw a figure ahead of her, running too. She had followed. So had the red eyes of the ragged shadow.

She yanked her hair free from the thorns. Ran, gasping. Small bare feet over dark loam and tangled roots, fear numbing the cuts of sticks and stones. A tall, twisting tree stood in the middle of a clearing ahead. Its bare branches reached up to the rictus face of the moon. Birds crouched upon them. Hundreds of birds. Hunched forms of white and black feathers.

She could see someone running ahead of her. It was one of the caravan guards. Morinar, the kind one with the gut that did not fit under his armour; who always gave her one of the dried fruits from his pack when she asked; who was never scared of the sounds that came from the night, and always smiling.

'Help!' she cried. He turned, armour plates and chainmail jangling. He had a sword in his hand. His face was pale, eyes wide with terror, air gasping from his mouth. 'Help! Please!' she called again. Her foot caught on a root.

She fell. Her knee hit the edge of a stone. Blood… Blood beading her skin, black under the moon's glare. She twisted to look back.

Red. Spots of red in between the trees. And jaws. She froze. A rattling sound of breath through long teeth came from behind her. The tears had stopped now. The birds shifted on their perches, beaks and feathers rustling. A rattling sound of something that could not breathe growling through a rotten throat. She was shaking. Her eyes clamped shut.

'Mama...' she whimpered, 'Papa...' It was the only thing she could think to say, the prayer of a child in the face of the unimaginable. It was right there, on the other side of her eyelids. She needed to be brave. Be brave and things would be all right. She turned, shaking, and opened her eyes. Glowing eyes looked back at her. Rotting skin and fur hanging from a long, yellow skull. Bits of red and pink hung from its teeth. It cocked its head. The ember light in its eyes flared. Two others padded from its shadow. Death-light and blood drooled from their mouths. Dead muscle tensed under flesh. Jaws hinged wide. She could see strands of hair and bits of cloth caught in the fangs. Be brave...

A sound like a scythe passing through wheat. Black, rotten blood splattering.

The nearest dead wolf twisted. The two halves of its split skull thrashed from side to side. A bubbling howl came from its throat. A shadow landed. It looked human. Almost human. It crouched on the ground between her and the wolves. A tattered cloak covered its back. It had a sword in its hand, bright under the grin of the moon. Two dragons coiled either side of the cross guard. She noticed rings on the thin fingers, black iron on pale skin. The wolves gave a growl. Their heads lowered. The figure in the tattered cloak looked back at her over its shoulder. Red eyes. Skin pulled taut around a mouth of knife-point teeth.

'Run,' it said.

The wolves howled.

The birds in the tree above took flight.

She ran.

Cado rose, looking at the other wolves. Ghost-light crackled silver in his sight. The fat caravan guard had his back against the tree.

The man raised his sword, undecided whether to run, climb or fight.

'This one is not yours,' said Cado. The wolves tensed. Dead muscles bunched. The hunger trapped in their rotting shells would not turn away now – any more than Cado would. He felt the weight of the sword in his hand. The silver runes in its steel breathed cold into the lengthening second.

The wolves pounced. The sword came up. The first wolf's jaws were wide. Cado rammed the tip of the blade through the top of its mouth. Force jolted down his arm. Another wolf landed on him, jaws fastening on his shoulder. Fangs shattered as they met the armour under his cloak. He pivoted, ripping the sword out of the skull of the first wolf and throwing the second onto the ground. It hit with a crack of shattering bone. Pale light fizzed in its mouth and eyes. Cado stamped down. The creature's skull shattered. He whirled. The rest of the pack were already past him. The wolves flowed towards him, blurred shadows, howling. Cado leapt, sword tracing a silver-sickle path through the moonlight. Bones parted. He landed amongst the mess of rotten flesh and guttering magic. The substance of the wolves was already turning to black froth as the sorcery animating them dissolved into the wind.

Cado turned to the fat guard. The hunched birds in the branches were quiet and still.

'They could smell the reek of your god on you,' said Cado, nudging a crumbling wolf skull with his foot. 'You brought them to the caravan. Did you think the innocent could mask you, or were they just a shield to be spent?'

'I don't know what you are talking about,' gasped the guard.

'You almost outran me, but this hunt is over.'

'I... Don't... Please don't. We just wanted to reach safety, please...' The man had started to move away from the tree, ready to run. Cado levelled his sword.

'You worship lies. You should know when one has run its course.'

He looked up at the fat man's eyes. They were suddenly steady, unblinking. There was no fear there now.

The man opened his mouth, paused, and then smiled.

Cado lunged.

The guard spat a word into the air.

Moonlight shattered into rainbow. The birds exploded from the tree branches. Cawing cries filled the canopy. The guard's shape unravelled. Fat and skin and armour and smile spun into blue fire. The sword in his hand melted. Sculpted muscle unfolded under translucent skin. A grinning mask of bronze now covered his face. He had a knife in his hand. The blade flickered like a flame.

The blow was fast, but Cado's sword turned the blade, and sliced the hand holding it. The man in the bronze mask flinched back. Cado rammed the pommel of his sword into the mask. Its bronze grin crumpled. The man staggered, and Cado was on him before he could recover, hammering blows into the face and chest. The masked man lashed out. Cado grabbed the fist and twisted. Force snapped up the man's arm. Bones shattered from wrist to shoulder. Then Cado slammed him onto the floor. He lay, gurgling, blood and breath forming pink bubbles in the mask's mouth slit.

Cado tied the man's limbs, broken and whole alike, then hooked his fingers under his chin and began to drag him back through the forest towards the caravan. Above him the birds were wheeling.

The caravan was still intact, but there was almost no one left alive. Almost. One guard, gasping last breaths, legs worried to ribbons, lay where he had collapsed, trying to crawl away. He looked too old and thin for the scraps of armour he wore. Most of his blood was now soaking the ground he lay on. Cado paused above him, looking at the worn dagger still clutched in the bloody hand. Others must have survived, he reasoned: travelling chests and bundles had been opened, possessions taken. Two of the five wagons were gone. He could read the hoof and foot marks where someone had harnessed the surviving horses to them. He wondered if the girl had been amongst them. Maybe. None of them had seen the dying guard. Or perhaps they had; perhaps they had heard his gasping pleas for help. Either way, they had not stopped to give succour. He was not surprised; the underworlds were not kind places for the living. Everything dissolved into agony and loss. Only revenge and justice remained true in such an age.

The beliefs of mortals had made the underworlds. Across existence the living had told stories and dreamed of what would follow death, and with time those beliefs had become real. Places of punishment, plenty, reward, reincarnation and eternity – conjured into being with all the variety of imagination, hope and fear that life could create. There had been mountains and forests crossed by rivers, the waters of which carried the souls of the dead; great networks of caves where grey shades moved between stone tables to set them with two cups and talk again to every person they had met in life; orchards that never seemed to end, where the trees always bore fruit and the dead lay in warm shadows under green boughs and winter would touch neither leaf nor air.

That had been the beginning of the Realm of Death: an archipelago of kingdoms made by the beliefs of the living, in which only the dead dwelt. But in time the living had come. Colonies of mortals had made the underworlds their homes. Cultures had grown. The ways of the newcomers had intertwined with those of the dead. It had been the first invasion of the afterlife, and from it the Realm of Death had become a Mortal Realm. Then Chaos had descended. The followers of the Dark Gods had stepped from the shadows. Realms and underworlds had burned. Blood had soaked the ground as daemons feasted on the souls of the dead.

The past had become fire and ashes. The lives of mortals became ones of cruelty and suffering. Long ages of pain, with no light of hope or rest from the hunger of the Ruinous Powers.

Finally, a change. There had been a war, a new invasion to add its layer of blood to those that had come before. This one wrapped itself in promises of hope and help. It echoed, to Cado's ears, the hubris of the past, spoken in a new voice. Faith, alliances, light, order and majesty... all of it so crushingly familiar. All of it empty of anything except inevitable failure. The Realm of Death was a broken dream still sliding into darkness. Chaos had breathed its taint into everything, and the unquiet dead took what little kindness remained.

In the great cities of the underworlds, the living clung either to the protection of the servants of the Lightning God of Heavens, or the tyranny of the undead and the shadow of Nagash. Both were a lie. Sigmar, Lightning Born, could not undo the poison poured by the Dark Gods into the Realm of Death. It ran too deep. Nagash and his legions tried to make empires of bone and shuffling corpses, as immune to corruption as they were to time: another bargain, made with a lesser torment.

The people who had led the caravan through the forests had been humans. Either their forebears had survived under the hand of Chaos, or they had come to resettle this land. Regardless, they were fleeing whatever life they had made. They were trying to find safety, Cado guessed: a city guarded by the forces of Sigmar, a way out, other mortals to join up with. All lies told like stories to soothe frightened children. Now all that remained of their credulity and hope was an old man in battered armour gasping his last in shallow, bloody breaths. Cado paused and knelt beside him. The guard did not react. Pain and the nearness of death had stolen his sight. Cado could feel the tug of hunger rise to the reek of the man's blood. Slowly, carefully, he reached out. The guard flinched at the touch of Cado's hand on his neck. Cado flexed his fingers and felt vertebrae crack in the man's neck. Then he stood and picked up his captive again.

He dragged his prisoner to one of the remaining wagons. It had slewed off the road and pitched onto its side when its wheels caught a rut. A tree bore its weight now, branches bunched against its side. The tree was in bloom, Cado noticed. Purple blossom covered its twigs and branches in thick clumps, petals open to the moonlight. He fastened the prisoner to a wheel with an iron chain and pitch-dipped rope. The man's head lolled forward, unconscious. The bronze mask still hid his face, blood dripping from under its edge. Cado watched the thick scarlet droplets slide down the man's chest. The heart inside that chest was still beating… Warm… soft… the rhythm of redness.

He had gone very still. The smell of the drying blood and torn flesh all around him was suddenly a haze threading his senses. Hollowness opened wider inside him, screaming with silent hunger.

He stepped back, closed his eyes. The world was red threaded with black. A high, dry shriek filled his head. The blackness was roaring up from inside.

Hunt now, run through the night and find the living. Rip, tear and feast…

Red warmth. Emptiness filled with crimson. The comfort of iron and copper on the tongue.

He held himself motionless. Slowly the shriek faded to a dry chuckle. He could still hear a remembered echo of that false laugh when he opened his eyes.